THE NETWORKING OF THE NATIVITY

Shiloh Ridge Ranch in Three Rivers, Book 9

LIZ ISAACSON

ISBN-13: 978-1638760191

The Glover Family

Welcome to Shiloh Ridge Ranch! The Glover family is BIG, and sometimes it can be hard to keep track of everyone.

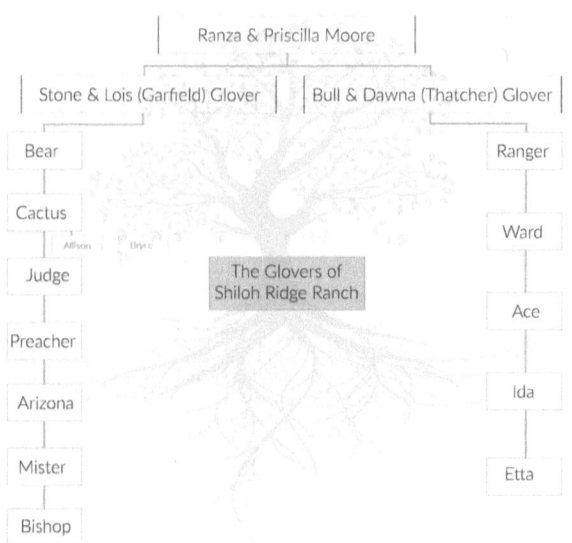

There is a more detailed graphic here, on my website. (But it has spoilers! I made it as the family started to get really big, which happens fairly quickly, actually. It has all the couples (some you won't see for many more books), as well as a lot of the children they have or will have, through about Book 9. It might be easier for you to visualize, though.)

HERE'S HOW THINGS ARE RIGHT NOW:

Lois & Stone (deceased) Glover, 7 children, in age-order: (Lois is now married to Donald Parker)

1. Bear (Sammy, wife / Lincoln (12), step-son, Stetson (2), son, Russell (6 mo), son)

2. Cactus (Allison, ex-wife / Bryce, son (deceased) // Willa, wife / Mitch (13), step-son, Charlie (5 mo), son)

3. Judge

4. Preacher (Charlie, wife)

5. Arizona (Duke Rhinehart, husband, living at the Rhinehart Ranch, just south of Shiloh Ridge / Shiloh (2 mo), daughter)

6. Mister

7. Bishop (Montana, wife / Aurora (18), step-daughter, Robbie (3 mo), son)

DAWNA & BULL (DECEASED) GLOVER, 5 CHILDREN, in age-order:

1. Ranger (Oakley, wife / Wilder (13 mo), son, pregnant and due in November)

2. Ward (engaged to Dot Crockett)

3. Ace (Holly Ann, wife / Gunnison (4 mo), son)

4. Etta

5. Ida (Brady Burton, husband / Johnny and Judy, (twins, 6 mo), son and daughter)

Bull and Stone Glover were brothers, so their children are cousins. Ranger and Bear, for example, are cousins, and each the oldest sibling in their families.

THE GLOVERS KNOW AND INTERACT WITH THE WALKERS of Seven Sons Ranch. There's a lot of them too! Here's a little cheat sheet for you for the Walkers.

MOMMA & DADDY: PENNY AND GIDEON WALKER

1. RHETT & EVELYN WALKER
Son: Conrad
Triplets: Austin, Elaine, and Easton

2. JEREMIAH & WHITNEY WALKER
Son: Jonah Jeremiah (JJ)
Daughter: Clara Jean
Son: Jason

3. LIAM & CALLIE WALKER
Daughter: Denise
Daughter: Ginger

4. TRIPP & IVORY WALKER
Son: Oliver
Son: Isaac

5. WYATT & MARCY WALKER
Son: Warren
Son: Cole

Son: Harrison

6. SKYLER & MALLERY WALKER
Daughter: Camila

7. MICAH & SIMONE WALKER
Son: Travis (Trap)
Daughter: Due soon

THE GLOVERS KNOW AND INTERACT WITH THE SEVERAL of the cowboys and their families at Three Rivers Ranch too... There's a lot going on in Three Rivers!

You'll see:

1. Squire and Kelly Ackerman

Mother / Father: Heidi (owns Ackermans bakery) / Frank

Son: Finn

Daughter: Libby

Son: Michael

Son: Samuel

2. PETE AND CHELSEA MARSHALL (CHELSEA IS SQUIRE'S sister)

4 sons: Paul, Henry, John, Rich

3. REESE AND CARLY SANDERS: THEY'RE THE ADMINS FOR Courage Reins, Pete and Chelsea's equine therapy unit at Three Rivers Ranch.

Chapter One

✤

J udge Glover put the last bite of his scrambled eggs in his mouth just as the door that led into the garage opened. Out of the two men he lived with—his cousin Ward and his brother Mister—he'd prefer it to be Ward.

He'd been getting along just fine with Mister since they'd made up several months ago. The younger man annoyed Judge from time to time—or all the time lately— but he kept his mouth shut.

He didn't tease his brother the way he would've in the past. He didn't play tricks on him—or anyone—anymore. It had taken him an extra-long time to mature, but he'd done it.

Mister walked in, a sour look on his face. Instant annoyance sprouted inside Judge. Still, he said, "Morning," and got up to wash the ketchup off his plate. Mister had said plenty of things over the years about how Judge ruined perfectly good eggs by putting ketchup on them.

He washed the red stuff down the drain and bent to put his plate in the dishwasher. He noted that Mister had not done that with his dishes that morning, and another dose of annoyance washed through him.

"Is June coming to Ward's wedding with you?" Mister asked, the chair scraping as he pulled it out from under the table. He sat in it with a big sigh. "I don't want to be the only one at the wedding without a date."

"I honestly don't know," Judge said, his mood only worsening with this topic of conversation. His relationship with June over the months could barely be categorized as such. She'd been called back to her house by her daughter and the police on their date after Christmas.

She hadn't been able to come to the impromptu New Year's Eve party they'd held at Shiloh Ridge Ranch, due to some previous plans she'd made with friends.

Judge hadn't given up there, but he probably should have. Days bled by, turning into weeks, and months, and while he sometimes talked to June on the phone, and they texted fairly regularly, he'd only seen her a few times.

He wasn't even sure he'd call running into her at the diner a date.

He'd asked her out a few times. She'd said yes. They'd made plans.

Something always came up—and not just on her end, so Judge didn't believe she was putting him off.

Lucy Mae had a band concert she hadn't put on the calendar. Judge had six calves born in the same day, so there was no way he could leave the ranch. June's car got hit in the parking lot, and she needed to take it to the body shop. Bear had called a family meeting after church, and Judge couldn't miss it. June had a massive system failure at her office in Oklahoma City, and she'd had to leave immediately to go fix it.

The list went on and on for what had gotten in the way of him taking her to dinner, going to her house after church, or the two of them simply getting together.

He was starting to think the Lord simply didn't want Judge to be with June. He'd backed off on texting and calling, and she hadn't made much effort to reach out to him either.

"Have you asked her to attend with you?" Mister pressed.

Judge cast him a glare, but the other man was staring at his phone. Probably looking through the long list of women's numbers he owned, trying to find someone he could ask to Ward's wedding. "Not exactly."

"Why not?" Mister looked up.

Judge turned back to the sink with a sigh. "Because, Mister, if I don't ask, then she can't tell me yes and then cancel later."

"At least she tells you yes," Mister grumbled as Judge picked up a butter knife. He contemplated stabbing it through his own eye, but just held it under the hot water and let the mayo melt off of it. He put it in the dishwasher as Mister continued, "Libby still refuses to tell me anything else about why she doesn't believe I like her. I've asked her out a couple of times, and she just says no."

"Maybe it's time to move on," Judge said, and he was telling himself as well as Mister.

"I don't want to move on."

"We don't always get what we want."

"Thanks, Dad," Mister said sarcastically.

"At least I don't," Judge said as if Mister hadn't even spoken. His chest vibrated in a strange way, and something told him not to say another word. "You seem to though."

The chair scraped again as Mister stood. "What does that mean?" He came closer to Judge, who twisted away from him to put a rinsed plate in the dishwasher. Probably Mister's, but who was keeping track?

Judge was, that was who.

"It doesn't mean anything."

"Yes, it does,' Mister said. "If you have something to say, just say it."

Judge paused, cocked his head to the side, and flew backward in time to another argument they'd had. He'd lost his temper; Mister had too. Cruel things were said. Judge wasn't going to do that again.

"I'm sorry," he said slowly. "I shouldn't have said that." He met Mister's eye, noting the darkness and unhappiness there. His heart ached for his brother, because Judge knew what bitter feelings came with unhappiness. He and Preacher had talked about how to help Mister, but they'd come to no conclusions or solutions yet.

"It means something," Mister pressed, and he was never one to let anything go. That was why he couldn't just let Libby walk out of his life, despite her rejections.

Judge had been rejected too, and it was never pleasant.

"I just...I don't want to hurt your feelings. It doesn't really matter what I think."

Mister nodded, his expression softening. "Will you tell me anyway?"

Judge paused, only the sound of the hot water running between them. "What if it upsets you?"

"I'm already upset," Mister said. "What's one more thing?"

He did seem to walk around in a perpetual bad mood lately. Maybe since New Year's, when everything with Libby blew up.

"I think you missed out on learning some things when you were younger," Judge said, trying to be delicate. He kept his voice low and his eyes trained on the mugs in the sink. Dark liquid spilled from them when he turned them over, and he rinsed them out. "Because you didn't have to go live in the cowboy cabin for a year, and work the ranch like a regular cowboy."

"I work the ranch just fine," Mister said, his default always defensive.

"I didn't say you didn't work hard," Judge said.

The door opened again, and Judge prayed it would be Ward. Preacher walked in, and that was ten times better than Ward. He was the perfect buffer between Judge and Mister, and he paused instantly. "What's goin' on?" he asked, looking between the two of them.

"Nothing," Judge said, reaching to turn off the water.

"Judge was just telling me how lazy I am."

"That is *not* true," Judge said. "At all."

"What did you say?" Preacher asked, his eyes still zipping from brother to brother.

"I said he missed out on learning some lessons because he went straight into the rodeo. The rest of us had to go live in the cowboy cabins, draw the cowboy's daily wage, and learn how other people live and work." He glared at Mister. "That's what you don't get. Not everything goes your way all the time. I learned that while sharing a cabin with three other men and barely having enough money to pay for groceries."

"It was a tough time," Preacher said, committing to entering the house. "What do you guys have to eat here? We haven't been to the store in a while, and Charlie's promised to bring you back whatever you want." He smiled at Judge and hugged him quickly.

Judge hugged him back and watched as he stepped over to Mister too. Mister stood unyieldingly in his arms, his frown still pinned on Judge.

"There's bagels and cream cheese," Judge said, moving back to the table to get his coffee mug. He started rinsing that too.

"What kind of lessons?" Mister asked.

Judge sighed and looked up to the ceiling, wishing he could see all the way to heaven. He needed some help from On High right now, that was for sure.

"Patience, for one," Judge said. "And for two, you have no idea how regular people live. What they have to deal with."

"I'm a regular person," Mister said.

"No," Judge said with a laugh. "You're not. We're not. None of us up here are. You learn that in the cabins."

Mister looked at Preacher, who set two halves of his bagel into the toaster. "What does he mean?"

"The fact that you don't know is how I know you don't get why Libby won't go out with you."

"Is this about Libby?" Preacher asked.

"It's always about Libby," Judge said, and a bit of sarcasm crept into his voice. He cleared his throat to tame it. He wasn't going to poke fun at Mister for his crush on Liberty Bellamore. He wasn't, because that was cruel, and not what brothers should do to one another.

"Mister," Preacher said, turning toward him. "He's right, bro. We're not normal."

"In what way?"

"In the billion-dollar way," Preacher said. "In the way that if we want a new house, we just build it. We don't have to get a loan. We don't have to worry about making mort-gage payments. We don't worry about anything, really."

"That's not how normal people live," Judge said gently. "They have more bills than money. They have to decide if they should pay their electric bill or buy the prom dress their daughter wants. Sometimes it's medical care or groceries. I learned that in the cowboy cabins. I met men who were desperately trying to provide for themselves or a family."

"You think I got off easy."

"You did," Preacher and Judge said together. They exchanged a glance, and Preacher's jaw tightened. Judge had seen that look before, and he knew Preacher was done talking. Judge should be too.

"You learn to lean on yourself," Judge said quietly. "Or the Lord, even though Dad is just a few steps away. That's what he wanted us to learn." Judge had learned it too.

"You think I'm spoiled," Mister said.

"You have a lot of money, and a lot of shiny belt buckles, and a lot of titles," Judge said.

Mister folded his arms and glared. "Do you think I never had to lean on anyone while traveling the rodeo circuit by myself?" He threw his arms up. "Because that was no picnic, Judge. I was alone all the time. There's *so* much pressure out there."

"I think it's different," Judge said. "Out here, when it's just you, and you have nothing? You have no idea what that's like. You've been privileged your whole life, even while on the rodeo circuit." He pointed toward the door, toward the whole ranch. "Those men we employ? That's all they have. They don't have big bank accounts waiting for them at home, or glitzy belt buckles. You walk around here like you own the world, and that's fine. You're a great guy, and you help others. I'm just saying...."

"What?" Mister demanded, dropping his arms and clenching his fists. "What are you saying?"

"I'm saying you're hard to relate to," Judge said, committed now. He swallowed and glanced at Preacher, who seemed to need to stare unblinkingly at his bagel while he spread cream cheese on it.

"It's no wonder Libby thinks you don't get it. You don't. You've been spoiled rotten your whole life. You work, but you don't have to, and you know it. For some of us, we had to live and breathe and work like a cowboy for a year, and all we got was the twenty grand."

"You knew you'd have a big bank account afterward," Mister said with a scoff. "Don't give me that."

"Okay," Judge said, holding up both hands. "I'm not going to argue with you about it anymore. I think you missed out on learning some really valuable life lessons. Stuff Dad and Uncle Bull *wanted* us to experience and learn. You never did, and in my opinion, it shows." He started for the front door, but he kept his steps slow and even. He wasn't mad. Mister could think what he wanted. Judge was just tired of listening to him moan and complain about how everything didn't go his way.

Welcome to the freaking club.

Judge had learned while living in a two-bedroom cabin with three other men that compromises could and should be made. He didn't have to get his way all the time. He could put his needs aside in favor of someone else's.

He'd learned to truly share—and not just his toys like when he'd been a kid. But share parts of himself with other people. Share his resources so they could all have a good life. Share the workload so one of them wasn't left doing all the dirty dishes.

No, he didn't have the bejeweled belt buckles or the titles Mister did. But he had more wisdom and knowledge that actually helped him in the life he was trying to live now. He didn't complain that life got in the way of him and June being together. Life did that sometimes. It happened, and it didn't always go the way he wanted it to.

He knew his life was charmed too. He wasn't delirious or blind to that fact. But he had put himself in someone else's boots and walked and worked for a full year. Mister never had.

His life had been, and still was, all about him. What he wanted. What he didn't have. Why Libby wouldn't go out with him.

"I'm gonna go get started with the horses in seven," he said. "Is that where you want me, boss?"

"I'm not your boss," Preacher said.

"But you are," Judge said. "I know you and Ward are the boss, and that's another thing I learned in the cowboy cabins. The work is hard, and it never ends, and the boss tells you what to do, and you do it."

Judge actually didn't mind that. He knew who he was, and it wasn't to be Preacher or Ward. He'd never survive as a leader the way they did. He didn't like all the pressure on him when tough decisions needed to be made.

He could work like a dog, and he often had around the ranch. He had around other ranches when their owners needed help. Judge liked to work. He just didn't want to be in charge.

"I follow orders too," Mister said.

"I'm not saying you don't," Judge said. "I'm saying, I don't think you have any idea what it means to bend your will to someone else's. After all, you're *still* asking Libby out, and she's still telling you no."

"You are?" Preacher asked. "Didn't she tell you no like six months ago?"

"The horses in seven?" Judge asked.

"Yep," Preacher said, and Judge reached for the doorknob. He yanked the door open and stepped outside—and right into someone standing there, their hand reaching for the doorbell.

Their fingers hit his shoulder, and he grunted at the same time the woman there yelped. He reached out and grabbed onto her so he wouldn't knock her down, and that was when Judge looked into the gorgeous, brown eyes of Juniper Nichols.

In the flesh.

His heart leapt to the back of his throat. "June," he gasped out, his hands moving down her arms and settling on her waist. He looked over his shoulder, quickly dropping his hands from her body so he could close the door.

He faced her, noting the nerves—and tears?—in her eyes now. "What are you doing here? Is everything okay?"

Chapter Two

❧

Juniper Nichols told herself to be cool. Play everything so cool. In reality, she was hot under the collar, with burning tears behind her eyes.

"You look upset, June," Judge said. "What can I help you with?"

"I was just down the lane at Ace's," she said, stepping with him as he pressed her toward the edge of the porch. This one only had three steps leading to it, and it was clearly decades older than the house she'd just visited. "They needed some help with their WiFI. I got them a new cord, and they're good as new."

"Great," he said with a smile. "I'm headed over to the stables. Do you have a minute to walk with me?"

"No," she said, and Judge continued down the steps before he turned back to her. "I just heard that Ward is getting married this weekend. Holly Ann was on the phone with someone."

"Yes," Judge said, looking toward the homestead. That house dwarfed this one, though where Judge lived was twice as big as what June had.

"Why didn't you ask me to go with you?" June went down the steps too, and when she reached Judge, she laced her arm through his. "Can I go with you?" Her voice broke on the last word, drawing the cowboy's attention.

"Can you come with me?" he asked. "Of course you can come with me." He leaned down and touched his lips to her forehead. "I didn't ask you, because I was afraid you'd say yes, and then cancel on me."

Instant defenses flew into place. "I didn't cancel any of the times because I didn't want to go out with you."

"I know that."

"You canceled on me too."

"I know that."

June let the morning silence settle over them. "Life has been really funny the past six months."

"Yes, it has." Judge tucked her arm closer to his body. "Plus, I don't believe you didn't know about Ward's wedding. You're on that text with all the women." He looked at her, his eyebrows cocked.

June's emotions stormed through her like an army of soldiers. "Actually, I asked Willa to remove me," she whispered. "It was too hard, knowing all the amazing stuff they were doing together and not being able to do any of it. I didn't...I don't...I don't belong with them."

"You could," he said.

"Judge Glover," June said, a smile dancing across her face. "You best not be sayin' things you don't mean."

He started to laugh, and June joined him. "It's been an interesting ride with you, Juniper."

She liked it when he used her full name, and she'd hated her full name since grade school. Somehow, when Judge said it, it became a term of endearment.

He drew in a deep breath. "I also didn't ask, because I know Lucy Mae graduates on Friday. I believe you told me she was leaving for California the next day—and that's the day Ward is getting married."

Those pesky tears entered her eyes again. She knew if she spoke, Judge would hear them. He'd look at her and see them again. "Yes," she said anyway, and he did exactly what she feared he would.

She let him look, and she let him see, and he did exactly what she hoped he would. He gathered her close to his chest, enveloping her in his strong arms, and whispered, "It's okay, June-Bug. It's okay."

She pressed her eyes closed, because her only daughter leaving Three Rivers wasn't okay. Such a thing wasn't even in the same realm as okay. "I don't know how to be alone," she said.

"Maybe you won't have to be," he said.

"I don't know how to have enough faith that she'll be okay in California."

"Maybe I can help," he said.

June pulled away slightly and looked up at him. "Why won't you go out with anyone else?"

"Have you?" he asked.

She shook her head. "I sort of have a policy about that."

"Yeah, but you'll break that policy for the right guy," Judge said, dead serious. "Right?"

"I guess."

"Have you been asked out in the past six months?"

"Yes," she said.

"By someone other than me?"

"Yes."

Judge frowned, and he obviously didn't like that. "Did you say yes?"

"No." A relationship with him felt impossible though. It was exactly as she'd told Ida months ago. Maybe God simply didn't want June to have someone as amazing as Judge in her life.

"I don't want to ask you to come to the wedding," he said. "If you're available and you want to come, that's fine. No one's going to turn you away." He stepped gently away from her, and they both looked up to the door when it opened again.

Preacher came outside, and he paused, surprise evident on his face. "Hey, uh, when you're done here, can I talk to you for a sec?"

"Sure," Judge said, looking from his brother to June. "I think we're done. Miss Nichols surely has a full schedule today to be at the ranch so early." He reached up and tipped his hat to her, his smile gorgeous and perfectly symmetrical, with all those shiny, white teeth.

She watched him go up the few steps and say, "What's up? I overstepped with Mister, didn't I?" before the two of them went inside and the door closed behind them. She knew Judge and Mister didn't always get along, and she wanted to know what boundary he'd overstepped.

She wanted him at her side this summer while Lucy Mae was gone. She'd wanted more of a relationship with him the past few months, but she'd let the tides of life push her this way and that one.

She wanted to see his Christmas display, and help him upgrade his network to make it run flawlessly.

She wanted to tell him that Adam was coming to pick up Lucy Mae, and she was scared out of her mind to see her ex-husband for the first time in thirteen years. She'd spoken to him when she'd had to, but she hadn't been in the same physical space as him since he'd left her and Lucy Mae all those years ago.

While still standing on the front sidewalk in front of Bull House, she sent a text to Judge. *Can you go to dinner tonight? I'll be done by five-thirty, and I have something I want to tell you.*

Sure, he said almost instantly, and she could hear it in his cowboy twang. The man said "Sure," as easily as he breathed, and with a date with him on the horizon, June finally felt like she could breathe again too.

"DID YOU GET YOUR CAP AND GOWN?" JUNE ASKED WHEN her daughter walked in from her after school job. She pulled the pan of lasagna from the oven. "Dinner's almost ready."

"I'm going out with Timmy tonight, remember?" Lucy

Mae dropped her backpack by the door and kicked off her shoes. "Yes, I got my cap and gown. You would not believe how many cars came through the line today." She smiled and reached for one of the caramels June had gotten out for herself.

"I forgot about Timmy." June frowned and looked at the pan of lasagna. She wouldn't have made it if she'd remembered. After all, she had a dinner date tonight too.

Maybe Judge could just come here, she thought, and she reached for her phone as Lucy Mae filled a glass with water.

"And some of them went through the line twice, saying we had to give them a free wash, because the first one didn't get the mud off."

"What are you and Timmy doing?"

"I argued with this one guy until Gerome came out and said to just give it to them." She shook her head and took a big drink. "But honestly, the entire town got the mud rained on them. It's all over everything, from the garbage cans to the fence posts. I should work on tips." She grinned, and June smiled back at her.

Lucy Mae had always been a talker, and she could go on and on—and on—about almost anything. When she'd been obsessed with Broadway, June had listened to the plot of every play Lucy Mae could get her hands on. And not a short synopsis either.

"Timmy's taking me to the senior hot dog roast," she said. "Tomorrow is the all-nighter."

"I don't want you out all night."

"I know, Mom. We already talked about it." Lucy Mae

rolled her eyes and put her glass in the sink. "Sorry about the lasagna. We'll eat it, I'm sure."

"I'm thinking of having Judge come help." She looked from the Italian dish to her daughter.

Lucy Mae's eyebrows soared toward the ceiling "Judge Glover? I thought you'd decided to let life play its course, and he wasn't included."

"Maybe he still is," June said. "I saw him today."

"Where?"

"The ranch. I had a job up there."

Lucy Mae cocked one hip and put her hand on it. "Did you, Mom? Or did you go seek him out?"

"What if I did?" she asked. "People can alter their course in life, you know." She put the oven mitts back in the drawer next to the stove. "I'm letting you go to California, and that's a complete life course deviation." She gave her daughter a glare, not wanting to admit how much she still liked and thought about Judge Glover.

"I will text you every hour," Lucy Mae said.

June scoffed, caught her daughter's grin, and drew her into a hug. "I love you so much, Lucy Mae."

"I love you too, Mom."

"I can't believe you're graduating and moving out. Moving on. You're going to have such an amazing life." She stepped back, used to letting her daughter see her tears. She didn't let them slip down her face, but they definitely brimmed in her eyes.

"So are you," Lucy Mae said. "You'll finally be free to do what you want."

"You have never been a burden to me," June said firmly. "Never."

"I know." Lucy Mae hugged her again, and June felt something extra in the touch. Her daughter held her tighter, and June did the same in return.

They stepped apart, and Lucy Mae wiped her eyes. "I'm going to go shower. If Timmy gets here before I'm done, please be nice to him."

"I'm always nice to him," June said.

"Mom, last time, you told him you could find out where he'd been on the Internet. "Two clicks, Timmy, and that history is mine.' That's what you said." Lucy Mae rolled her eyes again, but June only smiled.

She knew better than most of the dangers out there on the Internet, and she knew about the enticing things that teenage boys could get into.

Her daughter went down the hall to her bathroom, and June muttered, "That *was* me being nice, baby." She knew the ins and outs of routers, networks, security systems, and backend servers. She could sit outside Timmy's house and, within five minutes, be spying on what he was doing on his computer.

She wouldn't, of course. But she could.

She picked up her phone and called Judge, hoping he wasn't up to his elbows in manure or something. Now that summer had arrived, Judge would be pulling his Christmas supplies out of the basement, and the more likely scenario would have him wrapped up in old strings of holiday lights.

"Heya, June," he said, and it sounded like he was running. "Can I call you back in maybe ten minutes?"

"Sure," she said quickly, and he said, "Great, thanks," and the call ended.

June smiled to herself, because it sure felt like Judge would provide a life for her that would never have a dull moment. She looked around her house, feeling very much like a boring, old maid.

She needed some excitement in her life—and not the kind where her entire Oklahoma City office was offline.

But the cowboy kind.

The *sexy* cowboy kind, and she grabbed her phone and went down the hall to her bedroom and bathroom. If Judge was coming over, she needed to freshen up a little bit. She caught sight of herself in the mirror and gasped.

The manly polo with Nichols Networking stitched over the breast came right off. "I need new company shirts," she muttered to herself. Something with a V-neck or something that didn't make her look so boxy.

She stepped out of her work boots and pants and slipped into some black slacks made of something silky.

"Mom?" Lucy Mae called.

"I'm changing," she said, turning her back toward the door, as her daughter would come in whether she was changing or not. She searched her limited closet space for something appropriate for a date in her own home.

She glanced at her daughter as she entered the closet. She must've been able to read June's mind, because Lucy Mae said, "You want something to bring out your eyes." She stepped over to the rack and started flipping. "And since it's the beginning of summer, and you're a little pale from winter, you want—"

"I am not pale from winter," June said. "The sun's been shining in Texas for months."

"Something blue or purple, I think," Lucy Mae said, not bothered at all by June's protest. She plucked a purple blouse from the options and held it up. "This one's really cute."

The blouse had little white confetti blotches all over it, and June reached out to touch the material. It was light and airy, and June would feel confident in it. "Okay," she said, taking the blouse off the hanger. She pulled it over her head and then took the ponytail holder out of her hair.

"Up or down?"

"Down, Mom. Always down when you're trying to impress a man."

June's lungs seized. "I've always had it up when I've seen him before."

Lucy Mae smiled and reached over to fluff June's hair. "Then he'll be doubly impressed tonight."

"Yeah, the way I heated up that frozen lasagna is going to win him over for good."

Lucy Mae giggled and kept arranging June's hair. "Looks good now. Come and let me do your makeup."

"I don't want a lot of makeup."

"I'll choose three things," Lucy Mae said. "I won't do a single thing more." She opened the top drawer in June's vanity and started digging through her makeup bag. "Mascara, foundation, and lip gloss." She held them up, and the makeup looked so innocent. "Doable?"

"Doable," June said, and she followed Lucy Mae back

into the kitchen. She sat at the dining room table, and she closed her eyes and let her daughter start to paint her face.

The doorbell rang, and Lucy Mae left quickly to go answer it. As she greeted her boyfriend, June's phone rang. Judge's name sat on the screen, and she hurried to answer the call.

"Hey," she said. "You really called back."

"I was chasing a turkey, believe it or not," he said with a laugh. "Stupid thing got into some cord, and we needed to get it off his feet."

"Sounds exciting," she said. "I didn't know you had turkeys."

"We have a little bit of everything up here," he said with a sigh. "Let me guess—something came up?"

"Yes," June said, grinning to herself and then looking at Lucy Mae and Timmy as they came into the kitchen. "I forgot my daughter had a date tonight, and I made dinner for her. I'm wondering if you'd like to come to my place to eat instead of going out."

"Absolutely," Judge said. "I'm headed home now, so I just need to shower and make the drive. Say, an hour?"

"Can't wait," June said, hoping she'd used a flirtatious voice.

"Wow, Mom," Lucy Mae said as Judge said good-bye, and June hung up.

"What?" she asked. "You can't leave until you finish my makeup."

"Can't wait," Lucy Mae said in a falsely high voice, a poor imitation of June. She giggled and waved with the mascara wand. "Eyes closed. I'm going to make your face match that flirty tone, and you're going to show this cowboy he shouldn't let a day go by without talking to you."

"From your lips to God's ears," June said, immediately following that up with a silent prayer that the Lord would indeed help her with her at-home dinner date with Judge Glover in only an hour.

Chapter Three

J udge had walked up to June's door at least a dozen times in the past. Maybe two dozen. He'd brought flowers sometimes, and other times, he hadn't.

Tonight, he'd stopped for a twelve-pack of June's favorite iced tea, and he'd seen a bouquet of brightly dyed roses on the way out of the grocery store. So he'd gone back to get them, and he smiled down at the bubble gum roses, as they'd been labeled.

They were vibrant and colorful, in blues, pinks, yellows, purples, and greens, and they reminded him of an easier time in life. A time when he could ride his bike behind Bear and Cactus out to the pond their dad told them not to swim in.

Of course they swam in it, and Bear had even fashioned an old tire to swing out of the tree and over the water. The boys would take turns running toward the tire, grabbing onto it, and then dropping into the water. Sometimes, Cactus or Bear would push him and Preacher out in the tire and they'd just swing back and forth over the pond.

The roses reminded him of childhood and good times, and he smiled as the front door opened.

"Judge," June said. "C'mon in, cowboy."

"Aren't these the most beautiful flowers you've ever seen?" He held them out toward her, and she took a step closer to him to get them. She brought the scent of cotton candy with her, and Judge's stomach roared at him.

Sure, he needed to eat, but what he really needed was to dip his head and touch his lips to the soft spot on June's neck where she sprayed that candied perfume. He wasn't all that surprised by his thoughts. This woman had dominated them for about four years now.

Nope, he thought. *Five*. He'd asked June out after a Fourth of July picnic at the church, *five* summers ago.

He'd thought about dating other women, but he'd never done it. In his mind, Juniper Nichols was the one he wanted. He just needed the Lord to help him line up their schedules, and he needed June to realize that he was the one she wanted.

"They're fantastic," she said, taking the bouquet from him. "Where did you get them?" She leaned down to inhale the scent of the flowers. "Lucy Mae knows how to dye flowers. She took a class in high school where they did that."

"They were just at Wilde and Organic," he said, stepping inside her house. "Where I got this." He lifted the sweet tea, and June's smile only grew.

"I think someone's trying to earn some bonus points," she said, turning to go further into the house.

"Does that work?" he asked. "What do the bonus points buy me?"

"Nothing," she said. "But you can put that in my fridge."

She wore a purple blouse that made her lighter features pop, and Judge had seriously never seen a more beautiful woman. "You sure do look nice tonight, June."

"Thank you," she said, glancing at him as she reached for a vase. He opened her fridge and put the box of sweet tea inside, spinning when the sound of shattering glass reached his ears.

June moaned and said, "Oh, no."

"It's fine," he said, his default for everything. "Stay right there. You're not even wearing shoes." He looked from her bare feet to her face. "Tell me where the dustpan is."

"My foot is bleeding," she said, her voice oddly haunted.

Making an executive decision, Judge crunched right over the glass and said, "I'm picking you up, June-Bug. Hold on." He swept her into his arms, grunting a little at the effort required to carry her. She wasn't overweight by any means, but he wasn't fifteen either. He was forty-three, with a body which had worked hard around the ranch for most of those years.

He didn't just lift people into his arms and carry them around the house. Tonight, he did. He took June into the living room and put her on the couch. "The dustpan?"

"It's in the cupboard above the microwave."

"Really?" That so wasn't where Judge would put a dust-pan, but he retrieved it from the specified location and started to clean up. He hated the sound of glass scraping along the floor. To him, it was akin to someone scratching chalk along an old chalkboard or squeaking together Styrofoam.

"Judge."

"Oh, you're bleeding," he said, standing up. "Let me get a first aid kit. Where can I find one of those?"

"If you just get me a towel, I can do it," June said.

He grabbed the dishtowel hanging from the stove and took it to her as quickly as his feet would carry him. "How bad is it?"

"Just a couple of nicks," she said. "Finish with the glass and bring me some Band-aids. They're in the bathroom under the sink."

"You got it." Band-aids under a sink in a bathroom made sense to him. This wasn't how he wanted to start this date, and surely June wasn't in paradise either.

He worked as quickly as he could, and he cleaned as thoroughly as he knew how to get all the shards off the floor. "I think I've got it." He straightened, his back protesting all of this up and down and around movement. He'd had a pretty rough day on the ranch, and chasing down an injured and panicked turkey had just been the cherry on top.

Or rather, this broken glass was.

A strange smell met his nose, and he turned toward the stove at the same time June said, "Uh, there's smoke coming out of my oven." She got to her feet and hobbled toward him. "I forgot I put the lasagna back in there to warm it up."

"I'll get it." Judge picked up the oven mitts on the counter and opened the stove. June arrived as he took a blast of smoke and heat in the face. He grunted and flinched away, trying to find a pocket of clean air.

June started to cough too, and Judge reached back into the oven to remove the bubbling lasagna. "I think it just spilled over," he said. "Onto the bottom of the oven."

"Perfect," June said.

He closed the oven and turned on the exhaust fan above it. He clapped the oven mitts together and put them on the countertop. "Here's an idea. Let's order in." Judge tugged on his collar, though it sat in the right spot. "Or go out. You look amazing. I'm at least dressed to be seen in public. We can hit that sandwich shop you love and take the food to a park."

June looked down at her feet and back to him. "How far do I have to walk?"

"Not far," he said. "We can even just eat in the back of my truck if you'd like." That idea sounded like the best to him. "Grab some of those blankets you keep in your garage, toss them in the back, and just park somewhere. No walking at all."

"Parking?" she asked, her voice teasing now.

Heat filled Judge's face, especially when she said, "My mother always told me not to park with a boy."

"Good thing I'm not a boy," he said. "We could drive out to Squaw Peak if you wanted. I mean, it's not a peak hardly at all. It's the top of a hill. But it does have some amazing views."

"Your house has amazing views," she said.

"I live with Ward and Mister, remember?"

"Squaw Peak is too far."

He grinned at her. "We're back to parking, June-Bug." He held up one finger in the universal sign of please wait. "Let me get some Band-aids, and you can decide what you want to do while I play doctor."

"Now we're playing doctor too?" she asked as he left the kitchen.

"You're digging such a deep hole," he muttered under his breath. At least the Band-aids were easy to find, and he collected them and went back into the kitchen. He took the towel from her and got it wet, then wiped the dried blood from her feet.

"You're right," he said, reaching for the box of bandages. "These aren't bad at all. I think there's only one here that should be covered up. The others are fine."

"I'll put on thick socks before my shoes."

"It's summertime," he said, taping a Band-aid over the largest cut. She only had three or four others, and they'd stopped bleeding already. He straightened, groaning involuntarily again. "You don't want to wear shoes."

"I want to be comfortable," she said, a hint of warning in her voice. Judge remembered in that moment that she didn't like it when anyone told her what she liked or didn't like, should do or shouldn't do, or what she wanted or didn't want.

"Okay," he said. "I can get you some shoes, if you'd like."

"I can get my own shoes."

"Okay," he said. "Sorry, June."

"I'm the one who threw crystal everywhere and then burned dinner," she said, glaring at the lasagna. "It came from a box anyway. It's fine." She walked out of the kitchen, no limping this time.

Judge sighed as she disappeared down the hall. He had no idea if this was a good idea or not. He wanted to see June, spend time with her, hold her hand. They wouldn't even have to talk, as he knew sometimes the thought of carrying a conversation made June shrivel up and stay home.

When she returned, Judge had found a new vase for the flowers and he'd filled it with water. "They really are beautiful," she said, looping her arm through his. "Thank you, Judge."

"Mm." He leaned his head down and touched his lips to her forehead. "June, we can sit on the couch together. I don't care about anything else."

"I'm hungry," she said. "I know you are too, because if you hadn't even come in off the ranch yet, you certainly hadn't eaten dinner."

He hadn't, but he didn't say so.

"We don't have to talk."

"I feel stupid not talking," she said quietly.

"It's just me, June." He wasn't sure exactly what he meant by that, but he hoped she would be comfortable enough with him to just be herself. If she didn't want to talk, she didn't have to talk.

"Yeah, and you're amazing, and smart, and so darn handsome, and I've let so much time go by." She shook her head and slipped her hand away from him. "I don't want any more time to go by. How does driving through CW's sound? You can get that monster double bacon burger you like, and I'll get the fried cheese, and you can park us wherever you want. We'll watch the sun go down, and if there's something to say, we'll say it."

"That sounds like a little slice of heaven," Judge said, his voice low and barely reaching his own ears.

"Let me make sure this oven is off," June said. "And we can go."

Thirty minutes later, Judge balled up the wrapper on his burger and tossed it in the bag. "The sun's gonna go down right over there," he said, pointing west. He hadn't taken her to Squaw Peak, as that sat East of Three Rivers.

They weren't in his truck.

"Not for hours," June said, snuggling into his side. "This is amazing, Judge."

"Yeah." He could hold her for hours, and while he hadn't originally thought he'd end up on the roof of the tallest building in town with June that night, he wasn't sorry about it either.

Charlie, Preacher's wife, had called her friends at Heal-Now, and they'd gotten him and June into the building and up to the roof. The employees at the new pharmaceutical company in town had put couches, chairs, tables, and even a rug up on the rooftop, and June and Judge currently shared a lounger he'd dragged to face West.

They'd talked a little bit on the way to get food. He'd told her about Charlie and her connections, and they'd brought their food up to the roof. They'd both exclaimed about the furniture up here, and they'd eaten.

Judge didn't have anything to say, so he let his eyes drift closed. He breathed in and out, simply enjoying the heat, the fullness of his stomach, and the sensation of holding June in his arms.

"Judge?" she asked.

"Hmm?"

"I wanted to...I have to see Adam this weekend." Tension poured from her, and Judge's eyes flew open.

"Oh."

"I'm scared."

"Why's that, June?"

"I haven't seen him for thirteen years," she said. "Since Lucy Mae and I left California and came here." She sat up and faced the horizon, the slump of her shoulders so down-trodden. "He's taking her back with him." Now her voice sounded like cobwebs, just wispy shapes in the evening sky.

"How does she feel about that?"

"She's nervous but pretending like she's not. Like talking to a man who's essentially been missing for her entire life is just great. That she's *so excited* for the road trip, and of course she'll be fine."

Judge thought she probably would be fine, but that wasn't what June wanted to hear.

June sighed. "She just wants to go do this program, and she knows I'll let her if she goes with her dad."

"Lucy Mae is a smart girl," Judge said.

"Too smart for her own good," June said. "Am I over-reacting?" She twisted to look at him, and Judge could only smile at her.

"June, you have a big heart," he said. "And you're worried about your only daughter. I don't think you're over-reacting."

"You're just saying that so this date isn't a complete loss." She gave him a smile, but it didn't stay long.

"Maybe," he said, returning the smile. "But why are *you* nervous to see Adam? You don't have to drive halfway across the country with him."

"We just...we were never good together, you know? He's older than me, and he swept me off my feet, married me, and we had a baby all within the first year of knowing each other. I was eighteen, Judge." She had not spoken of her ex-husband, or her life in California, much at all. Judge had heard the man's name before, and that was about it.

He knew June had gone back to her maiden name after the divorce, but that Lucy Mae maintained her father's surname. He couldn't recall what it was at the moment.

"How long were you married?"

"Eighteen months," she said. "Lucy Mae and I stayed with my parents for a couple of years while I finished a cyber security program, and then I moved here to start Nichols Networking."

"Have you spoken with him?"

"When I had to legally," she said. "Otherwise, no."

"Did he reach out to Lucy Mae?"

June shook her head, and Judge could certainly see how she'd arrived at the conclusions she had. It did seem like Lucy Mae was simply using her father to attend the engineering program that summer.

"I wish I knew what to do to help you," he said. "I'd do it."

She lay back down in his arms, and said, "You're doing it."

ON FRIDAY MORNING, JUDGE PULLED UP TO THE appointed floral shop, Mother in the truck with him. "I'm going to need some help," she said.

"That's why you brought me." He put the truck in park and got down. "Wait for me, Mother." He rounded the vehicle and hurried to help his mother out of it. His truck was huge, and sometimes when he looked at it, embarrassment would coat him from top to bottom. All a truck like this did was call attention to it.

To him.

Once, he'd needed, sought after, and craved the attention. Now, he just wanted to live his life and be left alone.

The door of the shop opened, a chime filling the morning air. "In the back, Mrs. Parker?"

Judge actually looked around to see who the woman was talking to. When Mother said, "Yes, please, Sherryl," he realized *she* was Mrs. Parker.

Mother had married Donald Parker a year and a half

ago now, but Judge had never heard her called Mrs. Parker. It didn't seem right at all.

She stood at the tailgate and checked things off her clipboard as they were brought out. Daisies, tulips, gardenias, lilies. Baby's breath, roses, wisteria. Dot wanted a lot of flowers, as she claimed that was the only way she liked to be feminine.

Mother adored flowers too, and having a bride tell her she wanted a lot of flowers had awakened all her hopes and dreams.

"Help them with that pillar, Judge," she said, and Judge clued into his surroundings. He hurried to assist with the heavy item, and he carried one of the four out himself. With everything loaded, Mother paid the balance of the order and Judge helped her get back in the truck.

"Judge?"

He turned toward the familiar voice, his smile instant. "June." He laughed as he approached her. "We're just runnin' into each other all over the place."

"That we are." She glanced at the bed of his truck. "Those must be the flowers for Ward's wedding."

"Yes, ma'am." They'd had a mighty fine date a few nights ago, and Judge would love to see her at the wedding tomorrow. "Here getting flowers for Lucy Mae's graduation?"

"Yes," she said, indicating the tent that had been set up in the parking lot for graduation floral pick-ups. "I need to be over there." She didn't move, and Judge sensed she wanted something from him.

He couldn't imagine what, but he found he did have one question for her.

"June," he said. "Would you come to Ward's wedding as my date?"

June smiled up at him and tucked her hair behind her ear. "I thought you'd never ask."

Chapter Four

June took a deep breath as she went under the arch at Shiloh Ridge Ranch. She'd been up since six-thirty that morning, which was earlier than she rose for work. But Lucy Mae's graduation had been at ten o'clock in the morning, and June needed another seventeen and a half years to learn how to keep her tears contained.

Since she didn't have that kind of time, she'd settled for flat-ironing her hair so that it fell in completely straight layers. When she did that, she could see all the different colors in her hair. The individual strands came in red, brown, blonde, gray, and even black. Her sister had once plucked a pure white one from June's head when they were girls about ten years old.

Well, June had been ten, with Cypress closer to thirteen.

Her hair still looked amazing, and after the graduation,

June had enjoyed the help of her daughter, her sister, and her mother to get ready for this wedding.

She'd spent most of last night trying to get out of going to the wedding at all, but no one would let her. Truth be told, she didn't want to cancel. She simply carried some guilt that she'd left her family when she saw them so rarely.

Her mother had hooked her with her most maternal of glares, and she'd said, "This is the first man you've been excited about in two decades. You're going, and you're going to have fun."

June turned left at the top of the hill, determined to do exactly what her mother had said. "Have fun," she whispered to herself. June knew how to do that. She and Lucy Mae could get laughing so hard during their family game nights. She loved games in all their varieties, and she couldn't remember the last game of cornhole she'd lost. Somehow, she had impeccable aim, and knowing that made her smile.

She pulled to a stop behind the last car which had parked on the side of the road, but she stayed in her vehicle. People streamed down the road toward the barn, which stood tall and proud and blue against the summer sky.

June could taste the love in the air. It landed like sugar on her tongue, with an added bite of toasty marshmallow and that deep, rich chocolate that all good desserts possess. She could feel the excitement buzzing through the air, though she hadn't started toward the barn yet.

"Go on," she told herself. Backing out now wasn't an option, and June felt the hands and encouragement of her sister, her mother, and her daughter lifting her as she got out of the car. They supported each step she took toward the barn, whispering in her ear to keep going until she found Judge.

She'd texted him when she'd left her house, and there hadn't been too much traffic or any problems on the drive from the town of Three Rivers to Shiloh Ridge Ranch. The worst part was the very last lane up to the ranch, as guests of the wedding were all coming, the same as she was.

"June."

She heard her name, and she turned toward the sound of it. Judge waved to her from the corner of the barn, and a giddiness filled her that June didn't understand. A smile touched her face, but she controlled the spread of it so she wouldn't come across as too eager.

Turning, she started toward him, maybe adding a hop or a skip in there as she walked almost faster than she could. "Howdy, Judge."

"Look at you, beautiful lady." He took both of her hands in both of his and spread their arms out to their sides. "This purple on you is gorgeous."

She met his eyes, the sparkle in his downright dangerous to her health. "You look great too," she said, stepping closer to him so he'd put his arms around her. He did, and June leaned her palms into his chest. "There will be dancing today, right?"

"Have you never attended a Glover wedding?" he asked.

"This'll be my first," June said, though of course he knew that.

"There's dancing at this one," he said. "Ward and Dot

are doing the full slate. Ceremony. Dinner. Dancing. I think there will be fireworks if you stay long enough."

"You're kidding."

"Yeah." Judge grinned down at her. "It's three o'clock, June-Bug. If we're not done here by six, I'm going to take off my tie and stuff it down my throat."

June started to laugh, and Judge chuckled along with her. Her nerves butterflied through her, and she cleared her throat. "I was wondering...um."

Judge stepped away from the barn, and they linked hands as they moved toward the entrance. "You were wondering?"

"Did you go to the graduation this morning? I know you have a niece who graduated."

"I did," he said. "The whole family couldn't go, but I'm not important around the ranch, so I was able to attend."

June slowed her steps. "Judge, you are too important around the ranch."

He shook his head but didn't insist he wasn't, or admit he was.

She didn't know how to continue with his words hanging in the air. "Judge."

"I'm just fine, June," he said. "I was at the graduation this morning."

"I didn't see you, but did you see me?"

"I did."

"So you know my family is in town."

"I figured."

June looked toward the entrance, and it yawned ever wider, about to consume her whole. She wouldn't be able to ask him once they went inside. The music and noise pouring from the barn already muddled her thoughts.

"They'd like to meet you," she finally said. "I'd like you to meet them." She blew out a sigh and faced him. "What do you think?"

He searched her face. "What do I think? Well, honestly, June." He reached up and removed his cowboy hat. He ran his fingers through his hair and put his hat back on.

Her pulse bumped through her veins in a painful way. What if he said no?

"I think meeting your whole family from California is the job of a boyfriend." A smile twitched at the corners of his mouth.

"I agree," June said.

"So is that what I am?" he asked, lowering his voice and leaning toward her.

"If you want that label, Judge, I'm happy to give it to you."

"No," he said, pulling back. "Nope, it's not just a label."

The music inside the barn changed, and Judge turned that way. "I have to get inside. Let me take you to your seat."

June realized in that moment that he wasn't going to sit with her, at least not right away. Her nerves multiplied, especially because they hadn't finished their conversation.

Nope, it's not just a label. His words carved their way through her mind as he led her inside. "This place is called True Blue," he said. "A couple of my brothers and a couple of my cousins remodeled it when we discovered that it was structurally unsound. My father and uncle built the original barn decades ago." He gave her a smile, but June had so many other amazing things to look at.

Deep, dark-stained barrels stood at the entrance from this foyer part of the barn to the main hall beyond. Huge pots of flowers sat on top of the barrels, and June recognized some of them from the back of Judge's truck.

Flowers had been tied in the bows on the backs of the chairs. Blooms hung along the walls and floated in the air above the aisle and all the chairs, almost as if someone had gathered up every type of flower in the world and then blown them out of their hands.

Then time had been paused, and the flowers were all stuck in space, just where they'd been scattered.

A rich, dark wood covered the floor, and the scent of something buttery and something chocolatey filled the air.

"Wow," June said.

"Mother saved us seats," Judge said. "Do you mind sitting by her while I run back to the groom's room?"

"Meeting your mother feels like something a girlfriend would do."

"That it is," Judge said without missing a beat. He took her by the hand and started down the aisle. When they reached his mother, he paused and leaned so close his mouth touched her ear. "The difference, June-Bug, is that me calling you my girlfriend is not just a label for me."

He pressed a kiss to the tender spot just below her ear, sending pure delight through her in a white-cold blast. Shivers spilled down her spine, and all the skin on her body erupted in gooseflesh.

"Mother," Judge said. "Can June sit by you?"

"Absolutely," his mother said, rising to her feet and smiling. "Hello, June."

"Hello," June said, glancing at Judge.

"My mother, Lois," he said. "Her husband, Don."

"Nice to meet you both." June nodded at both of them, unsurprised when Lois drew her into a hug and then moved down so the end seat was empty for when Judge returned.

"Be right back," he said, and he walked away. June wanted to turn and watch him go, but she forced herself not to. Without him at her side, she was just a stranger at someone's wedding, and she glanced to her left.

Across the aisle, the chairs all remained empty, and she assumed more Glovers would fill them. She glanced to her right, and Lois reached over and patted her hand. June smiled at her, because it felt like something her mother would do.

"I'm so glad you could make it," she said. "Judge doesn't like attending these things alone."

"I wouldn't either," June said just as the music faded to silence. All the chatter did too, and June twisted and then stood as everyone else did. Lois's hand landed heavily on her arm, and June spun back to her to make sure she had the support she needed.

"Sorry, dear," she said, but she didn't let go of June's arm.

"Are you okay?" June asked, concern filling her now.

Lois nodded, her face taking on a faint pinkness. Her husband put his arm around her, and Lois finally released June's arm.

"You come up here," she said. "This is your nephew

getting married. I don't need a front-row seat." June switched places with Lois and Don just as a group of cowboys came out from the back right-hand side of the hall.

June had been enamored with cowboys her whole life, and seeing so many of them—so tall, so broad, so buttoned up in their white shirts, bowties, and deep, rich, dark jackets—had her head spinning.

She picked Judge out instantly, because the man called to her in a way no one else did. He wore his beard so neat and so trim, and with that midnight black cowboy hat on his head, he was literally male perfection walking down the aisle with everyone else.

They'd obviously practiced their walk beforehand, because every boot landed at the same time, the lead cowboy in the front of the V moving all the way to the altar while the others paused at various intervals along the aisle. June couldn't take in the festivities fast enough, and she realized it had been a long time since she'd attended a wedding at all.

The wedding march started piping through the speaker system in the barn, and it was clearly state-of-the-art. The bride and her father came out of the hallway too, and they walked down the aisle with full smiles. Every time Dorothy Crockett passed one of the cowboys, he handed her a flower and peeled off to go sit down.

By the time she reached the altar where her groom-to-be waited, Dot carried a bouquet in both hands and everyone was well on their way to finding their seats.

The crowd started to sit too, and June took the seat

next to Don. She looked around for Judge, but she couldn't find him.

"Welcome, everyone," he said, and she snapped her attention back to the altar. Judge stood there, beaming out at the crowd, and June could only gape at him—the officiator of the wedding.

She marveled at the altar, which appeared to be an antique wheelbarrow filled with rich soil. Vines, wood, and flowers—of course—filled it, and Judge indicated one of the larger sticks. "I invite the bride and groom to hold here during the ceremony, as it represents the way a husband and a wife must cleave unto one another in order for a marriage to thrive."

No one else seemed surprised to see Judge behind the altar, and June settled in for what had just turned into a very interesting wedding...even if she did have to sit alone for a few more minutes.

Chapter Five

❦

J udge spelled big words in his head—things like *Mississippi* and *lieutenant*—to keep his emotions in check. June being in the audience unnerved him, and he didn't even know why.

Oh, wait, yes he did. She'd said if he wanted the label *boyfriend*, she'd give it to him. No, he didn't want the label, thank you very much. Judge didn't need to be a boyfriend to know who he was and how to act around June.

Maybe you do, he thought, wishing anything but this lingered in his mind.

"Judge?" Ward whispered, and he blinked out of his thoughts and looked at his cousin.

Judge cleared his throat and didn't look at June in the front row, sitting right next to Don, with Mother on the other side of him.

H-A-P-P-E-N-S-T-A-N- C-E.

"Thank you all for coming. I'm sure if Ward and Dot could turn around and give you one message, it would be of gratitude." His cells didn't settle though his voice came out loud, clear, and controlled. Perhaps he'd simply learned to master a few of his emotions he hadn't eighteen months ago when he married Mother and Don.

"Marriage isn't easy. I myself haven't been married, but I've been around a whole lot of married people lately." He smiled broadly at Ward and Dot, noting the way they clung to one another, as their altar didn't rise very high and acted more as a prop than anything else. They both gripped the pole in the wheelbarrow too, Dot's knuckles so white that Judge looked at her to make sure she was okay.

She wore a smile, but tension radiated off of her in great, undulating waves.

"I've seen my brothers, my sister, and my cousins get married over the past several years," he said, deciding to cut some things out of his speech. "I even married my mother last year, and that was no easy feat." He didn't dare look at her either, for fear she'd push his quivering emotions over the edge.

"I've seen them fall in love," he said. "I've watched them struggle through misunderstandings. Through hurt feelings. Through car accidents." His voice did break then, and Judge took a moment to spell *pronunciation* in his mind.

"I've watched them endure pregnancies, and birthing seasons where we have the stubbornest cows on the planet trying to drive us all mad." A few people in the audience twittered, mostly Preacher and Bear, with a little bit of Ace and Bishop in there too.

Ward himself chuckled and nodded, because it forever seemed like life on the ranch was trying to separate good men from their wives.

"I've seen them come together for Sabbath Day meals. Witnessed them hold one another when bad weather came. Whisper to each other over the dinner table before they announce that our already loud, crazy, insane family of mostly males is going to get bigger."

He grinned, because he loved his loud, crazy, insane family so very much. "It sure would be nice if someone could have a girl. They're woefully underrepresented, and I know with this many of us, we can start to bring the numbers a little more even."

He'd grown up with five brothers and only one sister. How Arizona had survived them all, he'd never understand. She knew how to hold her own in the family, and she alone had the only biological girl in his side of the family.

Ida and Brady Burton had a little girl too, but other than that, all of the babies that had been brought to Shiloh Ridge had been boys.

"I've seen heartache, and I've sat with almost every Glover—whether by birth or marriage—for a few minutes when things felt overwhelming for them." He drew in a breath, because who would sit with him? If he was struggling, which he constantly felt like he was, who did he turn to?

Cactus, he thought, and he sought out his brother. The man reached up with his fist and pressed it over his heart, giving Judge courage.

"We're not a perfect family," he said, glancing to Bear.

He too touched his fist over his heart, giving Judge confidence. "We all make mistakes with each other." He didn't need to name specific incidents; everyone in the family knew of them, and the friends and other extended family members who didn't, didn't need to know.

"We always choose each other," he whispered, looking at Preacher. His brother brought his fist to his heart and nodded, giving Judge the recognition he so craved.

"That's what makes our family work," he said. "Free choice to put one another and our ranch first. And forgiveness." He looked at Bishop, who smiled and pressed his fist over his heart, giving Judge permission to simply be himself.

He drew in a long, deep breath and looked at Ward. His whole face shone with the light of heaven, stars, the sun, and the moon. Judge pressed his fist over his heart, hoping all of his brothers knew it was for them. He hadn't looked at Mister, but the two of them weren't speaking much lately.

They did, but Mister had retreated inside himself after Judge's lecture a few days ago, as he usually did. He'd come around, and after a while, Judge would seek him out, apologize, and they'd do exactly what he'd just said they would. They'd *choose* to be brothers; they'd forgive each other.

He looked at Zona, her tiny, two-month-old baby in her arms. She smiled at him, the water in her eyes easy to see. Her emotion gave him hope that it was okay to cry, even for a tall, tough cowboy.

"So Ward and Dot, that would be my pastoral counsel

today. Choose each other first. Come together when times are hard, and *choose* to be there for one another in your own personal Gethsemanes. Come together when times are good, and *choose* to thank the Lord above for your blessings. Come together when the family annoys you, and when we don't. Choose each other. Choose to forgive one another—and the rest of us."

He looked down at all the beautiful blooms before him. "It really is such a lovely gift, this idea of being able to choose." He faced the crowd again. "If it gets too hard to reason through your own thoughts to make those choices, I encourage you to seek help. There are plenty right here in this room who will give it, and plenty who do so for a living. Some of us know those people and can help you get to the right person who can help you straighten out your thoughts and make the best choices."

Dot's knuckles had loosened quite a bit, and when Judge looked into her face, he found the same, shining love which poured from Ward. "I can feel the love Dot and Ward hold for one another." He tilted his head to the side and closed his eyes. "Pause with me for just a moment. Listen. Reach out. Can you feel their love?"

The stillness and silence in the barn impressed upon Judge's heart, and he basked in what he could only describe as a golden glow. Gold, warmth, light, love.

"I've felt this same way at all the weddings we've had here at the ranch. All the weddings I've attended in other places. It's the same comforting feeling I get when I walk into the homestead when the whole crew is there. It's love, and while we might not know how to love perfectly yet, there's time to learn."

He exhaled and said, "Okay, the speech is done. It's time to get these two married." He grinned at Dot and Ward, so glad he'd made it through something that brought him to his knees every time he had to do it.

Something divine touched his mind, and Judge's eyes widened. "Ward, your father is so very proud of you." His eyes filled with tears, but he didn't care who saw him cry. "I can feel him here, and he is so happy we've restored this barn so he can come see his children do important things in their lives."

Ward's own eyes filled with tears and he nodded, his jaw tight, tight, tight.

"I can feel how at peace he is," Judge said, closing his eyes again, hoping he'd described the feeling correctly. "My father is here as well, and again, he is at peace." He opened his eyes. "I don't know who needed to know that, but well, there you go."

He smiled, once again releasing his emotions as the moments he could feel his dad and his uncle dissipated into the air around him.

"Dorothy Claire Crockett, do you give yourself to Woods Ward Glover, to be his legally and lawfully wedded wife, for now and for forever?"

Dot turned toward Ward, one hand gripping that pole and the other holding fast to his. "I love you, Ward," she said, her voice shaking. "I don't know much, and I don't know how to do or be any of the things I know I need to know how to do or be, but I love you, and I'm going to rely on that for right now." She nodded at him and released his hand to wipe her cheek quickly.

"Because I love you, I do pledge myself to you today, to be your legally and lawfully wedded wife, for now and for forever."

Judge liked this different way Ward and Dot had decided to do their vows. "Woods Ward Glover, do you take Dorothy Claire Crockett unto yourself, to be your legally and lawfully wedded wife? And do you give yourself unto her, to be her legally and lawfully wedded husband, for now and for forever?"

"Dot," he said, his voice strong and without all the wobbles found in Judge's. "I searched and searched for a woman like you. Even when you didn't like me very much, I was falling in love with you. Even when you annoyed me, I was falling in love with you. Even when we weren't sure we were going to make it, I knew we would, because I loved you. I do love you now. Love might not be all we need to make it through whatever the future holds, but it's a sure foundation where we can build anything else we need. So yes, because of that love, I do take you to be my wife, and I give myself unto you to be your husband, for now and for forever."

"I now pronounce you husband and wife," Judge said, the cheering starting before he'd said the last few words. He grinned at Ward and Dot, and the whole congregation. "You may kiss your bride."

He stepped back, stepped right out of the situation, and looked at it. Really looked.

Everything seemed to move in slow motion.

Ward bent toward Dot, both of them releasing the pole and moving their hands to the other's face.

Aunt Dawna, Ward's mother, had both hands pressed against her chest, her tears flowing down her face even as she grinned with bright light.

Ranger, Ward's oldest brother, was on his feet, his smile radiant and his hands moving ever—so—slowly together as he clapped. Beside him, his wife, Oakley, held their fifteen-month-old son on her lap, both of them clapping too.

Whoops and hollers entered his ears in slow motion, the sound warped and warbled.

Ace, Ward's younger brother, walked toward him, and the whole group hug thing would happen in seconds.

Ward and Dot kissed, sealing their marriage and beginning their new life together.

Judge saw Mother holding Don's arm, her face a picture of joy.

Then he looked at June. It seemed as though light beamed down from heaven, shining directly on her. She too glowed. She smiled. She remained seated. She applauded the wedding.

Judge had liked her for so long, and as her eyes drifted closed in a blink, he wondered if the two of them would ever be celebrated the way Dot and Ward were currently being cheered for.

He loved her already, and he knew that was a huge part of the problem between them.

As her eyes came open, they met his. Time rushed forward. The muted noises filled the hall and overwhelmed

Judge. He flinched away from the altar as more and more people swarmed toward it.

He automatically moved to his left, toward June, who stood and came to him. "That was wonderful," she said, her voice like music to him. She stretched out her arms and wrapped them around his waist. "You didn't tell me you were officiating. I didn't even know you could marry people."

"I can," he said. "At least in the state of Texas." He put one arm around June, and the two of them turned to face the newlyweds. Ward hugged his mother, then all of his siblings. Dot did the same, and then the two of them came together again.

They turned toward Judge, and they engulfed him, separating him from June.

"That was wonderful," Dot said. "You calmed me down so easily."

"Yes, thank you, Judge," Ward said, his grip on Judge's right shoulder so tight.

"Happy to do it," Judge said, though he hadn't been. Not really.

The moment Ward released him, Bear stood there, and since Bear gave the best hugs on the planet, Judge stepped into his embrace easily. "Good job, brother," Bear said in Judge's ear. "It'll be you next, right?"

"I doubt it," Judge said, smiling as he pulled away from Bear. "Roads are longer than they seem."

"Hey, that's a line I would say," Preacher said, grinning as he stepped into the circle and hugged Judge too. "You always say the right things. I don't know how you do it."

"I don't either," Judge said. "I can't even remember what I said right now."

"It's nice to know Dad's at peace," Bear said. "I worry about that sometimes."

"Do you?" Judge asked, as he never worried about their father.

"Yeah, thanks for telling us that," Bishop said, joining them. "I miss him so much sometimes."

Judge hugged him too. "He's always here, Bishop," he said. "He loves what we've done with the ranch, and he's happy with all of us."

"I hope so." Bishop clung to him, and Judge let him, because Bishop still seemed to carry things about their father's death that Judge didn't. If he could make that burden lighter, he would.

"I'm just going to steal you for a second," Zona said, and she pulled Judge into a hug too. "Your girlfriend looks a little lost, Judge."

"She's not really my girlfriend," Judge said automatically.

"Well, go sew that up," Cactus said, grinning over Zona's shoulder.

Judge grinned back at him, squeezed Zona one more time, and then stepped into Cactus's arms. Well, one of them. He held his five-month-old in the other one.

"You are one of my first choices," Cactus said quietly, so only Judge could hear. "Thank you for that speech. It reminded me so much of such truth. We *do* choose each other."

Since both Cactus and Judge had experienced times where they didn't choose someone in the family, what he'd said carried more weight. "Mister's mad at me again," Judge said just as quietly.

"Mister's mad at the world." Cactus looked over to him, as did Judge. He wore a smile as he stood next to Mother, but Judge could see how thin and plastic it was. One breath of wind would knock it off his face, revealing the unhappiness and fury beneath.

"I don't know how to help him," Judge said.

"Choose him," Cactus said. "Then get on over to June. She does look a little lost."

"Yes, well, we're easy to get lost in," Judge said, because that was the truest thing he'd said that day.

"You are never lost to me," Cactus said, and Judge nodded.

"Thank you, Cactus." He stepped away from that brother and approached another. "Mister." He took the man into his arms and closed his eyes. "I'm sorry. Please, please forgive me."

"Nothing to forgive Judge," Mister said, his voice rough and filled with emotion. Was it regret, like Judge had running through him?

"I love you," Judge said. "I don't mean to be critical of you. I just want you to be happy, and well, Libby doesn't seem to make you happy."

"No, she doesn't," he murmured.

"I don't either, and I'm sorry about that. I will keep my mouth shut." He pulled away and cupped Mister's face in his hands. "Okay? I will. I'm sorry." He couldn't say it more sincerely, and he didn't know other words to use.

Mister nodded, clapped Judge on the shoulder, and pulled him into another hug. "I have plenty of room to grow myself," he whispered. "You're not the only one who needs to keep their mouth shut and do better. I'm sorry too."

Judge nodded and stayed in the hug as long as Mister needed. Then, with his emotions once again teetering on the edge of a knife, he walked over to June, who'd smartly gotten out of the way. "Sorry." He sniffled as he took her hand in his. "I didn't mean to abandon you during all of this." He took in the fray before him, feeling part of it and also detached from it. "They're crazy. You should run while you have the chance."

"That's just it, Judge," she said, her voice barely loud enough for him to hear. "I've been trying to run from you, and I can't."

He stepped in front of her and looked at her. Her chin wobbled and her eyes filled with tears. "I just can't."

"Hey, don't cry." He wiped the tears as they spilled down her cheeks.

"You did," she said, giving half a laugh that he joined in with. "You're supposed to cry at weddings," she added.

"But not for this reason," he said, curling his fingers around her ear and then the back of her neck. He leaned down, and she let her hands drift across his chest and then come to rest on his shoulders. She tipped up, and the next thing Judge knew, he was kissing her, right there for anyone at the wedding to see.

A new kind of fire exploded through him, because while he'd kissed June nearly five years ago, this was different. This was five years' worth of waiting, of desire, of absolute uncertainty becoming clear.

He told himself to stop, but instead, he deepened the kiss and kept right on going.

Chapter Six

J une had not kissed a man in a very long time. In fact, the last man she'd kissed was the same man she was kissing right now. So many things streamed through her that she couldn't identify them all.

The love he'd spoken of. Attraction. Desire. Heat. Guilt, which she pushed against. She could kiss a man. She wasn't hurting herself or Lucy Mae by kissing Judge.

Judge pushed his hands through her hair, lighting her scalp and her soul on fire. "We should go outside," he whispered, finally breaking their kiss. They both breathed in together, and June felt like the air simply didn't hold enough oxygen after a kiss like that.

"The boyfriend label would not just be a label," she whispered back.

He took her hand in his and led her along the wall of the barn, where they could stay mostly out of the way.

People moved around them, setting up tables and pulling the chairs out of the rows to go around them.

Judge went left at the back of the hall, and they passed a restroom and then entered a small foyer at the rear of the barn. A door sat there, with two big windows which let in plenty of light.

He went through the door and outside, where the noise finally ebbed and the oxygen increased.

She released his hand and kept walking even when he stopped. He let her go, and somehow, that angered June. She spun back to him. "I'm scared, Judge."

"Of what?"

Everything felt so hot outside, which she supposed it was. Still, she felt wildly out of control, like the increased oxygen had somehow fanned the fire Judge had ignited with his kiss into a great, raging inferno.

"Of being your girlfriend," she admitted. She reached up and pushed her hair off her forehead, sighing. The sound only bore exasperation, and it was all directed at herself. "I've not been a girlfriend for a long time. What if I screw it up? I mean, I already did. I already said if you wanted this label, I'd give it to you. You weren't happy about that."

She paced away from him, bitterness coating the back of her mouth. "I don't know how to be a girlfriend. I don't know how to have a boyfriend." June took a deep breath and closed her eyes. She faced the sun and let the light paint the backs of her eyelids with bright red. Little veins ran through her vision, and she drew in a calming breath that smelled like sugar and hay at the same time.

Judge's footsteps approached, and he joined her at her side. He didn't touch her, and she appreciated that. He also didn't say everything would be okay, and she doubly appreciated that.

"I've been Lucy Mae's mother for so long," she whispered. "I don't know how to be anything but that." She opened her eyes and looked at him quickly. "If you come meet my family, it will be as my boyfriend, because that's what you are. Because that's how I feel about you. Because that's what I want you to be, even if I'm scared."

Her smile shook on her face, and she couldn't maintain looking at Judge. He hadn't looked at her, which had helped, but he was so...perfect. He said perfect things. He dressed the perfect way. He kissed her one-hundred percent perfectly.

"We can take things one day at a time, June," he said.

"Okay."

"You won't have to stop being Lucy Mae's mother." He did reach out and tentatively touch her fingers with his. "Okay?"

"Okay."

"Come on, now." He drew her into his embrace, and they stood in the sunshine together. "I'm sorry about kissin' you in there. It just...came over me."

"Don't be sorry," she said. "It was a good kiss."

"Yeah?" He chuckled. "I'm a bit out of practice, I suppose."

"You and me both, cowboy." She leaned into him and held him around his waist tightly. She was going to make so many mistakes with him, and she pressed her eyes closed and prayed that she wouldn't hurt him too badly. Prayed with all the energy of her soul that she'd know how to be with him, and what to say to him.

Begged the Lord to tell her who she was, so she could be the woman Judge deserved. *He's so good, and I'm so... normal*, she thought.

"I have to pick up the slack while Ward is on his honeymoon," Judge said to break the silence between them. "How long will your family be in town?"

"They're staying for another week," she said.

"So we have time."

"Yes," she said. "I'm making a big meal tomorrow after church. Lucy Mae is leaving right after that."

"I thought she was leaving today."

"She decided to stay so I could come to the wedding."

Judge shifted so he could look at her, his eyes wide. So much flowed between them that June didn't have to say how important he'd become to her. The fact that her own daughter had changed her plans so that June could be here with him said it all.

"I can come eat with you tomorrow," he said. "God willing and if the creek don't rise."

June busted out laughing, because he sounded so country and so not like himself. When he said things like that, he certainly wasn't the same man who also gave moving speeches about love, his deceased father being at peace, and always choosing to forgive.

"Come on, cowboy," she said. "You promised me a dance, and I hear some music startin' up."

"Mm, okay," he said. "But first...." He took her into his

arms and kissed her again, and this time, June lost herself in every stroke, unconcerned about who might be watching them.

"HE'S GOING TO BE HERE ANY SECOND," JUNE SAID, practically throwing the bottle of ranch dressing on the table. "Can you help me?" She threw a dirty look at her sister, who wore sunglasses and toed herself back and forth in June's deck swing.

"Why? Mama's helping. It's not like the food has to be ready the moment he appears."

Inside the house, the doorbell rang, and June spun that way. "I'm so nervous." She wasn't sure why. Her family was much smaller and much less intimidating than his.

Cypress stood then and left her sniffling five-year-old on the swing. "I'll get it, Juney."

"You be nice to him," June called as her older sister walked into the house. She looked at Forrest and reached to pick him up. For a five year old, he weighed a lot, but she cuddled him anyway. "You okay, baby?" He'd found a pair of Lucy Mae's old rollerblades in the garage, and he'd fallen about five seconds later.

Cypress had not been happy, because she'd told Forrest not to put on the skates. "He can barely walk without falling down," she'd said.

Her son had disobeyed her and gotten hurt because of it, which was why she'd retreated to the back deck and given June a little attitude about helping. June understood her sister's frustrations, but she also knew children were going to do what they wanted to do. They had to make their own mistakes.

"Yeah, Aunt Juney," Forrest said, hugging her tightly.

Cypress had not closed the sliding glass door behind her, and June heard her sister's laughter. "Okay," she said, her chest quivering with the effort it took to hold her pounding heart inside. "Let's go see who's here."

She, of course, knew who was here, and she looked down at herself. "Oh, jeez." She practically ripped off the apron that showed the carnage from making Lucy Mae's favorite food—tacos. June wasn't Martha Stewart in the kitchen—or any version of her—and she'd had a little mishap making the fresh salsa. It looked like she'd been in the barn, butchering pigs.

She tossed the apron behind the swing, took her nephew's hand, and entered the house.

Judge stood on the cusp of the living room, his smile gorgeous as he faced her sister, her mother, and her daughter.

June nearly passed out. How could she have left him to meet them alone? What had she been thinking?

Her nerves had blocked all rational thought.

She passed her nephew to his father, who also stood in the living room, just farther back. "Judge," she said, putting a smile on her face too. The sight of him did that to her, so it wasn't too terribly hard. She'd chosen to wear a sensible pair of khaki shorts for this meal, along with a silky tank top with a colorful butterfly on the front. Fine, Lucy Mae had chosen her clothes for her.

Judge's eyes slid down to her bare feet and back to her face in less time than it took for her to inhale. "Heya, June-Bug." He lifted his arm, and she stepped into his side effortlessly. He pressed a kiss to her temple, and June saw the sigh and softening on her mother's face.

"You met everyone?"

"I introduced him," Lucy Mae said, grinning at June.

"You used names?" June asked.

"Maple," Judge said, nodding at her mother. "Lucy Mae, of course. And Cypress." He indicated her sister. "She's older than you."

"Hm." June put one hand on his chest. "Come meet my dad. And Cypress's husband."

"She was just saying she has three children," Judge said, not an ounce of concern coming from him. He slipped his fingers between hers, and June could feel some tension there.

"Yes," June said. "Here's Forrest now." She grinned down at the little boy. "He's five, and he just survived a rollerblading fall."

"Heya, Forrest."

"This is my boyfriend, Judge Glover," June said, the words coming from her mouth easily. She'd been worried they wouldn't, which was why she'd allowed Cypress to get the door. She'd actually asked Lucy Mae to do it, and she wondered who had gotten there first.

"His daddy, Paul." She indicated the two girls sitting at the dining room table only a few paces away. "They have Aspen and Hazel too."

"Forrest, Aspen, and Hazel," Judge repeated. "Juniper. Cypress. I sense a tree theme happening here."

"Yeah," Paul said. "It's a Nichols thing, I guess."

"You guess?" June said, swatting at her brother-in-law.

"You didn't name your daughter after a tree," he said, and June couldn't argue with that.

"Yes, well, I'm the outcast of the family," June said, glancing at Judge. Surprise darted across his face so quickly, she wasn't even sure she'd seen it.

She led him past the girls and into the kitchen, where her father manned the refried beans on the stove. "Dad, this is Judge Glover. We're seeing one another."

Her dad turned, a smile on his face. "Of course. Judge. I've heard so much about you." He shook Judge's hand, a glint in his eye that June knew so well even though she'd been gone for the past thirteen years.

"Dad—" she started just as he said, "Do you know who your governor is here?"

"Nope," Cypress said, swooping into the kitchen. "We're not talking politics while in Texas, Dad. That was the agreement to let you out of the basement." She grinned at him and looked at June. Gratitude streamed from her, and she chanced a glance at Judge.

He seemed stunned, whether that was from the question about the governor or Cypress's comment about keeping their dad in the basement, she wasn't sure.

"Don't worry," June said, tugging on his hand to get him to move. "They don't keep him tied up down there or anything." She laughed, glad when Judge joined in with a chuckle. "Come on, everyone," she said. "We're eating out on the deck."

She let go of Judge's hand so she could grab the bowl of lettuce. "Everyone grab something and take it out."

The front door opened, drawing June's attention to it. Timmy Blevens walked in, which elicited a squeal from Lucy Mae and a frown from June. She couldn't be upset her daughter's boyfriend came to her send-off meal, but she didn't have to like it either.

She went outside and put the bowl on the serving table, glad her mother and sister had listened to her and brought out items too. Her father came out with the hot pot of refried beans, and June stepped back inside to find Judge bringing out the tray with all the smaller bowls of tomatoes, cheese, and sliced olives.

"Thank you," she said.

"Of course." He gave her a quick smile and took the food outside.

June heaved a sigh and went to greet Timmy, who had his arms around her daughter and was kissing her. "Come on in, Timmy," she said loudly. He'd met her parents and her sister already, so no introductions were necessary.

Lucy Mae turned, her dark eyes alight with happiness, and June couldn't deny her anything when she looked like that. "Come meet my mom's boyfriend," she said, adding, "And my dad will be here in a little bit."

June watched her lead Timmy over to Judge, who grinned like having the boy here was just grand, realizing the introductions weren't over yet.

Chapter Seven

J udge laughed at something June's father said. Sure, he knew the older gentleman was trying hard to make him laugh, and he didn't mind. He kind of liked the way all the women in the group rolled their eyes at Lester while what he said didn't bother Judge at all.

"If you keep laughing at him, you'll only keep encouraging him," Cypress said, pointing her fork at Judge.

He held up one hand in surrender and kept chuckling. This lunch with only eleven people felt downright cozy, and he reached for another handful of chips. "This salsa is to die for," he said. "Who's responsible for that?"

"Your lady over there," Lester said, to which Lucy Mae said, "Ew. Grandpa, don't call Mom a lady."

"Ew?" June asked from beside Judge. He sure did like the warmth of her beside him. Even if she'd been vampire-cold, he'd like her at his side. Something about having her there made him feel like he could face whatever life threw at him with a brave face.

"Am I not a lady?" She smiled at Judge and then looked past him to where Lucy Mae sat around the bend of the table. Just the fact that he could see and hear everyone at the table was a miracle to Judge. "I mean, I know I ordered those really ugly polos for work. They do make me look like a man."

"I'm sure that's not true," Cypress said. "You can't look masculine if you tried."

"So I'm not a lady, and I'm a weakling?" June shook her head. "I think we should stop talking about this before I develop a complex."

"The polos are fine, Mom," Lucy Mae said. "I just meant it sounded weird, being called...." She glanced at Judge, who simply looked at her, dying to know what she was going to say. He had some experience with girls her age, because Aurora had come into the Glover family a few years ago. Aurora and Lucy Mae were the same age, and so much about them was similar. At least he knew some of the terms June's daughter used, so he felt ahead of the curve.

"*His* lady. Sorry, Judge. It just sounds freaky."

"You don't have to be sorry. She's certainly not mine."

"She's not?" at least four people asked, one of them male.

Suddenly every eye had landed on Judge, and he shifted along the picnic bench. "Of course not," Judge said, dipping his head to block their gazes with the brim of his cowboy hat. He turned slightly toward June. "She doesn't belong to anyone. She's a real person, you know. Now, she might choose to be with me, and I choose to be with her, but she can leave if she wants. I don't *own* her."

June grinned at him and slid her hand down the side of his face. Her fingertips barely brushed his beard, and yet electric shocks traveled through his whole body. He wished they could be alone, because he'd *really* like to kiss her again.

To clear his mind from that path of thoughts, he lifted his head and looked at her family again. "Right?"

"Well-put," June said. "I choose to be with Judge, but no, I'm not his."

"Well, it's semantics," Maple said. She shook her silvering hair over her shoulders and half-closed her eyes, something Judge had noticed her do earlier when she'd said something she wasn't interested in debating. "You said he was your boyfriend. And you're his girlfriend."

"Sure, Mom," June said, obviously placating her. "Semantics."

"I was saying that saying 'your lady' like Grandpa did made it sound less romantic and more possessive," Lucy Mae said. "That's all."

"So what should I have said?" Lester asked.

"How about, Juney over there made the salsa. Isn't she the cutest cook you've ever seen?'" Lucy Mae threw her mother a smile.

"Ew," June and Cypress said at the same time. June held up her whole taco and used it as she added, "No woman in the middle age wants to be called cute."

"You are not middle aged," Cypress said with a laugh. "My word, June. Come on."

"What's middle aged?" June challenged, and Judge sure did like this show. He knew he was middle-aged, but June was several years younger than him. He was on Cypress's side with this one—which was just another reason to keep his mouth shut. Or full of chips and salsa.

"You can't be middle aged until forty-five," Cypress said. "You have almost a decade."

"Forty-five?" June asked, her voice pitching up. "Come on, Cy. Do you really think you're going to live to see ninety?"

"Forty then," Cypress said. "You still don't qualify." She quickly turned her attention to Judge, who heard the soft scoff June made. "How old are you Mister Glover?"

"Mister Glover?" June asked. "And you'd be mortified if he asked you that."

"I'm forty-three," Judge said. "I think June said you're three or four years older than her...." He glanced at June, who nodded. "You must be close to forty."

"She just turned forty three weeks ago," Lucy Mae said, grinning at Judge.

He nodded and polished off the last of his chips. "So, Lucy Mae. You're driving to California?"

"Mm, yep." She set down her half-eaten taco. "With Adam."

Judge once again glanced at June, who had gone cold on the bench next to him. "He's your dad, right?"

"Mm hm," Lucy Mae said, obviously not interested in talking about this. But she was the one who'd brought up

Adam. He looked down the line of people, most of whom wouldn't meet his eye.

"Okay," he said. "What did I do? Let in the elephant?"

Silence greeted him, only punctuated by a shocked look on Maple's face. Lester suddenly seemed interested in the pattern on the paper plates, and Paul, Cypress's husband, actually got up and left the table, muttering something about needing another napkin.

Judge looked at the stack of napkins on the table, not two feet from where the man had been sitting. "I know June's been married before. I know Lucy Mae has a father." He turned to June and leaned toward her. "Sorry." He kept his voice low, just in case he'd now been blackballed.

"It's not your problem," June said in a normal voice. "We obviously all know I've been married before too. And of course Lucy Mae knows she has a father."

"She just doesn't know him," Maple said. She reached over and patted Judge's hand as if he were a little boy. "Not all of us think Lucy Mae should go on an extended road trip with a stranger, dear. That's all."

"Mother," June snapped at the same time, Cypress said, "Mama, this is not your business."

"I'll be fine, Grandma," Lucy Mae added right at the tail of that.

Judge should've realized Lucy Mae's father would be a sore subject, but he was knee-deep in it now. "So you don't know him very well?" he asked Lucy Mae.

She started to shake her head, but Maple said, "She doesn't know him at all. We could put her on a train and tell her to find him when she got to the next station, and she wouldn't be able to do it. She's never even seen him."

"I've showed her pictures, Mom," June said, her voice quiet but oh-so-deadly. "And Adam has been in town for four days. She's spent time with him already."

"Sure, when it's convenient for him."

Paul came outside just in time to catch the end of Maple's sentence, turned around, and went back inside. Judge felt like doing the same thing, but he'd dug this grave for himself.

"No one is arguing that, Mom," Cypress said. "But what? You're going to blame June and Lucy Mae for Adam's choices? That's not fair."

"We video-called every week," Maple said, her voice rising in pitch and volume. "We can take her with us."

"We're flying, Mama," Cypress said. "God knows I would not survive a road trip from here to California with you." She gave her mom a smile, but Judge sensed some truth behind those words.

He reached under the table and put his hand on June's leg. She dang near jumped out of her skin, looking at him with wide eyes. "Sorry," he murmured, and he hoped she knew it was for more than scaring her just now.

"Mom," June said calmly. "We've been over this. She wants to do the road trip with her father. She is almost an adult, and she has a phone. She has a credit card. She is incredibly smart, and she knows how to listen to her intuition."

It sounded to Judge like June was reciting things she'd

told herself time and time again, simply to allow Lucy Mae to make this trip at all.

"Adam lives ten minutes from Cal-State Fullerton," June said, bending down to feed a bit of meat to one of her dogs. "It's going to be fine."

"She will not be an adult for another eight months," Maple said, and Judge wanted to come to June's defense.

"Mother, I'm done talking about this," June said. "She's my daughter, and believe it or not, I can handle this." She fed her other little dog. "Come on, guys. Let's go get the dessert." She stood and went into the house, her toy poodle and her Bichon Frise following her.

Judge looked around at her family. "I apologize for bringing it up. In my family, we don't really hold back."

"He has eleven brothers and sisters," Lucy Mae said, smiling at him.

"Not quite," he said, grinning back. "Just six. But I have five cousins too. We mostly all live up at the ranch, and our family dinners are probably three times this big." He shook some more chips onto his plate. "I'd never get extra chips up there."

That caused Cypress to laugh at least a little, which felt like a huge victory for Judge. "Are you and June serious then?" she asked. "I have literally never heard her mention anyone but you." She leaned her face into one palm. "And now, here you are."

"Uh, I'm not sure," Judge said. "It's been this sort of...." He glanced at Lucy Mae and swallowed. "On-again, off-again? Is that what you would say?"

"You guys know how Mom is," Lucy Mae said, standing

up and taking her plate. "Trust me, me going to California is going to be the best thing for her."

"No one's debating that, sweetie," Lester said.

Lucy Mae didn't stay, and Timmy got up and followed her inside too. Not three seconds later, June reappeared, saying, "Okay, but come back out. This cake is for you."

Cypress twisted, saw the enormous chocolate cake in June's hands, and said, "My goodness. Let's clear a spot."

Judge helped do that, and June set the delicious-smelling cake right in front of him. Lucy Mae, Timmy, and Paul re-joined them, and June put her arm around her daughter. "I'm going to miss my Lucy while she's gone, but I'm so glad she's getting this opportunity." Her eyes welled with tears, and Judge's own emotion choked in the back of his throat.

Opportunity. O-P-P-O-R-T-U-N-I-T-Y.

By the end of the word, he'd regained control of himself.

"It's only six weeks, Mom," Lucy Mae said, but her voice broke and she turned to hug her mother tightly.

June didn't let that go on for long, and hers weren't the only wet eyes. "Okay, okay," she said, wiping at her face. "I wore makeup today and everything." She gave a crying-laugh. "This is Lucy Mae's favorite cake. I've been making it since she was four years old." She beamed at her. "It's not her birthday today, but she's doing something very grown up, and I couldn't be prouder of her."

"Plus, Mom loves this cake," Lucy Mae said, beaming out at everyone. "Oh, thank you all for being here." She went around the table, hugging her aunt and grandmother,

her cousins, and when she got to Judge, she grabbed onto him and held him tight. "You take good care of her while I'm gone, ya'hear."

"Yes, ma'am," Judge whispered. "I will if she'll let me."

Lucy Mae pulled back and looked him right in the eyes. "I just don't give her a choice." She patted his shoulder and moved onto her grandfather.

Judge settled down with a big piece of cake, the taste and smell of it better than anything he'd ever eaten. He'd never tell Ida, Holly Ann, Etta, or Bishop that, but if June entered this cake into the bake-off, she'd beat the pants off of them.

Before he knew it, the doorbell ding-donged again, and June's little dogs went into a yapping frenzy. "Stop it," she said to them. "It's just Adam."

Judge got to his feet for some reason. His curiosity over who'd stolen June's heart and stomped the life out of it couldn't be qualified. He gathered a few empty cake plates, along with the plastic forks that went with them, and took them inside to the garbage can.

June had already answered the door, and a man taller than her stood in the foyer now. Her two little dogs barked and barked at him, both of them stretching up on his legs. He neither looked at them or bent down to pat them.

He said something and the two of them faced the rest of the house. In that moment, Judge saw June's true emotions, and they weren't good. She was worried, scared, and not happy to have her ex-husband here.

When she looked up and saw Judge, she smoothed over everything and put a smile on her face. "Judge," she said, reaching for him though she still had several paces to cross before she'd meet him.

He stepped toward her and took her hand, looking from her to the man behind her. Adam had dark hair that went to his collar and curled. His coal-black eyes could probably be classified as dangerous and alluring for the right woman. All Judge saw was his own displeasure for being there.

"Judge," June said again. "This is Adam Fernston. Lucy Mae's father." She turned back to him. "Adam, this is my boyfriend, Judge Glover."

"Pleasure," Judge said, swiping off his cowboy hat. He normally took it off in the house, but they'd been eating on the back deck, and the sun was bright back there. He tucked it under his arm and extended his hand to shake Adam's.

"Good to meet you, bro," he said, his voice not matching his physical appearance at all. Thrown for a loop, Judge didn't shake his hand very hard, and the touch only lasted for a moment anyway.

"Is she ready?" Adam asked, plenty of impatience in his voice. "We've got a long way to go before we can stop tonight."

"She's with my parents," June said. "Let me get her." Before she could leave, Lucy Mae walked into the house.

"Your dad's here," June said. "You're ready, right?"

"Yes," Lucy Mae said. She stepped past Judge and into Adam's arms. "Hi, Adam."

"Hey, cool cat. Where's your stuff? Let's get this show on the road." He turned away from June and Judge. Away from Cypress and Maple and Lester as they came into the house. Away from Timmy, who Lucy Mae was leaving behind for six weeks too.

Judge didn't like the man, but he held his tongue. It wasn't his place to judge anyway. He simply held June's hand, hoping his steadiness was enough to help her through this moment, and then the next.

Chapter Eight

M ister Glover tore off his glove with his teeth as his phone rang. He pulled it from his back pocket, sweat running down his back, and looked at the number. 580 area code. Oklahoma.

He quickly swiped the call on, his heartbeat tripling in rate. "Hello?"

"Mister Glover?"

"Yes, sir," he drawled.

"This is Luke Fenton. I was just lookin' at the job board, and you've got a mighty fine résumé."

"Thank you, sir," Mister said, glancing to his left. Preacher rode way down yonder, and he wouldn't be able to overhear this conversation. Not that Mister could keep anything secret for long at Shiloh Ridge.

He simply didn't want anyone to know he was planning to leave until he had another job somewhere.

"You workin' a family operation down there in Texas?"

"Yes, sir," Mister said.

"Why you leavin'?"

"Well." Mister blew out his breath and tried to find the right answer. He'd worked on his résumé for a couple of days, and then he'd put it all online that morning. Only a few hours had passed since. "That's a hard question, sir."

"Family trouble?"

"You could say that," he said. "There's a lot of us here. I'm not sure I have a place, me being one of the youngest and all." That wasn't entirely true; Mister knew he had a place here at Shiloh Ridge if he wanted it.

What he wanted was Libby Bellamore, and she wasn't willing to give him another shot. What he wanted was respect from his brothers and cousins, and he wasn't going to get it if he didn't go out there and do what they'd done.

"To be honest," he said. "My father required all of us to live in the cowboy cabins for a year. Draw a regular cowboy's salary. Live like real cowboys, and I never did that, sir. I joined up with the rodeo when I was nineteen, and I rode the circuit for a while."

"I see that here. Four national championships."

"Yes, sir," Mister said, the familiar pride beginning to swell in his chest. He tamped it down quickly. "But don't worry. I'm not going to cause any trouble. I just want...I want the opportunity to show everyone that I can be a real cowboy too."

"The salary's not great," he said. "It does come with a cabin. Enough for groceries. You're runnin' a cattle operation there in Texas? Shiloh Ridge, right?"

"Yes, sir," Mister said, realizing in that moment that he

shouldn't have put the name of the ranch on his résumé. Shiloh Ridge came up in Google searches.

"We've got about five thousand head," he said. "Not nearly as big as you boys."

"That's just fine," Mister drawled. "It's not about size for me."

"I run a three-hundred acre corn farm," Luke said. "I need help with somethin' all the time."

"I'm your man," Mister said.

"I'm sure you'll get a ton of calls," he said. "But my salary is thirty-five, with the cabin included."

Mister gazed around the pasture where he currently worked. He needed to hurry the lagging chickens along, as the goats weren't far behind him. "When can I start?" Mister asked.

"Any day you can get here, son."

"I need a couple of weeks," Mister said. "I need to talk to my brother and take care of a few things." He could literally pack his suitcase in less than twenty minutes. Have a conversation with Bear and Ranger in another twenty.

The thought of leaving Shiloh Ridge Ranch would take a lot longer for him to accept, and Luke said, "That's fine. Let's exchange some information, and I'll send you our standard packet. You can look it over. Choose a start date. Send in the contract I make my men and women sign."

"Sounds good," Mister said. He made sure Luke had his correct phone number and email address, and the call ended. "Pick it up, Dolly," he said to his horse, and she lifted her head and got back to work.

They plodded along, and Mister sometimes liked that

his job moving animals from one place to another gave him a lot of time to think. Lately, though, he'd hated it. He didn't want to think about kissing Liberty Bellamore on her front porch, only to be stood up by her a few hours later.

He didn't want to think about all the things he'd said to her that she hadn't said back. In fact, she'd *thrown* some of them back in his face. His mood darkened, almost like God had drawn a curtain over the sun.

Preacher's whistle met his ears, and Mister lifted his hand to acknowledge he'd heard him. He clucked his tongue at the chickens, and Dolly picked up her pace too.

He kept his head down and his mouth shut, and he got his work for the day done. After checking off with Preacher, he headed toward the Ranch House alone. The only person waiting for him there was Judge, and Mister didn't want to tell the brother he hardly got along with about his decision to leave Shiloh Ridge and go to Oklahoma.

At the same time, he didn't want to go to the homestead and try to have a conversation with Bear or Ranger in the evening. They turned into family men about five p.m., as they should, and Mister would need to schedule an appointment to meet with them.

He wanted to see what the welcome packet from Luke entailed, and he needed to at least know the name of the ranch where he'd be working before he started having conversations about it.

At the Ranch House, he found Sammy in the kitchen, mixing a pitcher of sweet tea. She looked up at him, smiling before she could possibly recognize him. "I brought dinner. I can't seem to make enough for just me and the kids at lunch, and it's your turn to eat my leftovers." She came around the counter and hugged him. "It's just mac and cheese and some broccoli slaw. Don't be expecting a gourmet meal."

Mister held her tightly, because he loved Sammy. "Thanks," he whispered.

"Oh, dear," she said. "What's wrong?"

"Nothing." But Mister couldn't let go of her. His chest vibrated as if thunder rolled through it, and he couldn't get it to stop. He didn't cry. That was Judge's role in the family. He didn't yell; Bear did that.

He didn't talk everyone's ear off—that was Bishop. He didn't rave at people—that was Zona. He didn't retreat into silence, as Preacher had cornered that market. He didn't simply walk away from everyone the way Cactus had.

Even as he thought through all of his siblings, he realized he was a little bit like each of them. He could yell if he had to. He was literally going to walk away from his family. He felt like bawling his eyes out, raving at everyone that they'd be sorry once he was gone and that he should be treated better.

Then he'd talk to each and every one of them, explaining everything so they knew it wasn't anything about them. There was something lacking inside *him*. Then, he'd fall into the silence and bask in it until the day he left the ranch.

"Michael," Sammy whispered. "You're scaring me."

"I'm so scared myself," he whispered back. He pulled

away with great effort and kept his head down. "I made a hard decision today, but I'm not ready to talk about it." He stepped past her and went into the kitchen, where a tray covered with tin foil waited.

"That just goes in the oven for ten or fifteen minutes when you're ready to eat," she said.

"Three-fifty?" he asked, turning toward the oven. He really didn't want to talk, but he sure had been glad he hadn't had to come home alone. On the new ranch in Oklahoma, he'd probably never have to go home alone. Hadn't Judge said he shared a tiny cabin with three other big men?

That didn't sound all that fun either, and Mister sighed as he pressed the buttons on the oven to start getting it hot.

"Are you sure you're okay?" Sammy asked.

"I'm sure," he said. "And Sammy, I'd really like you to keep this to yourself. I'm gonna talk to Bear soon enough." He turned and met her eyes, plenty of steadiness in his. "Please."

"When are you going to talk to him?"

"I'm going to text him about meeting with me right now." Mister even pulled out his phone, as if he literally meant right now.

"Okay," she said. "So he'll know as much as me."

"Should, yep." He swiped on his phone, actually checking to see if Libby had called or texted that day. Of course she hadn't. She'd gone completely silent on him, and he wasn't expecting her to call or text him first.

He hadn't called or texted her since their last argument either.

"You're my favorite Glover," Sammy said, and Mister smiled and shook his head.

"I am not," he said. "But thanks for saying so."

She gave him another smile, this one laced with trepidation, and left through the back door. Relief cascaded through Mister, and that made no sense. He'd been glad to see her there, and then glad to see her go?

Nothing made sense to Mister anymore.

He did put Ranger, Ward, Bear, and Preacher in a group text and sent them a brief message. *I need to meet with the four of you about my future here at the ranch. I'm good whenever Preach or Ward says I am.*

Send.

He didn't even bother to read over it twice. He wasn't going to back out.

He put the mac and cheese in the oven, turned, and took off his cowboy hat. He reached across the counter to hang it on one of the hooks by the back door, and he turned back to the kitchen with another sigh. He'd eat green stuff if someone else made it, and Sammy seemed to know the single cowboys didn't get the proper servings of vegetables.

He closed his eyes despite the dinging on his phone, and he thought about the last time he'd felt this level of devastation.

Definitely when he'd broken his femur in a bronc riding accident. That injury had ended his career and sent him down a long road of recovery. Sometimes, his right leg still had phantom pains from that break.

He'd felt so alone then. He'd felt utterly alone in the chute too, despite all the cowboys on the fence, making sure his hand was tied to the bull correctly and asking him if he was tight and ready.

In reality, it was just him atop that bull—and that animal was thirty-five hundred pounds of muscle. He was the only one riding it. He had to judge every move. Every tick of the animal. Every rearing of its head. Every split-second decision.

"This is not a split-second decision," he said to himself.

The doorbell rang, and then Mother's voice filled the house with, "...it's fine if we just go in, Don."

Mister pushed away from the counter to go greet his mom. Tears filled his eyes then, and he practically rushed at her. "Momma," he said, one of the only children to call her that and not Mother all the time.

"Oh, my dear boy," she said. "Don, take these." She handed him the white paper bag that Mister assumed carried sandwiches, and she opened her arms to Mister. He flew into them and lifted her right up off the floor.

"I knew I needed to come," she said. "What's wrong, son? Talk to me."

Mister pressed his eyes closed and just basked in the strength of the love and embrace from his mother. How could he leave this behind?

You have once before, he thought, and that strengthened him slightly. He made sure she was steady on her feet before he released her, and then he ducked his head low as if she'd caught him doing something wrong and he was embarrassed.

"Momma," he said. "I've decided to leave the ranch."

She pulled in a breath, her hand flying to her mouth. "No. Why?"

"Something Judge said."

"Oh, I'm going to kill that child." She spoke with fury, and Mister lifted his eyes to hers.

"He was right, Momma. It's not his fault."

Her eyes searched his, and he sometimes wished he'd gotten more of her fairer features. Everything about him was so dark, he felt like he simply blended into the landscape around him. "What did he say?"

"I never did live the year like a regular cowboy, Mother. He said I was spoiled, and I am. He said I didn't understand compromise, and maybe I don't. He said I don't know how to think of anyone but myself, and he's right about that."

He turned away from his mother and found her new husband sitting at the dining room table, a few sandwiches spread out. Mister wondered how much they cost, as he'd never really paid attention to such a thing before. A man who had to decide what to pay for would know. A man who couldn't afford any and everything he wanted would know. A man who knew how to share would know.

"You can have any one you want," Don said. "I think Lois said you like this ultimate pigpen. Ham, cheese, bacon, with crunchy pork rinds."

"I do like that one," Mister said, reaching for it. "Thanks, Don." He sat down across from the man and began to unwrap his sandwich. Mother took the seat next to him, and Don slid her a sandwich she ignored.

"Where are you going to go?"

"A ranch in Oklahoma," he said.

Mother sucked in a breath between her teeth. "So far?"

"I'll have a phone," he said with a smile that slid right off his face. "Judge and Preacher both said they learned lessons—vital life lessons—during their year in the cowboy cabin. They said it was what Dad wanted us to do, and I—well, I didn't do it. I'm going to go do it now."

"It's not necessary," Mother said.

"Lois," Don said, and Mister looked at him. He watched Don and Mother have a conversation without words, and he wanted that for himself.

Mother sighed. "I don't like this, Mister. You don't have to prove anything to anyone."

"I know that, Mother. But I do have to prove something to myself."

"What?" she asked. "What do you need to prove?"

"I'm not sure," he said slowly. "Which is why I need to do it. Why I need to go."

"This doesn't have anything to do with Libby, does it?"

"Honestly? It has everything to do with Libby." He took a bite of his sandwich and looked at her. She wore maternal concern on her face he wished he could erase.

"I'm going to miss you so much," she said, finally tearing her eyes from his and unwrapping her sandwich. "I hated my boys living in those cabins. Stone always said it would do them good, and maybe it did." She shook her head. "Even Zona did it."

"Exactly," Mister said just as the back door opened. Judge walked in, and Mister quickly turned back to Mother. "Not a word to him. About any of this. Promise me."

"Howdy y'all," Judge said in an overly cheery voice. Of course he'd talk like that. He got to work with the horses today, and he'd had, in his own words, "the most amazing date" with June last night.

"Howdy," Don said.

"Promise me, Mother."

"Fine," she hissed. "I promise." Then she stood and went to greet Judge with a "Howdy, son, I brought sandwiches for dinner."

"It smells like...burnt cheese," Judge said, frowning as he hugged Mother and then kicked off his boots.

"Oh, shoot." Mister flew from his chair and into the kitchen to remove the mac and cheese from the oven. "Sammy brought this by. We can eat it any old time."

"Sammy brought dinner too?" Mother asked.

"She said it's her leftovers from lunch," Mister said. "Nothing special, Momma. Come sit down and tell me how the back yard remodel is going."

Judge joined them, and Mister nodded to his brother. He got a nod in return, and Don passed Judge a sandwich too.

"Well, now that we've lost Dot for a little bit," Mother said with a smile. "Things have really slowed down."

Chapter Nine

Liberty Bellamore came to a complete stop, her heart pouncing up into the back of her throat, as well as down into her gut.

She knew that big, black behemoth of a truck.

"No." She shook her head, her resolve hardening into something way past steel. "Not again." She balled her fingers and marched toward her house. "Can't a woman come home for lunch without having to fight with a stubborn cowboy?"

Even as she bellowed the question to the sky, in the hopes the Lord would hear and answer her, Libby knew Mister's truck in her driveway was her fault.

Everything that had happened in the last six months was *her* fault.

She shouldn't have said anything about him to Preacher. She shouldn't have kept trying to be his friend. She shouldn't have agreed to go to dinner with him. And most of all, she shouldn't have kissed him.

She'd apologized at least a hundred times—more in her prayers. Ten times more.

Not only that, but she'd decided to do something about Mister Glover, and that was to get him out of her head. Out from under her skin. Out of her life completely.

She'd joined the dating app local to Three Rivers, and she had a third date with a man she'd met a couple of months ago this very night. No, she hadn't told Mister about him, because Mister wasn't her sister, and he wasn't her best friend forever, and it was simply time for him to move on too.

Her footsteps sounded like loud, clunky gunshots as she stomped up the wooden steps, and she dang near ran right into Mister as the front door opened and he came out with his back turned toward her.

"...just let her know I stopped by," he said. "She doesn't need to call or text or anything. I don't want to upset her."

"Too late," Libby bit out, and Mister spun around.

His eyes widened, and dang him from here until Mississippi. He was so darling and so good-looking that Libby's resolve slipped once again.

She hitched it right back into place and kept her glare on her face. "What are you doin' here?"

A slow smile touched his mouth, but his eyes only held sadness. Guilt ripped through her, and she nearly burst into tears. It *hurt*, and knowing that she hurt him only added to the pain spiraling through her.

"I'm leaving Three Rivers, Libs," he said, his voice the

quietest she'd ever heard a Glover speak. He focused on his hands, which fiddled around one another near his waist. "I just wanted to say good-bye. I didn't think you'd be home."

Mildred appeared behind him, and Libby looked at her sister. She wore anxiety in her eyes, and that further softened Libby's iron defenses around her heart when it came to Mister. "You're leaving Three Rivers?"

Glovers didn't leave their generational ranch, and confusion rippled through her the same way her pulse did.

"Dear Lord," she said, gasping. She spun away from Mister and ran back down the steps. Tears spilled over her cheeks, and a sob flew from her mouth as she reached the sidewalk.

"Libby," Mister called.

"I did this, didn't I?" she asked, her steps slowing from a run into a very fast walk. "Lord, I can't have done this. I'm not that powerful. He doesn't even like me that much." Her feet quickly ate up the sidewalk and went past his truck. "How do I fix this? Do I just go back and tell him he can't leave? I can't give him the wrong idea again."

Another sob racked through her, and Libby covered her face with both hands. "Help me," she begged. "Don't let him go. I can't live with myself if he leaves town."

And his family? How could he leave them? Didn't they need his help on the ranch?

"Libby," he called again, but she reached the fork in the road and took it without slowing. If she could just make it a few hundred more yards, she could hide behind the hay barn.

She broke into a run, knowing she couldn't truly hide

from Mister. There were no trees here, and nothing to conceal her. Still, her desperation to find a patch of shade and cry the afternoon away drove her to keep going.

She reached the barn and dove around the side of it, into the blessed shade. She couldn't sit though, and she paced toward the back corner, her chest heaving.

Libby didn't do a lot of running, see, and while she worked the ranch her father had put his entire heart and soul into, her chores didn't require heavy lifting. Her two older brothers really ran the ranchy side of things, while she and Mildred managed more of the commercial aspects.

Mildred kept their website updated; she sold all of their excess hay and corn; she designed flyers and maps and tickets for their Country Christmas each year. Together, they came up with the theme for the year, and they spent about five months preparing for the Christmas festival the Golden Hour Ranch put on every year.

Libby needed to return a phone call for their musical guest this year, something they'd never done. But bringing in a country music star—even a local one—would allow them to raise their ticket prices and draw a bigger crowd.

"Libby," Mister said behind her, his voice out of breath too.

She reached the edge of the barn and turned back to him. "I can't do this," she said, feeling wild and out of control. "I can't be responsible for driving you away. From Three Rivers? Really, Mister?" She reached him and looked up into his face. "Tell me it's not me."

"It's not you," he said woodenly.

She scoffed and sobbed again, spinning away from him. "I don't believe you."

He didn't try to reassure her, which didn't reassure her.

"When you were on the rodeo circuit, every letter was about how you couldn't wait to come home," she said, her voice thick with emotion. "You love that ranch. What is your family going to do without you?"

And the better question, the unspoken one—what was *she* going to do without him?

"They'll manage just fine," he said. "I've already spoken to everyone. They've known for a couple of weeks."

"A couple of weeks?" Libby turned back to him and put her hands on her hips, though she wasn't trying to be combative. "I can't believe the rumor mill didn't alert me."

"Zona said you blocked her texts."

"Not on purpose," Libby said.

Mister frowned. "How else do you block someone's texts, Libby? It's always on purpose."

"I didn't block her number," Libby said. "I asked her not to include me on the ranch wives group text. There's a difference." She wiped her eyes, feeling so hot and so leaky. She hated crying, and she especially hated crying in front of Mister.

"I'm so sorry," she said. "Please, please don't do this."

"I'm leaving today," he said. "I should be headed east by now, actually."

Instant fury reared through her. "You didn't tell me on purpose." He'd waited until the very last minute *on purpose*.

"What was I supposed to do? Call or text you and

confess everything? I've already done that, Libs. Two or three times."

"You didn't give me a chance to make you stay."

"You can't make me stay."

"I'm making you leave!" she yelled.

He didn't deny it, and Libby's tears started anew. She shook her head and looked at the grass, the weeds, and the dirt at her feet. She'd never felt this helpless before. "I'm sorry," she said. "If you'd have given me the chance, I would've said I'm sorry every day, every *hour*, so you'd stay."

She looked up and met his eyes again. He looked away quickly, blinking fast. He had told her how he felt about her a few times. The problem was, nothing he'd said had sounded true. Nothing was authentic with Mister. It was all contrived, all dreamed up *after* he'd found out she had a crush on him.

Yes, kissing him had moved the earth—for her.

For him, it felt like a conquest, and Libby wasn't going to devote herself to a man she'd literally set up on a dozen dates with other women, who wasn't serious about any of them, and who'd never even noticed she was female until *after* her insane comment to his brother.

She was *not*.

She was worth more than that. There would be someone who would fall madly in love with her, because of who she already was, who she could become, and what she believed in. That man simply wasn't Mister Glover.

"I'm sorry," she said again. "I'm sorry I kissed you. I'm sorry I said I'd go to dinner with you. I'm sorry I canceled. I'm sorry—"

"You didn't cancel," he said harshly. "You stood me up."

"I'm sorry I stood you up," she said. "I'm sorry I'm not a good friend. I'm sorry for anything I've done to lead you on, give you hope, or just anything that makes you hurt. That was not my intent *at all*. I'm sorry, Mister."

She paced toward him again, nearly falling into him as she reached to grip the collar on that maddeningly perfect plaid shirt. "I'm so sorry. You can't go. It'll ruin me if you leave because of me."

He gripped her elbows and looked down at her, his dark-as-coal eyes shining with unshed tears. "I'm going to miss you the most," he said, his voice gruff and rough and raspy. "Blast me anywhere, I *am* going to miss you the most. I wish I wasn't. I wish you'd believe the things I've said. But I can't change the past. I can't change *you*. I can't change what you think of me, because of what I've done in the past."

"I don't care about any of that," she said, desperate to make him understand.

"But you *do*, Libs. All those women I went out with? You *do* care about them." He released her, and she stumbled forward as he fell back. "I can't go back and not date them. I can't go back and not ask you to set me up with all your friends. I can't." He shook his head and gestured between them. "I can't do *this* anymore either."

He drew a deep breath and removed his cowboy hat. He looked like he hadn't showered that day, because his hair stayed stubbornly flat, even when he ran his hand through it. He resettled his hat on his head and took another giant breath.

"I am not leaving because of you," he said evenly, then blew out his breath. "I took a job in Oklahoma to get some experiences the rest of my siblings and cousins had years ago. I missed out on them because I joined the rodeo circuit, and it's simply time for me to learn what they all did. That's it."

That so wasn't it, but Libby couldn't argue with Mister anymore. So she nodded and turned away from him again. "How long will you be gone?" Surely his move wasn't permanent. It couldn't be.

"A year," he said. "At least."

She reached the corner of the barn and gazed out onto the ranch where she'd grown up. She'd spent too long wishing Mister would look her way. She'd spent countless days wishing for his attention, and plenty of time on her knees praying for it.

She drew in the same steadying breath he had a few minutes ago and wiped her face. His footsteps came closer, and when he slid his hand along her waist and rested it against her hip, Libby sighed and leaned into him.

"I'm going to miss you," she said, still focused on the blue sky out in front of her.

"Seems hard to believe," he murmured.

She turned into him and hugged him tightly, pressing her ear to his heartbeat so she could have a memory of how he looked, how he smelled, how he felt, and how he sounded before he left.

"I never meant to hurt you," she said to his shirt. "You're my very best friend in the whole world, and you have been for so long."

"I'll text you when I get there," he promised, his voice husky against her ear. He held her tightly too, and Libby couldn't imagine watching him walk away from her and then drive out of sight.

"You can call me too," she said.

"Maybe I will," he said. "You know my number too, Libs. It's not changing."

She nodded against his chest and looked up at him. He leaned down and touched his lips to hers in a beautiful, chaste, yet oh-so-meaningful kiss. Then he released her and walked away.

She couldn't stand to watch, so she turned and faced the ranch again, all of it blurring behind another waterfall of tears.

Chapter Ten

J udge pulled up to the diner, wondering why in the
world Mister wanted to meet him here for lunch. It
was out of both of their ways, though Judge hadn't
seen Mister for a couple of days. Sometimes he went to
stay with Preacher or Ward, but he always turned up at the
Ranch House again, usually when Judge was hoping for
some peace and quiet.

His younger brother's truck sat in the parking lot, a ton
of stuff in the back of it. Judge frowned at that, wondering
why he had everything tarped up and tied down. Maybe he
was taking something somewhere for the ranch. It wasn't
like Judge knew the ins and outs of everything at Shiloh
Ridge.

He wasn't one of the foremen, and he'd started pulling
out his Christmas decorations this week, so he'd been
extremely distracted.

Inside the diner, he found Mister easily, the man sitting

only two booths down. He wasn't wearing his hat, and Judge swiped his off his head too. He nodded toward his brother, and the hostess waved him on by.

"Heya," he said, sliding into the booth. "What's goin' on? What's in the back of your truck?"

"Something to drink, cowboy?" A waitress held a pot of black coffee in her hand, though it was way past breakfast.

"Some of that, please," he said, nodding to it.

She flipped over the mug in front of him and poured. "Cream and sugar?"

"Tons," he said with a smile.

"You know what you wanna eat?"

"Whatever he ordered." Judge looked at Mister, who simply smiled at him and then the waitress.

"You got it." She walked away, and Judge picked up his spoon and began stirring his coffee. He'd put forth the questions he wanted answered. Now Mister just had to start talking.

He cleared his throat and looked past Judge as the bell on the door chimed again, indicating more people had entered. He hadn't mentioned inviting anyone else to lunch, but maybe he had.

Judge twisted to see who it was, but he didn't know the two men. When he looked back at Mister, his face had turned a considerable shade of red.

"My truck is—I'm moving to Oklahoma today."

"What?" Judge stilled the spoon in his coffee. "Oklahoma? Why?"

"Cream and sugar," the waitress plunked the carafe

down and put a real bowl of sugar next to it. "Those cheeseburgers will be out any minute."

Mister waved her away, but Judge hadn't even looked at her. "Why?" he repeated.

"To do what you said to do," Mister said, grumbling the words.

"No," Judge said, horror striking him the way rattlesnakes did. Fast and deadly, his heartbeat spiked with every strike. "You can't."

"I am," Mister said. "I have. It's done. I moved out. My room is clean. I did the bathroom this morning after you'd gone out onto the ranch. I met with Bear and Ranger, Ward and Preacher. It's done."

He lifted his own coffee mug to his lips, but Judge saw the tremble in his hand.

"I can't believe this." Judge leaned back in the booth. "I'm—you can't do this because of what I said. I say stupid stuff all the time." He waved his hand toward Mister. "Especially to you. God help me, for some reason, you get under my skin and I say stupid stuff."

"Like right now," Mister said with a smile. The redness in his face had started to fade too, but Judge felt red-hot all over.

"Yes," he clipped out, reaching for the cream. He nearly knocked it down with his clumsy hands. "Like right now."

"You should be happy for me," Mister said. "I'm going to go figure out all the things you did when you lived in the cowboy cabin."

"Why would that make me happy for you?" Judge said. "It's a terrible time."

A dangerous glint entered his eye. "You said it would be good for me."

Judge poured way too much cream in his coffee, his own hand shaking as he did. It spilled right over the top, and he scoffed and pushed it all way. "I hate what I said to you," he said. "Whether it's true or not. I hate this."

The whole diner felt stuffed with awkwardness and tension, and Judge hated that too.

"It's true," Mister said, looking out the window. "What you said is true, Judge. I felt it in my soul, and the moment I decided to leave the ranch, I knew it was the right thing to do."

"It won't be the same without you."

"I would hope not, no," he said.

"Where are you going?"

"This part cattle ranch, part corn farm operation just outside Oklahoma City. It's called Winterhaven."

Judge nodded, his jaw so tight. "Sounds nice."

"Does it?" Mister met his gaze again, some measure of challenge in his.

"No," Judge practically spat. "It doesn't. It sounds like I drove you away because of something that didn't mean anything. Because you were pining over Libby, and it annoyed me for two seconds. I'm allowed to be annoyed for a few seconds."

"Of course you are," Mister said dangerously. "And I'm allowed to take what my older, wiser brother has to say and actually consider it."

Judge opened his mouth to reply but stalled. "What?"

"Weren't expecting that, were you?" Mister chuckled and looked up as the waitress appeared again.

"Here you go, boys. Double cheeseburger with bacon, no onions." She put the plate in front of Mister first. "Extra-crispy fries." She slid one in front of Judge. "Times two." She nodded toward the window. "Ketchup right there. Anything else I can get for y'all?"

"No, thank you, Miss Hattie," Mister said, all coy and flirtatious. It was just the kind of thing that Judge would've rolled his eyes at before.

In that moment, he didn't, because Mister had changed right in front of him. The moment Miss Hattie walked away, he leaned forward. "You listened to what I said?"

"For probably the first time in my life," Mister said. "Like I said, Judge, you were right."

"I don't feel right," Judge said. "I just feel guilty."

"Well, don't," Mister said. "Everyone I've told has said that, and it's no one's fault. It's my decision, and I'm telling you, it's the right one *for me*." He picked up a French fry and popped it into his mouth before reaching for the bottle of ketchup. "So be happy for me."

"Fine," Judge said, sounding the opposite of happy. "I'm happy for you."

Mister chuckled again, and then leaned over and took the biggest bite of his cheeseburger. The kind that usually made Judge roll his eyes and eat in disgust for the rest of the meal.

That might be the last time Judge saw him do that for a while, and he tossed his napkin at his brother. "Stop it." He laughed, glad when the melancholy atmosphere and extreme tension bled away.

Mister chuckled through his bite, and then he pierced Judge with one of his sharpest looks. "I am going to miss you, Judge. There's a reason everyone comes to you for advice, and a reason why they all want you to marry them."

"Only a couple of people asked me to marry them," Judge said quickly. "And no one comes to me for advice except Cactus."

"And Bear," Mister said. "And Ward. And Preacher. Willa, Sammy, Ranger, Bishop, Ace, *and* Zona," Mister said, ticking them off on his fingers. "And don't think I don't know about you and Etta meeting every Saturday morning." He cocked his eyebrows, daring Judge to argue with him.

Judge took a giant bite of his hamburger, not about to say anything else for Mister to think about. After all, he had a long drive ahead of him to Oklahoma City, and his truck seemed packed and ready to go.

"Mm hm," Mister said. "That's one of the things I've learned while observing you the past couple of weeks. You know, when I take myself out of the equation and try to see things neutrally, I've found you quite...wise."

Judge choked on the last bit of his burger, his eyes flying to Mister. He bit into a fry and didn't seem worried about anything. "I wanted to have lunch with you," he said. "To say thank you. To say good-bye." He looked up and met Judge's eye. The moment lengthened, and Mister finally cleared his throat and said, "To say I'm sorry for my part in all the misunderstandings between us. I'm sorry for all the hurtful things I said to you. I'm sorry I wasted so much time *not* saying I'm sorry."

Judge's emotions surged, making his chest tight and his eyes hot. "There is nothing you need to apologize for."

"And you're not a great liar." Mister grinned and popped another fry into his mouth. "I'm sorry to leave you alone in the Ranch House."

"It's far too big for just me," he said.

"Better get June up there quick, then." Mister's eyes glinted with dual emotions—one teasing Judge and one utterly devastated that he didn't have someone to bring up to the ranch and call his wife.

"I'm headed over to her place after this," Judge said.

"Things going well, then?"

"Well enough," Judge said. "She hasn't ended things yet, and I'm counting that as a win. She says yes when I ask her out, and our schedules have aligned lately, so that's a major win." He paused and stirred a crispy fry around in some ketchup. "I met her parents a couple of weeks ago, and ahem, she lets me kiss her whenever we're together."

"Oh-ho," Mister said, chuckling. "Sounds like it's going *really* well."

"I'm trying not to be too hopeful," Judge said. "Is that stupid?"

"Given your history with this woman, I don't think so," Mister said. "I understand how devastating a dashed hope can be."

Judge nodded, and the two of them simply ate together until their food had disappeared. When neither of them could put it off any longer, Judge stood. Mister threw some money on the table, and said, "That's almost all I've got."

"I'll get lunch," Judge said, digging into his pocket for his wallet. "You're gonna need that."

Mister hesitated, then reached for his money. "You're right. I signed my account over to Bear, and I opened a new one with a little seed money. I need this." He tucked the cash back into his pocket and looked at Judge.

Something wavered between them, and Judge grabbed onto Mister—because he was what was wavering between them—and held him as tightly as he could. "You're going to be amazing at Winterhaven. It's only four hours away. Come home anytime. There's always going to be room for you at the Ranch House, with me."

"I appreciate that." Mister said, his voice as tightly woven as a new drum. He drew in a sharp breath and stepped back. They went outside, and Judge followed Mister to his packed truck. He ran his fingers along the brown tarp there and hugged his brother again.

Then, just like that, Mister got behind the wheel, backed out of the parking spot, and made a left turn onto Main Street, heading East.

Judge watched him go until he couldn't see the black vehicle anymore, then he sighed and headed toward June's office building.

She ran her Internet and business network solutions company from one of the oldest buildings in Three Rivers, and Judge loved the beautiful, aged, red, orange, and white bricks. He loved the unique quality of it, because he sometimes felt like just another man in a cowboy hat. Up at

Shiloh Ridge, there were dozens of men like him, though he did have a bit lighter hair than most of the other Glovers.

He also kept a beard, one of the only Glovers to do that too. He tried to stand out in subtle ways now, instead of calling attention to himself in trickster ways.

He pulled into the parking lot at Nichols Networking, noticing one of her utility trucks right behind him. He parked out front, while that vehicle went along the side of the building toward the back. He'd just reached for the front door when he heard his name.

A moment later, June came jogging around the side of the building. "It is you," she said, slowing and smiling. "I thought so."

"I told you I was coming, remember?"

"Yeah, that's why I'm back already."

"Well, he's gone," Judge said as he walked toward June. Everything stormed inside him, and he didn't know how to hold it back. June should know how emotional he was anyway.

"Who's gone?" she asked.

He reached her and wrapped his arms around her. "Mister," he said, his voice way up in the back of his nose. "He's gone. He left. He's going to work a ranch in Oklahoma, and it's all my fault."

A sob wrenched its way through his chest, and he couldn't contain it. He didn't want to. "It's my fault."

"Sh," she said, holding him with a tight grip. "It's okay, Judge. I'm sure it's not your fault."

Twenty minutes later, Judge sat in June's kitchen while she bustled around, putting mugs, spoons, miniature marshmallows, and a can of evaporated milk on the counter in front of him.

He wanted to tell her he was fine, but he wasn't sure he was. She'd assured him she could take the rest of the afternoon off, which was great. He couldn't, and he had plenty of chores at the ranch to complete before the sun went down.

And yet, here he sat, unable to get himself to leave.

"I'm sorry," he said about the same time her electric kettle started to boil.

"Judge, you have absolutely nothing to be sorry about."

"I broke down and sobbed into your shoulder," he said, dropping his head until his only choice for a view was her floor. Picasso and Remmy lay there, curled into one another. Their love for each other filled the air and somehow gave Judge hope.

He looked up. "This is who I am, June. I'm weak."

"Your emotions don't make you weak," she said, coming around the island with two mugs with steam rising from them. She looked at him earnestly and passed him a mug. "They make you human."

"Women don't want a weepy man."

"You're not weepy."

Judge shook his head and reached for the evaporated milk. "You say this is good?"

"My mom calls it canned cow," June said with a smile.

She lifted her mug to her mouth and took a sip. "She says you can't have hot chocolate without it."

He poured in all the "canned cow" he could without making this drink overflow the way he had the coffee at the diner. "I don't think we should be having hot chocolate in June at all," he said, but he took a sip the same as she had.

"Oh, wow," he said, the richness of it coating his tongue. "Your mother is a genius."

June laughed and put her hand on his knee. "I'm glad to see you today, Judge."

He looked at her fingers against his jeans and then up into her eyes. "How are you doing without her?"

June's gaze fluttered away from his. "It's been...hard." She put a brave smile on her face as Judge's fingers curled around hers. She drew in a deep breath. "I'm so glad to see you today, because it sure is nice to have company."

"I agree," he said, thinking about the now-empty Ranch House, and how he didn't have anyone waiting for him at home either.

Chapter Eleven

June couldn't stop smiling. First, she wasn't home alone tonight, and that felt like she'd won the lottery. Second, Judge had so many Christmas decorations that he had to keep a clipboard with a wad of papers stuck to it for an inventory list.

"This one I used a couple of years ago," he said, holding up a nearly life-size version of Rudolph.

"Do you ever throw them away?" June took in the boxes and boxes and boxes. They seemed to go on for miles, and she wondered how Mister even managed to find a spot to be in this house.

"Oh, sure," Judge said, the joy in his eyes so different from the devastation that had been there several hours ago. "I threw out all my lights last year and replaced them." He set down Rudolph and dove back into his boxes. "I still got third."

"I'm sorry."

"Mister says I'm never going to win, because I can't get enough people to come up to the ranch to vote," he said.

"He might be right." June took a deep breath and got the golden scent of roasting chicken. She'd watched Judge truss the bird and put it in a baking dish with onions, carrots, and potatoes. He'd promised her a home-cooked meal, and they'd taken a walk on his ranch before starting in on the decorations.

"I know," Judge said. "I think this might be the last year I even put anything up." He sat back on his haunches and ran one hand over his beard, smoothing it down. "Then all of this will go in the trash."

He spoke with sadness about it, and the inkling of an idea sparked in her head. "If you can't get people physically up here, you should take the light show to them."

"How do you figure?" he asked, rising to his feet. He came to sit beside her on the couch, sighing loudly as he leaned back and lifted his arm over her shoulder.

She sank into him, the presence of another human being so comforting. She had no idea what it was like to truly be alone until Lucy Mae had gone and left her in Three Rivers by herself. Her parents and sister had stayed for a few extra days, but every moment since then had felt so...hollow.

Except for when she was with Judge, June just felt hollow. She still had her business and her work. All of her friends there. Her beautiful home. But none of them brought her the same joy and comfort that Judge Glover did. She wasn't sure what that said about her—or him. For now, she was just glad to be with him.

"Well," she said. "I *figure* that it's pretty easy to set up webcams these days. Why can't you broadcast your light show for people to see wherever they are?"

"Broadcast it?"

"Sure," June said.

"I don't think I have the bandwidth for that," Judge said.

"Yeah, you really should call someone who knows what they're doing when it comes to upgrading your network." She rolled her eyes, glad when Judge's chest vibrated with a deep chuckle.

"How much is that going to cost me?"

"Why?" June asked. "Is it something you can't afford?'

"No, I—"

"Yeah, so ask me a question I can actually answer."

"What does that mean?"

"It means, my sensitive cowboy, that I know you're really rich."

"You do? How do you know that?"

"You cowboys don't get off the ranch super often, do you?"

"Depends on who it is," Judge said. "Ace does a lot of grocery shopping for us. Cactus is forever going down to town for things. I came to town for lunch today."

"Lunch." June giggled and put her feet up on the couch, practically laying in Judge's lap. He ran his fingers up and down her arm, sending shivers through her whole body.

The man had a real way of lighting her up when she was dark and cooling her down when she got too hot.

"Since you're one of the ones who doesn't leave the ranch much, you obviously didn't see the VIP spotlight in the Three Rivers Times."

"I did not."

June swiped on her phone and started typing to get to the town newspaper website. "Let's see what it says... The spotlight was of one Ranger Glover." She tilted her head back to see him, but Judge wore a frown between his eyes, which he'd trained out the window.

June had come this far, though, and she might as well see this through. She cleared her throat. "Ranger Glover is a lifetime Three Rivers resident, who lives and works at Shiloh Ridge Ranch. He's a cowboy billionaire who not only runs a profitable cattle operation south of town, but he's the founder and developer of Two Cents, the town's robust recommendation app."

She stopped there, because Judge's body had tightened with every word she'd read, and it wasn't even about him.

"Does he know about this article?" he asked.

"I assume so," June said. "It had quotes from him and everything."

"Hmm."

"If he's a cowboy billionaire, aren't you?"

"What makes you think that?"

"Just answer the question, Judge." June sat up and looked at him, but she didn't need him to answer. The money was written right there in the three dozen boxes of lawn Christmas decorations. The remodeling of this house. The insane amount of building that had gone on up here.

"Yes," he said. "We all inherited quite a sum of money when my dad died. Ranger and Ward do a lot of investing that keeps us living in luxury."

"I didn't say you lived in luxury," she said, noting the sarcastic note in his voice.

He closed his eyes and sighed. "I know you didn't. Come back over here." He kneaded her back to his side, where they both sighed. June's eyes drifted closed too, and Judge's chest started to rise and fall in steady, even breaths.

"Something smells good in here," someone said, and June jerked back to full consciousness. "Judge?"

"I'm asleep," he said without moving.

Footsteps came closer, and June scrambled to sit up. Still, Judge didn't move.

"Oh, howdy June," a tall, bear of a man said.

"Bear," June said, jumping to her feet. She glanced at Judge, who was just now opening his eyes. He yawned and reached for her hand. She helped him to his feet, not that he really needed that.

"What's up?" Judge asked, stepping around the couch.

"Mister left today," Bear said. "I thought I'd come see how you were coping." He flicked a glance toward June, a quick smile appearing on his face too.

"I put in a chicken for dinner," Judge said. "You and Sammy and the kids could come eat with us." He took his brother into a hug, and Bear pounded him heartily on the back.

"I'll text her," Bear said, stepping back. "I think she was

giving Stetson a yogurt with Honey Nut Cheerios in it when I left." He pulled out his phone and sent a quick text. "Did you talk to Mister today?"

"Yeah, we went to lunch." Judge moved into the kitchen, leaving June with Bear. He had a presence about him that dwarfed June and rendered her mute.

"Sammy says Link is out with Mitch and Cactus."

"I'll invite them too," Judge said. "Wait. June." He set the roasting pan on the stovetop and met her eyes. "Is that okay?"

"It's fine," she said. "If you think that single chicken can feed all of us."

He looked at the chicken and back to her. "I think we'll survive."

"I don't know," June teased. "I've seen cowboys eat, and you lot aren't lightweights."

"She's right," Bear said, chuckling. "I can have Sammy bring over—"

"We're fine," Judge said, his focus on his phone. "It's eight pounds of meat, and I put in a ton of potatoes."

"Okay," Bear said.

Judge turned toward the cupboard and got down what looked suspiciously like a brownie mix. "I'll make dessert. That's all I want anyway."

"Oh, things are bad," Bear said.

"Things are fine," Judge said with a hefty bite in his voice. "The only problem is you interrupting my nap."

"Sammy's rounding up the kids now," Bear said.

Judge's phone sounded, and he peered at it. "Cactus is just comin' in from the ranch, and he'll talk to Willa."

June entered the kitchen and got out the eggs. "Oil?" she asked.

"Yes, please," Judge said quietly. "Is this really okay?"

"Are you kidding?" she asked. "It's great." She turned to get the oil out of the cupboard where she'd seen him put it after he'd finished with it earlier. "Better than sitting home alone," she muttered under her breath, and that was the gospel truth.

The house started to fill after that, not only with the scent of double-fudge brownies, but with people. Everyone greeted June with smiles and hugs, even the supposedly prickly brother named Cactus.

June fed off the energy of the two older boys, who Judge introduced as Lincoln and Mitch, who were twelve and thirteen respectively. She loved watching them interact with the little children—Stetson, who toddled after them as if he could possibly keep up—and the babies, who were both about six months old.

One of them—Willa and Cactus's son, Charles—started to fuss, and June found herself the closest adult. She bent to pick up the boy, who'd fallen forward onto his face. "It's okay, buddy," she said. He looked at her with wide, brown eyes the color of tree bark, his cheeks flushed a little.

A single tear clung to his eyelashes, and June smiled at him and wiped it away. "You're okay, bud. Let's get you a cookie."

"She's getting him a cookie," Willa said.

"Let 'er," Cactus said, not moving. "I had the worst day ever, and I wish someone would bring me cookies and feed them to me."

June grinned at him and joined Sammy and Judge in the kitchen. One of his cousins had come too, and Etta turned toward June. "The cookies are in the cupboard above the freezer."

"Thanks." June started to reach up, but she knew she couldn't make it.

"I'll get them, Juney," Judge said, and he stepped to her side and got down the graham-flavored cookies shaped like little teddy bears.

"Why do you have these?" she asked, shifting the baby to her other hip.

"Everyone has flaws," he said with a grin.

She scoffed. "If you're counting eating cookies as a flaw, I think you might be taken up to heaven in the twinkling of an eye."

Judge burst out laughing, drawing the attention of everyone in the house. June kept her eyes down as she opened the box and took out a single teddy bear. She held it very still for baby Charlie to take it from her. He did, and he missed his mouth the first time, sending the little bear to the floor.

He looked down, shifting his weight, and June nearly dropped him. "It's okay, bud," she said. "There's more." She took out another teddy and pinched it until he took it from her. He got this one into his mouth, and his big, beautiful eyes widened when he tasted it.

"It's good, right?" she asked, cuddling the boy closer. She'd never thought she'd want another child, but this baby had changed her mind in only five minutes. She handed him another cookie and took one for herself too. "Oh, these are fantastic."

Charlie leaned his head against her shoulder, all smiles even as he started to drool a little bit. She stepped over a few feet and grabbed a paper towel. The boy whined when she wiped his face, but she fixed that with another cookie.

"Time to eat," Judge said, his voice rising above the others chatting in the house. They weren't loud, as it was mostly the women catching up with each other. "Everyone come sit down."

Cactus dragged himself off the couch, but he didn't come get his son. Willa busied herself with Mitch and Lincoln, and Sammy had two little boys to wrangle. She and Bear each tackled one, with Stetson giggling as he ran from his mother.

"I got you," she said, scooping him into her arms and tickling him. His lighthearted, childlike giggles brought so much joy to June's heart that she couldn't help laughing too.

Surprisingly, Judge pulled two highchairs out of some-where, and Sammy strapped Stetson into one of them against his wishes. June dropped a cookie onto the tray, and the dark-haired child looked up at her.

"Shh," she said. "Eat it quick, bud."

He grabbed it and stuck the teddy bear in his mouth, and June turned toward Judge. "Does he go in a chair?"

"I'm not sure," he said, bending down to give the baby a kiss. "Did you get some teddies, you lucky boy?"

"Da, da, da," Charlie said, and June gave him another cookie.

"I can take him," Willa said.

June turned toward her. "Do you have to?"

"Absolutely not," Willa said, smiling at June. "It'll be nice to eat with both hands, for once."

"Does he sit in the chair?" she asked, glancing at Sammy. "It looks like Bear is going to hold Russ."

"You can try," Willa said. "He usually ends up screaming after about ten seconds." She wore a look like June was about to attend her own funeral.

June removed the tray from the highchair and set Charlie in it. She handed him a cookie, and while he was distracted with trying to figure out how to get the treat into his mouth, she buckled the strap and slid the tray back on.

Another teddy bear went onto the tray, and she sat down in the chair next to the baby.

"I'm going to say a prayer," Judge said, putting his hands on the back of the chair next to her. She wanted to watch him, but she closed her eyes and folded her hands into her lap. "Dear Lord," he said. "Thank you for sending my favorite people to spend time with me tonight. Bless Mister while he's away, and—" He ground his voice through his throat. "Bless the food. Amen."

He pulled out the chair and sat down. "Why are you so tired, Cactus?"

"Because," his brother said just as his son started to fuss. June reached for one of the baby carrots that had roasted with the chicken and easily pinched off the end of it. Carrots were so sweet, and she put it on the tray. Charlie quieted instantly, reaching with his chubby, little fingers to get what he thought was a treat.

"Some of us had to pick up the slack for the two cowboys who weren't at work today." Cactus smiled at Judge, though he did look a couple of breaths away from passing out completely.

"That," Willa said. "And Tank rang the bell to go out about every hour last night."

Mitch's fingers started to fly, and both Cactus and Willa looked at him.

Bear started to laugh, as did the boy's parents. Even Judge joined in.

"Is that true?" Sammy asked, but June had no idea what the boy had said.

"What did he say?" she asked.

"Oh, sorry," Judge said. "He said Tank was sick because he found Cactus's secret chocolate stash in the barn and ate it all."

"If that's true, I'm making a trip out to the Edge," Sammy said.

"Why?" Bear asked. "We don't have enough chocolate in the homestead?" He took a couple of slices of chicken and passed the platter to his wife.

"You can never have too much chocolate," June said at the exact same time as Sammy. Their eyes met, and June started to giggle along with the other woman. June had listened to Judge talk about Sammy, and he really liked and respected her. She had a knack for knowing when he needed to be checked on, and June thought he possessed the same gift for others.

He'd texted this morning to ask if he could see her that day after lunch, and she'd nearly burst into tears because of it.

"So," Sammy asked. "How's Lucy Mae doing at Cal-State?"

"Good," June said, glad her throat hadn't closed at the first mention of her daughter. Charlie fussed slightly, and June gave him a chunk of potato this time. "She got put on the team she wanted, which made her very happy."

"Which team is that?" Judge asked, handing her a full plate of food and picking up her empty one.

She looked at the meal, her heart expanding so many sizes she couldn't count. She couldn't believe she'd cut this man out of her life previously. At the same time, she had no idea if she had any right to be here with this family.

She was just Lucy Mae's mom. Sammy's first question was even about Lucy Mae. Not June herself. Not Nichols Networking.

But Lucy Mae.

"June?" Judge asked quietly. "Which team?"

She cleared her throat and said, "She loves building and working through problems related to buildings and cities. She got put on the civil engineering team, and she was thrilled."

"That's great," Willa said, and June nodded and smiled at her.

"Oh," Bear said. "I just got a text from Mister. He's at Winterhaven, all checked in with the boss, and in his new cabin." He held up his phone, and everyone smiled. June didn't have many experiences with Adam's family, but they weren't like this.

Even her own family didn't feel as close as this one, and they certainly didn't get along as well. Judge had told her that one of the reasons he'd been so upset that afternoon about Mister's departure was because they didn't get along that great.

"I'm putting it on the family string," Judge said. "Since he obviously only texted Bear."

June looked at him, the bitterness in his voice not hard to hear, at least as close as she sat to him. Sammy said something to Stetson, and Lincoln started laughing hysterically about something Mitch had said with his hands.

"Stop it," Bear said to Lincoln. "You're being so loud."

Lincoln quieted by maybe two decibels, and by the time Judge looked up from his phone and into June's eyes, she felt sure everyone had forgotten what he'd said.

"You okay?" she asked, sort of wishing they were once again alone. She'd enjoyed that peaceful, comfortable feeling of just lying in his arms while they slept.

"Yeah," he said. "He just said he'd text me when he got there, that's all."

On his other side, Etta said, "He's probably doing the best he can."

"I know." Judge sighed and stabbed a piece of chicken. He'd just put it in his mouth when his phone chimed. June caught Mister's name on the screen, and she smiled as Judge dove for the phone. "This is him. He said he's got two roommates, and their names are Billy and Wick. Oh, I like Wick."

"Sounds like a name we'd use in this family," Etta said.

"But not a real name," Willa said. "You'd have to name the baby Wendell or something. Then just call him Wick."

"Of course," Sammy said. "But not Wendell. William. Wendell's no good."

June listened to them talk, but she didn't really understand it. When there was a slight pause between people tossing out names that started with W, she asked, "What's with the dual names?"

"Everyone has a different given name," Cactus said. "Do you think my mother really named me Cactus?"

"Not everyone," Etta said, her voice firm. "Some of us weren't as favored by Grandmother."

"That's not it at all," Bear said.

"How do you know?" Etta challenged. "Besides, you were her favorite."

"I was not," he said, and that caused an uproar, with Judge actually tossing a bit of bread in Bear's direction. June grinned at him, because he obviously *was* their grandmother's favorite.

"All right," she said. "What are all your real names, then?"

"Bartholomew," Sammy said, grinning at her husband. "And Charles."

"Oh, I should've guessed that one." June looked at Judge, her eyebrows almost as high as her mood. This dinner had been exactly what she'd needed.

"My real name is John," he said.

"Not Jonathan?"

"No, ma'am. Just John." He smiled at her, leaned over

and kissed her forehead, and speared another carrot. "That baby is gettin' ready to scream." He nodded past her to Charlie, who June had been ignoring.

She hurried to get him another bite of food, but his little face was already all screwed up and bright red. In the next moment, he let out a wail that reminded June of a fire engine siren, and no amount of cookies could soothe that.

Chapter Twelve

Etta Glover rode alongside Montana, enjoying the wind in her face and the freedom of the sunshine warming her soul.

"Anyway," Montana said. "I'm sorry about Marshall." Her eyes landed heavily on the side of Etta's face. "What are you going to do?"

"Well, tonight, I'm going to babysit baby Robbie so he knows I'm the best aunt in the world." She flashed a smile in Montana's direction.

"We don't have to go," Montana said. "I don't want to anyway."

"Yes, you do," Etta said, scoffing afterward. "Your uncle is getting an award, Montana. You'd be so mad at yourself if you weren't there."

"It'll be stuffy," she said. "Full of men and women with too much money and not enough humor."

"Well, you and Bishop fit one of those," Etta quipped, smiling into the sun again.

"Aurora is going out with Ollie," Montana said. "She makes him come pick her up at the house, but Bishop and I will be gone."

"She's already told me," Etta said. "I told her I get to answer the door and ask him a few questions." Etta started to laugh, though she wasn't looking forward to watching the two kids go out tonight. Aurora and Ollie had been dating for years now, but Etta knew the summer honeymoon was about to end.

"Shouldn't she be starting her lessons soon?" Montana asked, twisting in her saddle to look behind her. "I don't see her."

Etta slowed her horse, a pale beauty she'd named Sugar Cube. "I'll go find her. I'm supposed to take two kids on their lesson today."

"You are?" Montana peered at her. "She's paying you, right?"

"Yes," Etta said, though she didn't need the money. She'd refused to take Aurora's money in the past, but the girl had offered. "I mean, she offered."

"Etta."

"She offered," Etta said, swinging Sugar Cube around. She knew right where Aurora would be. "I know she's saving for college, and I think it's great that she has so many kids taking lessons from her that she can't serve them all." She caught the look of displeasure on Montana's face. "I'm happy to help."

"I know you are," Montana said. "And Aurora knows it too. Don't you let her take advantage of you."

"I won't." Etta gave her a grin and added, "I'll be by your place by five."

"Thank you, Etta."

Etta got Sugar Cube going in the direction of the far stables, where Aurora had her kids come to take lessons. She did them in groups of five, but every so often, she had a pair of little girls who put her groups to seven.

Etta had been helping all spring and summer with this round of lessons, and she would until Aurora left for college in Stillwater.

Sugar Cube went around the corner of the stable, and sure enough, Ollie's truck sat there. The boy would leave again once the lessons started, and he'd show up at Bishop's and Montana's house for his date with Aurora at six-thirty.

The truth was, Oliver Walker wasn't a boy anymore. He was a man, and he too had a wide-open future in front of him. He was tall, dark, handsome, strong, and sweet, and Etta would not be surprised in the least if Aurora ended up marrying him.

"Probably before you get married," Etta muttered to herself, thinking of Marshall. She'd had fun with him on the few dates they'd been on. Etta thought herself a kind person, with an open mind about the type of man she wanted to have in her life. Her focus had once been quite narrow, and her own indiscretions had humbled her to the point that she didn't have any requirements for a potential boyfriend other than he be unmarried.

She supposed she could add "honest" to the list, as Marshall's lies had been the main cause of their break-up.

She clicked her tongue at Sugar Cube, who slowed and stopped. "Wait here, girl." Etta swung out of the saddle and dusted her hands together. She approached the stable door and banged on it. "I'm coming in."

A moment later, she did just that, and thankfully, Aurora and Ollie had stopped kissing by the time she found them standing over by the tack room door. "Your mother is looking for you," Etta said, pinning them both with a knowing glare. "And you best get that truck moved, Ollie. The lessons start in ten minutes."

"Yes, ma'am," he said, reaching for his hat, which had fallen to the ground at some point. Probably when Aurora pushed it off his head so she could kiss him. His cheeks flamed red as he stuffed the hat back on his head and strode out of the stable. "'Bye, Rory."

Aurora kept her back to both Etta and Ollie as she said, "'Bye, Ollie. See you at six-thirty."

"Yep." He walked out, and a few seconds later, the growl of his engine filled the air.

Etta approached Aurora, who kept her head bent. The braid her hair had been in had obviously been tampered with. "Want me to fix your hair?"

"Sure," Aurora whispered.

Etta took out the elastic on the end of the braid and started combing her fingers through Aurora's pretty, blonde hair. "You need to be careful with that boy," she said quietly as she started re-separating it into three strands. This wasn't the first time she'd caught Aurora and Ollie kissing in the stable, and it wouldn't be long until someone else did.

"At the very least, you might want to switch up where you meet him." She smiled as she said it, and a moment later, Aurora giggled.

Etta kept her own laughter to herself, which was easy to do because of the jealousy raging through her. She finished the braid and patted Aurora's back where the hair lay. "You're such a beautiful girl," she whispered, pressing her chin to Aurora's shoulder. "Does he know it?"

"I think so," Aurora said.

"Are you going to marry him?"

"I don't know," Aurora said, turning into Etta. She wore worry and fear on her face. "I'm leaving in only a couple of months, and he's not coming with me."

"I know." Etta offered her a sympathetic smile. "People date long-distance, you know. There are apps and videos and phones and all kinds of things to stay in touch. Not only that, but Stillwater is only a few hours away. Ollie has a truck—a nice one by the looks of it."

Aurora shook her head. "I don't want to date long-distance. Can you imagine what my mother will say?" She reached up and brushed the tears from her eyes.

"I know exactly what your mother will say," Etta said. "So...then what? Are you going to break-up with him?"

"I don't want to."

"But you don't want to go to college and not be able to do what college students do," Etta said. "They hang out with each other. They date. They kiss lots of boys." Etta giggled then, and Aurora smiled for a brief moment.

Etta sobered and drew in a deep breath. "What do you guys talk about?" she asked, exhaling. "I'm sure it's not all kissing, all the time."

"Savannah," Aurora said. "As always."

"And?" Etta turned away and reached for one of the children's saddles hanging on the wall.

"And nothing," Aurora said, joining her in the task. They had seven horses to saddle and have ready for lessons in only a few minutes. "It's never going to happen. Ollie mentioned it to his father, and he dang near went ballistic." She shook her head. "Bishop and Mom will react the exact same way."

"Why?" Etta asked. "You can't know that."

"I do know it," Aurora said with plenty of frustration in her voice.

"You're already going to college," Etta said. "Why does it matter if it's in Stillwater, Oklahoma or Savannah, Georgia?"

"The distance," she said. "What I'm studying."

"You're extremely talented with cloth and a sewing machine," Etta said firmly. "Do not let anyone tell you that's not something." She looked at Aurora, her resolve hard. "It *is* something, Aurora. You could be an amazing fashion designer."

"It's never going to happen," Aurora said. "They have a good design program at Oklahoma State."

"Oh, they do not," Etta said, opening the stall to let the horses out into the paddock so they could saddle them. "You should talk to your parents about Savannah." She'd mentioned as much to Aurora several times over the course of the past few months since they'd been doing this riding lesson session together.

"I'll think about it," Aurora said, the same as she always did.

"Okay," Etta said, taking the saddle out to the paddock to get the first horse saddled. She wasn't going to badger Aurora about it, and she wasn't going to tell Montana or Bishop either. Aurora had that right, and Etta wouldn't take it from her.

The first children arrived, and Etta smiled as she looked up to greet them. She loved children, and as she hugged a little girl named Petra, she prayed the Lord would send her a man who she could love, and who would love her, and who she could have a family with.

I guess I do have some requirements, she thought, lifting the child into the saddle. *But they seem normal to me, so if there's anything You can do, that would be much appreciated.*

Chapter Thirteen

I da Burton's fingers flew across the screen, her texts to her sister full of misspellings and missing punctuation. *You definitely need to go out with Henry Platt*, she said. *He's so good-looking, and I just watched him lift two hundred pounds straight up over his head.*

She giggled and glanced up at her husband. Brady's forehead shone with sweat, and Ida tucked her phone into her back pocket. "You did so great, baby," she said, throwing her arms around him. "I had no idea you could lift so much."

"I lost, Ida," he said, laughing with her as they spun around once.

"Who cares?" she said, gazing at him with love pouring from her. "I liked watching you try to beat Henry, and I just told Etta she should go out with him."

"Etta and Henry?" Brady glanced over his shoulder to

where the victor of the lifting competition stood grinning with several other cops.

Ida hadn't known what to expect at this police department Olympics, but lifting huge bags of medical supplies was apparently one of the main events.

"I could see that working," Brady said. "What did she say?"

"I don't know. I'd just finished texting her when you came over." She glanced over to where Lilly sat with the twins. "How are Johnny and Judy?" She didn't move that way, because it was nice to be free from the babies for just a few minutes.

"Lilly loves them," Brady said, smiling. "She's got plenty of help too. How about we sneak away and get some ice cream?"

"Like, leave the building?" Ida glanced back over to Lilly and the twins, who were now surrounded by a few other girls, most of them somewhere in their low teens. One girl lifted Judy into her arms and grinned at her.

"They'll be fine," Brady said. "Those are Chief DuPont's girls, and the ice cream parlor is literally right next door." He took her hand and led her toward the side exit. A thrill moved through her as they snuck away, and she giggled when they hit the alley between the police station and the courthouse next door.

"Brady," she whispered, as if this summer day wouldn't allow her to speak too loudly. "This is crazy."

"We need a night out without the twins," he said. "A whole weekend. A week."

"You getting a week off would be a miracle," Ida said. "Even a weekend is unheard of."

Brady turned back to her and smiled, the gesture twinged with sadness. "I know, baby. I'm not going to work so much after we get our new hires trained up, I swear."

"Is that so?" she teased, laying on her Texas accent. "And when is that, Detective Burton?"

He grinned at her. "Not more than three more weeks, I swear."

"And then we'll get away for a weekend," she said. "I can ask Etta to come sleep at the house to take care of the babies."

"Yes," Brady said, ducking back around the corner. "Then we'll get away for the weekend." He kissed her, and Ida remembered all the soft feelings she had for her husband. She remembered how much she loved him, and how much he loved her.

Her back pocket chimed, and she giggled as she broke the kiss. "That's Etta."

"Mm." Brady kissed her neck right there in the alley, with people walking by only a dozen feet away.

Ida's blood heated, as the temperature in Three Rivers that day neared a number that drove people inside to their air conditioned homes.

"Ooh, it is Etta, and she said she'd go out with Henry."

Brady stepped back and sighed. "I suppose I'm going to have to talk to him."

"Of course not," Ida said. "You totally messed up talking to Byron. I'm going to handle Henry." She turned as if she'd go do it right then, but her husband took her by the hand and led her onto the sidewalk.

"I did fine with Byron," he said. "Isn't Etta going to get sick of us setting her up with cops?"

"First off, it's been one cop," Ida said. "That you messed up, so she didn't even go out with him."

Brady chuckled and nodded to a couple walking in the opposite direction. "I had a hard enough time asking you out, my love. I don't know how to do it for someone else."

"We can try again with Byron if things don't work out with Henry," Ida said, the ice cream shop appearing ahead. "Oh, dear. Look at the line, baby."

"No problem," Brady said. "Excuse me, folks." He started stepping past the people waiting. "Official police business." He kept a tight hold on Ida's hand as they moved all the way to the front of the line.

"Hello, Officer," a woman standing there said. "Your usual?"

"You have a usual?" Ida asked, making it to her husband's side. "How often do you come here?" While she labored at home with pukey, demanding babies, the grocery shopping, the cleaning, the bills, the rain gutters full of leaves, he was here getting "his usual"?

"Yes, please, Hilde," he said. "And Ida here wants the mint cookie, please."

"Yes, sir," Hattie said, and not two minutes later, Brady and Ida walked out with their treat.

"You didn't even pay for it." Ida looked up at her husband, shocked at what had just happened.

"I have an account," he says. "I pay it every month."

"You're addicted to chocolate brownie ice cream," Ida said, teasing and surprised at the same time.

Brady burst out laughing, but he didn't contradict her. He did love his sweets, and that was simply another thing Ida was busy doing while Brady snacked on ice cream—making a dessert for dinner every night.

She'd grown up that way, with Mother making something sweet and flaky night after night. Mother didn't think a meal was a proper meal without pie.

Brady loved Ida's apple pie, and she didn't make a new one every night the way Mother had. It was just Ida and Brady eating the pie, and she could make one last three days. She also wanted more than pie, so she made chocolate cakes, brownies, cookies, and even a flan once. Brady hadn't liked it as much as the more traditional desserts, but he did love cinnamon rolls, buttermilk bars, and chocolate tarts.

A slip of resentment moved through her, and Ida swallowed against it. "Brady," she said. "I...hate that you're always here, and I'm at home doing everything."

"I—" He didn't say anything else, and the situation couldn't be fixed. "I won't get ice cream every day anymore."

"It's not about the ice cream," Ida said. "It's...I don't want to make dessert every night if you're already getting sweets while working."

"I never said you had to make dessert every night." Brady stopped in the shade of a huge oak tree and looked at Ida. "Or dinner, baby. You don't have to do those things. I've told you many times, I don't care if you nap all day long and wear sweats. I really don't."

Ida nodded, but her chest still felt too tight. "I'm going to keep working with Etta on the outreach programs."

"And you should," he said. "I've told you that a dozen times. Heck, more than that." He frowned at her. "Why don't you believe me?"

She licked her mint cookie ice cream. "I don't know," she said. "When we got married, we agreed to split things the way we have. You work a lot, and you help me with the dishes and the laundry. I love those babies, and I love you, and I don't want you to think I'm unhappy or dissatisfied."

"I don't think that." He sighed and glanced around. "Do you feel trapped, Ida?"

She ducked her head, but that only caused Brady to take a step closer. "Ida, baby, we agreed to be honest with each other in all things. You told me you'd tell me if you felt trapped at home with the twins."

"Yes," she whispered, a slip of guilt moving through her. "I feel trapped at home with the babies."

"Is this about the ice cream? Because I won't get it anymore if it bothers you."

"It's not about that," she said. "It's about what it represents. You, getting to get out and do whatever you want all day. I know you're working." She looked up into his troubled eyes. "I know you're working. I know that. But no one's bringing me ice cream. No one's throwing me a party for something I did. I just...I feel useless."

Brady wrapped one arm around her waist and pulled her closer. "I will throw you a party every day," he whispered. "For how well you take care of me, the house, the twins, and our life. You're an amazing woman, Ida, and I love you more every day for all you do."

"I love you too, Brady," she said. "Now, my ice cream's going to melt all over your shirt."

He chuckled and stepped back. The laughter didn't last long before the moment sobered again. "Are we okay, Ida?" Brady asked. "I'm sorry I don't help as much as I should. Let's get dinner before we head home this afternoon. Then no one will have to cook tonight, and we can eat the leftovers for lunch tomorrow after church."

"You've got yourself a deal, Detective," Ida said, linking her free arm through his and raising her ice cream to her mouth. "Okay, now help me decide how to approach Henry. Just come straight at him and ask if he'd like to go out with my sister? Or do a more probing approach? Find out if he's seeing someone, and then suggest Etta?"

"I know he uses that dating app," Brady said. "Etta's on there, right?"

"I don't think we should mention she's on the app." Ida cleared her throat. "And we should tell him not to mention he's there either. Etta's not too keen on guys on the dating app right now."

"Just because one man lied, doesn't mean they all do," Brady said.

"I know that, and you know that," Ida said. "Etta will understand that too. Right now, though, let's stick with he's one of your cops, and he's handsome and strong. She's my sister, and she's *stunningly* beautiful, smart, and willing to go on blind dates."

"I think you've got the pitch down pat," Brady said,

smiling at her as they went around the corner and toward the side entrance. "She said she'd go out with him?"

"Her exact words were, 'set it up, Ida, and don't be teasing me about the two hundred pounds.'" She trilled out a laugh, and as they re-entered the workout room at the police station, she heard the fussing of one of her babies. "Oh, that's Judy," she said.

"I'll get her," Brady said, stepping in front of Ida. "You sit right here, baby, and finish your ice cream. I've got the twins." He walked away, his step sure and long, and he swept their daughter into his arms. The little girl stopped fussing, and Ida allowed a soft smile to cross her face.

She loved him, and she loved her life with him. Now, she just wanted to find someone for Etta to fall madly in love with too.

Chapter Fourteen

O akley Glover sat behind her desk in her office at Mack's Motor Sports. She came down from Shiloh Ridge Ranch a couple of times each week, because she did need to keep up with her payroll and her employees.

She'd taken a leaf from Ranger's book, and she held a mandatory meeting every Tuesday morning. That way, she could keep up with who was leaving, who wasn't, who was happy, and who wasn't. She could meet with individual employees, grant raises, go over customer comment cards, and review the service reports.

She worked all day Tuesday, and then took work home with her, because she didn't go back to Mack's until Saturday.

On Saturday, she got to work the floor for half the day, and that fed her desire to talk to people—real people who could talk back, not the fifteen-month-old she spent most of her time with. Yes, she talked to Sammy and Etta, the two women who lived in the same house she did. She spoke with Ranger, and she spent time with Ward and Dot, who'd returned from their honeymoon a week or so ago.

She let Holly Ann feed her at the house down the road in the clearing, and she loved getting together with her mother-in-law and her two sisters-in-law to go shopping for a couple of hours.

In a lot of ways, however, Oakley still felt completely isolated. She knew now that she was attending therapy that those feelings of loneliness stemmed from her estranged relationships with her parents. She also never seemed to do anything at the same time as her friends, as all the other Glover women had just had babies, and she was currently the only one expecting.

She'd told no one yet, and as she breathed in the scent of orange wax in her office, she knew why. She wanted the first person she told to be her mother, though she knew she wouldn't get the reaction she wanted.

"Oakley?" Vanessa knocked on the open door, drawing Oakley's attention from her phone.

"Yep, c'mon in," she said, spreading her hands across the desktop. She'd turned nearly all of the day-to-day operations over to Vanessa, who now bore the title Executive Manager of Retail Operations.

Oakley had another person as the manager out in the service bay, and a manager over sales, with sub-managers over vehicles, ATVs, motorcycles, boats, and RVs, as Mack's sold so many different things.

Vanessa entered the office, and she reminded Oakley so much of herself. She wore a cute little pencil skirt, her hair all curled, and a pair of heels that made Oakley's feet hurt just looking at them. She sat down in the chair across from Oakley, her bottom lip trembling.

Oakley's heartbeat bounced up to her throat. "What's wrong?"

"I hate to do this, because you're my favorite boss in the whole world. I love this job with my whole heart." She sucked in a breath as the last word shook coming out of her mouth. Her eyes filled with tears, which she quickly swiped at. "I'm due with my first baby in January, and I'm not going to be able to keep working as much as I do."

Oakley jumped to her feet and hurried around the desk. "Oh, Vanessa, that's so great. Congratulations." She sat in the second chair and hugged Vanessa from the side. "Are you thinking you'll quit completely? Do you just want reduced hours?"

Vanessa drew in a deep breath. "I don't know," she said. "I've been talking about it with Jackson, and we might not be able to afford me quitting completely."

"So we'll talk about a part-time schedule."

"I can't do this part-time," she said. "I can barely do it full-time, and do you think it's a job that two people can reasonably share?"

"I don't see why not," Oakley said gently. "I know you and Walter get along great. Perhaps you could work with him."

"Then you have to find someone to manage Sales, and honestly, I wouldn't move anyone from our sales team onto the management team."

"No one?" Oakley asked. "I almost made McCray the

Sales Manager before. He's been here for twelve years, and he's great with clients."

"He went through a divorce last year, and he's...not quite the same."

"I'll talk to him," Oakley said. "Maybe this promotion is something that will bless his life."

Vanessa smiled and sniffled. "You're always so forgiving," she said. "It's something I really admire about you."

Oakley looked at her, her eyes wide. "No one's ever called me forgiving before."

"You're just so...open to everyone," Vanessa said. "You accept people as they are, and you act like they're better than they are."

Oakley didn't know what to do with that information. She did look for the good in people, and in life. She'd learned how to live life at a slower pace, and she had Ranger and the ranch where she lived to thank for that. She wanted Vanessa to have all the time she needed with her new baby, because she wanted that for herself too.

"Okay," Oakley said. "I'm going to make a note to talk to Walter today, but I think it's McCray's day off." She got to her feet, a twinge in her stomach making her move her hand there as she walked around the desk. "So I'll call him tonight and talk to him." She met Vanessa's eyes. "This is going to work out just fine. Don't you worry at all."

"Thank you," Vanessa said, standing and lifting her phone. "Sorry, Travis just reminded me I was supposed to be sitting in on an interview with a new mechanic."

"Go," Oakley said, watching Vanessa leave the office. She had a lot of paperwork to do, emails to catch up on, and now two new huge tasks to complete. She'd learned from being a mother that the only way the work got done was to wade right in and start.

Instead, she picked up her phone and typed up a text to her mother. *Hey, Mom, it's me Oakley. I heard you got a new phone, so here's my number for it. I wanted you to be the first to know that I'm expecting another baby in November.*

Oakley paused and read over the message, fixing the spelling mistakes. She didn't want just another *congrats!* from her mom. She wanted her mom to be here when the baby came.

"Be brave," she told herself. "Tell her what you want."

She started typing again. *I want you to be there when the baby is born, Mom. I'm due November sixteenth, but I can stay in touch as the date gets closer. There's plenty of room to stay on the ranch, or we can put you in a hotel in town. Then you'll get to meet Ranger finally, and you'll get to meet your other grandson, and I love you, Mom.*

She quickly deleted the last sentence and retyped, *I love you, Mom* after the bit about the hotel. She wasn't entirely sure where her mother lived at the moment, and she had no idea what her mom's finances looked like.

She just wanted her to be there.

She'd put off inviting her, and she hadn't with Wilder at all. She regretted that, and she'd really like to patch things up and make things right. Panic bolted through her, because her mother had never responded the way Oakley wanted her to, and she might not this time either.

That enormous fear alone had kept her from telling her mother about the baby, but she was starting to show in a way she couldn't hide from Sammy, Willa, and the others for much longer. Ranger wanted to tell the family, and Oakley needed to send this text.

So she did.

Then she picked up the phone and called her husband. "Hey, sweetheart. How are things at Mack's?"

Oakley sighed; she could tell him about texting her mom later. "Vanessa is due with her first baby in January, and she wants to pull back to part-time."

"Oh, wow," Ranger said.

"I've been thinking," Oakley said, pushing the papers on her desk to the side, her unrest doubling. She'd texted her mom. Her main manager wanted to reduce her hours. The work never ended. "Maybe it's time to sell Mack's."

"Whoa, what?" Ranger asked.

"Maybe it's time to sell Mack's," Oakley said again, the weight of it heavy in her mind. She had been stewing on it for a while, but she hadn't mentioned it to Ranger yet.

"I was not expecting you to say that." He let out a sigh and added, "I don't know, Oakley. You love that place, and you love your time away from the ranch."

"I'm going to have another baby too," she said. "Bear and Sammy are moving out, and that means that whole homestead is going to be mine to take care of. Etta will find someone wonderful to marry, and she'll be gone, so I won't even be able to take Wilder to her when I need help." She rolled her neck, feeling the weight of a huge motorsports dealership and the hundreds of pieces it took to run it settling into a knot at the top of her spine. "I'm just...maybe it's time to start talking about selling it."

"I...I don't know what to say."

"You don't need to say anything," Oakley said. "It's just been on my mind, and I wonder if we can talk about it more, when we both know what to say."

"Yeah, of course," Ranger said, his gentle strength such a comfort to Oakley.

She ran her hand through her hair, remembering when she'd invited him to this very office for lunch with her. He'd walked right out on her without eating anything, after telling her he wasn't willing to go out with her if she was dating other men.

Choosing him, the way Judge had talked about at Ward's wedding, had been the best decision of Oakley's life.

"Range," she whispered. "I texted my mom about the baby."

"You did?" More shock filled his voice. "And? Has she responded?"

"Not yet." Oakley's tears pressed behind her eyes. "I'm so scared. What if she doesn't respond at all? What if she won't come?"

"Did you tell her you wanted her to come?"

Oakley nodded and sniffled. "Yes."

"Just like that? In those exact words?"

"Yes," Oakley said, smiling at his questions. He'd told her to be direct, but having hard conversations was very difficult for Oakley. He wasn't particularly eloquent either, but the two of them managed to have important conversations like these.

"Wow, Oak, I'm so proud of you. No matter what she

says, you did it. You invited her."

"I can't change her," she said. "I can't change the past."

"No one can," he agreed.

"I just...I want her to know our kids."

"I know you do, sweetheart. She gets to make her own choices."

"Yes." Oakley drew in a sharp breath. "Yes, she does."

"Do you need me to bring lunch? I'm going to bring lunch. How about barbecue?"

She laughed and felt the rays of sunlight and joy in her life that Ranger gave her so freely. "I will love you forever if you bring barbecue for lunch—and actually stay to eat it with me."

"You've got a deal, Mrs. Glover."

"Thank you, Mr. Glover." She hung up and sighed as she looked at the huge white board across from her desk. It used to be full of colors—red, black, blue, and green—as she made notes of what she needed to do around the dealership. Now, it showed November of last year, and Oakley hadn't updated it in far too long.

She didn't need to update it, and she got up and crossed to the board. She erased the marker from it, because it was better it sat empty than outdated. Across the top, she wrote today's date in black marker and added, *Texted mother about the baby due in November. Waiting to hear back.*

She stepped back and read over the words. Her joy for the life growing inside her bloomed and expanded, and she closed her eyes and said, "Thank you, Lord, for the great blessing of being a mother. Bless me with a forgiving heart, so that when my children make mistakes, I can forgive them and always be involved in their life."

She felt herself strengthen with the prayer, and she added, "Thank you for my parents, and bless them wherever they are to know how very much I miss them and love them."

With her heart calm and her faith reaffirmed, Oakley returned to her desk and dug into the work that needed to be done. Her phone never chimed.

Chapter Fifteen

J udge plugged in the giant Christmas tree, the huge, triangular piece of cardboard practically setting sail in the wind whipping across the ranch. Thankfully, it had holes for the lights to go through, and he held it steady while he checked each light.

They all seemed operational, and he moved the decoration back into the corner of the room where he kept most of his light show items. He wasn't sure what he wanted his theme to be this year, and that frustrated him.

With July now upon them, he needed to make a decision and start pulling out the decorations he was going to use for sure. Some of them had to be cleaned. Some had to be touched up with paint or duct tape. He'd have to arrange them in the yard in a new, unique way.

He thought about taking his show online, the thought never far from the center of his mind whenever he came downstairs or contemplated the theme for his Christmas light show. He'd ask June for more details tonight on their date.

As he went upstairs, the air grew steadily warmer, and somewhere outside, a horn honked. "Judge," Preacher called. "Ward's here."

"I'm comin'," Judge yelled, increasing his pace so he took the stairs two at a time. "Is there really room for me?"

"Yep," Preacher said, handing him the bag of glo-sticks they always took to the evening parade. "You can ride in the back with me and Charlie." He grinned at Judge and headed for the front door.

"I'm going to go off with June," he said, following his brother. "Maybe I should take my own truck."

"Why can't you and June hang out with us?" Charlie asked as she brought up the rear. "Me and Preach. Ward and Dot. You and June. It's perfect."

"Judge likes to get her alone," Preacher teased, grinning at Judge as he went down the front steps.

"Of course I do," Judge shot back. "Who was it again that kept his girlfriend hidden from the family for ten months? Oh, yeah, that was *you*."

"It was only eight months," Preacher said easily. "And *you* knew about Charlie."

"I knew *about* her," Judge said. "I didn't ever get to *see* her." He glanced back at her as she came down the steps behind him. "And she's so amazing, I'm actually mad at you still."

Preacher just laughed, and Judge stopped talking, because he knew Preacher's attitude could change on a dime. He also knew Preacher still carried some guilt for how Charlie had been introduced to the family.

"Nice save," Charlie said, giving him a smile. "But really, Judge. I'd love to get to know June better. I won't bite." She climbed into the truck, moving past Preacher, who held the door for her. He got in next, and then Judge got the window seat behind Ward.

"Out of all the women, me and Dot are the tamest," Charlie said. "Right, Dot?"

"What are we talking about?" Dot asked from the front seat. She turned around and smiled at the three of them.

"Judge thinks he wants to go off with June alone, but I told him we should all hang out," Charlie said. "And I was saying you and I are the tamest of the Shiloh Ridge wives."

"For sure," Dot said, looking at Judge.

"She's not my wife," Judge said. "It's awkward."

"It is not," Ward said. "You're dating her. What's awkward about hanging out with us?"

"You're both married," Judge said. "Do you not remember being single at all? You've been married for a month." He didn't want to continue this conversation, so he folded his arms and looked out the window.

Preacher said something he hummed at, and thankfully, his younger brother moved the topic to something else.

Judge had said he'd meet June at the parade, and he gripped the glo-sticks as if trying to strangle them. He finally forced his fingers to relax once they hit the highway, and when they arrived in town, he focused on being with his family again. Sometimes he got too lost inside in his head, and he didn't want to stay there for much longer.

"Look," Ward said after they'd parked and gotten out their chairs. "June's already there." He patted Judge's chest and grinned at him. "When does her daughter come home?"

"Two more weeks," Judge said, an accompanying wave of nerves threatening to engulf him. The past month with June had been near-perfection for Judge. She talked about Lucy Mae, but the girl didn't influence any of her decisions, and Judge had a suspicion that would change when her daughter returned to Three Rivers.

"Hey, June-Bug," he said, putting down his camp chair. He didn't take the time to set it up; he simply drew June into a hug and drew in a deep breath of the scent of her hair, skin, and clothes. "Mm, I missed you."

"We went to dinner last night," she murmured, but she didn't laugh at him.

Judge definitely wanted to sneak off with her and take a while kissing her, but he wanted to spend time with Ward and Dot, Preacher and Charlie, too. He swayed with June for a moment before asking, "After this, do you want to go wander the fair and get food with Ward and Preacher and their wives?"

"Sure," June said easily.

"We could do our own thing too," he said, stepping back and unclasping the buckle that kept his chair together. It expanded, and he widened the legs and set them in the grass beside hers. "But I rode with Ward and Dot, so I kinda need to be with them at some point."

"I like them," June said, sitting down in her chair. "I like all of your family members. It's fine. It'll be fun."

Judge sat beside her and laced his fingers through hers. "You didn't bring the dogs?"

"I did," she said, nodding down the row of people who'd beaten Judge to the parade spot Bear had driven down to town and saved over a week ago. "They're down there with Cactus. That man speaks canine, I think."

Judge smiled down the row at his brother, who had both dogs sitting in his lap. His own dogs—Galaxy and Tank—were far too big to be lap dogs, and they lay at his feet, obviously put out June's smaller dogs could fit on his thighs.

"That he does," Judge said, glad Cactus had changed so much in the past few years. His transformation was a real example for Judge, who felt like a completely different man than he'd been when he'd first met June. He wondered if she could see all the ways he was different, but he'd never asked her.

"This feels weird," June said. "To be here without Lucy Mae. The first time we came, I sat in the worst spot ever. It was right next to the Dumpsters for the funnel cake trailer, and wow, every time the wind changed, I got a whiff of rotten garbage." She laughed, and Judge smiled at her.

She seemed so carefree and wild, and Judge didn't get to see her like that very often. He'd dated a couple of other single moms years and years ago, but neither of them were anything like June.

"I suppose I'm going to have to get used to doing things without her," June said. "I just don't know how."

"You're here," Judge said. "How did you do that?"

"I knew you'd be here," she said. "I knew you'd be

waiting for me to show up, and I didn't want to disappoint you."

Judge nodded, but he didn't really like that answer. "So if I wasn't here, and we weren't dating, you wouldn't have come?"

"Probably not, no," she said, sighing.

"You sound frustrated," he said, glad all of his siblings and cousins seemed to be engrossed in their own conversations.

"I am," June said just as Bear asked, "Can we sit by you, Judge?"

He looked up at his oldest brother, who carried three camp chairs while his wife pushed a stroller with both their little boys in it.

"Of course," he said, watching Link make a beeline for Mitch and Cactus. Judge and June shuffled over a few feet to make room for the chairs, but they didn't have to leave the shade of the tree. Judge might mutiny if he had to, because July Fourth in Texas could make a man's blood boil before nine a.m.

Once they were all settled, Sammy unbuckled the boys and let Stetson get out of the stroller. "Stay here, bud," she told him. "They'll throw candy once the parade starts."

"Come on, Smiles," Judge said, and the little boy toddled over to him. "Yes, you come sit with Uncle Judge. I'll muscle those other kids out of the way for you."

There were no other kids to speak of, at least not right now. Judge knew that once the candy came out, all bets were off. He reached down to the ground where he'd dropped the glo-sticks. "You want one of these, Smiles?"

The boy smiled and said, "Yes, pwease," in the cutest voice possible. Judge grinned as he ripped open the package and held up a few of the sticks. "What color? Blue? Red? Green?"

"Gween," Smiles said, and Judge cracked it up and down and handed it to the child.

"I want one of those," Bear said, and Judge handed him the package, thinking him a great, big little boy. Bear had always enjoyed life, and he selected a blue glo-stick and cracked it to get the lighting elements to start working.

Judge turned and looked at June, who watched him and Smiles. "You're good with him."

"A couple of the nieces and nephews like me," Judge said. "I have no idea why."

"Probably because of the glo-sticks," she said with a smile. She looked tired, with heaviness in her eyes Judge wanted to erase for her if he could.

"What are you frustrated about, June-Bug?" he asked, shifting Smiles to his right side so he could hold June's hand on the left.

"I don't know who I am," she said, her voice almost muted.

"I do," he said. "You're Juniper Nichols, smart business-woman, Internet genius, and...." He cleared his throat, the words he wanted to say right there. He'd never said such things out loud, and perhaps a public park with his nephew on his knee wasn't the best place.

"Sexiest woman alive," he finished anyway.

June's fingers in his tightened to the point he met her gaze. "You best not be sayin' things you don't mean."

"I never do," he said, dead serious.

"You didn't say Lucy Mae's mom," she said.

Everything clicked into place then. "You think you're no one without her."

"Something like that, yes."

"That's just not true," he said. "You were your own person before her, and you'll be your own person after her."

"There is no *after her*, Judge."

"Sure there is," he said. "You'll always be her mom, but she won't need you day-in and day-out like she has in the past."

"And see, there's part of me that really dislikes that."

"Uncle Judge," Smiles said. "Look." He squirmed off Judge's lap and ran on his chubby legs toward the curb. "B'loons." He faced the row of adults with pure, unadulterated wonder on his face. "Momma, b'loons."

Judge got up and followed the two-year-old. "Yep, balloons. There'll be horses in a minute, bud. Come back here so you don't get clip-clopped on." He drew Smiles back to the chairs, where he stood and leaned against Judge's knee after Judge had sat back down in his chair.

"Don't suck your thumb, bud," Bear said, reaching over and brushing Smiles's hand away from his face. "Big boys who get candy at parades don't suck their thumbs."

"Candy," Smiles repeated, but the candy-throwing part of the parade hadn't started yet.

The horses approached, because Judge could hear all the clipping and clopping of their shod feet on the asphalt. For the Fourth of July evening parade, a few cowboys and cowgirls rode at the front of the procession, bearing the

Texas state flag, which was lowered slightly to the United States flag.

Judge got to his feet and swept Smiles into his arms. "Hand on your heart, bud," he said, catching sight of Old Glory as the horses and riders came into view. "We love God and our country," he told Smiles. "That flag represents our country. The red and white one with all the stripes, with all the stars."

"Bwue," Smiles said, and Judge smiled as he honored the flag.

"The other flag is for Texas," he said. "We love Texas too. Best state in the Union."

"You realize the Texas state flag is also red, white, and blue," June said.

"Just the one stripe though," Judge said, eyeing that star. "Just one star."

"It's a nice star."

"Stars," Judge said, and suddenly his Christmas light show came to life in his mind. It was all about the stars— one for Texas, fifty for the US, and one special one that had appeared when the Savior of the world had been born.

He knew he wouldn't be using soldiers, trees, or snowmen this year. No reindeer. No sleighs. No nutcrackers.

Just stars.

The flag passed, and all the riderless horses followed. Their hooves made such a racket on the road that Smiles covered his ears with his hands saying, "Loud," in a loud voice.

Judge laughed and pressed the boy into his chest to

help muffle the sound further. Because yes, a couple hundred horses trotting by with metal shoes on hard road was very, very loud.

June's unrest and her comments about not knowing who she was also sounded loudly in Judge's soul, and he wanted to get back to that conversation.

He realized he was still standing when he didn't need to be, and he sat down.

"Licorice?" June asked, offering him a bag of the red treat.

"I never say no to licorice," he said, taking a couple of pieces.

"I some?" Smiles asked, his face the picture of childlike hope. "Pwease?"

"You have to ask your daddy," June said, smiling at Smiles. "I don't want to get in trouble."

"Daddy." Smiles slid right off Judge's lap and went around his knees to his father. "Daddy." He climbed up into Bear's lap, who was talking to Wade Rhinehart about something. He helped his son, but he clearly wasn't paying attention to him at all.

"Bear," Smiles said, and that got Bear to look at his son.

Judge choked back his laughter, the stunned look on his brother's face almost too much to contain.

"Did you just call me Bear?" Bear asked.

"Daddy," Smiles said. "I have lick-rish?" He pointed toward June, who held up the bag of red licorice for Bear to see. "Pwease?"

"Did you ask her?"

"He did," Judge said. "She said he had to ask you."

"Pwease, Papa Bear?" Smiles asked, and Judge couldn't hold back any longer. He burst out laughing, especially since the frown lines between Bear's eyes got deeper.

"Papa Bear?" He turned to his wife. "Where does he come up with this stuff?"

"Hey, he's your son," she said, grinning too. "He can have some licorice. He ate dinner."

"You can have some, Smiles," Bear said. "Say thank you."

Smiles wore a radiant look of happiness as he slid from his father's lap. He approached June, his face taking on a measure of nervousness.

"Smiles," Judge said. "This is June. She's with me. She's real nice."

"Pwease?" he asked, and June gave him a full piece of licorice.

"Tank you," Smiles said, coming back to Judge and turning to stand between Judge's knees.

He looked at June, who was watching Smiles with a look of pure love on her face. Joy, love, and wonder, and Judge wondered if she'd be willing to have more kids.

His kids.

The things he needed to talk to her about doubled, and he cursed himself for agreeing to stick with Ward, Dot, Preacher, and Charlie.

"Candy," Smiles said a moment later. He twisted and looked at Judge, everything about him so wonderful and so joyful. Judge got reminded about how good life was whenever he was with Smiles. "You help me, Uncle Judge?"

"I'll help you," he confirmed. "Let's go sit on the curb, bud. Do you have a bag?"

"Right here," Sammy said, and Judge took the plastic grocery sack from her and gave it to Smiles. Then they went to get the candy the queens and princesses were throwing. Judge wished his life was as carefree as Smiles's, that he didn't have to riddle through what June had said or wonder if she'd want to essentially start her life from scratch when she married him.

If, he told himself. *If, not when.*

Chapter Sixteen

"Oh, it's so good to see you." June gripped her daughter in a strong hug, not caring that they'd created a little roadblock in the flow of traffic out of the airport. She pulled away. "You seem thin. Are you eating?"

"Yes, Mom," Lucy Mae said, plenty of dryness in her voice. "I ate every day in California." She bent to pick up her bag. "Come on, I'm starving. We can get some food, right?"

"Yes," June said.

"You didn't bring Judge?" Lucy Mae asked.

"No," June said, hoping she could keep her answers to one word when it came to Judge Glover. She reached for Lucy Mae's bigger bag. "Tell me everything. I haven't gotten an email from you for eight days."

Lucy Mae could talk and talk, which June was counting on. Her daughter stepped up to the plate and delivered, telling June about their final projects, the team she'd bonded with, and "Leon, James, and Fiona" as if June would know who those people were.

The stories kept them both entertained through the drive-through and all the way back to Three Rivers from Amarillo.

When June turned into their driveway and saw Timmy's truck sitting there, her mood soured. Lucy Mae, however, let out a squeal that could've called the dogs up at Shiloh Ridge Ranch and practically leapt from the vehicle before June had even brought it to a complete stop.

She launched herself at Timmy, who caught her around the waist, his smile big and broad on his face. Their laughter carried across the space and through June's cracked window.

June watched them in her rearview mirror, wishing she could show Judge how she really felt about him the way Lucy Mae did. She wasn't sure what Lucy Mae and Timmy would do when she left for college for good. No coming back after six weeks. No big reunions, where they kissed right there in the front driveway.

June got out of the car and cleared her throat. "Come inside at least," she said. "We don't need to give the neighbors a show."

Lucy Mae broke away from Timmy and took his hand in hers, her mouth already moving a mile a minute. *Bless the man who marries her*, June thought, exhausted from the trip to Amarillo and back.

Lucy Mae didn't act as though she'd said a word on the drive home, and when she entered the house, Picasso and Remmy went nuts, whining and jumping up on her, she dropped to her knees and scrubbed them along the back, cooing at them about how much she missed them.

June put her purse on the sideboard and sighed, kneading her fingers along her forehead, where a headache had started. In her purse, her phone chimed, and she pulled it out to see Judge's name flash across the top of her screen.

Let me know when you make it back to town. I have something to show you.

"You better ask your mom," Timmy said, and June turned without answering Judge. She knew what he had to show her—his mysterious Christmas lawn display. He'd been very tight-lipped about the design for this year, claiming he didn't want to show her until it was just right.

She knew he worked on the display all the way through October, getting opinions and suggestions from every single one of his family members. Then he'd make adjustments to the timing, the songs, the lights, all of it. So he probably just wanted to show her the preliminary drawings.

Yes, actual drawings. He'd told her he was almost done with the sketches on one of their dates earlier in the week, and she'd asked a bunch of questions until he'd admitted that yes, he drew everything out before a single decoration touched the grass in front of the Ranch House.

"Ask me what?" June asked, and she saw her quiet evening at home, reunited with her daughter go up in smoke right in front of her eyes.

"We want to go to the concert in the park," Lucy Mae said, putting in her puppy dog eyes. "Please, Mom? It's the Lone Star Dads tonight. You love them. You should come."

She exchanged a glance with Timmy, who took a moment too long to nod.

"I thought we were going to put on *Emma* and make caramel corn," she said. She could see the movie night clearly in her head. Picasso would lean against her thigh, acting like he didn't care if he didn't get a bite of popcorn when he did. Remmy would stare her down, and June would do her best not to give in to his canine pressure.

She'd crack, of course, and let him lick the sticky caramel from her fingers. There would be no bright lights, no phones ringing, no interrupted Internet, and no expectations. June's clothes were starting to choke her, and she wanted to slip into her sweats while the microwave popcorn popped.

"We can do that tomorrow," Lucy Mae said, a certain level of whininess in her voice. "It's the Lone Star Dads."

June sighed, because she'd always been terrible at telling her daughter no. "Okay," she said. "You two go. I'm tired."

Lucy Mae squealed again and launched herself at her mother this time. June hugged her back, laughing, but the moment she and Timmy left the house, June's giggles dried right up.

She looked back at her texts, wondering if she could invite Judge down to the house to watch *Emma* with her. A new kind of movie night bloomed before her eyes, and her daughter was nowhere in sight in that fantasy.

June frowned, because something he'd said at the parade a couple of weeks ago had bothered her. *She won't need you*, he'd said, speaking of Lucy Mae.

She didn't want to admit it, but he was right. Lucy Mae

didn't need her. She could've gotten Timmy to come pick her up at the airport. She'd already run off to spend time with someone else besides June.

"So who am I without her?" she asked, staring at Judge's text. He'd called her smart and sexy at that same parade, and June really wanted to see herself the way Judge did. When she looked in the mirror, she saw the mom-jeans, the split ends on her hair because she didn't have time to go to a stylist, and the emptiness in her own eyes.

When she thought about Judge, she couldn't get the image of him holding his nephew out of her mind. The boy had dark hair and bright, bright blue eyes like his father. Judge sported lighter hair and eyes than his brothers and siblings, but June had seen a new future for herself in those minutes where she'd watched him and Stetson—aka "Smiles"—interact.

He was very good with kids, and she still had some time to have another baby. Probably two or three.

"And then what?" she asked herself. "You start a brand-new life? It would be like leaving Lucy Mae behind."

That's not true, she heard Judge say in her mind, as if he were there, participating in this conversation. She'd worked hard to be mother and father for Lucy Mae. She hadn't brought any men until Judge into Lucy Mae's life. She hadn't wanted her daughter to believe for a single second that anyone was more important than her.

She still didn't, but she stood in her kitchen while Lucy Mae had chosen to go spend time with her boyfriend that night, not her mother.

"Choices, choices," June muttered to herself, thinking

of what Judge had said at Ward's wedding. It really is such a lovely gift, this idea of being able to choose.

Choose each other.

If she chose Judge over Lucy Mae, was that okay? Would she become Judge's girlfriend instead of Lucy Mae's mom?

Who did she want to be?

Instead of texting Judge, she called him. "Hey," she said when he answered. "We made it back. Do you want to come down and watch a movie with me? I'm a pretty dang good caramel popcorn maker."

"I'd love to," he said, and her hopes lifted. She really didn't want to be alone tonight. "But I'm up to my neck in stars and lights." He chuckled. "Can I take a raincheck?"

"Of course," she said through a narrow throat.

"You could come up here," he suggested. "I put a turkey breast in the oven a while ago, and now I'm just wrestling with a few things."

June thought about it for a moment. "I don't think I can," she said. "Lucy Mae just got home today."

"Of course," he said, his voice turning slightly diplomatic. "I'll send you a picture of what I wanted you to see, okay?"

"Okay," she said, and just like that, the call ended.

Emptiness and silence descended upon her, and she hated that she'd used her daughter—a daughter that wasn't even home—as a reason she couldn't go to Shiloh Ridge to see Judge.

But she did want to be home when Lucy Mae returned from the concert. Responsible parents didn't go on dates and stay out later than their teenagers. She was Lucy Mae's mom, and it seemed she couldn't turn off that role even if she tried.

As she put the bag of popcorn in the microwave and went to change, she wondered, *Can you be Lucy Mae's mom and Judge's girlfriend? Does it have to be one or the other?*

She didn't know the answer to that, because she'd been switching from compartment to compartment for the past six weeks. Lucy Mae's mom whenever her daughter called. June would literally drop everything to talk to Lucy Mae on the phone.

Judge's girlfriend when he called, texted, or when they went out together.

"And somewhere in there," she said to her empty master suite, stripping off her restrictive clothes and stepping into a pair of sweats and a loose T-shirt. "You have to figure out how to be Juniper Nichols."

The problem was, she still didn't know who that was or how to find her.

"OH, WOW," JUNE SAID AS SHE GOT OUT OF HER NICHOLS Networking truck. "This looks just like the picture."

Judge had sent her a picture of the yard, and the whole thing was decked out in stars. The whole thing. And not just the yard, she realized, as she let her eyes follow the lines of the stars upward. They perched on windowsills, the shutters, the rain gutters, and the roof as well.

They came in a variety of sizes, from the massive, ten-foot monster on the very pinnacle of the roof, to an array of smaller stars no bigger than one of her hands.

In the middle of the day, they weren't nearly as magical as when they lit up in violets, reds, greens, blues, whites, and oranges. June could still see the amount of work Judge had put into setting them all up. He'd sent her pictures about a week ago, the night Lucy Mae had returned from California.

She hadn't seen him in the flesh since the night before that, and guilt ate at June's stomach. He'd asked her out twice, but both times, Lucy Mae had needed her for some reason or another. Desperate to hold onto her daughter and her role in her daughter's life, June had chosen her over spending time with Judge.

He didn't walk out onto the porch to greet her, and she lifted her phone to dial him. His line rang and rang, eventually going to voicemail. She texted him that she'd arrived at the Ranch House, though she'd texted him just before making the drive up here and he'd responded then.

He'd sent her a couple of videos of the preliminary light show taken at night, and he'd realized he needed an update on his system to be able to run things the way he wanted them to run. Then he'd asked her to come do the upgrades, and he'd really liked her idea of streaming the light show online in order to get more Three Rivers residents watching it and voting for him.

She walked over to the porch and sat on the steps in the shade, the Texas heat cooling a little bit.

Her phone went off, but it wasn't Judge's chime. It was Oakley, who'd said, *The luncheon this month is at the homestead, hosted by me. The theme is BABIES! We'll be eating all kinds of baby foods—baby butter lettuce wraps. Baby eggplant parmesan. Baby spinach salad. Don't bring your baby appetite. ;) Next Thursday at noon.*

June had been put on the group text for all the women up here at the ranch, but it had made her uncomfortable. This wasn't that, as Oakley had texted only her. She didn't see how she could possibly commit to coming in the middle of a weekday. Sometimes her appointments were longer than she anticipated, and sometimes they were shorter. All she knew was she didn't really have the luxury of escaping for a baby-themed luncheon in the middle of the day.

Congratulations on your pregnancy, June sent to her, because she'd heard through the grapevine—Judge—that Oakley was due with her second baby in November. The baby theme made sense, and it did sound fun.

I might be able to sneak away from work, but it's impossible to know until the day of.

You're always welcome, Oakley said, and June nodded to herself. If there was one thing the women up here excelled in, it was making people feel welcome and comfortable.

She sighed and waited, the air dead up here today. She was just about to return to her truck so she could turn on the air conditioning when Judge rounded the corner of the house. "Huh?" he asked, grinning at her. "It's great, right?"

"It's great," she said, getting hastily to her feet. She hurried toward him, suddenly missing him so much. She wanted to thread her fingers through his hair and tell him just how much she'd missed him.

Her emotions surged, causing her to launch herself into his arms the way she'd seen her daughter do to Timmy last week. Instead of getting swung around and then kissed, Judge just grunted and stumbled backward.

"Sorry," she said when he didn't grab onto her.

"It's okay," he said, but he still didn't reach for her. "So I think we need a camera out here." He turned away from her and went down the front sidewalk and past the edge of the grass. "We need to put up a few things and test to see what the angle gets for the show. I did put stars all the way up on the roof." He shaded his eyes and tipped his head back, as if anyone could miss that enormous star.

When it was lit up, June was willing to bet good money that the astronauts would be able to see it from space.

"Is something wrong?" she asked him as she opened the back of her van.

"No, why?" he asked.

"You're acting funny." He hadn't even said hello, his attention straight to his lights. With horror, June realized exactly what was going on. She'd seen him act like this around her before—right after she'd ended things with him and told him she wasn't dating until Lucy Mae graduated from high school.

Judge acted aloof, cool, and focused only on the business side of things whenever she'd put the brakes on their relationship.

She frowned, because she hadn't done that this time. It felt like *he* was the one doing it.

"Fine," he said, though she hadn't pressed him for more explanations. "I'm upset with you. Happy now?"

Chapter Seventeen

Judge's whole body stormed with something he couldn't quite name. He'd felt it before, many times. Usually when dealing with Mister. The man pushed all the wrong buttons, and he hated that this time, June had her fingers pulsing against his nerves.

He glared at the stupid metal star he couldn't get to go where he wanted it. He lifted it out of the ground and saw the tip of the spike he needed to drive into the ground had bent slightly. "Probably a rock here," he said, hefting it up, moving it over six inches, and driving it back into the ground.

He'd probably move every single star in the display fifteen times before they found their permanent home, but right now, he didn't care. He just wanted to work, and work, and work. Then he'd be too tired to think at night. Too tired to even think during the day.

He'd seen Preacher turn into a complete zombie last

year when he hadn't gotten enough sleep, and Judge actually envied him that right now.

"Are you going to tell me what I did?" June asked.

Judge didn't want to. He sounded like a petulant child —like Mister had, complaining about Libby—as the words rotated through his own head. No way he could say them out loud.

He turned toward her, standing there at the back of her van. She hadn't made a move to get out the equipment she claimed she could help him set up. It had taken her a week to get up to the ranch, and he told himself she was busy. She had a thriving company to run, and she couldn't drop everything and come help him film stationary stars.

Everything in his life felt so pointless right now. He wanted to kick down the star he'd just reset, stomp inside, and go back to bed. Judge's exhaustion all came from the mental toll the past week had taken on him, and he didn't quite trust himself to say much right now.

"Judge," June said, clear exasperation in her voice.

"I just want to set up the camera," he said. "See what the field is, so I can make adjustments and start to code the songs and lights."

She folded her arms and cocked her eyebrows at him, a very good version of *Nice try, buddy*, on her face.

He sighed and reached up to remove his cowboy hat. With his long sleeves to protect him out on the ranch, and this suffocating hat squeezing his head all the time, Judge's body heat rocketed off the charts. Maybe that came from the way June looked at him, but he wasn't sure.

"How many times did I ask you out this week?" he asked, keeping his voice calm and cool.

June opened her mouth, sudden realization entering those brown eyes, and stared at him. "We've—I've been busy."

"Yeah," he said. "Your daughter came back, and suddenly I'm back on the shelf." He glared at her too. "You need to be honest with me. I can't keep doing this yo-yo thing." He gestured between the two of them. "I like you. I don't like you. Up, then down. Maybe you throw me away for a little bit in this weird walk-the-dog move."

His chest heaved, but he still had more to say. "And then, you reel me back in. Wind me back up. Throw me away again." He mimed the yo-yo motions as best he could, but he hadn't played with a yo-yo in a very long time.

June gaped at him, and he frowned back.

"I'm tired of being second," he said. "I know you told me Lucy Mae came first. I guess I just...didn't realize it would be forever. I didn't realize that literally meant she couldn't come second sometimes. I mean, just *some*times." He sighed, feeling like a real jerk. He took a couple of steps away from her. "It's fine. I'm not a parent, so I don't get it. Forget it. I'm sorry I said anything."

He walked away, sure June would call him back. She remained silent until his boot touched the bottom step. "Judge," she said, his name in her voice like music to his ears.

He paused, and she came running up after him. "That's not fair, you know?"

He looked down at her out of the bottom corner of his eye. "Which part?"

"The part where you said she never comes second."

"Did she come second this week?"

June lifted her chin, her dark eyes sparking with a current Judge wanted to get burned by. The very idea was crazy, because he was upset with this woman. "No," she said.

"That's my point."

"I've chosen you over her before, though."

"Have you?"

"Yes, of course. Just the fact that we're dating is me choosing you over her."

Judge sighed and looked up at the big house. He couldn't see his stars from this position, but he did stand in the shade. "I don't want to make you choose. This is not a competition. She's your daughter. I'm...no one."

He started up the steps.

"You are not no one," June said after him, her work boots landing on the stairs as she followed him. "Don't say stuff like that."

"It's true," Judge said. "You know, my dad used to say that a man had room in his life to do three things really well. Just three. Otherwise, everything started to suffer. He was a mighty fine rancher. He took his religion seriously." Judge held up a finger with each point. "That left just one thing. He couldn't be the best painter in the world. Or an amazing woodworker. He couldn't volunteer in the community, or dedicate a ton of time, energy, or money to other charitable causes."

"What did he choose for the third thing?"

"Mother," Judge said. "And in turn, us. We were very important to Mother, and Mother was very important to Dad. Therefore, we were important to Dad. He spent time with us. He taught us. He loved our Mother, and he was very good at it."

June nodded, part of the blazing fire in her eyes dampening. "He sounds great."

"He was great," Judge said, missing his dad more than he had in a while. He needed to call Cactus and get out to the cemetery. He hadn't read his letter in a while either, and he determined to pull it out that evening and go over it again.

When he'd first gotten the letter from his dad, Judge had poured over it. Read it day and night, memorizing the words. After a while, he hadn't needed it so much, and he'd tucked it away in his nightstand.

He met June's eyes. "So you have Nichols Networking. That's one very big thing that can sometimes be two. And you have Lucy Mae, who can also be two things sometimes. You like your dogs, and they require care. You have friends, and relationships with them take time and work. You go to church, and your religion takes a spot."

He shook his head. "I'm just not sure you have room for me."

"I do," she said quickly. "Judge, don't say that. There's room for you always. I want you in my life."

The words were nice to hear, and Judge dropped his chin to his chest. He only felt worse and worse, bringing this up. She had enough on her plate without him adding to it. "I'm sorry," he said, stepping over to her and taking her into his arms so he didn't have to look into her eyes. "Forget I said anything."

"I'm not going to forget it," she said into his shoulder. "You have a valid point. And I...I *did* choose Lucy Mae over you this past week. I guess I was just hoping you wouldn't notice."

"I want to see you every day, June-Bug," he whispered into her neck. "I want to hear you laugh. I want to know about your day. I want to share my light show ideas with you, and I want you to tell me how you're nervous Lucy Mae's going to go off to college, fall in love with the wrong guy, and get married too young."

June started to laugh, but the sound quickly morphed into something that sounded like weeping.

"Don't cry," he whispered, pulling back to look at her. "I'm sorry. I'll keep my frustrations to myself from now on. I really will."

"Don't you dare," she said, her voice choked. "I want to hear them. Isn't that what people do? Confide their worries and frustrations in each other?"

Judge didn't know. The only person he ever wanted to talk to was her. He cradled her face in his hands and leaned down. "I miss you," he whispered. "I can *feel* it when you're pushing me away, and I hate it."

"I'm sorry," she whispered, her eyes already drifting closed. "I'm trying to find the right balance of things. I'm trying to figure out what my life is going to be without my daughter."

Judge looked down at her, this perfectly angelic creature he'd been in love with for so long. "I don't want to upset you." She dealt with so much, and he certainly didn't need to be adding to it. He wanted to alleviate her workload, mentally and physically, if he could.

"Then kiss me, cowboy," she murmured.

Judge didn't waste another moment to fulfill her request. He touched his lips to hers, this kiss after a hiatus one of the sweetest things he'd experienced in his life. June seemed hungry for him, and she accelerated the kiss, dislodging his cowboy hat as she pushed her hands through his hair.

Judge had no complaints now.

"OKAY, SO I CAN GO ALL THE WAY TO THE FENCE." HE peered at the tiny screen June had in the van. "We can see the star on the roof, so that's good. Is there a way to move it so there's not so much dead space over here?"

He pointed to the left side of the screen, which showed the lawn on the east side of the sidewalk. "I don't want to have to put up stars over there. These were hard enough to find as it was."

Surveying the lawn in front of him, he could see the colors. The blues, whites, reds, and greens. He was going to go simple this year. A Texas-themed Christmas show, with four colors, and one shape—the beloved Texas star.

He was going to broadcast his show online, so people didn't have to come up to Shiloh Ridge to see it and vote.

If he didn't win this year, Judge wasn't going to do the

show anymore. He told himself it was okay. Dreams changed. Sometimes a person could practice and practice and practice and never get off the bench. He'd been that person his whole life, actually playing baseball in high school without ever swinging a bat.

In adulthood, he'd been easily overlooked, something that had bothered him quite a bit. That was why he and Preacher had tried to stand out by making jokes, being obnoxious, and playing tricks on the other Glovers.

Preacher, though he was younger than Judge, had matured first and figured things out faster. He knew who he was, and it had taken Judge a little bit longer to do that. He now knew his role in the family, and he could admit his father's letter had helped him settle into it completely.

"I can," June said. "I'm afraid we're going to lose that star on the roof, though."

"Maybe I could bring it down and put it on the window."

"You want the biggest one on the top though." She fiddled with the camera, and as Judge watched, she zoomed it in until the east side of the lawn couldn't be seen. "See how we lose that top tip?"

Judge leaned in closer to the screen, and also June. She smelled like lemons and sunshine, and he wanted to kiss her again. Before that kiss on the porch, he'd felt like he hadn't kissed her in ages. He vowed to never let that many days pass without kissing June again.

"I see that." He frowned. "So I need to bring it down."

"Do you need four on the rooftop?"

"I mean, no," he said. "Maybe a group of three. I can

put the big one where that galvanized metal one is, and position the other two around it." That meant another trip up onto the roof, but it wouldn't be the last one, Judge knew that.

He fiddled with his light shows relentlessly, and he'd most likely be up on the roof in November, after reading a comment from an online viewer about one of the stars there.

"That would work," June said. "Do you want to do it now so we can test it?"

"Might as well." Judge had plenty to do around the ranch, but his brothers knew the light show was important to him. "Give me a minute."

He hurried around the back of the house and went right up the ladder he'd left there. The sun beat down on the roof, and every pore in his body started to sweat. His stomach growled, and he wondered if he could get June to stay for lunch. Then she probably had another appointment, and Judge could get back in the saddle and get the horses moved from one pasture to another.

Most of their cattle were out in the hills, though they still rotated some through the grass fields on the ranch. The goats, chickens, meat birds, turkeys, and pigs rotated through them too, and the horses had their own fields to graze in.

He crested the roof and started down the slope on the front of it. Setting something upright on a slanted surface wasn't easy by any stretch of the imagination, but Preacher had built stands for the stars. Convincing him to do it hadn't been hard for Judge either.

Grateful for his brother now, Judge simply picked up the huge star and took it down several paces to where a different one sat. None of the stars had lights on them, and Judge had a lot of work looming in front of him.

He reminded himself that he loved putting on this light show, and he didn't mind stringing lights. He didn't mind working a lot, and he didn't mind staying up late to code the things the other cowboys would come see in the morning.

He'd get their feedback, make adjustments and improvements, and edge closer and closer to the perfect final show.

"Right there," June called. "I can see the top of it right there."

Judge set down the giant star, picked up the one he wasn't going to use, and headed back to the ladder. Getting down with the star in his hand wasn't easy, and Judge slipped about halfway down.

He yelped, his mind blitzing through what to do.

Drop the star! shouted in his mind, but he'd paid a lot for that blasted star, and he didn't want to dent it.

His hands burned. The ladder actually swayed, coming off from where it rested against the roof above him.

His slippery cowboy boot couldn't find the rung to hold onto.

Judge felt the world hurtling through space at millions of miles per hour, and all he could do was go with it.

Chapter Eighteen

A terrible crashing sound brought June's head up from the screen she'd been adjusting. "Judge?"

Something told her to move, and move now. She ran toward the side of the house, calling, "Judge?" He didn't answer, which spiked her concern and helped her move faster.

The house went on and on, but she quickly reached the back corner. Judge moaned from his position on the ground, the ladder he'd been using only inches from him. The star he'd removed from the display stood straight up and down out of the earth, as if he'd impaled it there before falling backward off the ladder

"Judge," she cried out. She ran toward him, skidding on her knees in the grass the last few feet. "Judge, talk to me."

"I fell," he said, stirring slightly.

"Don't move," she said, her hands hovering above his

body, not sure where to touch. "Do not move. I'm going to call the ambulance."

"No," he groaned. "I'm okay."

"You are not," she insisted, the motherly instinct inside her screaming at her to keep him still. "Do not move, John. That's an order."

His eyes opened, and he focused on her as she dialed nine-one-one. "You used my real name."

"You're not listening to me," she said, just as the operator asked her to state her emergency. "Yes, hi." Her voice sounded so nervous to her. She *was* nervous. "My boyfriend fell off a ladder onto his back."

"How far did he fall?"

"How far did you fall?" she asked.

"I was about halfway down," he said, lying very still, his eyes closed as he let the sun bathe his face in golden light.

"About a story," June said, taking a chance by looking away from him and toward the house. He lay quite far from the building. "Backward, so the ladder probably picked up some speed before he hit the ground."

"I did try to jump off," Judge said.

"Ho there!" a man called, and June spun back toward the ranch to find a cowboy riding a horse toward her.

She stood and waved her free hand above her head while the operator asked her another question. "I don't know," she said, done with this conversation. Her pulse skipped through her body. "He's hurt, and he needs an ambulance. We're up at Shiloh Ridge Ranch, and I'm afraid to move him."

"Is he in pain?"

"Are you in pain?" she asked Judge.

"My head is killing me," he said. "I think I might have sprained my ankle. That thing's throbbing."

"What about your back?" June asked, finally switching the call to speaker just as Ward arrived amidst thundering hoofbeats.

"Yeah, that hurts too," Judge said. "I feel like I can't get a full breath."

"The ambulance is on the way," the operator said, and June nodded.

"What happened?" Ward asked, dropping to his knees in the grass too. "Judge?"

"He fell," June said. "He went up on the roof to get a star, and he fell coming down."

"Did the star get damaged?" Judge asked, his voice so quiet and so far away.

"Not important," Ward said. "They're sending an ambulance?"

"She said they would."

"They're fast," Ward said. "They'll be here in ten minutes." He leaned over Judge again. "Talk to me, Judge."

"It's so hot," Judge said. "I'm hungry and thirsty."

June and Ward looked at one another. June had raised Lucy Mae on her own, but the girl had never fallen off of a ladder. She'd never had a head injury. She had no idea if she could feed Judge or give him something to drink.

"I think we should wait for the ambulance, cowboy," she said. "Right, Ward?"

"I think she's right," he said. "Stay down, Judge."

Slowly, his awareness came back to him, and June didn't

think for a minute he'd obey her. But he did, and he stayed down. Ward had sent out some supersonic message, because by the time the ambulance arrived, so had every cowboy and cowgirl on the ranch.

The paramedics asked him questions, and June found herself with her arms folded, trying to stay warm. Hugging herself would surely work, but it didn't decrease the nerves. Her head felt light, and her feet felt heavy, and when one of Judge's brothers put his arm around her and said, "C'mon, June. I'll drive you down to the hospital," she simply went with him.

He didn't take her to her van though. He led her inside the Ranch House and started making a sandwich.

June blinked, things around her making no sense. "Cactus?" she asked.

"Did you eat lunch, June?" he asked with a level of calmness she didn't understand. They'd just carted his brother off to the hospital, and he was worried about peanut butter and jelly?

"No," she said.

"Great, me either." He continued slathering raspberry jam onto two pieces of bread. "I figured we'd take these with us, as we head down to the hospital to check on Judge."

"Do you think he'll be okay?"

"Judge? Yeah, sure," he said, topping the jammed bread slices with the peanut buttered ones. He handed her a sandwich, a genuine smile accompanying it. "Let's hit the road. I'll drive your van so you can stay down in town, okay?"

She nodded, and they pulled out only moments behind the ambulance, and June looked at her sandwich. She supposed she could eat it, and she took a bite. Tangy jam and creamy, salty peanut butter made a party in her mouth.

"This is great," she said. "Thank you."

"Always best to go into the hospital on a full stomach," Cactus said, grinning at her. "Do you need to call in to your work?"

"Probably," she said, reaching for her phone. "I'll take the rest of the day off."

"Good idea," Cactus said. "I'm sure he'll be fine, but being fully prepared isn't a bad idea."

Fully prepared for what? she wanted to ask. Instead, she simply took another bite of her sandwich, thinking this day had been up, down, and around—so much like that yo-yo Judge had talked about earlier.

A COUPLE OF HOURS LATER, JUDGE SWUNG HIS LEGS OVER the side of the bed. "I'm leaving. I don't have to stay here, and I'm not going to."

"Are you sure, Judge?" Preacher asked. Cactus watched with interest too. They'd both been here as long as June, only leaving when absolutely necessary.

"I'm sure." He pulled the IV out of his arm without a second thought. "I need some Advil and a cool soaker tub. Then I'll be good as new."

Cactus looked less than convinced, but Preacher's face

showed very little emotion at all. "We don't have a soaker tub," Preacher said.

"Etta does," Judge said. "I've already texted her, and she's already filling it for me, with bath salts and oils and all that junk." He looked up at his brothers. "I'm not staying here. I'm fine. I don't have a concussion. Nothing's broken. I'm not even in any pain anymore."

"Then why do you need the Advil?" June rose to her feet and looked at this giant of a man. She didn't think for a single second he wasn't going to get what he wanted. When he looked at her, everything pulsed between them.

"June," he said, and that was all. The four-letter name held enough emotion to prompt her to action, and she walked toward the door.

"You're unfair," she said, though she didn't really mind. "I'm going to go talk to the nurse. You best get dressed if we're leaving." She had her van, and Cactus could get back to the ranch with Preacher and Bear. They'd all been at the hospital for a couple of hours now, and June had simply rescheduled her appointments for that weekend.

She typically hated working weekends, but Lucy Mae seemed to be snipping apron strings left and right, and June figured she better figure out how to do the same. She couldn't hold onto her daughter forever, even if she wanted to.

Forty-five minutes later, Judge signed the final paper, promised he'd come back if he had any problems, and he walked out of the hospital by himself. He did hold onto June's arm a little tightly, and she moved slowly so he could. His brothers walked behind them, their presence in a row powerful and intimidating, and June saw more than one person looking their way.

"I hate this place," Preacher said. "I hope I never have to come back here."

"Tell me about it," Cactus said, and he actually gave a scoff. They both took big, deep breaths once they stepped outside, though the Texas summer air could burn a woman's lungs in a matter of seconds.

"I'm going with June," Judge said, turning to face them. Another silent battle of wills happened, and June really didn't want to get in between all these brothers. They were the four oldest siblings in Judge's branch of the family, and they seemed to be able to communicate without even looking at one another.

June supposed they did spend a whole lot of time together, as Judge was forty-three years old and had been living and working at Shiloh Ridge for his entire life.

"It's okay," she said about the same time Bear asked, "Are you going back to the ranch, June?" He met her eye and then switched his gaze to Judge's. "Maybe she has work to do. It's only three o'clock."

June wanted to be with Judge. The ground between them felt like it might crack open at any moment still, despite the kiss they'd shared on his porch. The discussion preceding it had been tense, and for several horrifying minutes, June had thought Judge would break-up with her.

The moment she'd realized how upset that made her, she'd told herself to fix things. Apologize. Choose him.

"I called in," she said with as much bravado as she could muster. "I'm not working the rest of the day."

"See?" Judge's hold on her arm tightened. "She's going to mother me, so the lot of you can stop doing so. You can go back to your regularly scheduled lives." He glanced at her. "She knows how to cook, and I'll be just fine."

"I'd be shocked if there's not fifteen plates of something or other at your place by now," Cactus said dryly. "I know Willa was planning to bring over the rest of our pecan pie." He didn't sound too happy about it either. He looked at the hospital, something dark in his expression.

He had *stories* to tell, and June wanted to hear them. She'd been slowly learning that these particular cowboys weren't as shallow as she'd once thought. They had a rich history, with real life experience.

"Tell 'er she doesn't need to do that," Judge said. He started walking again. "C'mon, June. I never get done working at three o'clock, and I'd love an afternoon nap."

She smiled at him, glad he hadn't been hurt more than he'd been. She praised the Lord as she stepped with him that there'd been no concussion, no fractures, no internal bleeding. Nothing. He had a headache and a backache, and he claimed it felt about the same as when he rode all day moving cattle.

He leaned closer to her, and while his extra heat wouldn't usually be welcome, right now, she sure liked it. "You'll stay with me while I sleep, right?" he murmured.

"Yes," she said. "I'll stay with you while you sleep." She'd also love to know why Cactus and Preacher hated the hospital, though she suspected Preacher's dislike had to do with the car accident he'd been in last year. She distinctly remembered Judge telling her about it and asking her to pray for his brother.

She had, and as the three of them hovered around the van while she waited for Judge to climb in, she sent up another prayer very similar to the one she'd offered last year. *Bless him, please.*

Sometimes simple prayers were all that was needed, and June felt her spirits lift. Not only did she want God to bless Judge, she wanted the same favor. She wanted to know how to keep herself in his life. How to be the Juniper Nichols she was supposed to be. She'd been searching for herself for thirty-six years, and she hoped when she found herself, she was a woman she could be proud of.

She wanted to be a strong woman, like the other ranch wives. She wanted to be a faithful woman, like her mother and sister.

She closed the door behind Judge, and as she turned to face his brothers, parts of June she hadn't known she needed fell into place. She felt more sure of her role in Judge's life, and it was at his side. Not behind him. Not in front of him. He didn't have to lag behind her and Lucy Mae.

They could be companions. Partners who worked together to achieve their goals and dreams.

Just like with the light show, she thought.

"Thank you for staying with me," she said, stepping quickly into Bear, the brother who stood in the middle of the threesome. "It was so scary coming around the house and seeing him on the ground."

Bear enveloped her in a hug that said more than words ever could. "Of course," he said quietly.

"I'm going to take good care of him," she said. She moved from Bear to Cactus and hugged him too. He seemed a bit more rigid, but he softened almost instantly.

"He's very lucky to have you, June," Cactus said. "He has a phone, and all of our numbers are in it."

"We have a family text," Preacher said, and June moved over to him. He didn't bend down as far as the other two. "I know Judge keeps it pinned to the top of his texts, right next to your string."

June didn't know what to say, so she just basked in the warmth of his embrace and then stepped out of his arms as he added, "If you have trouble, just text that family message. All of us will get it, and you'll have more help at the Ranch House than you know what to do with."

"That's the truth," Bear said, smiling.

"We can be overbearing," Cactus said. "But sometimes that's okay."

Judge opened the door behind her. "I'm suffocating in here," he said. "If you're going to stand in the parking lot and talk about me, can I at least have the keys to start the van?"

June's gaze swept the three Glover brothers in front of her, and the four of them started laughing at the same time. She nodded to them, hurried around the van, and got behind the wheel, still giggling.

She started the van and got the air conditioning blowing. "Sorry," she said. "And we weren't talking about you."

"Mm hm." Judge adjusted his vents, as June didn't have

passengers in her work van that often. "I know my brothers, and I'm sure they were telling you everything about me, including how I don't like mushrooms and to call them if you need help."

"No," June said quickly, wanting to defend his brothers for some reason. "There was no mention of mushrooms at all."

Chapter Nineteen

"I've got him," Bishop Glover said for at least the third time in twenty minutes. He was tired of saying it. Tired of reassuring his wife that he could take care of their son for an afternoon. He wasn't an invalid, and while he knew Montana didn't mean to make him feel like that, the fact was, she still did.

He picked up the five-month-old, everything about him brightening at his son's sudden smile. "Yeah, see? He's happy to come with daddy for a couple of hours."

"I'm sure he is," Montana said, everything about her voice stuck up in her head. Bishop hated being sick, but even worse was being sick in the summertime.

"I'm meeting Charlie and Preacher in a few minutes. Did you take your pills?"

"All of them." Montana lay on the couch, a blanket tucked around her legs.

"Do you want me to help you into the bedroom?"

Bishop looked at the body sling Montana had gotten out for him. He had no idea how to put it on, and he thought a stroller would be just as easy.

"Yes, please," she said, sighing. "I hope I start to feel better fast. This is terrible, and we're moving Aurora in only a few days. I can't miss that."

"You will now that we got the antibiotic," Bishop said. He cradled his son in one arm and helped Montana off the couch with the other. He steadied her and walked slowly with her down the hall to their master suite.

She climbed into bed, and Bishop noticed the sweat shining on her forehead from the effort simply walking down the hall had taken. He covered her up and tucked her in, and she let her eyes drift closed immediately.

"Sleep as long as you want," he whispered, pressing his lips to her forehead. She felt hot and clammy at the same time, and concern spiked in his blood. He reminded himself that she'd taken her medication, and she'd taken fever reducers, and she needed to rest. They were doing all the right things.

"Come on, bud," he said quietly to Robbie. "Let's leave Momma alone for a while." He retraced his steps out to the living room just as Aurora came in the front door. "Hey, there." He threw her a smile and gave her Robbie when she reached for him.

"Hey," she said, grinning at the little boy. She loved her half-brother, and Robbie absolutely adored Aurora. She grinned at him and laughed with him as he started flailing his arms.

Bishop picked up the sling, deciding it would be far

easier to not have to push a stroller over the uneven ground down at the Kinder Ranch. Things were coming along down there, and they did have a road base in, but he had a few things he wanted to show Charlie and Preacher that were off-road.

"Can you help me with this?" he asked Aurora.

"Sure." She put Robbie back in the playpen where Bishop had gotten him, and the baby wasn't happy about that. "Oh, hush," she said. "Your daddy's gonna take you, so stop freaking out."

She faced Bishop, her expression turning serious. "I, um, wanted to talk to you about something."

Bishop stopped fiddling with the sling, and Aurora took it from him, her gaze dropping to it. "Okay," he said, feeling like Montana should be here. At the same time, sometimes Aurora needed a sounding board before she approached her mother with something. Bishop was usually a lot more accepting, and he helped her reason through things before Aurora talked to her mom about what was on her mind.

"I'm leaving for school this weekend."

"Yes," Bishop said. "We're all aware. Holly Ann's been cooking for days and days." He smiled at Aurora as she went around him, lifting one part of the sling for him to put his arm through. "You still want the big send-off party on Saturday, right?"

"Yeah, sure," Aurora said. "Oliver's family is planning to come and everything."

"Great." Bishop didn't mind Aurora's relationship with Oliver, though it terrified Montana to the core. She wanted her daughter to have the freedom to experience all life had to offer, and she didn't think that happened very well when kids got married right out of high school.

Bishop had tried to stay neutral on the subject. He hadn't even thought about marriage until age thirty, and by then, Montana had a ten-year-old. Aurora was eighteen now and about to leave home to go to college, and if she and Oliver got married, Bishop could easily be a grandfather by age thirty-seven.

His son and his grandson would be nearly the same age, and his brain tripped over itself.

Aurora went around his back, taking the sling with her. She paused back there and said, "I need to make this bigger somehow. Just a sec."

"Mom said it had a buckle." Bishop twisted to look over his shoulder, but he couldn't quite see the sling.

"Yeah, it's right here."

"Keep talkin', baby," Bishop said. "What's on your mind?"

Aurora stayed silent for another moment. Then she said, "Georgia, Bishop. I want to go to school in Savannah, Georgia."

Bishop pulled in a breath, his mind reeling. "That's a lot farther from Texas than Oklahoma."

"People go all over to go to college," Aurora said, talking fast now. "They have a design school there, and it's amazing. The best in the country. I could do fashion design or interior design. They have sewing classes and runway shows. They have this furniture design course that looks so fun. There's fashion management and marketing. It's everything I want. So many things I could do there."

Her voice broke, and Bishop abandoned putting on the sling. He faced her and drew her into a hug. She wept against his chest quietly, and he just let her. Robbie fussed, but both of them ignored the boy.

"Sounds like you've done a lot of research on this place," Bishop said gently.

"My home economics teacher told me about it last spring," she said. "I've been looking at their website every day." She pulled away and wiped her eyes. "It's fine. Oklahoma State is fine. It has a decent program."

"But it's not what you want."

Aurora eyes filled with tears again, and she shook her head.

Bishop reached out and pushed back the loose strands of hair that had fallen out of her braid. "Aurora, you know I'd give you anything you wanted."

"I know that." She looked at him, and the only thing coming from her was misery. Pure misery. How had he missed it before? How had he not seen it in her face every time they spoke about her moving to Stillwater?

While most of the Glovers had been shocked and worried when Mister had moved there a couple of months ago, Montana had been thrilled. He could help to look after Aurora if she needed him, and Montana had been texting Mister for weeks. He was planning to meet them on Sunday when they arrived to move Aurora into her student apartment.

Bishop didn't know what to do. He had no idea what to

say. He knew he couldn't send Aurora to Stillwater as miserable as she was.

"What do we need to do?" he asked. Aurora was a smart girl, and so much like her mother. She had a plan for everything, just like her clothing had a pattern.

"I want to apply to go there in January," she said, sniffling. "It's not too late for that. It's a private college, Bish. It's expensive."

"That's okay," he said. "Could you get a scholarship there?"

"Maybe," she said. "I have a few things I can put in my portfolio, but I don't know. They might have given out all their money for people starting in the fall."

"Money isn't an issue," Bishop said, looking down the hall. He knew what the issue would be—Montana. She was already struggling with the fact that Aurora was old enough to leave home. He couldn't remember how many times she'd said Stillwater was less than four hours away.

We almost drive that long just to get groceries, she'd said.

Bishop had laughed and laughed, because that so wasn't true.

"She just worries about you," he said quietly.

"I know that," Aurora said. "But Bish, people really do move across the country to go to college. It's normal. I'll be fine. I'll have some experience living away from home already, and you'll fly me home anytime I want." She flashed him a smile and moved back around his back to work on the sling again.

Bishop would fly her home anytime she wanted. He'd

fly Montana out there. He'd do whatever it took to make them both happy.

"What about Oliver?" he asked.

"He's thinking he might try the SCAD too," Aurora said. "They have a graphic design course *and* an animation course. His dad does that, and no, it's not UT-Austin, but Ollie says there are other schools. The best animators don't always come out of Austin." She spoke with some disgust in her voice, and Bishop wondered if he should call Tripp Walker.

The two men were in very similar situations, raising step-children as their own and trying to give them the best chance at life possible.

"They also have an advertising program," Aurora said. "Arm up, Bish."

He lifted his arm, and she slung the fabric around it. "And an equestrian studies program that caught Ollie's eye."

"That's a wide range of things."

"He doesn't know what he wants to do. He's not even going to UT-Austin this semester, because he's afraid to choose the wrong thing."

"He doesn't have to choose right now," Bishop said.

"That's what I keep telling him." She fastened the buckle across Bishop's chest after making the strap longer. "There. Do you want him in right now?"

"Yeah, I'm late already to meet Preacher and Charlie."

"I'm sorry," she said. "I didn't realize you had an appointment."

"I don't care at all," he said quickly. "Let me text them."

He pulled out his phone while Aurora bent to get Robbie. "This is more important, Aurora."

He sent the text and met his step-daughter's eyes. "*You're* more important to me than anything, okay?"

"Except Mom," she said with a smile.

"Right," Bishop said, grinning too. "Except Mom."

Aurora sobered so quickly, that unrest inside her bleeding out everywhere.

"I'm sorry I didn't see how much turmoil you were in," he said, taking the baby and positioning him in the sling. Aurora strapped him all in, making sure everything was tight and secure.

"I'm okay," she finally said. "But I don't think I'm going to be happy at Oklahoma State. I can just feel it. It's not what I want, and Mom's always talking about going out there and experiencing life. Doing what I want. Achieving my dreams." She swept her arm in front of her body. "Just getting into the SCAD would be a dream come true."

"Then you better apply," Bishop said. "And we better talk to Mom about this soon."

Aurora nodded. "You're so much easier to talk to than her."

Bishop grinned, pride swelling within him. "Don't ever tell her that." Their eyes met, and they both started laughing. He pulled her into a hug, despite Robbie's gurgled noises and the way he sort of smashed the baby between them.

"I love you, baby," he whispered to Aurora. "If this will make you happy, I'll step up to the plate for you."

"I love you too, Bishop," she said, stepping back from him and Robbie. "I'm going to talk to Mom. I am."

"Before you leave for Oklahoma?"

Aurora took a deep breath. "Yes," she said as she blew it out. "Before I leave for Oklahoma."

Bishop nodded, so proud of her. He beamed at her. "You're going to do amazing things with your life, I can feel it."

She gave him another smile and walked toward the kitchen. "I'll get dinner started while you're gone," she said.

He watched her for a moment, marveling at how wonderful she was. His phone went off a couple of times, and Bishop turned toward the door. "All right, Robbie," he said to his son. "You better be takin' notes from your sister, because I don't want any trouble this afternoon."

Chapter Twenty

Preacher Glover kept his hand securely fastened in Charlie's. Bishop could talk fast, and he used words that Preacher felt like he needed to look up to know the meanings of them. He got the general gist of most things, but his head still spun.

"All of the utilities have been stubbed in," Bishop said. "The road base is here, but we need to expand it out to the other buildings. We're still clearing the land for the barns and stables, but the main homestead site is ready, as is the area for the cowboy cabins." He pointed to the various sites on the horizon in front of them.

"How many barns and stables?" Charlie asked. "I didn't think we were having a whole new ranch down here."

"You're not," Bishop said. "But we want a few outbuildings here, simply for storage. Ward mentioned being able to sell our excess hay from the barns here instead of up on the ranch, and then customers won't have to go all the way up on our road in their big trucks."

"Makes sense," Preacher murmured. Everything at the Kinder Ranch site made sense. Bishop, Ward, Bear, and Ranger were very smart men. Preacher had sat in on all of their meetings, as he was going to be responsible for taking care of this patch of land.

It suddenly felt so much bigger than just having a house. Judge just had to take care of the Ranch House. Bishop had half an acre with a house and a small patch of lawn.

This was at least thirty acres of land, with cowboy cabins, a house, a yard, gardens, barns, and stables.

Preacher felt like throwing up. Charlie wasn't particularly outdoorsy, though she'd gone horseback riding with him a little bit this summer. His back couldn't take much, and he'd rather walk or ride in a truck. If Bear would let them use ATVs on the ranch, Preacher could easily see himself riding one of those instead of a horse.

An idea sparked in his mind, and he asked, "Will there be an equipment shed?"

Bishop swung toward him, and his baby flailed his arms and legs, looking like he was having the time of his life. Bishop had put a big hat on the child to protect him from the sun, and Preacher couldn't help smiling at the baby.

He did want kids of his own, though he and Charlie weren't in any hurry to start a family. Preacher still had days where he couldn't do much, and Charlie's life was filled with broadcasting, and now that school had started again, chemistry demos.

She'd kept Below Zero open in the mall, but she didn't do fairs or events anymore. She went down to town when she felt like it, but she'd hired people to work the ice cream kiosk for her, not quite ready to give up on her liquid nitrogen treats yet.

"An equipment shed?" Bishop asked. "For what? We're not going to be cultivating the land down here."

"I thought we were," Preacher said, turning in a circle. "We own it all. I thought Ace said we should be planting it. Selling what we could. Utilizing it."

"It really will be like a second ranch then," Bishop said.

"No," Preacher said. "An extension. That's why we have more cowboy cabins, right? To hire more people to work the ranch as it grows?"

"Yes," Bishop said. "I suppose that's right. I didn't think of an equipment shed."

"I want ATVs too," Preacher said, his voice sticking in his throat. "So something big enough for tractors and ATVs."

Bishop opened his mouth and then closed it again. He looked down at his clipboard, the silence between them now charged in the hot afternoon.

"I'll talk to Bear," Preacher said. "I can't ride a horse for long, and it would be nice to jump on an ATV and zip up to the homestead or whatever."

"Ranger tried to get ATVs on the ranch," Bishop said. "He failed."

"It's been a few years," Preacher said.

"True." Bishop shaded his eyes and drew a deep breath. "We could put an equipment shed on that side of the road.

It'll take up some room, but I think you're right. It's probably necessary."

"Sorry to change the plans," Preacher said.

"That side of the road is in better condition than this side," Bishop said, as if adding a huge building was no big deal. "We'll still want to get your house and the cowboy cabins in first."

He lifted the clipboard toward Preacher. "I've got the cement truck coming next week. They're going to pour your foundation on Tuesday morning."

"Tuesday morning?" Charlie exclaimed, grabbing the clipboard before Preacher could take it. "You're kidding."

Preacher smiled at her enthusiasm, and while he didn't mind living in the Top Cottage, Charlie wanted somewhere that was theirs. She wanted her own bed, and her own dining room table. She wanted a huge office for her computers and monitors, and she wanted a little alcove for her cats, Paulie and Archie.

With the design Bishop and Montana had come up with, she'd get it all.

"Tuesday," Bishop said. "We'll build from there. I've hired Lira and Barney Lowenstein to work on this project until it's done. They're going to be here next Saturday, and I expect the pace to pick up considerably with their help."

"That's great," Charlie said, but Preacher knew what it cost to bring in more builders. The Lowensteins had come for a month or two last spring, when Montana had stopped working to have Robbie. They'd finished Zona's and Duke's house in record time, and Bishop had used them to help get the remaining outbuildings completely fixed after the wind and snowstorm that had come last Christmas.

"They're bringing a crew of four," Bishop said. "So between all of us, I think we'll have the homestead here done by summertime. Cowboy cabins very soon after that, and then we'll see."

"So earlier than your original timeline, at least for us," Preacher said.

"Definitely." Bishop nodded. "Of course, Bear and Sammy are building a new place, and Micah Walker's going to be here doing that. He's asked me and Montana to help, so I'll be divided a little bit." He drew in breath, and added quickly, "Not much."

"You have a son now," Preacher said quietly. "You'll be divided a lot. You can't do everything, Bishop."

"I know," he said airily. "I just don't want you to think we're abandoning you, or passing everything off to Lira and Barney."

"I don't think anything," Preacher said. "I will give thanks to the Lord because of his righteousness."

Charlie beamed up at him, looping her arm through his and leaning her head against his bicep. "It's going to be spectacular, Bishop," she said. "Thank you so much. We're very grateful we'll get to start and raise our family here."

Silence poured through the sky then. Even Robbie didn't make a single baby sound. Preacher basked in the peacefulness of the land, and he felt closer to the Lord and closer to his wife in that very moment.

"Uh, is that an announcement?" Bishop asked.

Preacher choked, his gaze flying to Bishop's. "What?"

Bishop burst out laughing, and he bounced his baby as Robbie started to cry at the sudden, loud sound. "It sounded like Charlie was saying y'all were going to start your family."

"Eventually," Preacher said, glancing at his wife. "That was *not* an announcement."

Bishop kept chuckling as he reached into his pocket and pulled out a pacifier for his son. "Hey, we had an agreement, bud. You'd behave, and you'd get to come work with daddy. Hush up, now."

Preacher did like watching his brothers and cousins interact with their wives. He liked watching Zona soften and become a wife and mother. He'd been up to her new place a few times now, and he didn't mind holding her tiny baby girl while they both took a nap. Zona liked it, because she got to get a few things done Shiloh prevented her from doing, and Preacher liked the extra body warmth that lulled him to sleep faster.

In fact, he and Charlie were going to dinner at Duke and Zona's that night. He still needed to clean out a stable, and then check on Judge, so he took the clipboard from Charlie and glanced at it. "What else?"

"Just you facing the grizzly about ATVs," Bishop said, another chuckle coming from his mouth. "I'm going to meet with Rufus Randolph in about five minutes." He twisted and looked toward the highway. It sat several hundred yards from the Kinder homesite, but it was a heck of a lot closer than Shiloh Ridge Ranch.

Preacher's excitement to be close to his family but not right on top of them redoubled. This was the perfect spot for him, and he thanked God he and Charlie could start and raise their family on this land.

"He's going to tell me what else we need to do to get approval from the city to pour the roads." Bishop took his clipboard back, and Preacher turned toward his truck.

"Thanks for everything," he said.

"Anytime," Bishop said, flipping pages and already distracted by something else on the clipboard.

Preacher helped Charlie up into their truck, and he took several moments to get in and get comfortable too. They started up the hill back toward the ranch, and Preacher let his mind move wherever it wanted to.

He and Charlie had been married for eight months now, and he did love the married life. He loved seeing her first thing in the morning, and he loved listening to her breathe evenly when he first woke himself. He always fell asleep before her, but he was definitely more the morning person.

"When are you going to talk to Bear?" she asked. "Would it be better if I went with you?"

Preacher sighed and looked out his window. "I don't know. The house won't be done for nine more months, at least. I just think it would be easier for me to get up to the ranch on an ATV. I wouldn't have to drive and park, and I can't ride my horse that far." He refocused on the road in front of him. "Bear's reasonable. I might actually have a legitimate need. Ranger just wanted to use them for things to be easier."

"Making things easier is a legitimate need," Charlie

said. "More efficient. You guys are all about efficiency. I'm surprised Bear doesn't use all the technology he can."

"He just wants to maintain the integrity of Shiloh Ridge," Preacher said. "My dad wouldn't have wanted helicopters or ATVs. He was old-school." He grinned at her. "Kind of like you and that alien game you like."

She grinned at him, her smile slipping after only a few seconds. "I do want to start a family with you." She clasped her hands together, pressing them into one another until they shook. Then she set them in her lap. "I think I'm ready whenever you are."

Preacher didn't know how to answer. He loved Charlie, and he did want children. Did that mean he was ready? "I have no idea how to be a dad," he said.

"You'd be just fine," she said. "I work from home. I don't have to do the chemistry demos. I have someone else running Below Zero. I can still do my broadcasts, and I've seen how much Zona's baby sleeps. I'll have plenty of time to play my video games and do my sponsorships." She cleared her throat. "If I even still want to."

"Charlie," he said, surprised. "You want to. I know you do."

"Yeah, but...." She trailed off and looked out her window as the arch over the road came into view. "I don't know, Preach. I see how things change for people once they bring home that precious little human. I know they'll change for me too. Maybe I won't care so much about getting the best games first or consulting on the chemistry for a new game that will be out in three years."

"I don't—" He cleared his throat, because he wanted to

give her whatever she wanted. He simply didn't know how to say what looped in his head.

"What?" she prompted.

"I don't want you to regret it," he said. "I don't want you to give up what you love doing. I don't want you to give up who you are."

"I'm not going to do that," she said. "I'm going to enhance who I am. Expand it." She gave him a smile as they bumped onto the ranch. "You're always so worried about me. When was the last time I did something I didn't want to do?"

"Well, you tried that kimchi last week." Preacher grinned at her, and Charlie burst out laughing. He loved making her laugh, and he hoped he could continue to do so for many years to come.

They drove up the rickety road to the Top Cottage, and Preacher took Charlie's hand as they went inside the small, two-bedroom house. It sat in the middle of a grove of trees, and the air conditioner didn't have to run here as often as it did at the Ranch House.

"So what do you think?" Charlie asked as she went up the steps with him.

"About what?"

"Starting a family." She reached for the doorknob and turned back to him. She tipped up onto her toes and kissed him, and Preacher sure did like that.

"I guess I could stand it," he whispered, and she claimed his mouth again, opened the door, and walked backward inside, still kissing him.

Surprise darted through Preacher. "Oh, we're starting right now?"

"Mm hm," Charlie said, and Preacher tapped the door closed with the heel of his boot and twisted the lock behind him.

Chapter Twenty-One

M ontana Glover wiped her forehead, the air conditioning in the lovely home where she lived already working overtime. She felt so hot from the stress too, because today, she was feeding everyone at the ranch from her own kitchen.

Then, she, Bishop, Robbie, and Aurora would load into the truck and drive the four hours to Stillwater, towing a small trailer with everything her daughter needed to survive for the next several months.

She pulled back on the emotions, determined not to let them choke her today. She mixed Italian dressing and poured it over pasta and veggies. She covered the huge bowl with plastic wrap and put it in the fridge.

She emptied the ice maker again and set the bag of cubes in the freezer. She checked the mini meatballs in the oven and set the timer for three more minutes.

Nearby, Robbie babbled to himself, a plastic set of keys

making a racket while he waved them around. Montana grinned at the child, smitten by his chubby cheeks, shock of dark hair, and those Glover blue eyes. He looked so much like Bishop, and the man adored his son. Montana loved watching the two of them interact, because while Bishop was loving and Robbie clearly had his father wrapped around his little finger, he was also stern with the boy.

"Do you want a cracker, baby?" she asked, getting down a box of goldfish-shaped crackers. She put a couple on the floor in front of Robbie, who bent right in half to get them. At six months old, the baby still didn't seem to have bones in his body, but he could stay sitting up now.

Montana knew her life would get exponentially harder once Robbie learned to move around on his own, and for now, she enjoyed the fact that she could put him on a blanket near her, and he'd stay there.

Aurora certainly wasn't staying anywhere, and another round of sadness hit her. She continued her work in the kitchen, frosting the miniature cupcakes she'd made last night and then pulling out the vegetable tray to add in extra dill to the store-bought dip. That was a trick Aunt Jackie had taught her, and Montana's heart filled with love for her aunt and uncle that had accepted her, let her live with them, and loved her no matter what.

Montana's mother hadn't made the trip for this little shindig, because it was just a send-off party. She'd come for Aurora's graduation in the spring, and that alone had been ultra stressful for Montana. She did send her mother pictures of Robbie, and in fact, she paused in her work again, snapped a photo of him with his fat fist in his mouth, and sent it to her mother.

The door leading to the garage opened, and Bishop said, "...got it? Let me prop open the door." He did that with the toe of his boot and then continued backward into the house, carrying a long, folding table.

She watched him and Judge bring in four more tables, push furniture out of the way, and start setting up chairs.

"How's June holding up?" she asked Judge once they'd stopped. Bishop filled a couple of glasses with precious ice and then water, giving one to his brother.

Judge drank greedily from it and wiped his brow. "Good, I think? I don't know."

Montana exchanged a glance with Bishop, who gulped his drink too. "It's so dang hot today," he said. "Terrible day for moving."

"Maybe she won't go," Montana said, only half-kidding. She couldn't believe half of her wasn't.

"I think that's how June feels," Judge said. "She should be here soon. She said she'd skip church too and bring up all the decorations."

"I texted her a while ago," Montana said. "She said she'd be here at ten." It was five minutes till the hour, and then she had a feeling things would get even crazier. June would fill the house with decorations. All the Glovers would return from church and come straight to the house for lunch.

Good-byes had to be said. Hugs given. Tears shed. They were leaving at two o'clock, and Montana wasn't looking forward to sharing a tiny hotel room with her baby, as

Robbie slept down the hall in his own room and always had.

"Hello," Aunt Jackie trilled out, and Montana turned toward the sound of her voice.

"Pour this over those meatballs, would you, Bishop?" She handed him the rubber spatula she'd been using to stir together a sweet and sour barbecue sauce. Her husband was a better cook than her, but Montana did about half the cooking.

She rushed toward her aunt and uncle, diving into the embrace of Aunt Jackie. "Oh, I'm so glad you're here."

"You're going to be fine," Aunt Jackie said, and Montana nodded against her shoulder.

"It just feels so far away." She watched her daughter walk in with Oliver Walker, and tears pricked her eyes. She stepped over to Uncle Bob and let him reassure her with hugs and kind words too.

"Heya, baby," she said to Aurora, those tears so hot and threatening to spill over.

Aurora held her tightly, and Montana knew the girl put on a brave face. She possessed courage too, and she had no doubt she'd be fine in Stillwater. The feeling of peace and love descended on her, and she pulled back and said, "You're amazing. It's going to be so great on your own."

Aurora's eyes widened slightly, and she glanced over to Ollie. Montana had accepted his place in her daughter's life. It didn't seem to matter what she said anyway, and Aurora had enjoyed high school with him as her boyfriend for a lot of years now.

"Can I talk to you for a sec?" She took Montana's hand and led her out onto the porch.

Montana's heartbeat bumped rapidly through her neck. The heat didn't help, nor did the seemingly insurmountable task list she still needed to accomplish in the next couple of hours. "What's going on?"

The ranch sat in silence. No breeze, no nickering horses, no lowing cattle.

Aurora paced to the edge of the porch facing west and leaned against the railing there. Montana wasn't sure if she should follow or not. She told herself to get some of her daughter's courage, and she reminded herself that she'd talked to this girl about everything. About her father. About boys. About sex. About *everything*.

She walked toward Aurora and put her arm around her shoulders. "What's wrong?"

"I don't want to go to school in Oklahoma."

The rate of Montana's pulse tripled. She had no idea what to say, so she stayed silent. The Glovers jumped in after every sentence, but Montana knew if she stayed quiet, Aurora would continue.

She looked out over the pasture next to their house, praying to God to give her patience and strength for whatever Aurora said next.

"Mom, I want to go to the SCAD in Georgia." Aurora turned toward Montana, her eyes wide and scared. They also held hope.

Montana's immediate reaction was to say no, of course not. Georgia was much too far away, and she was already dying with Aurora moving four hours from the ranch. She could drive four hours every day if she had to, but Georgia?

No.

She blinked, still trying to think of what to say.

"I've looked up all their programs, Mom," Aurora said. "They're the best design school. They have amazing fashion opportunities." She cleared her throat, her eyes filling with tears. "I'm not going to be happy in Oklahoma. I don't even want to go."

"Then don't go," Montana said through a scratchy throat. Her thoughts slowed, and what she should say came forward in her mind, a gift from the Lord above.

Aurora scoffed and turned back to the horizon. "Of course you'd say that. You've never wanted me to leave Three Rivers."

"Don't got to OSU," Montana said slowly. "Stay here and keep doing the horseback riding lessons and working on the ranch. Save your money, and go to Georgia in January." She barely recognized her own voice. She couldn't believe what she'd just said. "Or next fall. There's not a rule that says you have to start college the very moment you finish high school."

Everything moved in slow motion, and Montana could hear every little sound, smell every precise scent coming from the house.

Tires crunched over gravel, and Aurora turned toward her, shock on her face. The tangy smell of barbecue sauce and vinegar met her nose.

"Are you kidding?" Aurora asked, her voice barely more than a whisper. It sounded like a shout in Montana's ears.

"Howdy," someone called, and Montana turned toward June. She and her daughter, Lucy Mae, had gotten out of their truck and were both carrying boxes toward the porch.

"Hold that thought," Montana said to Aurora, the world rushing forward in real time again. As she walked toward the top of the steps, the front door opened. Aunt Jackie held Robbie in her arms, big, fat tears on the boy's eyelashes.

"Montana, dear, he needs to be changed, but he's got some diaper rash. Do you have any cream? Bishop can't find it." She snuggled the little boy and bounced him in her arms. "I had to diaper him up without it, and he wasn't happy about it. You poor thing. Aunt Jackie's so sorry."

"I bought a new tube," she said. "It's probably in my bathroom. Sorry, Aunt Jackie."

"No problem. Let's go find it, baby." She went back inside, but she didn't close the door.

"I have another box in the back," June said, reaching the top of the stairs. She wore a smile that thinly covered her own stress, and Montana connected with her in a way she never had before.

Boots landed on the porch behind her, and Judge said, "Howdy, June-Bug."

"Give that to Judge and come show me," Montana said, glancing down the porch to where Aurora still stood. She watched Montana, her arms folded. Montana held up one hand as if to say, *Patience, baby. I'll be right back.*

"Heya, Lucy Mae," Montana said as June passed her box

to Judge. "Are you excited to go back to California? They're in a real heat wave right now."

"Ugh, I know," she said, as if she really wouldn't go because of the temperature. "But it can't be worse than Texas, right?" She grinned and followed Judge into the house.

Montana went down the steps with June, her mind regurgitating what she'd just said to her daughter. *Don't go to Oklahoma. Go to Georgia.*

What in the world had she been thinking? Aurora had already stopped her horseback riding lessons. People had found other instructors. She couldn't just pick that back up. She could work around Shiloh Ridge, and Bishop would give her four times what she'd earn somewhere else. The man had a real soft spot for Aurora, and Montana adored that about him most of the time.

"How are you holding up?" she asked June.

June sniffled as they reached her truck. "It's fine. I'm fine. Everything is going to be fine."

Montana took her into a hug and held on tight. "I know you're going to miss her."

June clutched her in such a desperate way that Montana didn't dare let go. "I don't know who I am without her."

Montana understood that feeling. She'd been just as torn in the past couple of years as she'd brought Bishop into her life, and then a new baby.

"How are you doing?" June asked. "I feel like we interrupted something."

"You did, but it's okay," Montana said. "I'm...okay." She

glanced up to where Aurora still stood on the porch. "I just feel old. I don't feel like I'm old enough for her to leave. I have this brand-new baby, and yeah." She shook her head. "Everything in my life is a little bit at odds with one another."

June looked toward the house too. "I know what that feels like." She raised her hand, and Montana saw Judge as he came to the top of the stairs. "Just one more box, honey. We've got it." She made no move to get it out of the back of the truck though.

Montana didn't either. She didn't want to pry into a private relationship, but she understood a lot of June's reservations about being with Judge. "He could help you, you know."

June focused on her. "What do you mean?"

They kept their voices low, and Montana saw the anxiety in June's expression. "I mean." She sighed and looked away. "I don't want to assume you're just like me. I don't want to put feelings and thoughts into your brain. I'm just...I mean, he could help you understand that you're more than just Lucy Mae's mom. We wear these badges as mothers, you know?"

She wasn't even sure what she was saying, but June nodded. "I think I'm having an easier time letting go of Aurora," Montana said slowly, trying to find her clarity of thought. "Because she's not all I have. I have Bishop, and he's so important to me. I have Robbie, who I love dearly. He's my child too, and he's not Aurora. Even if I didn't have him or Bishop, I have my construction firm. There are *other* parts of me." She smiled and reached for the box.

"Does this make any sense at all? I'm sorry; I feel like I'm rambling."

"It makes sense," June said quietly.

"And I'm not losing Aurora. She'll always be part of my life, no matter where she goes or what she does." The words gave her strength and spoke truth to her heart. "You're not losing Lucy Mae either." She pulled the box to the end of the tailgate.

"I've never really thought about it that way," June said. She touched Montana's arm. "Thank you, Montana. I needed to hear all of that." She hugged Montana again, and this time it was less desperate and less frantic. "Thank you for letting us crash your going-away party, and thank you for including us in your luncheon."

"You can come to all the luncheons, June," Montana whispered. "I know Oakley invites you specifically, and I know you see those texts on the group chat."

June pulled away and wiped her eyes. "I do. I just...." She looked at Montana, and Montana found such a beautiful spirit in the woman. She felt a sisterhood with her, and she sure hoped she and Judge could work things out. Even if they didn't, Montana wanted to keep June as a friend.

"I'm not one of you," she said simply.

"Yet," Montana tacked onto the end of the sentence quickly. She picked up the box and nudged June to start walking, her eyes on Judge still standing on the porch. "And June, look at that man. You could be one of us easily."

"You think so?" June whispered.

"Honey, he's been waiting for you to be ready for *five* years," Montana hissed at her. "*Look* at him."

June looked, and Montana hoped and prayed she could see the adoration on Judge's face. Montana sure could.

"Let me," he said, coming down the stairs to take the box from her. "You guys okay?"

"Yes, thank you, Judge." Montana brushed her hands together and looked at her daughter. "I'll be in lickety split."

June and Judge went up the steps together, and Montana waited for them to close the front door behind them before she moved. She went right back to her daughter's side and asked, "What are you thinking?"

"I'm actually thinking about doing exactly what you said." She looked at Montana and let the tears fall down her face. "How hard would it be not to go? Will we lose a bunch of money on my housing? I'm so sorry, Mom. I should've talked to you months ago."

Montana folded her sobbing daughter into her arms and held her tight. "I don't care about the money," she said in a very Bishop-like statement. "It'll take a couple of phone calls, baby. You'll make them, and you'll unpack, and it'll be fine."

She smiled as she said the word "fine," because she sounded like June. "You'll ask Bishop for a job, and he'll pay you ten times the normal cowgirl rate." She laughed, the sound getting choked in her chest as her own tears started to fall. "And then, you'll go to Georgia, and you'll get into those amazing design programs you want, and you're going to have a spectacular life."

She pulled away and held Aurora by the shoulders. They looked at one another, and Montana only felt love for her daughter and the human being she was becoming. "I love you, okay? You can talk to me about anything."

Aurora nodded and wiped her face. "I'm sorry, Mom."

"Don't be sorry," Montana said, brushing her hair back off her face.

"I love you too." Aurora grabbed onto her again, and Montana held her, glad she could be the strong one and lend support to her daughter when she needed it.

"Sweetheart?" Bishop asked, coming out onto the porch. He looked right and then left, his eyes locking onto Montana's. "What's going on?" He moved toward them quickly, then stalled completely.

Montana knew in that moment that Aurora had talked to Bishop first, but this time—for the first time—she didn't mind. She knew Aurora found him easier to talk to and confess things to, and she'd had to deal with that in the past.

"Aurora?" Bishop asked.

She stepped out of Montana's embrace and wiped her face again. "I'm not going, Bishop," she said, rushing toward him. "I'm not going to Oklahoma."

He caught her and hugged her, and Montana's emotions rippled through her. Tears tracked down her face as Bishop mouthed, *I'm sorry, love* to her and then bent his mouth closer to Aurora to say something to her.

He motioned for Montana to join them a moment later, and she did, sandwiching Aurora between her and her husband.

"Okay," Bishop said, his voice thick. "This is okay." They separated, and Montana took a moment to clear her tears away. Everyone would be able to tell she'd been crying, but she didn't care. She was allowed to cry today, even if Aurora wasn't leaving.

"What are we going to do?" Aurora asked.

"We're going to have a party," Montana said. "At the beginning, you're going to make an announcement about your plans."

"Did you apply to the college in Savannah?" Bishop asked.

Aurora nodded. "Just on Friday. I won't know for a few weeks. Mom said I could maybe work around the ranch and save some money?" She looked hopefully between the two of them.

"Of course," Bishop said, as Montana knew he would. "And you'll go...whenever you go." He met Montana's eyes, and she nodded.

"Maybe in January," Aurora said, squaring her shoulders and facing the house. "Maybe not till next fall. There's no rule that says I have to start college the moment I finish high school."

"No," Bishop said, shock in his eyes. "There's not."

Aurora nodded like that was that, and then she entered the house, leaving Montana standing with Bishop on the porch.

"I told her that," Montana said as Bishop put his arm around her waist, a hint of pride blipping through her. "That bit about not having to start college right after high school."

Bishop pressed his lips to her temple. "Well, at least now you know she listens to you." They started to laugh together, and Montana did the same thing her daughter did. She lifted her chin and faced the house, preparing herself to go inside.

"And we'll have enough food for a couple of days," Montana said. "So that's another bonus."

"And your daughter isn't moving today," Bishop said, starting to slide away from her.

"Triple bonus." Montana tugged on his hand to get him to stay. Their eyes met, and she added, "Thank you for being my partner with her. Thank you for loving her."

His eyes searched hers, and Montana fell in love with him all over again. "Thank you for loving me." She kissed him, keeping it sweet and beautiful, and then they went into the house together, a united front. And with Bishop at her side, Montana could conquer the world.

Chapter Twenty-Two

A ce Glover scrambled the eggs in the bowl and stepped over to the stove. "I'm just saying, you don't have to do it," he said, not able to look at Holly Ann right now. "Bethany Rose can do it. Heck, someone else entirely could do it."

"Bethany Rose can*not* do it," Holly Ann said from behind him, plenty of disgust in her voice. "She has a two-week-old baby."

"And you have a seven-month-old baby, and a husband that works a ton during birthing season." He poured the eggs into the hot pan, relishing in the sizzle that resulted. Then he didn't have to hear Holly Ann's sigh.

He turned back to her, hating that he had an opinion about this. But he did. "I know your family's been the Santa at the mall for years. A lot of years, but I just don't see how you can keep doing it. It's four days a week, and you'll be gone for hours at a time. I can't be Gun's only parent during those times."

"Bishop just straps Robbie to his chest." Holly Ann glared at him. "Lots of women work a ton. There are single moms all over the country."

Ace hung his head and pushed his hand through his hair.

"Besides," Holly Ann said. "I'm not asking you to babysit your own son. Montana is willing to help out."

"And what?" Ace asked, raising his head. "You'll tell her you're putting on a Santa suit and sitting on a throne decorated with candy canes and pine boughs?"

Holly Ann looked toward the spot on the carpet where their son played.

"I thought this was a huge family secret," he said. He picked up the rubber spatula and turned to stir up the eggs. "Are you going to lie to her?"

Lying was still a sore subject with Ace. He didn't think there was much worth lying about, this included. Montana would keep her secret. Bishop would too.

Holly Ann hadn't wanted to tell anyone in the Glover family, because there were so many of them, and news traveled fast. Maybe not outside the family, but she didn't want to take any chances. Ida lived in town, and she suspected Etta would too, once she met the right man.

Ace took a moment to think about his sister, and he faced the counter again. "Maybe Etta...." Holly Ann met his eye, and he sighed. "Maybe Etta would take Gun and keep things quiet. I bet she'd come here."

His wife searched his face. "I want to do this," she whispered. "Etta feels...right."

Ace got out two plates and started serving breakfast. "Talk to her. She's discreet. She works with the schools, but you're doing late afternoon and weekend stuff."

The barstool scraped, and Holly Ann came to his side in front of the stove. "Are you sure you're okay with this?"

"I'm fine," Ace said. "I just want you to be happy, and I want our son to be cared for. I remember what it was like that year before we got married, and I was so busy, and you were always disappearing...." He shook his head. "I don't look forward to the holidays, that's all."

"I can talk to Bethany Rose about sharing Santa with me. We could do every other year."

"We'll have the angel tree," Ace said.

"And Daddy wants to do a kick-off dinner the Sunday before Thanksgiving," she said.

"I'd love that," Ace said, smiling at her and handing her a plate of scrambled eggs.

"We've got a couple more months before things get really crazy." She took her plate around the island and sat back down. "And then it's only a month, Ace. It's the few weeks between Thanksgiving and Christmas."

Gun started whimpering, and Ace went to get him before he sat down. He settled the chunky baby on his lap and put a piece of scrambled egg on the counter in front of them. Gun immediately reached for the egg, his arm flapping a little before he got his fingers around it.

Ace grinned at his son as he fisted the egg and moved it

toward his mouth. The baby ate it and bounced in Ace's lap, grunting for more.

"Here you go, sonny," Ace said, thinking they should call Gun something like Greedy. The boy sure did like to eat, but he'd never suggest such a thing. Holly Ann didn't want him to have a nickname at all. She called him Gun or Bull without exception, and she'd already told him she wanted him to go by either of those names, not something else someone made up.

Ace wasn't sure how to tell the family that, but it hadn't become an issue yet. He thought of Ward's confession over Christmas that it had bothered him that he didn't get a special nickname like everyone else. Ace didn't want that to happen to his son.

He'd decided not to worry about it until he had to. In all honesty, he sure liked Gun and Bull for the name of his son, and he couldn't think of anything better—especially something that started with a G.

Ace had just finished his eggs when someone knocked on the door. "That'll be Cactus," he said, sliding Gun from his lap to Holly Ann's.

"Ace," Cactus called. "I'm comin' in."

"Come in," Ace yelled back to him, and the man's cowboy boots came through the house. He usually had a couple of pairs of smaller boots following him, but the boys had started school a few weeks ago. Mitch and Lincoln were both at the junior high this year, and that made driving them to school easy.

Cactus did the morning run, and Bear took the afternoon. Sometimes Willa or Sammy went in the morning, especially if Sammy was spending the day in the mechanic shop. She still loved working on cars, and she had a gift for it. She'd been helping them at Shiloh Ridge for years before becoming Bear's wife, and she still had that opportunity.

Ace saw her in the equipment shed from time to time, both of her little boys with her. She sat and talked to them about carburetors and spark plugs while Stetson drew on her tablet and Russell napped.

"I'm a little early, but they've got the cemetery fence done, and it's all ready for us now." He grinned as he looked at Ace. "I'm headed over there for a couple of minutes, and then we'll head out to find those cows."

There'd been some sickness moving through the herd this fall, and Cactus had recruited some of the family to help him find them all, get the medicine delivered, and keep the rest of the cattle from getting infected. This week, Ace was the one going around with Cactus.

"Yeah," he said. "I didn't realize it was going to be done so soon."

"They moved us up." Cactus nodded to Holly Ann. "Morning, ma'am. Could I take Bull?"

"Yep," Holly Ann said, twisting to give the baby to Cactus.

Bull clapped and grinned at his favorite uncle, because Cactus had a special way with children. Ward did too, and Bull loved him too.

"Yes," Cactus said. "Come on, boy. Let's go see your grand-daddy's grave. You have his name, you know." He turned to leave the house without waiting for Ace.

Ace stepped over to the garage door and pulled on his boots. "You want to come, love?"

"I'll go out later today," Holly Ann said. "I'm going to go through my inbox this morning."

Ace paused and looked at her. "When are you going to talk to Etta?"

"I already texted her," she said. "I told her there would be a delicious lunch in her future if she'd come talk to me about something I need help with."

"Are you going to show her the suit?"

"No one sees the suit," Holly Ann said with a smile, one that didn't shine nearly as bright as it usually did. "You've barely seen it."

"I'll be a good boy if you show it to me later," he said with a grin, but Holly Ann just laughed at him and shooed him out of the house.

He hurried after Cactus, finding the man moving around the corner and out of the meadow. He turned right, and Ace went jogging after him. "Cactus!"

Cactus came back and waited for him, Gun babbling with almost his full fist in his mouth. Ace caught up to him, and they continued down the road toward the family cemetery. It wasn't very far, and Ace saw a small group had gathered.

The cemetery used to sit down the hill a little bit, the slope not secured. There wasn't even a path to take. It was just a field with a fence around it, with the family burial plots inside.

But a landslide had transformed the ridge coming onto the ranch over Christmas, and they'd had to do a bunch of work at Shiloh Ridge. The road had been re-graded and made safer, should another landslide occur.

The road around the side of the ranch to the Ranch House had been fortified with a retaining wall, so another slide wouldn't cover it. The cliffs under Ace's deck had been shored up and strengthened with wood and steel, so they wouldn't lose anything in the future.

The cemetery had been the last piece, and they'd needed family unanimity to raise it to the same level as the road, the homestead, True Blue down the lane, and everything else up on the ranch.

They'd all decided to do that, and that meant excavating graves and headstones, raising the land, securing it, fortifying it, and then rebuilding the whole thing.

The fence along the road stuck straight up into the autumn sunshine, and Ace found himself moving faster to join everyone.

A sidewalk now left the gravel road and went right past two thicker fence posts, no gate necessary. Ace let Cactus go first, and he followed, moving to stand next to him and Bishop at the back of the crowd.

Ranger, Ace's oldest brother, glanced around. "Is everyone here who wants to be?"

"Did they send a text or something?" Ace whispered to Bishop, who nodded.

He pulled his phone out, realizing he'd left it on silent. He normally turned off the sound at night, though Ward had questioned how he could do that. What if there was an emergency like what had happened with Dot over Christmas?

Ace had a hard time sleeping as it was, and any little bleep or chime woke him up and kept him awake for a while afterward. He cursed himself as he saw how many texts he'd missed, and he quickly fired one off to Holly Ann.

Everyone's here. Are you sure you don't want to come?

"We're still waitin' on Ida and Brady," Ward said. "They said they're ten minutes away."

"No problem," Ranger said. "There's not a ceremony or anything."

His phone chimed, and he read Holly Ann's text. *I just saw the family text. I'm getting dressed, and I'll be there in five. Don't let them start without me.*

I won't, Ace promised.

People started to chat, and Ace edged his way over to Ward and Etta, who stood with Stetson in her arms. Dot held Russell, and one thing Ace could say about his family was that there were always people around to take the babies.

"What's going on with Holly Ann?" Etta asked. She looked at Ace, swaying with such a cute little boy on her hip.

"Oh, uh, I'm gonna let her tell you," Ace said. "You got her text? When are you guys meeting?"

"Tomorrow, for lunch." Etta glanced at Ward, who hadn't missed a word.

Ace swallowed, because he didn't want anyone in his family to feel any inkling of the betrayal he had when he'd learned about Holly Ann's family secret. "Great."

"What's goin' on?" Ward asked, and Dot looked over at Ace too.

"Nothing," Ace said. "I'm going to go see what's taking my wife so long to show up." He edged away from his siblings, cursing himself for saying anything at all. His thoughts about telling Etta, because she was discreet, came into question, and he'd have to tell Holly Ann.

As he faced the copse of trees which secreted his house from the rest of the ranch, Holly Ann stepped out onto the gravel road. Her beauty still struck him straight in the chest every time he saw her.

He went up the sidewalk to the road and strode toward her. "I may or may not have said something to Etta," he said when he was only a few paces away.

"What? Why would you do that?" Holly Ann looked past him to the group in the cemetery.

"I just...wasn't thinking."

Holly Ann sighed and took his hand. "It's fine. I'll explain everything to her tomorrow, and it won't be anything." She nodded toward everyone. "Ida's here. Let's go."

They returned to the back of the crowd, and as Ida arrived, Holly Ann took Judy while Brady kept Johnny to himself.

"We're all here," Ida called up to Ranger. "Thanks for waiting."

"Yeah, it was very last-minute," someone said.

"Thanks for coming this morning," Ranger said. "Doesn't the cemetery look amazing?" He turned and faced everyone. "We've been working with some landscape experts on this for months, and everything is structurally sound now. Even if there was an earthquake here, this cemetery wouldn't be going anywhere."

"Everyone is back where they belong," Ward continued. "And it's easier than ever to come here. We cleaned up the headstones, and they look great. There's room for many more generations of Glovers now."

"There's obviously a new fence," Bear said. "I think my dad would've loved this."

"Mine too," Ranger said.

Ace thought so too, and he patiently waited his turn to edge toward the headstones, taking Gun back from Cactus. He finally looked down at his father's name on his grave marker. Bull Harrison Glover. He felt such a connection to his father when he came here, and he wasn't sure if that was ridiculous or not.

He didn't care if it was. He crouched down and balanced his son on his knee. "This is your grand-daddy, Gun. He's who you're named after, and he was such a huge giant of a man." He smiled at the name his son and his father shared. "A real bull. If you're anything like him, you'll be amazing."

Holly Ann put her hand on Ace's shoulder, and they stood there for only a moment before he straightened and handed Gun to her.

"I love you, Ace," she said. "Thank you for letting me continue my family traditions too."

He slung his arm around her waist and pressed his lips to her temple. "Always, my love. Always."

Chapter Twenty-Three

L iam Walker answered the door, the chatter behind him quieting the further he got from it. "Howdy," he said, grinning at Bishop and Montana Glover. "Come in, come in."

His wife, Callie, came rushing up behind him. "Hi, guys," she said, not even glancing at Liam. "Come in. We've got a whole soda bar, and I know you love your soda, Bishop."

"He does love sweet things," Montana said, stepping into the house. She and Bishop seemed nervous, and Liam supposed he would be too. This dinner wasn't exactly just a few friends getting together to eat good food.

Tripp, Liam's twin, had been smoking brisket for hours on the back deck, and his nerves had kept Liam on-edge all day long.

See, Tripp's step-son and Montana's daughter had been dating for a long time. Years. All through high school.

They'd graduated now, and Bishop had called Tripp and asked if they could get together and talk about the kids.

They weren't legally kids anymore, but Liam couldn't even imagine making such grown-up decisions as who he wanted to marry when he was eighteen years old. Both Aurora and Oliver were eighteen, and neither knew about this dinner.

"Hey," Tripp boomed from behind Liam, and he brought the door closed after Bishop entered the house. "You guys made it. Sorry we have to do this here. Our house is still full of water."

"Still?" Bishop asked, stepping down the hall to shake Tripp's hand. They both wore smiles, but the tension in the house had never been this high.

Liam watched Callie take Montana further into the house, and he moved to follow them. "Denise, honey," he said. "Will you go help your sister?" Liam nodded toward the sliding glass door, where Ginger nearly had her fingers caught. "You two can go out, if you want. Isaac is out there."

"Can we go down to Auntie Simone's?" Denise asked. "She made cupcakes and said we could."

"Not tonight," Liam said. "Besides, she and Uncle Micah are coming here tonight." As if on cue, the doorbell rang again, and Liam turned back that way.

Micah opened the door without waiting for Liam, who hadn't taken a single step anyway. "Hey, hey," he called. "We're here." He stepped into the house and held the door for Simone, who entered with four-year-old Trap's hand in hers.

She was due with their second baby any day now, and Liam hurried forward to take his nephew. "Come on, Trap," he said. "Come with me, buddy."

The little boy's face lit up and he skipped awkwardly toward Liam, who scooped him into his arms. "Look at you, skippin'. Did your momma teach you that?"

"Uncle Jeremiah did," Trap said in his high-pitched voice. "I got to go play with the dogs today, Uncle Liam. It was so awesome!" He put both hands on Liam's face and squished his cheeks together, the intensity in the little boy making Liam chuckle.

"You do love a good dog," Liam said.

"Daddy says if I'm real good when the baby comes, he'll get me a pup." Trap squirmed to be let down, and Liam lowered him to his feet. "Where's Deni?"

Micah chuckled as he joined Liam in the hall and watched his son run through the house. "We brought the cupcakes." He indicated the tray he carried. "In the kitchen?"

"Yep." Liam's mouth watered at the sight of them. "Maybe I can sneak one before dinner."

In the back of the house, where the living room, dining room, and kitchen all existed in the same huge space, Liam found Callie laughing with Ivory and Montana. Simone waddled that way, and the women got louder as they exclaimed over her size and started asking questions about when the baby would be born.

Tripp drank from his soda, and Bishop reached for a cupcake the moment Micah set down the tray. "Are you having a boy or a girl?" he asked.

"We don't know," Micah said.

"He's already got his hands full with that little boy," Tripp said, grinning at Trap, who'd finally gotten the sliding glass door open and was trying to squeeze through a too-small opening.

"He's a busy one," Micah admitted. "I hope it's a girl, honestly. I don't think I can handle another boy."

"Think of your mother," Bishop said, laughing. "And mine, I suppose."

"Yeah, she had seven kids too," Micah said, reaching for a sweet. Liam took a cupcake too, noting how quiet Tripp was. Sometimes he could be loud, and sometimes not, especially with something pressing on his mind.

"But one of them was a girl," Bishop said. "Besides, us boys were very nearly perfect for our mother."

"Oh, yeah," Micah said dryly. "Us too, right, guys?"

The lot of them erupted into laughter, and Tripp did participate in that. He glanced at the women, and he quieted first. "Well," he said. "I think dinner is ready. Let me grab Ivory." He stepped away from the counter laden with cans of soda, a bowl of ice, and all the tall bottles of flavored syrups.

Liam loved sweet things, and once he'd been introduced to the concept of vanilla and coconut in his Diet Coke, he hadn't been able to drink it any other way.

"Is he okay?" Micah asked.

"It's my fault," Bishop said with a sigh. "I told him we wanted to have a sit-down to talk about the kids." He lowered his voice and looked over to Tripp and Ivory. "He called immediately, and he was so worried."

"What does he have to be worried about?" Liam asked. "Ollie's a great boy."

"And Aurora's a great girl," Micah said, shooting Liam a look.

"He literally asked me if Aurora was pregnant," Bishop said, his voice nearly a whisper. "I think they're really worried." He lifted his head as Montana started toward them. "Hey, baby. Are we going to eat?"

"They're getting the kids." Montana surveyed the group of men at the counter, and Liam suddenly wanted to study the depths of his soda. "What are you lot whispering about over here? You're worse than women."

Micah grinned at her and drew her into a hug. "Right," he said. "Worse than women. Did you guys hear yourselves squeal when my wife came in?" They laughed together, and Liam did enjoy the warmth of Bishop and Montana's friendship.

Ivory came back into the house, waiting at the door for her son, Isaac. Then Denise and Ginger entered, with Trap racing in last.

"Sit down, baby," Simone said, pulling out a chair at the dining room table for the little boy. "All the kids, right here." Every Walker child loved Aunt Simone. She baked for them specifically. She had them over to her house for little tea parties, complete with tiny cakes with a ton of sprinkles.

Denise and Ginger adored her, and Liam wasn't complaining that he got some alone-time with his wife from time to time.

Simone made hand-crafted, thoughtful gifts for every

member of the family, for birthdays, anniversaries, and the holidays. Whatever struck her fancy. No matter what, Micah had hit the lottery when he'd gotten Simone Foster to marry him.

Liam felt the same way about his wife. He adored the ranch they worked together, and he praised the Lord for his children every single day.

He picked up Ginger, his five-year-old, and said, "What are the birdies doin' out there?"

"They've flown away," she said, her smile turning upside down. She'd started kindergarten a couple of months ago, and Liam missed her more than he'd anticipated. Some days, she was his shadow on the ranch. Other days, her mother's.

"Maybe some new ones will come back in the spring," he said, taking her over to the table. "Do you wanna sit by Isaac or Trap?"

"Isaac," she said, wiggling as he put her in the chair. With the kids contained—and only having to wrangle four was easy when it came to the Walkers—Liam looked at Callie. She looked at Ivory, who had historically been the quietest and highest-strung of the sisters-in-law.

"Thanks for coming to dinner," she said. "I want to thank Liam and Callie for hosting us. Our house should be put back together soon enough."

They'd had a pipe break, flooding their house for hours while none of them were home to stop it. Consequently, the floors had been soaked and had to be completely removed and replaced. The water had seeped up the walls, and the lower third had been cut out. They didn't want any chance of mold, so they'd been living in a hotel while fans blew twenty-four hours a day, while a restoration company treated the wood beams and sheetrock with chemicals, and while everything got rebuilt.

Tripp was exhausted, as he'd picked up an online professorship job for UT-Austin this semester. His worry over Ollie took a lot of mental energy too, especially since his son had opted out of going to his alma mater that fall.

Liam could still remember clearly the day Tripp had entered the barn, the words, "He's not going, Liam." He'd banged his open palm against the stall door. "I can't believe he's going to give up the opportunity to go to college."

Liam had spent a couple of hours with Tripp that afternoon, trying to reassure him that all was not lost. In the end, Tripp wasn't listening to Liam. It had been Momma who'd reminded him that dreams never died. That advanced degrees were earned by people from age eighteen to eighty-eight.

With the reminder of their mother's law degree—which she'd earned in her older age and only a couple of years ago—Tripp had calmed down.

"All right," Tripp said. "I'll pray, and then we'll eat." He braced himself against the back of a chair near his son and closed his eyes. "Dear Lord, we're grateful to come before Thee in prayer."

Liam felt that gratitude swell and bloom within him. It was such a blessing to pray to the Lord, and while the tension didn't dissipate, and hard conversations would be had tonight, for this one breath, he experienced peace.

"We ask for Thy guidance in all things. Patience too.

Help us to be open and honest with those we love, and we ask a special blessing on Oliver and Aurora, that they'll remember who they are and what values they've been taught." He cleared his throat, only ticking up the tension. "Amen."

"Amen," Liam chorused loudly, immediately glancing to Bishop and Montana. "Hey, I just realized you didn't bring Robbie."

"My cousin's watching him," Bishop said with a smile. "They've got a son only a month older than Robbie."

"You guys have a lot of babies about the same age," Ivory said with a smile. She let Tripp pull a chair out for her, and she sat down. Liam jumped to do the same thing for Callie. He watched Tripp as he sat, and once Micah and Simone had sat too, he turned toward the kitchen and started bringing over the food.

He pulled the pan of brisket out of the oven and set it in the middle of the table. "Wow," Bishop said. "We're going to eat like kings."

"Mashed potatoes comin'," Liam said, returning to the oven to get them. Lastly, he took a sheet pan of roasted beans, asparagus, and Brussels sprouts to the table.

"Ew," Denise said, frowning at the vegetables. "Do I have to eat some of that, Daddy?"

"Yes," Callie answered for him. "They're green beans, Deni. You like them." She put three on the girl's plate and reached for Ginger's. Their younger daughter would eat anything, and Callie put some of every veggie on her plate, a healthy dollop of potatoes and a few slices of meat.

Once everyone had food, and Bishop had said how

THE NETWORKING OF THE NATIVITY

good it was four times, Montana cleared her throat. "I don't know what you guys know," she said, surveying Tripp and Ivory. They wore their tension right out in the open. "But Aurora is moving to Savannah at the end of December to start a fashion design program at the Savannah College of Art and Design."

"Yes," Ivory said. "Ollie told us she got in. Scholarship and everything."

"Mm." Montana nodded and looked at her husband.

Bishop jolted slightly and reached for a napkin. After wiping his mouth, he said, "She told us a couple of days ago that Ollie was moving there with her."

"What?" Tripp bellowed, nearly coming across the table.

Ivory put her hand on her husband's arm, as if holding him back. "Baby, calm down."

"I can't calm down," he said, shaking his head. "This is insane. He's eighteen years old, Ivory."

"They have an animation program," Montana said. "He came over for dinner last night, as I'm sure you're aware." She paused, her eyebrows going up.

Liam couldn't even take a bite of food. He wanted Tripp to just simmer and listen. *Please*, he prayed. *Help him calm down.*

"Yes," Tripp clipped out. "We're aware of that."

"I asked him about it," Montana said gently. "He said he got in too. He's going to do the animation program, and take classes in equine studies."

"I asked him what he was going to do after he graduated," Bishop said. "He said come back here and work at

Seven Sons, like you." He glanced at Liam. "And his Uncle Liam. He said the two of you help around the ranch, but you do some animation on the side."

With Bishop's supportive smile, Liam was able to pick up his fork. He nodded as Bishop added, "He wants to be just like you."

A silence filled the air, and Micah met Liam's eye. It almost felt like the two of them shouldn't be there, but Liam knew why they were. Tripp couldn't hear everything when he was stressed, and he'd rely on Micah and Liam to help him riddle through things later. He'd wanted them there; he'd asked both of them to come.

Montana cleared her throat. "I think they'll get married before too long." Her voice sounded like she'd inhaled the brisket instead of swallowing it. "I asked them about it, and neither of them acted embarrassed or afraid. Aurora actually said they've talked about it."

"My word," Tripp said, getting to his feet. "The boy is *insane*."

"Sit down," Liam said as his twin came toward him. Tripp met his eye, and Liam actually got to his feet too. He took Tripp by the shoulders and looked him straight in the eyes. It was like looking into a mirror, something he'd been doing his entire life. There was nothing Liam hadn't done without Tripp for many, many years.

"He's a good kid," Liam said. "He's smart, and he loves her."

"He doesn't know what love is."

"Yes, he does."

Tripp broke his gaze and shook his head. "They're so young."

"That's only one more reason why he's going to need you to show him how to be a man," Liam said, bringing his brother's eyes back to his. "He needs your support, Tripp. Not your judgment. Where's your faith, brother?"

Tripp's eyes stormed with rage, quickly dropping into regret. "You're right." He drew in a deep breath and faced the table. "He's right. I need to have more faith that this will be okay."

"I feel you," Bishop said. "I have no idea how to be Aurora's father. She's not my biological daughter, though I love her like she is. I worry about her too."

"We'll have to go horseback riding sometime," Tripp said, retaking his seat. His emotions hadn't cleared, but he wasn't angry anymore. Liam could *feel* it. "Have you been out to Courage Reins?"

"No," Bishop said. "But Cactus speaks highly of it."

"It's great," Tripp said. "We should go sometime. Talk about the kids. About how to be a step-dad to insanity." He grinned, and Bishop chuckled.

Everything lightened after that, but Montana didn't let much time go by before she said, "Thank you for letting us come to dinner. I think they really will get married, and I think you're both such fantastic people." Her chin shook, and Ivory reached across the table and took one of her hands and squeezed it. "I couldn't ask for better examples and in-laws for Aurora."

Liam suddenly saw the situation in a new light, and he watched that bulb brighten above his brother's head too.

Bishop and Montana weren't lightweights. They were fantastic people too. Ollie felt safe with them, and he loved their daughter.

It was actually a beautiful thing. Insane, yes, in Liam's opinion. But beautiful.

"At least they won't say I-do and not mean it," Callie said, grinning at her husband.

"Oh, boy," Liam said, glancing at his brothers. Everyone in his family had experienced some form of false marriage before they'd fallen in love with their spouse, and Simone burst out laughing.

"Right? I mean, Micah and I got married during an audition, when we were barely even speaking to each other."

"What?" Bishop asked. "What does that mean?"

Tripp glanced at Ivory, who looked right back at him. She shrugged one shoulder, a pretty smile covering her face, and he grinned and leaned toward her to kiss her.

"And we all worked out," Callie added, squeezing Liam's thigh under the table.

"We sure did, baby," he said, covering her hand with his. "Ollie and Aurora will work things out. We just need to have faith."

Chapter Twenty-Four

Judge pulled up to the homestead, June in the passenger seat beside him. "We're not last," he said, noting there were still spots on the gravel in front of the house.

"How can you tell?"

"There's only five trucks here," he said, glancing down the row. "Zona's not here. Mother's not here. Ida's not here."

He hadn't wanted to be last for some reason. It would call too much attention to him. Too many eyes on him and June, who he'd invited to the biggest Glover family tradition they had: the angel tree decoration.

"There's dinner first," he said. "We usually have a big family meeting too. I don't know what they have planned, because I'm not in charge of anything. Then we decorate the tree."

June reached over and took Judge's hand in hers. "I'm

not nervous to meet them," she said. "I know all of them already."

"No, I know," he said.

"Then what are you nervous about?" she asked.

"I don't know." He peered up at the house, wondering if he could just take June to the Ranch House and show her the light display.

"Maybe you don't want to show me your show," she said. "We're doing that after the tree-decorating, right?"

"Maybe I don't want to be the only single one here," he said, not quite sure where the words came from.

June's grip on his hand tightened, and he looked at her. "You're not single," she said. "We're together."

"Mister's not here," he said, not that he normally spent a lot of time with Mister anyway.

"You're not making any sense," June said, and Judge felt her words deep down in his soul.

"I know I'm not." He shook his head to try to get his thoughts right. "I don't know why I'm so anxious tonight. Only that I am."

"I know how that feels," June said quietly. "I paced in my house, Picasso and Remmy whining at me for hours before Lucy Mae texted and said she'd made it to her apartment and everything was fine."

Judge lifted her hand to his lips and kissed her wrist. "She was okay."

"And you'll be okay tonight." June drew in a deep breath.

"How's she doing at college?" Judge asked. June didn't hesitate to tell him about Lucy Mae's adventures at Cal

Tech. She hadn't taken her boyfriend with her, and she'd been enjoying the single co-ed life in California. Her grandparents and aunt and uncle lived there, and so did her father.

"She's doing great," June said with a smile. "She decided to come home for Christmas and not Thanksgiving. She gets a longer break." She brushed her hand across her eyes, dislodging those pretty eyelashes that made her look made-up and ready all the time.

"That's great," Judge said, stealing some of the energy in her smile and using it as his own. "Well, I'm all dressed in my nicest jeans, and you look like a million bucks. I guess we should go in?"

June giggled and released his hand. He met her at the front of the truck, admiring her in the pair of black slacks hugging her legs and the light green blouse she'd chosen for their beginning Christmas celebration.

In October.

Judge was used to living and breathing Christmas for many months out of the year, so he didn't find their angel tree celebration that odd. "I love this blouse," he whispered, taking June into his arms so he could feel the soft, silky quality of it.

"It's got a wreath on it," June said as she took hold of his shoulders and embraced him back. "Very festive."

"That it is." He leaned down to kiss her, pausing when another truck came onto the ranch. "Oh, there's Mother and Don."

"You owe me a kiss," she teased, and Judge grinned at her.

"Definitely." He took her hand and led her over to where Don swung the truck into a spot at the end of the fence. He opened his mother's door and helped her down.

"Hey, my son," Mother said, taking him into a hug. "I brought your letter, baby. You left it at the house last week."

"I did?" Judge pulled away and searched his mother's face. She wore such light in her eyes, and seeing how happy she was made Judge's heart grow wings.

"Yep, it's right there in the glove box. You should get it out now and put it in your truck so you don't forget again." She moved out of the way to go greet June, who grinned and greeted his mother with enthusiasm.

Judge stepped further into the truck and opened the glove compartment. A plain white envelope sat there, and he took it out. He opened the flap and slid out the letter.

She'd folded it, which Judge didn't mind. He'd creased it first. He'd gone down to Three Rivers to visit Mother last week, and he'd taken his letter so he could ask her about something Dad had written in it.

Dearest Judge, sat at the top of the letter. Judge hadn't seen very many of his siblings' letters, but his was quite short. Only three-quarters of a single page, though each word carried such weight to Judge.

It's not easy being third, son, but you were created exactly to come to our family in that spot.

Winds could've howled around him, and Judge wouldn't have known. He reached out and touched the printed, black letters of the message, feeling his father's spirit in them.

His dad worked hard. He'd been a task-master to be certain. But he tempered every demand with love. With kindness. With an attitude that he was willing to do just as much as he expected everyone else to do.

"Sweetheart." June's voice cut through the turmoil in Judge's soul. He looked at her, and it took an extra moment for her beautiful features to come into true view. Her gaze dropped to the letter and rebounded to his. "What's that?"

He immediately refolded the letter and stuck it back in the envelope. "This is the letter from my dad," he said, getting out of the truck and causing her to fall back a few steps. He paused, once again the world falling away until only the two of them remained.

"I want you to read it," he said. "Tonight. After I show you the newly improved light show."

June's eyes widened. "You do?"

"Yes," he said firmly. "You won't ever get to meet my dad in this life, but this letter will tell you a lot about him."

"I already know a lot about him," June said. "I see him reflected in *you*, Judge."

If Judge wasn't in love with her before that statement, he finished falling by the time her voice reached his ears. "That's the best compliment ever," he whispered, taking her into his arms and kissing her. He didn't care who was watching now, and his whole soul lit up when June kissed him back with as much passion and movement as he put out.

She broke the kiss before he did, saying, "We should go in."

Judge took a moment to gather his wits about him, then he faced the homestead.

"Are you nervous about showing me the lights?"

"Yes," he admitted. "But I have a couple more hours." The sound of another truck came up the road, but Judge led June up the sidewalk, catching only a glimpse of Ida and her family as they arrived at the ranch.

Inside, the house pumped out sound like a frat party. Loud laughter came from the kitchen and living room combination room beyond the arch, but Judge took a moment to admire the flocked Christmas tree someone had already set up.

"So we put the tree here," he explained, wanting to talk to June for a minute out in the cooler air, without so many eyes on them. "We got a new one last year, and it's usually pure white. Zona bought a flocked one, and I think it's nice."

He indicated the boxes all lined up next to the front wall. "The ornaments are in there."

"And your grandmother made all of them?" She looked up at him with wonder in her eyes.

"That's right," he said. "She taught me to crochet and knit. I can still do it too." He smiled at the fond memories.

June laughed and clung to him like she needed to be touching him to stay standing. "Judge Glover, are you telling me you can make me a sweater?"

"I'm probably not all that good," he said. "But a scarf I could do." He hadn't picked up his knitting needles in a while. He worked so much with his hands, from the ropes and knots on the ranch, to playing the piano, to stringing lights and making minute adjustments in the code with clicks and a quick tap on the keyboard.

He didn't want to do anything else that required small, precise movements, though he had enjoyed crocheting with Grandmother.

"She made a set of reindeer at my request," he said. "I hang those for her each year."

The front door opened, and Ida and Brady entered the homestead. "June," Ida said with plenty of honey and surprise in her voice. "Is Judge explaining our angel tree tradition to you?"

"He has in the past, yes," June said with a smile. She stepped over to Ida and hugged her. The ten-month-old baby in Ida's arms protested, and June giggled as she took Johnny from his mother. "Ida, they're *huge*."

"Especially that one." Ida rotated her shoulder as if her son had torn her rotator cuff. "He's a little piggy." She grinned at him though, and Johnny let out a squeal and grinned back.

"Their outfits are so cute," June gushed, adjusting the collar on Johnny's shirt. "Look, Judge. It's a big reindeer nose."

"I see that," Judge said, grinning at the black shirt with the nearly neon red nose in the middle of it. He greeted Brady and took Judy from him. Ida and Brady continued into the kitchen, and Judge heard someone ask where the babies were before the swell of noise swallowed their answers.

He looked at her, and June looked at him, her eyebrows kicking up. "You want some of these, don't you?"

"I can't lie about it," he said, glad she'd brought it up. "I'd take a couple."

"Just a couple?" She perched Johnny on her hip, cocking it out as she held him.

"I don't have a set number," he said, clearing his throat. "Do you, June-Bug? Have you reached your limit for children?"

"Judge," Preacher said from the doorway. His gaze flickered to June, and he smiled at her too. "Heya, June. Bear was wondering if you'd play the piano for something during the family meeting." He came a little closer and took Judy from him. "I was supposed to ask you earlier, and I forgot, so if you don't want to, I'll shoulder the blame and deal with the Grizz." He grinned at the baby, who reached for the towel Preacher had thrown over his shoulder.

"I can do that," Judge said. "We're not caroling or anything, right?"

"No, he just wants some upbeat party music during the announcements."

Judge blinked, trying to comprehend. Preacher chuckled and shook his head. "I was befuddled too. When I asked more questions, he just told me to ask you, and well, I forgot."

"I can do something upbeat," Judge assured him.

Preacher glanced at June. "Great. Thanks, Judge." He stepped to June's side and gave her a quick squeeze. "So good to see you here too, June."

"Thanks," she said, and Preacher left.

"Wow," Judge said. "That's amazing for Preacher. He

doesn't normally have an opinion on who brings dates to things."

"He likes me," June said with a grin. "Just like this baby."

"You never did answer my question," he said.

June gave him a playful look out of the corner of her eye. "I don't think I've reached my limit yet."

A grin exploded across Judge's face, and he swiped off his cowboy hat and hung it on one of the hooks on the wall between the arch and the stairs. He kept his face turned away from June, but he couldn't straighten his smile.

He faced her again, and she laughed as she shook her head. "Good to know," he said, taking her by the arm and leading her toward the kitchen. "All right, now gear yourself up for a wall of noise...."

Chapter Twenty-Five

June basked in the warmth inside the homestead. The furnace wasn't running, and she hadn't heard it kick on. The side door stood open, letting in the October evening air, which was pretty spectacular tonight.

Darkness had fallen sometime during the meal and family meeting, and June let Judge slip away from her as Bear rose to his feet. "We're almost done," Bear said. "But we've got a couple of announcements."

"Here we go," Cactus grumbled, and June shot him a smile. She sure liked him, as he had something dry and sarcastic to say about almost everything. Willa tempered him, and June liked watching the pair of them interact with each other, as well as Mitch, their deaf son.

Judge had given her a great family history lesson before this evening, so June knew everyone's names. She'd been studying hard, pulling open the cheat sheet he'd texted her, every night for the last week since he'd told her about this family tradition.

The food had been spectacular, and they'd enjoyed dessert first today, something Judge had said they'd never done before. Bishop had apparently made all the tarts, cakes, and pies, and June was full before the steak fajitas had been served.

The kitchen island—the biggest June had ever seen in her entire life—still bowed under all the leftovers, and June wouldn't refuse if someone wanted to send something home with her. Without Lucy Mae to pretend to cook for, June rarely did more than make a grilled cheese sandwich or heat up a microwave lasagna.

Judge sat at the piano, and Bear signaled to Ranger, who also stood. "We're going to take all the sales from Market Day this year and donate it to Cowboys Provide Christmas," he said. "Ward's running that organization this year, and we thought it would be an amazing opportunity to make sure ranchers and their families around the state have a good holiday."

"I'm not in charge," Ward said. "I'm the co-chair in charge of fundraising, and this just made my job non-existent." He grinned at his brother and cousin and sat back down.

Bear looked at Judge, and he burst into a jovial, upbeat song that only took four notes before every Glover—well, at least most of the males—joined in with their voices.

"...Your lucky day today. It's your *lucky* day today! Congrats to you, because it's your lucky day to-day!"

Judge played four or five more notes and promptly lifted his hands from keys.

One of the babies in the room wailed, and June knew why. That had been *startling*.

"My word," Willa said, giggling. "I was not expecting that."

"My dad used to make us sing that whenever we brought home good report cards," Bear said, grinning around at the group. He actually held a note card in one hand, and June found him adorable. "Or when Mother would make a chocolate cake for dinner. Or when we got to go camping, sleepover with our cousins, anything that was good."

"We sang it when Preacher won his debate championship once," Zona said.

More surprise moved through June, because Preacher didn't seem like a debate champion at all.

"And when Bishop took first in his sprint," Preacher said.

"Right," Bear said. "I thought it would be fun for us to bring it back. I sang it for Sammy a week or two ago, and she just looked at me like I'd grown horns."

June knew the feeling, but she said nothing. A lot of what had happened tonight made her feel completely out of her league. She and Lucy Mae had been mostly alone for the last thirteen years, and this large, loud family could easily overwhelm her.

She'd seen Dot step out onto the deck right after dinner, and Cactus had followed her. They'd stood out there for a few minutes before Sammy had joined them, and June realized she could come and go if she wanted to.

Since she'd been enjoying herself talking to Montana and Aurora, then Holly Ann, who let her hold Gun, June had stayed in the house.

"So now you're ready," Ranger said. "Our next piece of news has to do with Bear, so I'll let him tell it." He grinned at his cousin, and June felt the love the two men had for each other. That was the kind of warmth she missed in her life, and she'd already texted her mom and her sister while here with the Glovers.

It wasn't about the temperature in the house at all. It was a spiritual warmth June craved.

"Sammy and I are expecting again," he said with a grin. "A baby come spring, and a house about the same time." He pointed at Judge, who gave them a few notes to get ready, and this time June opened her mouth and sang with everyone else.

"Hey, howdy, ho, it's your lucky day today. It's your *lucky* day today! Congrats to you, because it's your lucky day to-day!" She laughed along with several others once the little ditty finished, and she seriously wanted to spend so much time with these people.

"Micah and Montana are collaborating on the house," Bear added. "They've said it'll be done in March or so. It's about halfway between here and the Edge, and it's on the same road as the Ranch House." He glanced at Ranger. "We approved the site as a ranch management team, and Ranger will maintain the homestead with Etta."

June's eyes flew to Etta, who hadn't brought anyone

with her to this family activity. Preacher had called his brother in Oklahoma City, and Mister sat on the phone in the windowsill, listening in.

Everyone else had a significant other, and June met Judge's eye. He grinned at her, and she mimed applauding for him and his stellar piano playing.

"Is that it?" Bear asked, surveying the group. "Anyone have anything to share?"

"Charlie is walking," Willa said, and no one had to cue Judge this time. He played the notes, and everyone burst into song.

Willa waved her arms and laughed. "That doesn't make me lucky. Now I'm chasing him everywhere."

Judge played the intro, and the voices doubled in volume. "Hey, howdy, ho! It's your lucky day today. It's your *lucky* day today! Congrats to you, because it's your lucky day to-day!"

She shook her head, still laughing, but she didn't say anything.

Bear couldn't stop laughing, and he waved to Zona, who stood. "Come on, everyone," she said. "We're moving into the foyer to decorate the angel tree."

People broke out in chatter as they stood and started moving. It took a colossal amount of time to move over two dozen people from one room to another, especially with how loud this bunch could be. Finally, they all stood in the foyer, and Zona brought the first box forward.

"We've been having a few people say a few things about what the angel tree means to them while I get the ornaments out." She glanced at Bear. "Are we doing that?"

"Sure," he said. "If someone would like to say something about the angel tree, please go ahead."

"I will," Montana said, raising her hand. She stood only a few feet from June, and she wore the same thing she usually did. Jeans and a T-shirt. She didn't dress up. She didn't pretend to be something or someone she wasn't.

June could still hear her saying, "There are *other* parts of me." She'd been trying to figure out what other parts of her she wanted to cultivate. She'd always be Lucy Mae's mother, but she was also a business owner. She was a chocolate-lover. She was a dog person.

She was Judge's girlfriend.

She watched him as Montana said, "I thought I'd be hanging an ornament for my daughter this year, because I'd be missing her so much. It was comforting to know that I had this to look forward to, that I could pick through the ornaments to find the sewing machine that Aurora usually puts on the tree herself and think of her. Send her good thoughts. Pray for her. Thinking about that person you're missing is why I love the angel tree. It's comforting, even when it's not up."

When no one else said anything, Zona said, "All right. There's enough open to start. There are a lot of us. You know the rules."

June didn't, not really, but she hung back while a few others surged forward. She noticed they were Glovers, not the olive branches that had been grafted into the family tree. She smiled at Montana's Aunt Jackie, who beamed back at her.

"How are you, dear?" she asked. "How's Lucy Mae doing in California?"

"She's doing great, ma'am," June said. "Thanks for asking." She'd met Montana's aunt and uncle at the dual going-away party for Aurora and Lucy Mae that had turned into a single going-away party when Aurora had announced she actually wouldn't be moving to Oklahoma that day.

That too had shown a level of courage June didn't feel like she had, and she'd been reflecting on it since.

"Do you want to hang something?" Judge asked, appearing at June's side with another slice of cake on a plate.

"Yes," June said instantly. "Do you think she ever made anything like what I do?"

"What do you do, June-Bug?" He glanced at her, a smile in those dashing, blue eyes.

"What are you going to hang?" she challenged instead.

"This year it's easy," he said. "A star. A bunch of stars. I'm wishing on and putting all my faith in stars this year." He stuck the last bite of cake in his mouth while June laughed.

He set the crumby plate on the steps and took her hand. They went over to the tree and started looking through the boxes of ornaments. Judge found his stars easily, and there seemed to be plenty more where he'd found those. He also hung up a cute set of reindeer, a fond smile on his face.

June took her time, picking up one ornament at a time and considering it. She touched a snowman, then a sleigh. She handed a cowboy hat to Stetson, who chirped, "Thank you, ma'am," at her and toddled over to the tree, where his father lifted him up so he could hang the hat on the tree.

She moved from one box to the next, and she dug through it, finally finding the perfect thing. "Oh," she said, speaking before she even realized it. She held up the box TV, the kind she'd had in her house growing up in the late eighties.

It wasn't exactly the epitome of the Internet, or WiFi networks, or what June really did for a living. But to her, it did represent technology, and June felt the electricity buzzing through her veins the same way she always had.

"That's cute," Oakley said. "I've never seen that TV before."

June straightened, the television cradled in her palm. "I like it."

"It's perfect for you," Oakley said, grinning at June in a kind way. "Almost like Priscilla Glover knew you'd need to find it to feel like you belong here."

June gaped at her, but Oakley had already turned her attention back to the boxes.

"Oh, that's perfect," Judge said, and June turned to him. "You found a TV."

"I do love to watch TV," June said.

He chuckled and shook his head, gently taking the TV from her. "No, it represents your love of technology, even though this is old-school technology." He looked at her, really looked, and June felt herself falling in love with him.

"Hang that, Bug," he whispered. "Then I want to sneak out of here and show you my lights."

June wanted to escape with him, so she stepped over to

the tree and hung the television on an available branch. Then she took Judge's hand and went with him. They walked through the kitchen and out that sneaky side door, down the steps, and back to his truck.

He didn't say anything as he went back under the arch and made the turn to go around the edge of the cliff toward the Ranch House. June had been there many times before, but her nerves grew with every rotation of the tires.

The house hulked in darkness, and Judge killed the headlights and the ignition. "Wait here. I'll go turn it on." He looked at June, the only light coming from the sky above. She could barely see him, but his voice took on his business-like tone when he said, "I want your honest opinion. Like, the truth. I want this to be the best it can be."

June took out her phone and swiped to her notes app. "I'm ready."

"The show is eight minutes," he said. "It can be up to ten, but I find the shorter shows win every year, so I don't really want it to be longer."

"Got it," she said. "I'm ready, Judge."

He nodded and said, "I wish I was."

"I've seen your other shows," she said. "Besides, if you can't show it to me, who can you show it to?" Their eyes met, and something powerful connected them.

He leaned over and kissed her, this one a bit rougher than the one they shared in the driveway at the homestead. He withdrew quickly and said, "Okay, here goes nothin'."

Chapter Twenty-Six

J udge clicked the mouse on the computer in the office. The monitor started to brighten, a clicking noise letting him know the machine was gearing up to do the work. He had less than thirty days to get this show right.

"Maybe this is a mistake," he muttered to himself. June waited out in the truck, and Judge would grab a box of ice cream bars before he returned to watch the show with her.

He'd seen it dozens of times, and every time, he found something else he'd change. He'd make the adjustments right then, then watch that portion again. The software he used allowed him to see it on the computer screen, but it wasn't the same as standing outside and watching the actual show.

Everything about this show superseded anything he'd done before. The decorations took up a lot of space, but they weren't cluttered. He'd never left out the classic shapes, like soldiers or trees or snowmen. This year's show made a statement. This year's show was about more than Christmas.

"Definitely a mistake," he said, looking up and out the window. Darkness looked back, and his eyes couldn't adjust from the bright lights inside the office to the deep blackness outside. He'd never seen a light show in Three Rivers that wasn't entirely Christmas, but this felt like the right thing to do.

If this was going to be his last show, he wanted it to be memorable. No matter what, it was going to be memorable to him. He clicked the delay start button and put it at sixty seconds. With that coded, he had nothing left to do but hit the lights, grab the ice cream, and hurry to the truck.

Judge drew a deep breath, as June would be the first to see the show besides him. After tonight, Judge would have his siblings, his cousins, and all the cowboys on the ranch come watch the show and give feedback. The general public could start coming the day after Thanksgiving, and the voting continued through Christmas Day.

With technology the way it was, Judge could see real-time results online any old time he wanted. For a few years there, he checked several times each day, as if it mattered if he pulled ahead for a few minutes. Now, he knew it didn't matter. He still landed in third place every single time.

He thought of the letter in his glove compartment and closed his eyes. "I hope you like the show, Dad." With that, he hit play, and hurried to get the lights off and get back to the truck.

He climbed in and handed the box of ice cream to June. "It's chocolate chip."

"And the fat ones," she said. "I love these." She ripped open the box and handed one to Judge.

"Thanks, baby," he said, his nerves making his voice a bit lower than usual.

"How do you delay the start?"

"With a start delay code," he said. "I put the same one at the end of the loop, but it's only six seconds. I gave myself a full minute to get out here."

The lights flashed in front of him—every single star burst to life at the beginning of the show—but there was no sound. His hand flew to the radio as he said, "Duh. We don't have it on the right channel." He got that fixed, but they missed the first several notes of *Have Yourself a Merry Little Christmas*.

Frustration built within Judge. He said nothing, and June smartly didn't either. He'd programmed the smaller stars to brighten and hold on double-time beats, with the main melody pulsing through the larger stars in the front.

The song didn't last long before the tune moved on to *We Wish You a Merry Christmas*. He'd used music this year without words, only the instrumental tracks. The classic instrumental tracks. He was done trying to be trendy. He wanted to produce a show that meant something to him.

"My dad loved this song," he said. "He'd go around whistling it for all of December."

"Is that right?" June asked, not looking from the lights playing through the windshield.

"That's right," Judge confirmed. "He was a great

whistler. He used to joke that he could've been famous if only anyone cared about whistling." He chuckled, because he had fond memories of working with his father while he whistled.

We Wish You a Merry Christmas moved into *Little Drummer Boy*, and the stars started to "march" to the beat. The lights went from red and green and white—the only three colors in the show so far—to red, white, and blue.

"Wow," June said, leaning forward. "This is spectacular."

Judge said nothing, but he did love watching the stars march to the beat. He'd designed them in pairs, like boots, and he wasn't sure if anyone saw it but him. Left, right, left, right. Each star in the left-side pair lit up, then the right-side pair. Scattered as they were across the lawn, he wasn't sure it would be noticeable.

He didn't want to ask either. He'd learned to let people give him the feedback they had and not influence it. June had gotten her phone out to take notes, but it sat in darkness on her lap.

Several of the smaller stars pulsed with each *pa rum pum pum pum*. And as the drums in the background increased, the stars went dark. For the finale, he'd split the yard in half—two boots for the march. The music slowed in a ritardando, and Judge pulled in a breath.

The stars marched—left, right, left, right—four times, and June started clapping as the song ended.

A new one started instantly—no delay there—but June said, "Judge, that was *phenomenal*."

"Yeah?"

"I love that one. I want to see it again right now."

God Rest Ye Merry Gentlemen had started, and Judge had chosen a semi-fast recording of it. He only used half the stars in this song, and he'd chosen them based on depth in the yard from the observers point-of-view to give a sense of swelling up and pulling back in the music. This was another short song—just enough to whet someone's appetite and appeal to something familiar for them—before the show moved on to *Holly Jolly Christmas*.

The lights had gone back to red, green, and white after Little Drummer Boy, and Judge hoped people would get the nod to Texas with the stars and the patriotic colors of that song. Blue lights were always a hit, and he hoped that by using them sparingly this year, people would remember the show. Vote for the show.

Judge's heart started to pound. The part of the show where he deviated from anything he'd ever done before sat only seconds away.

Holly Jolly Christmas faded into a slower song that took even Judge a moment to recognize. June cocked her head, and then she looked straight at Judge. "It's I'm proud to be —an American," she sang along with the music.

"The song is actually called God Bless the USA," Judge murmured. Only blue stars pulsed and swayed to the song, and he loved the rippling effect he'd done from left to right to make it look like the flag was blowing in the breeze.

A thrill ran down his spine that she'd recognized the tune. He heard the beat from *Little Drummer Boy* come back into the song, and right on cue, so did the white lights.

"Oh, that's fantastic," June said. "You mixed songs."

And it wasn't done yet.

God Rest Ye Merry Gentlemen fit in between *God Bless the USA*, with the latter song fading. The blue lights disappeared too, leaving only white to fill the sky. As *Carol of the Bells* started low in the background and grew, so did the lights in the show.

They came in yellow, green, red, blue, white, purple, pink, and aqua, the rhythm of, *dunn—dun-dun-dun*, moving across the whole yard with perfect precision to the music. As it swelled and grew in the truck, so did the lights in the yard.

With only *Carol* playing now, with an intense orchestra and electric guitar, all the stars in the yard went out, leaving only the three on the roof to play the tune. Judge had programmed the biggest, brightest center star to play the slightly longer note at the beginning of the four note pattern. The two side stars took turns playing two notes in a row.

He'd only used white lights as an homage to the new star that had appeared on the night of the Savior's birth, and as the last note filled the truck, only the tall, broad, middle star remained lit.

The music faded to silence, but that star beamed on for four more seconds. Judge was just starting to wonder when it would go off when it did.

They sat in silence for another few seconds, and then June burst into applause again. "Judge!" She grinned at him for all she was worth. He felt her joy all the way down in his toes, and he couldn't help smiling back at her.

"That was incredible," she said. She stopped clapping and reached for him, drawing his face to hers. "Absolutely stunning."

"You're just saying that," he whispered, his lips nearly catching on hers.

"I am not," she said back. "I've seen your show lots of times, Judge Glover. That was the best it's ever been." She kissed him then, and Judge decided in that moment that he'd done the best he could with this show. He wasn't going to tweak it to death, not this year.

He didn't care if he won or not.

Kissing June was better than any prize he'd get from the town of Three Rivers, and he wanted to focus on getting better at that.

Chapter Twenty-Seven

R anger Glover could get lost inside Two Cents in a matter of seconds. He spent about as much time developing and improving the app now as he did out on the ranch. He'd just come in from the stables, showered, and taken Wilder so Oakley could take a nap. She was due in two weeks with their second child—this one a girl—and Ranger wanted to be home more so he wouldn't have to come running in from the ranch when she went into labor.

He only worked in the nearby buildings, and he wasn't helping with birthing season at all this year. Preacher as the second foreman at Shiloh Ridge had been a Godsend, and while he and Ward weren't the same at all, they sure did get along well. They knew how to run a ranch well. They had the love and respect of every man or woman who came to work at Shiloh Ridge.

Ranger lifted his coffee mug to his lips and glanced at his son. Wilder had fallen asleep about ten minutes ago, and pure contentment with his family life moved through Ranger. Now, if he could just get this new feature on the app to play nicely.

He dove into the code, moving through it step by step, trying to find the bug that prevented users from logging out. He himself never logged out of the app, but apparently some people shared the app on one device—he'd expanded to tablets in the past six months—and they wanted to use their own accounts.

Two Cents saved recommendations now. They were more personalized, and a user could save lists, mark restaurants or other businesses they wanted to visit, as favorites, and more.

So each user needed their own account, and Ranger needed to figure out a way to make sure they could logout on one device, and then login under another username on that same device.

He'd never gone to school for computer science. He'd dabbled in a few community courses, written a few programs, and been inspired to do more. He'd taken CS languages online and then started an app development training. It had been self-led, so he worked on it when he had time, and Two Cents had been born after three or four other apps that weren't good.

"Ranger," Oakley said, and it took him a moment to look up from all the letters and numbers on his screen. She leaned heavily in the doorway, and Ranger jumped to his feet.

"Are you okay?"

She held one hand on her pregnant belly, and the

moment Ranger stepped toward her, he saw the blood. She was not okay.

Panic reared through him, and he rushed toward her in a jog now. "Let's go," he said. "Can you walk?" Could he carry her down the steps? He was getting older, and he didn't do a lot of lifting around the ranch anymore.

Oakley said nothing, her face pale and her breath coming in pants. Ranger couldn't allow the tension to overcome him. He took Oakley by the arm and cast a glance to his sleeping son. There were plenty of people to help, and Ranger just needed to call one of them.

Wilder would be fine while Ranger got his wife into the truck. She could walk, albeit slowly, and he got her downstairs with some gentle encouragement and reassurances that she'd be okay, that they'd make it to the hospital just fine.

He didn't like the look of that blood, but he was no doctor.

"Etta," he called, though he wasn't sure if his sister was home or not. She didn't answer, and he kept Oakley moving toward the door as he yelled, "Sammy?"

"Right here," she said, appearing in the arched doorway. Ranger would be sad when she and Bear moved out, but he understood why they were. They'd have four kids in just six more months, and the three-bedroom suite in half the upstairs wasn't big enough for their family.

Ranger wanted to be the one to find somewhere else to live. Bear had designed this homestead for him, not for Ranger, and it felt wrong to be staying.

Sammy had insisted they move, though, and not many people argued with Sammy.

"Wilder's asleep upstairs," he said. "She's bleeding, and I'm taking her to the hospital."

"I've got him," Sammy said, her eyes wide. "I'll tell everyone."

"Thanks," Ranger said, opening the front door. The sky glared angrily down at them, but Ranger paid it no mind. "You're doing great, hon," he said to his wife.

"My mom's not here," she said. "I don't want to have the baby yet."

"I don't think you have a choice, Oak." He spoke in a quiet voice so as to not upset her. "Your mother is coming. She'll get to see the baby, and she'll be here to help for a while."

He was glad Oakley had been talking to her mother for the past several months. That had been hard for her, though she'd wanted to rebuild that bridge. The truth was, rebuilding a relationship was a lot of work. It took a lot of forgiveness and a lot of faith. His wife continued to impress him, even to this day.

Ranger had to boost her into the truck, because she couldn't get in herself, and she wept as he got behind the wheel and started the pilgrimage to the hospital.

"I'm bleeding all over," she said. "This isn't normal. There's something wrong."

"We're on the way," he said, his fingers flexing on the wheel. He hadn't done a lot of research about giving birth. She'd done it before, and things had gone well. "Are you having contractions?"

"No," she said.

"Did your water break?"

"I don't know."

Ranger stopped asking questions at that point. He just drove. When he got to the hospital, he raced inside to get a wheelchair and yell for help. Two nurses helped him get Oakley into the chair, and they took charge after that, pushing her toward an elevator that would take them to maternity.

"Who's the doctor?" one of them asked.

"Doctor Karen Monroe," Ranger said, glad his memory could produce that for him. He trailed along like someone who shouldn't be there, and he stood helplessly while the maternity nurses took over from the hospital nurses. They helped Oakley change out of her clothes and get into a bed. Wires and monitors started getting attached and readings started appearing.

A doctor entered the room, but it wasn't their obstetrician. Ranger moved to Oakley's side and took her hand.

"I'm Doctor French," he said. "I hear you're thirty-seven weeks pregnant." He grinned at Oakley like they'd share laughs and coffee later. Ranger was used to other men ogling his wife, but he didn't like it. It reminded him too much of her dating days, where she'd go out with multiple men in the same day.

"Yes," she said. "I was taking a nap, and I woke up with pain in my abdomen. I noticed I was bleeding, and we came in."

"Let's see what's going on." He positioned himself at the end of the bed and got to work. Ranger's anxiety tripled in the few seconds of silence. The doctor stood, his face definitely more grim than before. "I'm going to wait for Doctor Monroe, as long as you and the baby are okay." He checked the monitors and took the chart from the nurse. "Looks like last time, you'd been in labor for days and delivered quickly."

"Yes," Ranger said. Oakley hadn't even had time for an epidural last time. "What's going on? Tell us straight."

Dr. French looked at Ranger and then Oakley. "You might need a Cesarean-section. Part of the placenta has moved over the birth canal, and the baby's head is pushing against it. That's why you're bleeding."

"Okay," she said calmly, and Ranger marveled at that.

"The placenta is usually high in the uterus in late pregnancy," Dr. French continued. "You had some pain, which could be it tearing or coming off the uterus. That could also cause bleeding." He looked back at the chart. "No matter what, we don't want you to start hemorrhaging, and it would be my recommendation to deliver the baby as soon as possible and make sure you're okay."

Hemorrhaging sounded bad to Ranger too, and he nodded. "Okay," he said. "Let's do that."

"Doctor Monroe will be here in a minute," he said.

"I want to start now," Oakley said. "Surely you can't cut into me without drugs. I want those now." She sounded a bit hysterical, and Ranger squeezed her hand.

"I can do that," Dr. French said coolly. He turned to the nurse. "Let's get her on an epidural drip." He looked at Oakley as the nurse left the room. "We'll move you over to a delivery room and get the drugs going. Then, when Doctor Monroe gets here, she can fill you in on the rest."

"Thank you," Oakley said, finally laying her head back against the pillows. Everyone left the room, and Ranger sincerely hoped some sort of alarm would ring if they needed to return.

"Montana had a C-section," Oakley said. "I can do it."

"Of course you can." He kissed the back of her hand as she started crying again.

"I just wish my mom was here."

"I'll call her right now." Ranger stood and pulled his phone from his back pocket. He had only spoken to Oakley's mother, Blanche, a couple of times. They'd been video calls so he could "meet" her, and she was planning to fly in from Barbados next week.

Her line rang and rang, and Ranger's frustration grew and grew. He faced the tall, narrow window that faced the parking lot below. When Blanche's voicemail picked up, he said, "Blanche, it's Ranger Glover. Oakley went into labor early." That wasn't entirely true, but he couldn't explain everything in a message. "You're welcome to keep your same schedule and come next week, but she wanted me to let you know."

He hung up and sighed. "Dear Lord," he whispered to his faint reflection in the glass. "Bless my wife. Bless her mother that she can get here safely. Bless me that I'll know what to do with two children."

The weight of the world descended on him, and he let his head drop as he finished his prayer. He trusted the

Lord. *Whatever will be, will be*, he thought. Surely God wouldn't let him damage his children too much.

A loud beep screamed from behind him, and Ranger spun around. Oakley lay in the bed, her face the color of cement and her eyes closed. "Oakley," he called at the same time the door burst open and hospital personnel poured into the room.

He stayed out of the way as they worked on her, and when Dr. Monroe came into the room, he rushed toward her. "Help her."

"We're going to help her," Dr. Monroe said. "Let's move." They wheeled Oakley out of the room, and Ranger wasn't sure if he could go or not.

A nurse hooked her arm through his and said, "You come with me, Dad. I'll get you suited up so you can go into the operating room."

RANGER ACCEPTED HIS NEW BABY FROM THE NURSE. THE tiny girl had just been given a bath, and Ranger marveled at her perfect nose, her pink lips, and her head full of dark, wispy hair. He smiled at her, glad he'd been in the room to witness her birth.

"How's my wife?" he asked the nurse without looking away from his child.

"I'll go check," she said, and Ranger's gut screamed at him. Oakley had not woken up during the delivery, and she'd be upset she hadn't been able to see this baby the moment she'd been born.

They'd talked about names for this baby, but Ranger didn't feel comfortable choosing something without her input. He needed her to wake up and help him, and a quiet voice in the back of his mind told him he needed her to wake up, period.

He had no idea what he'd do if she didn't wake up.

Don't think like that, he told himself. "You're going to meet your momma soon," he whispered to the little girl. "She's going to love you so much." To him, this baby had Oakley's facial shape, and she definitely had the same shade of dark hair.

"Your grandma's coming too," he said. "All the way from another country. One of your grandmothers lives right here in Texas, and I bet she's in the waiting room." Ranger hadn't checked his phone since hanging up with Blanche, and he hadn't looked at any of the messages he'd had before making that call.

He suspected Sammy had rallied the troops, and that they'd all make the trek to the hospital. "Should we go meet everyone? There's so many of them, but they're all great. They all mean well. Maybe your brother will be out there."

Ranger looked up and around the nursery. No one seemed to care what he did, so he took his clean, fresh-from-heaven baby and left the nursery. He knew the way to the waiting room, and he whispered to his daughter, "See? There they all are," when he stepped into the area.

Ward approached, his face anxious and questions streaming from him. "How is Oakley?"

Ranger didn't want to say he didn't know. But he didn't

know. He just shook his head and passed Ward the baby. "Take her to Mother for me, would you? I'll go find out." He stepped back through the door without his daughter, his heart pounding.

He pressed his back against the door, his own breathing coming faster and faster.

"Sir," someone said, and Ranger didn't even realize he'd closed his eyes. He opened them and looked at the nurse who'd bathed his baby. She smiled at him. "Your wife is awake and asking for you and the baby."

"I just gave her to my mother," he said, his voice stuck in his throat. Tears filled his eyes, and the nurse cocked her head at him.

"I'll get her." She stepped out into the waiting room and came back a few seconds later with the tightly bundled baby girl. She fussed a little bit, her newborn cry making Ranger's heart take flight.

He hurried after the nurse to a recovery room, where he found Oakley with plenty of color in her face, sitting up in bed. "Oak." He ran to her and hugged her. She groaned as she lifted her arms up to hold him in return. "You're awake."

"I missed it all," she whispered. "I'm so sorry."

"It's fine," he said. "I was there, and she's here, and she's wonderful." He pulled away so Oakley could hold their baby.

The nurse slid the baby girl into Oakley's arms, and she gazed down at the infant. "Oh."

"I didn't give her a name," he said.

"What do you think?" she asked.

"I like Fawn," he said. "She looks like a Fawn to me."

"She's so beautiful." Oakley stroked her fingers softly down the baby's face. "I love Fawn." She leaned down and pressed a kiss to the girl's head.

"Fawn Eliza Glover," he whispered.

"That's perfect," Oakley said, leaning her head back and closing her eyes. "I can't wait to hear how she came."

"I'll tell you all about it," Ranger said, bending down to kiss his wife and then his daughter.

Chapter Twenty-Eight

Mister drove the tractor along the edge of the corn that needed to be cut, mowing under the old stalks and mulching them into silage. They didn't do a lot of that in Texas, but the ranch here in Oklahoma operated differently in a lot of ways.

He didn't hate the work, because Mister liked working. The people were decent, but they weren't family. He missed his family terribly, and that was actually one of the biggest lessons Mister had learned. He'd forgotten how important his siblings and cousins were to him. How much he loved his in-laws and seeing their babies, dogs, cats, and more.

He'd missed them while he'd toured with the rodeo circuit too, but working someone else's ranch was completely different than riding bulls and horses for a living. He'd had a trailer to himself, with a manager staying nearby. He'd had a phone, and he could talk to his mom and Bear anytime.

He could still do that now, but he'd determined to see how he did on his own. In his opinion, he thought he'd been coping really well. He'd been living and working in Oklahoma for five and a half months, and part of him thought, *That's halfway done, Mister. Keep up the good work.*

The truth was, he wasn't sure he'd return to Shiloh Ridge the moment he'd been gone for a year. He didn't have anything to prove to anyone, but he did feel like he still had something to learn.

He finished the square in the corn field and took the freshly bladed corn to the silo. There, it dumped onto a conveyor belt that went up to the roof and allowed it to fall down in. A filter sat up there to keep out bigger rocks and chunks of earth he might have vacuumed up, and Mister sure did like all the mechanized things at Winterhaven.

He thought Bear could use a lesson or two that would take Shiloh Ridge into the future. He'd just climbed back into the huge tractor to go finish the mowing and deposit one more load in the silo when his phone rang. Preacher's name sat there, and Mister smiled.

"Howdy, brother," he said, the chugging of the tractor loud until he closed the door and sealed himself in the cab. When he'd first come to Oklahoma, he'd used the air conditioning in the fancy tractors. Bear didn't invest in that either.

Mister could admit he liked seeing how different ranches and farms operated, and he'd been toying with finding another one and learning as much as he could there too.

He certainly didn't have anyone really waiting for him back in Three Rivers, even if he did miss his family and the comfortable house he used to live in.

"What's goin' on?" he asked Preacher.

"I'm just wondering if you're going to be coming home for the holidays at all."

A strong round of missing filled him, and Mister didn't put the tractor in gear. He sighed and looked right out the dirty window. "I don't know, Preach. I think...I think if I come home for the holidays, I'll want to stay, and I'm fine here."

"Okay," Preacher said, and he sounded disappointed. "We're prepared to tell you over the phone, but you're the first to know, and we're not going to tell anyone else until Thanksgiving. So you have to keep this a secret."

"I'm excellent at keeping secrets," Mister said, grinning.

"Charlie and I are expecting a baby at the end of May."

Mister whooped, giving Preacher the exact reaction his brother wanted, because Preacher started laughing. Charlie too, so Mister must be on speaker with them. "That's amazing," he said. "You two are going to have the calmest, quietest baby in the whole Glover family."

And Mister wanted to be there from the very first day. He wanted to meet that little bundle of joy and start working on himself being the favorite uncle. That shouldn't be too terribly hard to do, because all the other uncles would have their own children to spoil and take care of.

Mister had no one. Just himself.

And anyone you choose to involve in your life, he thought. Here at Winterhaven, he'd made a few friends, mostly the three cowboys he lived with in the cabin.

"It's too bad you can't come for even a day," Charlie said, her voice farther away than Preacher's. "Overnight. We have so many bedrooms, and I've learned how to make the *perfect* Texas pecan pie."

"It has chocolate," Preacher said. "It's not really true Texan...."

"It is too," Charlie said. "The recipe even says so. Don't make fun of my pie. You certainly eat enough to it to not be complaining."

"I'm not complaining," Preacher said, chuckling.

Mister's heart pinched painfully in his chest. He sure did miss the two of them. He missed seeing them. He missed the energy at the Ranch House. He even missed Judge's front yard full of decorations.

"I guess I could come on Thanksgiving," he said. "Stay over one night and drive back here in the morning."

"Then you won't get to see Judge's show," Preacher said. "It's amazing this year, Mister. You should see it at least once."

"He can watch it every night," Charlie said.

"How?" Preacher asked.

"Oh, shoot," Charlie said. "I wasn't supposed to say that. Forget I said anything."

"What do you know?" Preacher asked.

"I'm not saying another word about it." Charlie sounded really firm about it too.

"We're not done talking about this," Preacher said.

"Yes, we are," Charlie said, her voice moving away from the speaker.

"There's something going on," Preacher said.

"Obviously," Mister said with a chuckle. "You're removed from everything up at that cottage."

"I normally like that," Preacher said.

"So you'll text Judge and ask him."

"Nah, he probably has some big announcement planned too. We're doing that a lot now too. Bear even makes us sing that lucky day song Dad used to force on us."

"Oh, I love that song," Mister said. "Everyone sang it for me when I got accepted on the pro rodeo circuit."

"That they did," Preacher said. "You have to come for Thanksgiving." He sounded like he really wanted Mister to be there, and Mister felt his resolve slipping.

"I don't know, Preach," he said. "If I come...I won't want to leave again."

"And that's a bad thing?"

"Yes," Mister said. "It was hard enough leaving the first time."

"Have you met anyone there? You don't send great updates, by the way."

"I do too," Mister said. "You're getting way more than I'd tell you if I lived there."

Preacher burst out laughing. "You've got to be kidding. I heard about you and Libby *constantly*, day in and day out, when you lived here."

Mister opened his mouth to protest, but he stopped himself. Instead of arguing back, he said, "I'm sorry, Preach. I'm sure I was ultra-annoying."

"Only a little," Preacher said. "We all do stuff like that." He let a healthy pause go by. "So...are you seeing anyone there? A pretty blonde from Oklahoma is going to steal your heart and steal you away from Shiloh Ridge?"

Mister scoffed, because he wasn't into blondes. That was all Preacher. "No," he said. "I'm not seeing anyone. When you try to find yourself, Preach, it's best done alone."

"I see."

"I'll think about Thanksgiving," Mister said. "And the reason you don't get what you call an update is because there's nothing to tell. I'm working on the ranch."

"Is Brock putting his dishes in the dishwasher these days?"

"No, he is not," Mister said, finally moving the tractor into gear. "I swear, that guy has way more life lessons to learn than I do."

Chapter Twenty-Nine

L ibby climbed the ladder after Franklin, yelling at the stupid dog to get down from the roof. "You can't come up here, Frankie." She found the golden retriever standing with his front paws on the pinnacle of the roof, gazing into the sunshine as if he had just claimed the world.

When she'd seen him start up the ladder, she'd nearly choked on the hot apple cider Mama had brought out to the site of the Country Christmas their family had been putting on for several years now.

She and Mildred set it all up and ran it for seven weeks in November and December. They'd open next weekend, and Libby didn't think they were even close to ready. Not that it mattered. No one voted on the Country Christmas lights on the barn, but Libby did like to have everything in place before they started charging people.

"Come on," she said, climbing onto the roof. She was getting too old to do stuff like this. Mildred had already claimed that status, and that meant Libby had to climb the ladders and secure the lights to the gutters.

Mildred had designed the map this year, as a few things had moved around this open, flat space close to the entrance at the Golden Hour Ranch.

"I have no idea how to get you down," Libby said, approaching her stubborn retriever. Frankie hardly looked at her at all. "Can you go down the way you came up?" Maybe the dog would go face-first. Maybe she should call Jack for help. Her older brother would know what to do, as Frankie lived with him and usually stayed with him on the ranch.

Jack and Cord lived in big houses closer to the homestead, and they ran the private operation with Libby's father. They raised ten thousand head of cattle, worked the land, and raised their families.

Libby loved her nieces and nephews, and she enjoyed her life in the house where her grandfather had lived before he'd passed away several years ago. Neither she nor Mildred were married, and Libby's thoughts always went to Mister when she thought about weddings and babies.

She hated that she did, but she did.

She texted him from time to time, and as Frankie ignored her calls one more time, Libby gave up trying to get the dog to come down. Let him wander around on the roof and figure out how to get down. He'd obviously figured out how to get up there.

Libby sighed as she reached the peak in the roof too,

and she stepped to the other side of it. "This is a beautiful view, bud." She patted the top of Frankie's head and sat down. The wind blew up here, and Texas had existed in shades of gray for a few days now. Today was the first day the sun had shown its face, and everyone would be lined up to wash their cars and get their lawns trimmed for the last time before winter set in.

Libby was trying to get the lights hung before another round of rainstorms arrived.

She took out her phone and snapped a picture of the horizon in front of her. This barn faced west, and while Libby couldn't see Shiloh Ridge Ranch in the distance, she knew it sat there.

Thankfully, her front door opened to the east, so she didn't have to think about Shiloh Ridge and the Glover family every time she left. She hadn't gone to any of the "ranch wives" luncheons, though she liked the women who lived up there, particularly Arizona. She'd been invited a time or two over the past year, but she simply couldn't go.

She didn't belong there. She still clung to a tiny shred of hope that Mister would come back to Three Rivers a completely different man, but that wasn't likely to happen. Not only that, if he was a completely different man when he returned, would she even like him? Would she even know him?

She cropped the picture and brightened up some of the blues in the sky. She then sent the picture to Mister and said, *This is the view from the barn roof. It's beautiful in Texas today.*

He'd sent her a few photos from his farm in Oklahoma,

and the landscape they saw each day had become something safe for them to talk about. The weather qualified, as did the chores they had to do.

He didn't talk about his friends there, if he had any. He spoke of his boss a little bit, but always in positive terms. She'd told him that Jack and his wife, Suzy, were having another baby in the spring. She talked about her parents, and the new square foot gardening classes she'd started teaching at Wilde & Organic.

That was about it, and Libby missed her real friendship with Mister more than she could articulate. She never told him she missed him. He never acted like he'd rather be somewhere other than Winterhaven. It felt like they'd simply buried the hatchets and axes and other sharp tools between them and determined never to speak of them again.

Libby wasn't sure if that was healthy or not, but she couldn't change the situation unless she was willing to dig up the past between them. At this point, she wasn't.

She turned to her right and found Frankie sitting next to her, his tongue hanging out of his mouth as he panted. His eyes squinted up happily in his golden retriever smile, and Libby grinned at him as she took a picture.

"This is goin' to Mister, you know," she said. "He's going to be so surprised to see you on the roof of the barn." She edited and cropped that picture too, then sent it to Mister in Oklahoma. *He climbed the ladder himself while I was getting another box of lights for the roof.*

What? Mister answered almost immediately. *That dog is crazy!*

"Dogs don't belong on roofs," Libby said to Frankie, tucking her phone against her chest, knowing Mister had gotten her texts. He hadn't blocked her number. He didn't bring up uncomfortable things. He'd probably found a way to move past her, and he'd probably been out with a half-dozen women since he'd moved to Winterhaven Farm.

Libby pushed away the poisonous thoughts. Number one, they might not even be true. Number two, she had no right to make assumptions about Mister Glover. Number three, he wasn't a bad person and he never had been. Plenty of men went out with a lot of women, and Mister hadn't been cruel to any of them.

She heard machinery working in the distance, and she contemplated getting back to work. But the afternoon existed in perfection, and Libby didn't feel like getting up and stringing the lights. Mildred wouldn't care, and Papa simply asked his daughters if they were ready. Mildred and Libby said yes or no, and Papa would send help if they needed it.

Her phone chimed and she glanced at it. Mister had sent a picture too, and she swiped to see it more fully. She peered at it, something about it....

She sucked in a breath and got to her feet as quickly as she could without sliding down the pitched roof. Her heart pounded in her throat, because Mister had just sent her the same view she'd sent him, but from the ground level.

Before she could move, Mister poked his head up above the edge of the roof. "Mister," she said, not quite sure what else to say.

He grinned at her, but he seemed so different. Mister

Glover came all the way up the ladder and laughed, the sound rich and deep and wonderful. Absolutely wonderful.

Libby's emotion welled in her chest, and she pressed her phone between both of her palms. "You look great," she said, waiting for him to approach her. "It's so amazing to see you. Just amazing."

She wrapped her arms around him and he gathered her into a hug too. "Mm," he said. "I've missed you, Libs."

She pressed her eyes closed and took in a long breath, getting the scent of leather and cologne, something salty and warm at the same time. "I've missed you too."

He exhaled and released her. "The view is better up here." He bent and patted Frankie, and the dog just panted and smiled at all the attention. "I see why you climb up here to play hooky."

"Hey," Libby protested. "I wasn't playing hooky. I was trying to rescue Frankie, but the devil doesn't think he's in any danger."

Mister nodded and sat on down. Libby did too, putting the golden retriever between her and Mister. He didn't say anything, and that was another difference emanating from him.

"How long are you in town?" she asked.

"Just this weekend," he said. "It was easier to get a few days off now, as others had already asked for Thanksgiving off."

She nodded, the tension between them not exactly awkward. Things were just different. He was different, and Libby felt different too.

"Have you been up to the ranch yet?" she asked.

THE NETWORKING OF THE NATIVITY

"Yeah," he said. "I had lunch with Preacher and Charlie. Ward's planning a big dinner tomorrow after church, and I'm rolling out on Monday morning."

"Sounds nice," she said.

"Yeah," Mister said. "It was nice not getting to work before dawn this morning." He smiled without truly looking at her and Libby returned the gesture.

She didn't know what else to say, and he hadn't asked her anything. She told herself not to keep the conversation going. They'd had plenty of instances where they didn't fill every ounce of silence with sound, and it hadn't been awkward then.

"Want me to help with the lights?" he asked.

"I'd love that," Libby said, getting to her feet. She extended her hand for Mister, not that he needed her help to stand. He seemed even more fit now, with plenty of muscles he'd had before he'd left for the farm in Oklahoma.

He wore a full beard, as if he hadn't shaved in the nearly six months since he'd left, and Libby sure did like it. She wanted to reach out and touch it, but she didn't. Enough of a thrill passed through her when he put his hand in hers and got to his feet.

"I'll help you get this canine back on the ground too," he said. "Crazy thing." He chuckled and scrubbed Frankie's head. "Did you see him climb up?"

"Yeah, the last several steps," Libby said. "It was insane."

"I wish you'd gotten it on video. I'd have loved to have seen that."

"Right? It was video-worthy, just to see it with your

own eyes." She met his eyes, and he held hers. So much about him was the same, but so much had changed.

Mister ducked his head and cleared his throat. "How's your mother?" he asked. "Did she get her pickles done?"

Chapter Thirty

J udge laughed at something June said, the furnace blowing warm air into the Ranch House now that cooler weather had finally arrived. It seemed that no matter the weather in Texas, it was having a personality crisis. A bad hair day. A complete break-down.

"No, I'm not a genius in the kitchen," he said. "It's fudge, June. It's literally four ingredients, and I melted them in the microwave." He peeled the plastic wrap off the top of the fudge and started to cut it into squares.

"It's marbled," June said, peering at the chocolate-peanut butter fudge.

"Yeah, because I can take a spoon and drag it through the melted stuff." Judge mimed doing that, still chuckling. "It just looks impressive."

"I'll say."

Judge handed her a small square of the marbled choco-late and peanut butter fudge. He'd really only melted together some chocolate chips, some butter, and some sweetened condensed milk. Stir vigorously. Repeat with peanut butter chips. Swirl—or marble, in June's terms—and let it cool down.

He did put plastic wrap over it to prevent it growing a skin, and he put it in the fridge, because he'd thought of the treat two hours ago and it was that or no-bake cookies. He made those almost every week, and he'd wanted something different.

"It's so good," she said around a mouthful of fudge.

He grinned at her and stacked up three cubes for himself. "All righty," he said. "What are we doin'? Movie? Walk around the ranch? Want to go find a dog and take it for a walk?" Bear and Cactus were always letting people take their dogs, and Preacher hadn't gotten one yet because of that.

"The dogs will just go with you?" June asked.

"Yeah, I mean, Cactus's dogs are Cactus's dogs, but he'd let us take them. Benny is more of a community dog. In fact, I think Preacher has Benny almost all the time now. He's wanted one for a while." Judge didn't say why, but when Preacher had first come home after his accident, Bear had wanted him to get a dog to help him on the ranch. Alert others if Preacher had gotten hurt and the like.

He never had, because there were enough people around to take care of Preacher.

"Mm." June quickly finished her last bite of fudge. "You promised me you'd show me your horse, remember? And your letter."

Judge's heart grew at the mention of Pantomime, but skipped over a beat at the mention of the letter. It had been almost another month since Judge had sat in the front seat of his mother's truck and read a little bit of his letter. He'd told June about it, and perhaps it was time to let her read it.

"All right," he said, ducking down to pull out a plastic container with a tight-fitting lid. "We're going to take some of this with us if that's what we're doing."

"You don't have to," June said.

"I want to." Judge gave her a reassuring smile and filled the shallow container with as many fudge cubes as it could hold. "Be right back." He trekked into his bedroom, which sat down the hall past the office, another bedroom, the guest bath, and two storage closets.

In the nightstand drawer, the letter waited. Judge didn't hesitate as he reached for it. He'd spoken true. He did want to share this with June. He wanted to share everything with June, because he was in love with her.

His pulse did a crazy spin through his veins then, and he wondered if he could tell her that afternoon. Her daughter wasn't coming home until Christmas, and June would be such a huge support to him during the holidays as he took his light show online for the first time in Three Rivers history.

"Yeah," he murmured. "Or she might shut down and shut you out again." He didn't want that, and he determined to keep his big mouth shut about the L-word. There was no reason to say it until he knew for certain she'd say it back.

He returned to the kitchen and pulled his jacket from the rack by the back door.

"Do you ever use the front door?" she asked, copying him. She had to go toward the front of the house to get her coat, which she'd laid over the back of the couch.

"Not really," he said. "I park in the garage and come in that way. Or I come in the back. There's nothing out front."

"There's the most amazing view of the world out front," June said, her eyes widening. "You're telling me you don't sit on that glorious front porch and watch the town of Three Rivers go to bed every night?"

"I get up by five a.m," he said with a smile. "*I* go to bed before the town of Three Rivers does."

"Well." She shook out her hair and zipped up her jacket. "If I lived here, I'd sit out there every night, watching the stars come to life in the sky above and the street lamps flare in the town below."

June could make one day fading into night into the biggest deal. It sounded so romantic when she said it like that.

"Come on," he said. "If we don't get goin', we'll find ourselves out in the dark tonight." The sun had been disappearing in the west a little earlier each night, and Judge liked to be inside when it was dark.

With the fudge in one hand and June's in the other, Judge walked toward the stables in the distance. "See that one furthest to the west? It's just peeking out from behind the green one."

"I see it."

"That's the family stable. Preacher, Ward, and I take care of the horses there."

"Does everyone have a horse?" she asked.

"Yes," he said. "Bear has three."

June giggled and shook her head, creating the most beautiful picture in Judge's mind. "Sounds like Bear."

Judge couldn't argue with that, and his nerves tapped at him until he gave in to their needling. "You like my family, right?"

June swung her attention toward him, and the easy stroll on the ranch turned a bit more tense. "Yes, of course," she said. "I love your family."

"They're loud," he said.

"Everyone has a loud family."

"They're big."

"Well, I will give you that."

"Overwhelmingly big." He watched her for half a heartbeat and then looked away. A couple of ranch dogs lay in the shade under a tree, and Judge whistled at them. They poked their heads up and got to their feet, approaching him at an easy trot. "Howdy, fellas."

"Do those dogs have names?" June asked, pausing as they both went to her to give her a hearty sniff.

"They're blue heelers," Judge said. "Cactus does all the training with the cattle dogs. He feeds them and I'm surprised they're this far in today." He looked toward the Edge, but he couldn't see the cabin or barns where these dogs usually lived. "He names them all some shade of blue. That one you're patting is Navy. This one is Perry, short for Periwinkle."

June grinned at the dirty dog and crouched down to keep patting Navy. "You're just adorable, aren't you? Can you smell my dogs? They're not going to be happy to smell you." She grinned at Navy, and then straightened, taking Judge's hand in hers again.

"This is nice," she said as they continued toward the stables. "I feel so...content. Free. It's freeing up here."

"Is it?"

"The air is clear. The earth smells good. There are dogs who'll just trot along beside you."

"Not to mention I fed you and brought fudge on our journey to see the horses."

She laughed a little, and Judge joined in. She quieted, clearly contemplating something, and Judge just gave her a moment to herself.

"What are you thinking?" he asked when he couldn't stand the country silence for another moment.

"I'm thinking I should leave my phone somewhere and come up here every Sunday. This is so *nice*."

"You left your phone somewhere?"

"Just on the counter in your kitchen," she said, glancing at him and grinning. "I actually forgot it on accident, but it sure is nice to not feel chained to it. Don't you ever just feel like that slim, lightweight device weighs you down?"

Judge had never really thought about, but now he did. "Yeah," he said slowly. "It's definitely always there, in the back of your mind."

"Who's going to call me? Will it be an emergency with their WiFi? Maybe Lucy Mae will have some amazing news from this past week. She hasn't texted yet? Maybe text her first to prompt her." June sighed and shook her head. "Sometimes I want to throw my phone in one of the three rivers here."

Judge chuckled, but he knew the feeling. "Sometimes, especially during the holidays, I'll check my standing in the polls ten times a day. I can, because it's right there on my phone. I just open up the website, and all I have to do is pull down to refresh. Refresh, refresh, refresh."

The weight she'd spoken of hit him like a punch to the gut. "I should leave my phone behind more." He could just hear Ward and Preacher lecturing him if he did that. "We do a lot of business with our phones. It's how we communicate out on the ranch."

"I've seen some people with radios," she said. "Maybe you could carry one of those, at least during the holidays."

"It's not a bad idea." They arrived at the family stable, and Judge unlatched the door to go inside. An odd scent met his nose, and he paused.

"What?" June asked, only halfway through the door behind him. "Why'd you stop in the doorway?"

"Hello?" Judge called, because his nose told him someone else was here. Someone wearing perfume, and a lot of it.

The stable had a door on each end of it, with stalls lining the wall to his right from one to the other. On his left, more stalls stood as well, but halfway down the aisle that ran between the stables, they stopped. The space opened up there, and that was where the Glovers stored their tack, their winter clothes, and other odds and ends. A ladder went up to a loft above the stables on the left, where they kept hay, buckets of oats, and water pellets. Ranger had been known to buy butterscotch candies in bulk and keep them up in the loft too.

He spoiled his horses, and Judge could admit that he liked to give Pantomime a treat every now and then. He had to haul Judge around every day, for crying out loud. Horses loved to work, but they liked to be rewarded too.

"Judge?" June asked, edging past him to stand at his side in the wider aisle. "Is someone here?"

"I thought so," Judge said, his skin still prickling along his neck. But that could've been from June pressing into his back as she slipped by. "No one's answering though."

Down the row of stalls, a horse nickered. June giggled and started toward it. "Is this one yours?"

"No, that's Ace's," he said. "He's really vocal, and he's tellin' you he wants a treat."

"Do you have treats for them? We should've brought those sad apples from the house."

"Hey," Judge said, though he really didn't have any room to protest more than that.

"You're just going to throw them away," June said, stroking both hands down the sides of Ace's horse, Gemini's, face. His eyes drifted halfway closed in bliss, and Judge shook his head at the silly animal.

"Pantomime is down here." Judge went past the other horses, a couple of the prissier ones snuffling at him for his lack of butterscotch, to his beautiful friend. "Hey, buddy." He stepped in close to the stall, but Panto had his head over the gate already. He scoffed out a greeting, his lips tickling Judge's neck and ear.

He chuckled at the horse and said in a low voice, "You can have one little bite of fudge, okay? It's not good for horses." He opened the plastic container and held the square of fudge in the palm of his hand. Panto vacuumed it right up, then tossed his head, his black mane flying out as he did.

"He's gorgeous," June said, joining Judge in front of Panto's stall. "What kind of horse is he?"

"He's a seal bay," Judge said. "That just means his coloring. We call it seal brown. He's dark. His tail and mane are a different color than his hair." He glanced at her. "You've probably seen chestnut bays. They're the lighter brown ones—almost reddish?—with the black mane and tail."

"You're just stunning, aren't you?" She coddled this horse like she had the other one. Judge stepped back and let her, because June seemed to have a real kind heart for animals, something he hadn't known about her. "Fitting too, that this stunning man would have a stunning horse." She grinned at Panto like they'd just shared a juicy secret.

She turned to Judge. "Can we feed him? He needs a treat."

"He does not," Judge said, smiling. "He just got fudge, and I'll probably pay for that by having to clean up his stall in the morning."

"Oats or something?" June turned to survey the tack room, which was one more stall down. "I know how you guys run this ranch. There's oats here."

"For special occasions," Judge said, stepping to block the ladder as if she wouldn't see it. "He just got fudge."

"So you're telling me I can't give him a handful of oats?"

She glanced at Judge and kept searching the shelves. "Oh, I see something." She moved, and she moved fast, heading for a candy jar on one of the shelves.

She couldn't reach it, and Judge grinned for all he was worth. "Too bad, Panto," he said. "The little lady doesn't have quite the arm-span to get you one of those strawberry candies."

"Who put these here?" she complained. "A giant?"

"That would be Bishop," Judge said. "He loves those strawberry candies. They're not for the horses." He neglected to say where they kept those, though he glanced toward the ladder as he went toward June.

"You can get it," she said, a whine in her voice. "Just one, Judge. You got to give him a treat, and I want him to like me too."

"Why's that?" Judge asked, reaching up for the jar of red-wrapped candies. He adored these too. They had a hard shell on the outside, with a liquid, strawberry-flavored center.

"Because." June nudged him with her hip. "I need someone or something to like me as much as you."

"That's just silly," he said, the moment turning sober between them. He leaned down, the candy jar still fixed firmly in his hand, and kissed June. He sure did like doing that, and he liked the way she kissed him back too, matching him stroke for stroke, as if she was just as hungry for him as he was for her.

Something scraped behind them, and Judge pulled away from June to see who was there. No one. The door hadn't opened. The horses barely seemed to be moving.

His eyes flicked up to the loft, and he wasn't sure, but he swore he saw something move. His skin prickled again, and Judge handed June the candy. "Just one," he said under his breath.

"What's going on?" she asked, her voice just as quiet as his.

"Someone's here," he said, his mouth not moving. And they'd just watched him kiss June. A sliver of embarrassment heated his face, but he'd called into the stable when he'd gotten here.

"Who?" June asked, standing partially behind him as she searched the stable too.

"I don't know." Judge kept his voice low and then walked toward the ladder. "I'm going to get the butterscotch Ranger keeps up here," he said in a loud voice. He prayed as he took the first rung that whoever it was didn't have a weapon.

They didn't get people wandering the ranch here, as far from town as it sat. It couldn't be someone looking for shelter for a night; it had to be someone who lived and worked here at the ranch.

They employed women and men in their cowboy cabins, and Judge remembered the perfume he'd smelled.

He made his boots land heavily on every rung, announcing his arrival in the loft. He sighed and dusted his hands down his jeans, looking around in every direction. At first glance, there didn't seem to be anything amiss.

"Who's here?" he asked, because *someone was there*. He just knew it.

Aurora stepped out from behind a stack of hay bales in

the back right corner. She lifted one hand in a weak wave and kept her eyes on the ground. "Just me, Judge."

Oliver Walker appeared behind her. "It's not just her, Judge." He put his arm around Aurora, and Judge could only blink at them. At least they were clothed.

His brain spun, because he didn't know what to do in this situation. Below him, June called his name, and he frowned. "You guys scared us."

"Sorry," Aurora said, her voice with a tiny tremble in it. "You won't tell my mom, will you?" She met his eye then, and Judge once again spun.

"What would I tell her, exactly?" Judge asked, taking a step toward them, the butterscotch discs in sight now. "I don't think it's wise for you two to be sneaking around in stables together."

"No, sir," Ollie said, his eyes blazing. "We shouldn't be."

"I'm not judging you," Judge said. "Despite the name." He smiled at them, still wondering if he should tell Montana or Bishop about this incident.

"We just need to get away from the house sometimes," Aurora said.

"It's still probably better to stay where someone can see you," Judge said. "It's easier to remember who you are and what you really want out of life." He couldn't believe it, but he'd just quoted from his letter.

He gestured for them to come with him. "Come on, now. I brought fudge, and we're just talkin' to the horses." He dug into the bag with all the butterscotch and took a handful with him back down the ladder.

June waited there with round eyes, which only got

bigger when Aurora and Ollie followed Judge. "Here you go, Juney." He gave her the butterscotch. "Treat them all if you want."

She blinked, still staring at Aurora and Ollie.

"Ma'am," Oliver said, reaching up to touch the brim of his hat. He hadn't been wearing one upstairs, and Judge knew exactly why a man didn't wear his cowboy hat in the presence of a pretty girl. He looked at Aurora. "I should go."

"Don't you dare," June said, her voice more momma-bear now. "What were you two doing up there?" She moved past Judge to stand in front of the kids. She put one hand on her hip and said, "You better start talking, else my imagination is going to go wild. The truth now."

Aurora's eyes grew wide too, and she blinked at June, clearly frozen and afraid. Judge couldn't help smiling, though he turned his head away from the kids so they couldn't see it. And Aurora had been worried about her mother.

"Just a little kissing, ma'am," Ollie mumbled.

"A little kissing?" June repeated. "Young man, do not insult me." She reached up and plucked something from Aurora's hair. "You have hay all over in your hair." She clucked her tongue and shook her head. "Listen to me very carefully, both of you. Do you know how old I am?"

"No, ma'am," Oliver said, obviously the one who was going to talk.

"I'm thirty-six," June said. "Do you know how old my daughter is?"

"Eighteen, ma'am," Oliver said. "Same as us."

"Almost." June folded her arms, and Judge could only marvel at her. At the strength in her. At the fact that she could have this conversation at all. He was so out of his league when it came to teenagers. "Now, seeing as how y'all are both high school graduates, I'm assuming you can do some simple math. I'm thirty-six. She's nearly eighteen. I was pregnant for nine months. I think you're both probably older than I was when I got pregnant. Unless you're married, you can trust me from here to Jupiter that you do not want to have a baby in the next nine months."

"No, ma'am," Oliver said. "We don't. We aren't doing that. It was just a little kissing, I swear."

"In a private hay loft, in a stable where no one can see you," June said. "For two smart people, that's a really dumb thing to do. I know what this feels like. It's exciting and passionate, and you love him so much. He loves you. It's very easy to go from a little kissing to a lot of sex."

Judge sucked in a breath, and Aurora actually started crying. "I'm sorry," she said, grabbing onto June and holding her tight. "Don't tell my mom, okay? I swear, we're just kissing."

June held her too, finally raising one arm to beckon Oliver into the hug. He went willingly, and Judge had no idea how to process what he'd just heard and what he was now seeing. June said something to both of them, her voice too low for him to catch. They both nodded, and Aurora wiped her eyes.

"I'm sorry, June," she said. "Honest, I am." She looked at Judge, and everything was uncomfortable between them. "I'm sorry, Judge."

He waved his hand like this was no big deal, because he honestly wasn't sure if it was or not. June seemed to think it was. Oliver repeated the apologies, first to June and then to Judge, and the two of them left.

June deflated the moment the stable door closed, and she turned back to Judge. "Kids can be so stupid."

"You told them," he said as she returned to his arms.

She looked up at him. "I wasn't married when I got pregnant with Lucy Mae." Her own eyes filled with tears. "We got married before she was born, but I was once a stupid kid too. They're so...good. They have so much in front of them. I just don't want them to do what I did." She drew in a deep breath and blew it all out. "Okay, enough of that. Time to read your letter."

Chapter Thirty-One

J une couldn't believe the unrest in her soul that seeing Aurora and Oliver had caused. She'd been reminded so strongly of the mistakes she'd made, and she really didn't want anyone to repeat them.

Judge hesitated to get his letter out, and June wondered if he had more questions about her previous deeds. She'd never told him she and Adam weren't married before Lucy Mae was conceived, and her own chest quaked with nerves.

Would that change things for him? She felt like she'd worked hard to overcome the mistakes she'd made. She'd put her daughter first for many years. She'd worked hard to get training and special skills so she could support herself. She'd repented and returned to church. Surely that mistake from so long ago wouldn't continue to haunt her now.

He finally pulled out an envelope and flipped it over in his fingers. "I'm nervous about letting you read this."

"Why?" He'd said it would show her what his father was

like. But she had a feeling it would expose some things about him too.

"I don't know." He handed it to her. "I want you to see it, June-Bug, because I want to share everything with you." He swallowed, and June catalogued the movement in his throat. He didn't say *I love you, June*, but he might as well have.

She heard it ringing in the words he had said, and she saw it shining in those gorgeous eyes. She wasn't sure how she felt about him, but it hovered dangerously close to love. She wasn't sure she'd ever been in love before.

She'd been attracted to Adam, and yes, they'd gotten married. But she wasn't sure she'd ever loved him, not the way the men loved their wives in this family. Not the way her mom and dad loved each other.

She cleared her throat and lifted the flap on the envelope.

Dearest Judge,

It's not easy being third, son, but you were created exactly to come to our family in that spot. You were needed to lead the way before Preacher, Mister, and Bishop, exactly the way John came just before Jesus.

You are the part of our family that spoke of companionship. Everyone turned to you for help and advice growing up, and you somehow knew exactly how to judge every situation for what it was and give that advice.

Bear was larger than life, and I'm sure he'll continue to be himself. Cactus was always so steady and yet tainted with just a bit of salt. You toddled around after them, and I'd laugh when you couldn't get over the fences or get your legs to move fast enough to keep up.

Bear always came back for you, Judge. He never abandoned you, and I want to caution you not to abandon him. He's hard to deal with sometimes, but he needs you.

Cactus needs you, because you're reasonable when he feels unreasonable.

The other brothers and Arizona need you, because you never judge them. You love them perfectly, and Grandmother should've named you Savior for that. Continue to love them how they need to be loved. It's not always with uplifting words, because sometimes, they'll need to hear the truth.

Stay in the light, Judge. It's easier to remember who you are and what you really want when you stay in the light. I trust you will always do that, just as I trust you with any task around the house and ranch. You were a Godsend to both me and Mother, the perfect mix of a son who could and still can do anything.

I love you forever and always,

Dad

JUNE KEPT HER EYES ON THE LAST WORD ON THE PAGE, needing a moment to absorb everything she'd just read. It wasn't a very long letter, but his father had been able to say so much in so few words.

"This is wonderful," she finally murmured, moving her eyes back to the top of it again. "You always said you weren't a leader, but you are."

"I'm not," he said.

"He says you're like John."

"Just because my name is John."

June refolded the letter and slipped it back inside the envelope. "I don't think so, Judge."

"What do you think?" He took the envelope from her and put it in his back pocket. His eyes flitted around, never really landing on any one thing. The plastic on the candies in his hand crinkled as he started to unwrap one of them. "I really want to know what you think of what he said."

"I think he knew you extraordinarily well," June said quietly.

Judge walked away from her and down to the horse in the end stall. She simply watched him busy himself so he wouldn't have to look at her.

"I think you are a leader for Mister, Preacher, Bishop, and Zona. I think people do come to you for advice, because they trust you. They know you aren't going to spread their troubles around, and they like being with you, because you're calm and steady. You think rationally. You solve problems without telling them what they should do."

Judge nodded, but he didn't say anything. His phone rang, and he pulled it from his pocket. "It's Bear."

"He always came back for you," June said.

Judge's expression softened as he finally met her eye. "We all have things in our past we're not proud of," he said, swiping the call away. "Remember how I used to play tricks on everyone? They all hated me."

"I'm sure that's not true."

"It's why Mister and I don't get along," Judge said sadly. "Then I got this letter, and it was like my father rebuking me for being the prankster. It still took me a little bit before I figured out how to get into that light he talks about. He said if I'd stay there, I'd remember who I was and what I wanted."

He shook his head. "And it wasn't to be the mean brother, the one who hides trucks and steals people's phones." He dropped his chin to his chest, his shame evident. June knew exactly how he felt, because she'd dipped her toes in the depths of such shame in the past.

"It took me a while to change, and even longer for everyone to realize I had. By then, Preacher was being promoted, and I was once again left behind. Unable to get over the fences and get my legs to keep up. He moved past me, and every time I start to feel left out or overlooked, I come back to this letter."

"It's a beautiful tribute to you," June whispered. "I think your father is absolutely right. You're a Godsend, and you're a trusted confidante. You're steady and strong, and while you might've made mistakes in the past, you fixed them."

She felt the light of heaven shine on her too, and she felt forgiven for what she'd done wrong in the past all over again. A smile touched her face, because it was impossible not to smile when the mercy of God fell upon her.

His phone rang again, and Judge looked at it. "Bear must really need me." He swiped on the call. "What's up, Bear?" He started to turn away from her, but quickly came back. "Yeah, she's right here...okay, I'll tell her. Thanks."

He lowered his phone and said, "June, Adam's been trying to get in touch with you. There's been an accident in California."

THE WORLD HAD FALLEN OUT FROM UNDER JUNE'S FEET. The sky had opened. Everything felt like it was on fire, and June stared out the tiny window on the airplane, praying.

Praying, praying, praying. That was all she'd done for the past two hours, and she still had a couple to go before she'd land in Los Angeles.

She's okay, Adam had said. *But she wants you here. You'll want to be here to see for yourself.*

Those words, of course, had come after the angry ones, demanding "Where the devil are you?" and "Why in the world would you not take your phone with you?"

June gripped her phone in her fingers now, the bones aching with how hard she squeezed it. She'd enjoyed being free from it so much, but she could now see the irresponsibility of that. She had a daughter to worry about, for crying out loud.

Tears pricked her eyes, and her nose started to run. She would not cry on the plane in front of strangers. Doing that in front of Judge had been bad enough. He'd been nothing but amazing as they raced back to his house to get her phone. He'd dropped everything he had to do that evening to drive her an hour one-way to Amarillo. She hadn't even stopped at her house for clothes. She'd bought a ticket on the way there using her phone, and she'd boarded the plane with only her purse as luggage.

It didn't matter. She had family in the area, and Los Angeles had plenty of stores. She hadn't been able to get in touch with Lucy Mae yet, though her daughter had texted right as the plane had taxied down the runway.

Sorry I was in x-ray. We'll talk when you get here.

June closed her eyes, and the word *x-ray* imprinted on the backs of her eyelids. She just wanted to sleep, but she knew she wouldn't. Her mind raced in circles and then figure eights, trying to find a solution to her identity crisis.

Just when June thought she knew who she was and what she should be doing with her life, a string would get pulled. She'd get tugged right back to the place she'd been for the past eighteen years.

Perhaps that's where you're supposed to stay, she thought, though she'd enjoyed breaking out of her Lucy-Mae's-Mom box and exploring other options. Options like *strong female business owner* and *Judge Glover's girlfriend*.

With Lucy Mae happily off to college and living her dreams, June had started to believe Montana. She'd started to truly believe that networking was what she did for a living, it wasn't who she was. Mothering was something she was very good at, but it wasn't the only thing that defined her.

But now, the string pulled, and her mind screamed, and June reeled.

You were wrong, she told herself. *Stupid and wrong.*

By the time she touched down in California, darkness had fallen. She felt disoriented, and not only because she hadn't been back to this state in a few years. Since she had no luggage, she lifted her phone to her ear, the line ringing to call her ex.

"I'm here," she said when Adam answered.

"I'll circle around again," he said. "Text me what stop you're at."

"Okay." June jogged now, though she hadn't done a lot of running in the past. Her breath hitched, and she didn't want to make anything harder for Adam. Why she cared about him, she wasn't sure. He certainly hadn't made anything easier for her or Lucy Mae for a lot of years.

She ran outside, forgetting that it never really cooled off in California, especially in LA. She looked up and saw she'd exited near pick-up six, and texted the number to Adam. She crossed the street and looked left. His huge, hulking Hummer stuck out in the crowd of vehicles, and he'd barely come to a stop at the curb before she opened the door.

"Hey," he said, easing back into the flow of traffic.

"Hey." June clutched her purse on her lap, every muscle in her body as equally as tight as her grip. "How far to the hospital?"

"They released her about twenty minutes ago," he said. "She's waiting for me to come pick her up."

A dose of relief hit June. "She's released already? Must not be bad."

"I told you it wasn't bad." He cut a glance at her, a frown on his handsome face.

Yes, June still thought her ex-husband was handsome. Too bad his goodness only existed on the surface. She'd found a way to forgive him and accept him, and that was through Lucy Mae. Without him, she wouldn't have her daughter, and she could tolerate him and be kind to him because of that fact alone.

"What happened?" June asked. "I couldn't get in touch with her. She was in x-ray, doing something."

"They thought she'd broken her ankle," Adam said. "I got a text from her when she said she'd been released that she hadn't. It's pretty badly sprained, and she's shaken up."

"What happened?" June asked again. "All you said was there was an accident."

"Yeah." Adam reached up and ran his hands through his long, dark, surfer-boy hair. She wanted to tell him he was two decades too old for such a haircut. He looked semi-ridiculous with the curls at the ends. "June, I don't want you to freak out."

"What do you think I've been doing since you called and told me my daughter was in the hospital? Oh, and you yelled at me for not being chained to my phone, so thanks for that."

"Well, it was no picnic for me either," he shot back. "Having to call your boyfriend's brother and practically beg him to help me find you."

"I'm not apologizing for having a boyfriend," June said, though her gut poked at her. "You've had at least a dozen girlfriends since we got divorced, and you have two other children, with two other women. Do *not* lecture me about having a boyfriend."

"This is unbelievable," Adam said, yanking the wheel to the left to change lanes.

June fumed in the passenger seat, changing her thoughts to prayers for her own safety.

A few minutes passed, and the storm in the Hummer blew out. "I've done right by you, June," Adam said, his voice quiet. "I pay my child support, and I always have. I didn't fight you for custody, though I could have when you left California."

June had plenty to say about what it meant to be a father, and paying child support and sending a birthday card once a year wasn't it. He may have "done right" by her, but he'd disappointed Lucy Mae over and over and over.

With horror, June realized she'd just done the same thing. She had been distracted by her boyfriend—and someone else's kids making out in the loft—that she hadn't been available for her own daughter.

The pesky tears came again, and June turned away from her ex so she could have a measure of privacy.

He made another lane change and got off the freeway. As the hospital came into view, June quickly took out her phone and tapped out a message to Judge.

I made it to LA. Lucy Mae has apparently been discharged and we're picking her up now. It seems like she's fine.

She read over the message, her heartbeat like a big, bass drum in her ears.

"There she is," Adam said, pulling up to the curb. June looked up from her phone, and the sight of her daughter on crutches sent her pulse into a tailspin. The tears fell whether she wanted them to or not, and June leapt from the huge SUV.

"Baby doll," she said, rushing toward Lucy Mae. "My precious girl, are you all right?"

Lucy Mae started crying too, and she said, "I'm okay, Momma." But she wasn't okay, and June had known it before she'd even gotten out of the car. She'd looked tired. Worn down. Underfed. Broken.

June's daughter was *broken*, and she hadn't even known it. She hadn't known it, because she'd been too busy with her own life back in the Texas Panhandle.

"Come on, honey," she said, her voice sounding quite Texan in that moment. "Momma's here now, and you're going to be just fine." She helped her daughter to the back door and up into the car. "There you go. I got these."

She took the crutches to the back of the Hummer, where Adam took them from her and put them in the rear space. He closed the hatch and said, "She was in a car with some friends. The driver was high, and he rolled the car."

June sucked in a breath and looked up at her ex-husband. "You're kidding."

"I'm not," he said. "June...it's possible she was high too. She told me she wasn't smoking, but her clothes reek of pot, and no matter what, she had some second-hand inhalation. That can impair a person."

"But she wasn't driving." June couldn't even imagine the legal repercussions of that.

Adam shook his head. "No, she wasn't driving." He sighed and wiped his hand through his hair again, his tell for the amount of stress he carried. "But June, the driver died."

June didn't know how to keep standing. Her knees buckled, and Adam caught her before she collapsed to the ground in a puddle of worried tears. "That could've been her," June sobbed into his shoulder. "One second, Adam, and that person died."

One bad decision. One moment in time. One degree different, and Lucy Mae could've smacked her head against the glass and been gone.

"But it wasn't her," Adam said, his voice thick. "Come on, now, June. It wasn't her."

One bad decision to leave her phone in Judge's kitchen. One moment in time where she chose him over Lucy Mae. One degree different, and she could've lost her daughter because she'd been so focused on herself.

"She needs you to be strong," Adam said. "None of your lectures about her friends or smoking. At least not today."

June nodded, thinking through her work week. It was Thanksgiving on Thursday, and she always closed Nichols Networking the Wednesday before that. She'd have to call her office manager and explain the family emergency. It was only two days.

Lucy Mae was worth two days.

She wiped her face, her thoughts flying ahead to spending time with her parents on their sprawling property to the northeast of LA, and enjoying her father's roast turkey for Thanksgiving.

As she followed Adam to the passenger side of the Hummer, where he opened her door for her, June thought of the Thanksgiving she was supposed to share with Judge. With all the Glovers.

Her heart mourned the loss of them already, but she knew she'd never forgive herself if she lost Lucy Mae because she focused somewhere she shouldn't.

"I'm okay, Mom," Lucy Mae said from the back seat, but her voice sounded hollow and false.

"Of course you are," June said, because Adam was right. Today was not the day for lectures and piling on more hurt and guilt to the shame Lucy Mae already felt.

June couldn't do that anymore either. So she took out her phone while Adam got behind the wheel and said he was taking them to his house for the night.

She added more to her text to Judge and sent it, every cell in her body now quietly weeping at what she'd just done.

Chapter Thirty-Two

"Knock, knock," Etta said as she opened the back door at the Ranch House. "I come bearing—" She looked down at the bright yellow cereal box in her hands. "Pops." She glanced around the empty kitchen, dining area, and living room. "Judge?"

"Coming," he called, and a couple of seconds later, he came out of the hallway. "I was just in the office." He didn't smile at her, and Etta didn't really expect him to.

"Sammy sent over some cereal," she said, setting down the box on the counter that ran perpendicular to the back door entrance. She looked at Judge, who seemed normal on the outside.

Oh, but Etta knew the storms that could rage inside a person's soul. She could feel them emanating from him in pulsing waves that hit her directly in the chest with every beat of his heart.

Her compassion overflowed, and she rushed at him, taking him into her arms. "I'm so sorry about June."

He'd been at the homestead last night, after driving June to the airport. Her daughter had been in a car accident, and he'd been waiting for news. June had sent the news...well, a small snippet of it.

"Have you heard anything else from her?"

He nodded but didn't release Etta. "She sent me an article that she said is pretty accurate. She's staying there until next Sunday."

So June wouldn't be coming to Thanksgiving dinner at True Blue, something Judge had been so excited about. She wouldn't be there on the first official night of his light show. He'd been serving hot chocolate and crispy rice squares from his porch the night after Thanksgiving for years.

Everyone who could gathered to the field in front of the Ranch House and watched the inaugural show. Etta had seen this year's show three times now, as Judge had asked her for her feedback.

"I'm so sorry, Judge," she said again. The last part of June's text last night had been horrible. Judge had thrown his phone onto the couch in disgust and left the homestead with the words, "This is so stupid. What am I supposed to do now, huh?"

Bear and Sammy had called after him, but Judge needed to rage sometimes, just like everyone else. He did have Glover genes, after all.

"Five years," he'd bellowed as he'd yanked open the

front door. "I've been wasting my life on this woman for *five years!*"

Bear had wanted to go after him, but Sammy had wisely cautioned him to stay put. Ranger and Oakley had come downstairs, and even Blanche Hatch had made an appearance.

Etta had been the one to pick up his phone and read June's text. It was still imprinted in her brain, and she didn't think she'd ever be able to get rid of it.

I made it to LA. Lucy Mae has apparently been discharged and we're picking her up now. It seems like she's fine. I'll know more tomorrow, but we're not in any state to discuss it tonight.

I'm so sorry, Judge, but I can't see you anymore. I should've been there for my daughter, and I wasn't. It's not you, Judge. It's not. I just don't know how to be with you.

Etta had thought about that last line for hours. She'd laid in bed, trying to sleep, thinking about it.

I just don't know how to be with you.

She wondered what it meant. She wanted to call June and ask her, but she absolutely would not get between June and Judge. They had to work things out between them, just like every couple did.

Judge had not returned to the homestead last night, and Etta stepped out of his embrace and withdrew his phone from her pocket. "I brought this."

"I don't want it," he said, eyeing it like she'd brought a live rattler into his house. "I've already been to town and got a new one." He held up the new device. "Cactus took me."

That was code for, *wow, news spreads fast on this ranch*, and all Etta could do was smile sadly at him.

She drew in a deep breath. "Don't tell me you're still fiddling with the stars."

Judge picked up his old phone and held down the power button to turn it off. As he walked over to the trash-can, he said, "I'm thinking of bowing out of the light show this year."

"What?" Etta practically screeched. "You can't, Judge. It's the best show ever, and with the broadcasting, everyone will get to see it."

"I don't want them to see it," he said quietly. That was Judge-code for, *I only care if June sees it.* "Besides, there's something wrong with the drums from *Little Drummer Boy* in *God Bless the USA*. I'm recutting the music."

"So you haven't given up on it."

"I want to," Judge said miserably. "I don't know how. It's just like with June. I want to get over her. I want to move on. I want to cut her loose the way she so easily does for me. I just don't know how."

"I don't think it's easy for her," Etta said, her voice barely more than a murmur. Even as she finished saying it, she realized she shouldn't have. "I'm sorry," she quickly added. "Let's go fix that music, and I'll tell you all about this disastrous date I went on on Friday night."

Judge's eyes actually grew hopeful. "Really?"

"Yes, really," Etta said. "Trust me, you're going to think your love life is the gold standard after this story." She shook her head and grabbed the box of Pops. They didn't look sugar-free, and she needed something to snack on while she talked.

In the office, she sank into the cushy couch and opened the box of cereal. "It starts with him wanting to meet me at The Hole in the Wall. I get it. Shiloh Ridge is a long drive from town. Two hours round trip by the time you do it twice in one evening. So I agree to meet him."

She threw back a handful of cereal while Judge played the drum track from *Little Drummer Boy*. When he silenced it, Etta continued. "First off, he looks fourteen. He tells me he's a urologist, but there's no way. He's *fourteen*."

Judge chuckled, and that only spurred Etta to spill the whole story. "He proceeds to spend the whole evening drinking while telling me all about these horrible surgeries he's done. He used the word *bladder* about fifty times. The Hole doesn't have anything good to eat, and I don't drink, so I sat there sipping Sprite, trying to decide how to interject myself into this long-winded story about some guy's urethra. The *urethra*, Judge. Do you know what that is?"

"I kind of need to use mine right now," he quipped.

Etta laughed. "It's not first-date conversation material, let me tell you."

"Noted," he said. "These are such great tips, Etta. You should do a list for Two Cents."

The idea embedded itself right into her mind, and she seized onto it. "I should," she said. "I'll talk to Ranger about it. Maybe he could push it out as a featured post." She sighed and ate another handful of cereal. "Anyway, after about an hour of this, I tell him I have to go, and he actu ally asked me for a ride home. He was so snockered by then, you know?"

Judge spun around in his seat. 'This is crazy. You don't even like guys that drink. I'm surprised you made it to meeting him in person."

"He's a friend of Joanie's," Etta said. "She vouched for him. I didn't meet him on the app."

"Go on." Judge grinned at her, clearly enjoying this dating mishap. Etta had more where this came from too, because she'd given up the app. Every man on there was legit crazy or a liar, and Etta didn't have time for either of those.

"So I get him home—he can barely tell me where to turn—and as I'm helping him up the sidewalk—he's no lightweight either, let me tell you. At least twice as big as me—the front door opens."

"Oh, boy."

"This woman comes out, and she goes, 'Daniel, where have you been?' She comes marching down the steps, but not to help me get him up them. She lectures him about leaving her just because she wanted to go to some aesthetician school somewhere. All the way up the steps and to the couch. I wasn't about to take him into the bedroom."

"No kidding."

"So he's nearly passed out, and he says, 'Of course we'll be together again, baby,' and that's when I realize she's his ex-girlfriend. But she still had a key to his house. She was waiting there for him. She even kissed him with me standing right there." Etta shuddered with the memory.

"So what did you do?"

"I got out of there," Etta said. "I called my friend on the way home, and she admitted that yes, Daniel had just broken up with his girlfriend, and he—and I quote, *needed someone like me* to help him." She shook her head in disgust. "So now I can't use the app, and I can't trust my friends. I'm going to live in that single-room suite under the stairs in the homestead forever. Alone."

Forever.

Forever alone.

The words reverberated through her head. "Honestly, Judge, I'm tired. I don't want to date anymore. It's exhausting."

"Preach, sister," he said, turning back to the computer. He didn't say anything else, but his presence spoke volumes. She hoped her presence in the office was comforting for him too.

She closed her eyes, the taste of the sugary cereal still in her mouth. She desperately wanted to meet a good, faithful, grounded man. Without the app, and without any setups from her friends, she had very few options left. She worked the ranch outreach programs, but she didn't come in contact with a lot of dating prospects.

What about one of the cowboys who works here? she wondered. None had caught her eye in a while. No one made her sing. No one sparked anything inside her.

She thought of Noah Johnson again, her heart only wailing for a moment. She'd moved past Noah, and she'd been comforted to know that he'd moved past her. With only a twinge of regret still there, Etta knew she was ready to move on. She was ready to meet her Prince Charming.

"Maybe I need to get out more," she said miserably, opening her eyes and staring into the bright sunshine pouring in through the front window.

"You and me both," Judge said. "Let's do it, Etta." He turned back to her, that hope back in his eyes. "It's the Christmas Festival, and there are a ton of activities coming up. There's the Shop for Santa event this weekend. Cactus is always telling me the best place to meet women is in the grocery store. Maybe the same applies for the mall."

"Yeah, *women*," Etta said. "How is that going to help me?"

"There's Stories for Soldiers," he said. "Maybe you could start writing someone overseas and fall madly in love." He grinned at her. "There's the movie in the park. The tree lighting. The apple cider tasting. They do live caroling to the senior centers and preschools. Maybe an amazingly good-looking man will be visiting his mother at the center, and you'll knock his socks off with your high soprano." His face became more animated, and he said, "Wait. The present wrapping event. Single dads go to that, I'm *sure* of it. We could judge the yard decorations this year. You might knock on some hot, single guy's door to tell him he won for most festive display of Rudolph."

They laughed together, but Etta thought his idea had teeth.

"All right, Judge," she said. "I'm in if you're in."

He sobered slightly, a pinch of darkness returning to his gaze. "I have to do something," he said. "I've wasted enough of my life on Juniper Nichols, that's for dang sure."

Etta knew how he felt, because she felt like she'd

wasted enough of her life with such high requirements for a partner that she'd missed some stellar opportunities. Maybe the Lord wouldn't give her another one. Maybe she'd already blown her chance at love, marriage, and happiness.

I hope not, she thought. *Please, Dear Lord, don't let that be true.*

Chapter Thirty-Three

O liver Osburn saddled his horse, his father's eyes never too far from him. He'd been doing this for a decade now, and his dad's attention on him felt like the hottest spotlight in the world shining directly onto Oliver's bare skin.

He cinched the buckles and turned toward his dad. "Ready?"

"If you are," Dad said, and Oliver swung up into the saddle as his answer. He was ready. He'd been coming out to Courage Reins for a couple of years now, maybe longer. He liked to come with Uncle Wyatt and Uncle Jeremiah the most, because they didn't talk. They didn't ask him questions about his girlfriend and his life plans, as if he should have his entire future mapped out at age eighteen.

Ollie was aware of the bitter note in his thoughts, and he pushed against it. He hadn't come here to fight with his dad. He'd come to have an honest conversation with him.

They set out along the trail, one they'd both been on a dozen times before. Because of that, they didn't have a guide with them, and Ollie finally felt the air go into his lungs properly.

"Dad," he said, and the man that had been raising Oliver for the past decade looked at him. Ollie did love this man like a father, though his biological father would not allow Tripp Walker to adopt him legally. He felt more like a Walker than an Osburn, because it meant something to be a Walker.

"What's up, son?" his dad asked.

Ollie took another breath of air, and it still settled into his lungs right. "I've been doing a lot of thinking," he said. "I need your help."

"Okay."

"I don't want you to get upset."

His dad had been upset when Ollie had told him he wasn't going to go to UT-Austin last September. He'd come home about five weeks ago to a very angry mother and father, both of whom had known about the Savannah College of Art and Design when Ollie hadn't told them.

Apparently, they'd had dinner with Aurora's parents, who did admittedly know more. He was going to tell them, he'd said. He was.

"I will do my best not to get upset," his dad said.

"I think I'm in love with Aurora Martin," he said slowly. "I think she loves me. We're going to Savannah together, and it's been...." He cleared his throat, trying to find the words for what he needed help with. "We sneak off to the barn to, uh, be together."

Dad sucked in a breath, but Ollie was committed now. "I want to be intimate with her," he said in a rush. "It's getting harder and harder not to be, and I think once we move to Savannah, it'll be even easier to be alone. I...need help."

To his credit, his father said nothing while the horses plodded along. "Sounds like you better marry her," he finally said without a trace of emotion in his voice.

"I don't want to let you or Mom down," Ollie said, his voice cracking. He'd been trying so hard to hold everything together for so long. "I hate that it feels wrong to be in love with her. People fall in love early, right?"

His father looked over at him, surprise on his face. Oliver very rarely showed emotion, something Aurora had told him he better figure out, because she expected him to tell her how he felt. She expected him to be human, not a robot who did his chores with a yes, sir, no, sir attitude.

"I'm the oldest Walker grandchild, and I feel like I have all this pressure on me to be perfect. Get perfect grades. Go to college and be as smart as your daddy. Get my degree in what you got yours in. And the crazy thing is, I want that too. I love animation and app building, and I think I'm dang good at it."

His dad said nothing, and that only made Oliver keep going. "But I love Rory. I do, Dad. I know it. Your parents got married young, and they had babies right away, and it all worked out."

"It was hard in the beginning," he murmured.

"I know," Oliver said, though he didn't really know. "But Mom's always telling me I can do hard things, and I've seen the two of you do hard things. I think I can do this. I can go to school and have a good career. I can come back here and work the ranch. I can do anything—but only if I have Rory at my side. When I think about my life, she's always there, Dad. Always."

His dad nodded, something thoughtful touching his expression. Oliver calmed, because this yammering on wouldn't do anything. His dad knew how he felt.

"I'm sorry your mother and I have made it seem like it's wrong to love her," he said, the words nearly getting taken by the wind they were so quiet. "It's not wrong to be in love with a good person."

Hope burst through Ollie. "Would you help me?" he asked, his throat so sticky now. "Buy her a ring? Figure out how to ask her to marry me? Would you hate me forever if I married her when I'm only nineteen years old?"

"Of course not," Dad said, and that alone buoyed Ollie in a way he hadn't known he needed. "And you know who we should take along? Gramma. She married Gramps when she was only nineteen."

"I thought she was twenty," Ollie said.

"Somewhere in there." Dad smiled at something far away in his memory. He focused on Ollie again. "I don't have to agree with you to help you," he said. "Every couple has to work out their own relationship. I don't understand falling in love early, but yes, people do it. They have long, successful marriages too. You'll learn and grow with Rory, and the two of you will have to figure out what's most important to you and do those things."

"I'm going to finish school," Oliver said. "I am, Dad."

His dad smiled again, this time with an edge of sadness in his barely upturned lips. "You might," he said. "You might not. The truth is, Ollie, you have no idea what the future holds. My parents had to live with my grandparents for a few years because we were so poor. And are we poor now?"

"Not even close," Ollie said, half-laughing. "But I'm going to make my own way in the world, Dad. I'm not going to rely on you for money."

"But you can," his dad said. "Why can't you? We certainly have enough. And Bishop Glover has more than we do."

"We want to try it on our own," Ollie said firmly.

"So you've talked with Rory about this."

"Yes." They did sneak off to the barns to kiss, but they talked too. They talked about serious things, and they talked about the future. *Their* future together. "We want a family, but it doesn't have to be now. She wants to design clothes. I want to build apps. We have dreams, and we're not going to squander them if we get married. It's not an exclusive situation."

"I understand," Dad said. "Your mom and I just worry. We know what it's like to be single and carefree. It is easier to go to school. It is. We know what it's like to be newly married and struggling. You think you know Rory now, but you'll see a new side of her. She'll get to see all your flaws too, Ollie, and I don't even think you know how to put your cereal bowl in the dishwasher." He grinned at Ollie, who smiled back and shook his head.

He surveyed the land before them, and out here at

Three Rivers Ranch, the air held something special—a spirit that only existed in Texas. "I'm not going to be in Savannah forever," he said. "I love Texas, and I'm going to come back here."

"Again, maybe," Dad said. "Fashion designers don't usually live in Podunk towns in the Texas Panhandle." He gave Ollie another sad smile. "We want the best for you. We want you to spread your wings and fly. We'll miss you, but you know you can always come home to us. Always. You know that, right?"

"I know that," Ollie said.

His father reached over, and Ollie reached out and took his hand. "I love you, son," he said. "And yes, I know a great jeweler if you want to stop on the way back through town. Getting a ring sometimes takes a little time."

Ollie hadn't known that, and it felt like the whole world of things he didn't know loomed before him, jaws snapping. "I'm afraid to move to Savannah without marrying her," he admitted. "It's so hard to be with her and be good right now, and one of her uncles walked in on us a couple of days ago."

"Just kissing, right?"

"Right," Ollie said, but he'd wanted to do more. He respected her though, and he didn't want to let his parents down. He absolutely would not do that. Not again. He'd seen the look on his dad's face when he'd told him he wasn't going to UT-Austin last fall.

"Maybe it can be done over Christmas," Dad said. "They have that big barn up there. Perhaps you should ask Bishop what the schedule looks like before you and Aurora move. If you don't need two apartments in Savannah, that will save some money."

Ollie just nodded, his task list suddenly doubling and then tripling. "Will you help me?" he asked. "Know all that stuff? I didn't even think about the housing in Savannah." He looked at his dad, feeling so raw and so underprepared. "Maybe this is stupid. I can control my hormones."

His dad shook his head. "It's more than hormones, son, and you know it. You love her, and you want to be with her in a beautiful way, the way men and women are *supposed* to want to be with each other when they're in love. It's not dirty, and it's not disgusting. It's normal."

Ollie nodded, because he'd had this talk with his father before.

"We'll help you," he said. "Your mother is an amazing woman, and she'll be able to think of anything we can't ourselves." He swung his horse around. "Now come on. We better cut this riding a little short if we're going to stop and look at diamond rings."

Ollie let his horse go a few more clops, not wanting to leave the tranquility of this ranch. At the same time, his future hung just out of sight, and he was finally reaching for it and pulling it toward him.

He did love Aurora Martin, and he was finally going to do something about it. For her, he could cut anything short, including this therapeutic riding that had helped him so much over the years.

He swung his horse around and headed back too, because for Aurora, Ollie would do *anything*.

Chapter Thirty-Four

J udge mixed in the bag of mini marshmallows, some of the sticky, chocolately, gooey mixture getting on his fingers. He tipped the bowl with the coated Golden Grahams and marshmallows onto a sheet pan and used the back of the rubber spatula to spread and press it down.

Then he licked the chocolate from his fingers, satisfied that this panned version of s'mores would be amazing for Thanksgiving dinner. At the very least, Ward would like it. He'd been out at the fire pit last night, for crying out loud. Only the brief rain had driven him back into Bull House.

Judge smiled to himself, the radio playing in the Ranch House keeping him company this morning. He hadn't been able to get himself to go back into the family stable this week, and Ward and Preacher had been covering for him. Preacher had even brought Pantomime out to Judge every day, and he appreciated the kindness and thought of his brothers and cousins.

He'd mostly kept to himself, though Etta nor Cactus would let him completely fade into nothing at the Ranch House. He supposed he should be thankful for that, as he knew how hard Cactus's journey back into the family had been. He knew how isolated Etta felt.

Today, they were attending the family dinner in True Blue as each other's date. He at least knew he'd have someone to sit beside and talk to, even if it wasn't precisely the woman he wished he could see that day.

He'd never answered June. He had no idea if she'd texted him again. He doubted it. If she had tried to get in touch with him, she hadn't tried that hard. Yes, he'd gotten a new phone, but her ex-husband knew Bear's phone number, so Judge believed June could get any phone number for any of his family members up at Shiloh Ridge.

June didn't normally go back on what she said, though she had left the door open for them to remain friends for the past five years.

This, though? This felt like she'd snatched his heart and then slammed the door in his face.

He slid the tray of indoor s'mores in the fridge and started washing out the bowls and putting the utensils in the dishwasher. He'd given his new phone number to Bear, who'd distributed it to the family. Judge didn't have many friends outside of the ranch, but those he did, he'd messaged through social media and told them his new number.

This way, if his phone chimed—and it was a different

sound than his old phone, praise the Lord—he wasn't jumping as adrenaline shot through him. He knew it wasn't June, because she didn't have his number.

He braced his palms against the counter in front of the sink. "Dear Lord," he prayed right out loud. "Help me to move past her. It's time, isn't it?" He sighed and paused, letting his head droop. "I've clung to her for far too long. I'm not getting any younger. If I want a family at all, I need to find someone—and someone younger than me."

A lot younger than him. He'd be forty-four in six short months, and he knew women couldn't have babies forever. June was seven years younger than him, and perhaps that was why she couldn't figure out how to be a mother and be in a relationship.

"No," he said. "You're not making excuses for her. You're not." She was a grown woman who stood up to teenagers—the scariest beings on the face of the planet. "The truth is, Lord, she doesn't want to be with me. She thinks it costs too much. Takes too much from her." He rolled his neck from side to side, stretching it out. "Help me take a leaf from Etta's book and follow Thy will. Whatever it is, I'll do it."

He fell silent again and then added, "Amen." He stood still and let his thoughts quiet. He listened, trying to hear the guidance from On High. He had the distinct thought to go enjoy his family, so he switched off the radio, whistled for George to get his lazy hound dog bones up off the couch, and he slid the tray of indoor s'mores out of the fridge.

"Come on, Georgie-Boy," he said to the old dog Dot

had leant him for a couple of days. "Let's go see your momma." He grinned down at the hound, who tipped his head back for a scratch. Judge did love dogs, and he was glad to have a friend as he walked the half-mile around the bend and down the road to the homestead.

He kept going past the cemetery to True Blue, which had a dozen cars parked out front. He heard the family before he saw them, as the doors had been thrown open to let in some of today's perfect breeze. The Texas sky shone with pure azure, and Judge took a moment to breathe in the tranquility of the earth itself before he went inside.

A zoo opened up before him, and he grinned at it. Yes, his family was large and loud. They wore their cowboy hats inside this building for weddings and dances, something that would've probably made his dad roll over in his grave. They gave each other strange names. They argued sometimes, and some of them could be really prickly and really grizzly and really withdrawn.

But Judge loved them all so much, and in that moment, he realized the truthfulness of his letter from his father. He did love them, and he hoped he loved the way they needed to be loved.

"Wish you were here, Mister," he whispered as Mitch came running toward him, his hearing dog hot on his heels.

Judge, Judge, Mitch signed. *You have to come see this trick Link can do with Frost.*

"Okay," Judge said as he signed the word to Mitch. He could barely sign, but he understood more than he could say.

The lanky teenager ran off toward the back of the hall,

and Judge smiled at Holly Ann, handing her the pan of treats. "Could you take these to Bishop? I'm apparently needed back here."

"Sure thing," she said, taking the tray though she bounced her sister's baby in her arms. Bethany Rose and Doug came to all the family events here at the ranch. Holly Ann usually brought her father too, and Judge wasn't surprised to see the man talking to Bear and Preacher.

Montana brought her aunt and uncle to everything, and they both sat with her and Zona, the two of them holding their babies on their laps and listening to something Bob said. The group broke into laughter as Judge passed, and his heart warmed.

Montana looked past him to the doorway, quickly getting to her feet. He turned to see who'd arrived, and a tickle of shock moved through him when he saw Oliver Osburn there, with both of his parents and his little brother. Behind them came the older generation of Walkers—Penny and Gideon, Ollie's grandparents. Seeing Ollie wasn't new, but the whole family *was* a bit different.

Montana gave Robbie to her aunt and went to greet the Walkers, their arrival drawing the attention of more than one person. Mitch gestured to him from the back of the hall, and Judge decided he'd learn what was happening when everyone else did.

He went around the corner, where Mitch's pretty cocker spaniel sat next to Link's feet. "What's goin' on back here, boys?" He looked at Mitch as he spoke, and then smiled at Link.

"I taught Frost a new trick," Link said, using his hands

and his voice. "Watch." He whistled a low tone, and Frost looked at him. "Down," he commanded.

The cream-colored dog went right down onto his belly. "Forward," Link said, and he took a step back while Frost shimmied forward on his stomach. Link used the fingers on his hand to wave the dog forward, and as he stepped back again, he didn't speak.

The dog still moved, and then Link said, "Hug," and Frost barked, leapt up, and put his front paws on Link's thighs. Link grinned at him and grabbed onto Frost, hugging him. "Good boy," he said. "You're such a great dog."

"Mitch," Willa called behind them, and Frost got down and got back to work. Judge turned toward Willa as the hearing dog went to Mitch and sat in front of him. He barked and put his paw on Mitch's leg.

Then he trotted down the hall toward Willa, and Mitch turned and saw his mother. He started talking to her in a flurry of signs that Judge couldn't read.

"No," she said back to him with a frown. "I don't want you two back here training that dog. Come sit down with Grandma Lois. She misses you and wants to hear about your science experiment."

Her son continued past her, but Judge got the feeling he wasn't very happy. Judge looked back at Link. "Are you in trouble?"

"Yes, sir," he said miserably as Willa called for him too.

"It was a great trick," Judge whispered as the boy went by, and Link's head came up as he grinned.

"Sweetheart, I love you to death," Willa said, putting

her arm around Link's shoulders as he arrived in front of her. They went out into the hall together, her talking to him in a quiet, loving voice. Judge took a moment to thank God that he had examples to look to for how to deal with teenagers, though he didn't have any of his own and wouldn't for a long, long time.

Judge moved to the back corner of the hallway and paused, taking in the activity in front of him. Low music played, and people chatted in small clumps. Some sat at tables, and some stood in clusters.

His phone rang, a strange chime Judge hadn't heard on this device yet. Mister's name sat on the screen, and he was calling via video chat. Judge grinned and tapped on the call. "Mister, howdy."

"Howdy, brother," Mister said easily. He'd come for a short visit last weekend, but he hadn't been able to get the holidays off. He'd be back for a week at Christmas, and Judge found himself looking forward to that.

"Where is everyone?"

"Out in the hall," Judge said. "I'll turn you around. Just a sec." He tapped the button that flipped the camera, and a view of the hall came up on the screen. "We haven't started yet."

"Is Bishop in the kitchen?"

"Yep." Judge didn't attempt to move, though he caught sight of Etta looking for him. "What are you doing today?"

"Brock is actually pretty good in the kitchen," Mister said. "He's making the turkey and mashed potatoes. I made Mother's pecan pie last night. Matty is making a pumpkin pie right now, and we're going to have corn as our vegetable."

"Shocking," Judge said dryly. Mister had said he ate corn for every meal. At Winterhaven, they made corn into puddings, pies, breads, and pancakes. They had corn milk and corn on the cob and corn salads and corn dips.

"Right?" Mister chuckled. "But Sheila—the boss's wife —she made this corn and bacon dip that lit me all up toward corn again, so it's not so bad. We all got a big bowl of it for our Thanksgiving Day meals."

"Sounds good," Judge said, because anything with bacon was delicious. "Oh, Bishop is plugging in the microphone." He turned the phone so Mister could see.

"This must be the thing he told me he wanted me to watch," Mister said.

"He did?" Judge asked.

"Yeah, he said to call you just before two, for the family announcements."

Judge hadn't even known they were having family announcements just before dinner. He said nothing, because it didn't really matter. In the past, not knowing everything would've ruffled his feathers and left a bad taste in his mouth. Now, he didn't care. Whatever. If it didn't concern him, why did it matter?

His chest pinched, because it surely did matter. He was part of the family, and he felt left out, which was stupid. So many people had been so good to him this week, and he'd felt loved and accepted.

Bear had not let him get too far from the homestead after June's text, and he'd found Judge hanging out in the equipment shed, a wrench in his hand while he twirled it around. He wasn't mechanically inclined, but he hadn't wanted to be outside for some reason.

Bear had never abandoned him, and his oldest brother had come by the Ranch House every night that week. He'd sent out Judge's new number. He'd made sure everyone knew about the family gathering at the Ranch House tomorrow night for the light show.

Nine o'clock, Judge thought. He wasn't going to broadcast it the way he and June had set up. He was still deciding if he'd do the show for more than his family at all.

"Light show tomorrow, right?" Mister asked. "Should I call Ward?"

"Yeah, call Ward," Judge said. "I'll be crazy with it."

"Okay," Mister said at the same time Bishop did. He glanced toward Judge, who lifted his phone slightly to let him know Mister was on the line.

"Welcome to our Thanksgiving feast," Bishop said. "Holly Ann, Ida, Etta, and I have been laboring for days over this. If you don't like it, don't eat it, but don't say anything either." He grinned out at the crowd, but it didn't hold its usual wattage. The smile slipped off his face almost instantly, and Judge tensed.

"Something's up," he whispered.

"Seems like it," Mister said back, equally as quietly.

"We have a few announcements," Bishop said. "Each person is going to make their own, so I'll give the mic to Preacher."

Preacher stood from a table very nearby and took the few steps toward Bishop. He took the mic and drew in a breath. "Short and to the point, Charlie and I are expecting a baby in May."

"I knew that," Mister said, obviously proud of himself. "He called me a week or two ago."

"That's great," Judge said as the crowd clapped and cheered. Preacher's ears grew bright red, and he practically threw the microphone back to Bishop. Bear took it next and said, "Stetson's official nickname is Smiles, so you can call him either thing."

Judge tried to find the happy two-year-old, but he couldn't see him right that moment. A swell rose in the chatter, and he finally found Sammy grinning at her little boy. Nearby, Dot held Russell, and Sammy and Bear would have another child come summer.

Judge felt so left behind, and there was no way Bear could come back and get him this time. He didn't expect him to, and Mister hissed, drawing Judge's attention back to the microphone.

"Is that Ollie?" he asked.

"Yes," Judge said slowly as Oliver Osburn took the microphone from Bear. He cleared his throat, and his normally tan skin was so pale he looked like a sheet of copy paper. "He's going to throw up."

"What's goin' on?" Mister asked. "I can't see."

"You're seein' what I'm seein'," Judge hissed at him, his heart pounding, pounding, pounding through his whole body.

"Rory, will you come up here?" he asked, and Aurora got to her feet.

"She looks like she's going to be sick too," Mister said.

"Is he going to propose?" Judge whispered, noting how Oliver had kept his right hand in his pants pocket. "I think he's going to propose."

"Well, I feel like a real loser," Mister muttered.

"Join the club," Judge said back, his eyebrows drawing down as Aurora reached Ollie and looped her arm through his.

"I love you," Ollie said into the mic, his focus singular on Aurora now. "Whenever I picture what my future looks like, you're right there inside it. You've been such a support to me already, and I'd like to think I'm a support to you. I don't want to go to Savannah with different last names. Will you marry me?"

He handed the mic back to Bishop, who did not look happy, and dropped to both knees. Sure enough, his right hand came out of his pocket then, a glinting diamond ring throwing light around the barn.

Aurora wore nothing but pure delight on her face. She nodded enthusiastically and then bounced on the balls of her feet as she said, "Yes!"

"My goodness," Judge said, completely stunned. He'd known Oliver and Aurora liked each other. He'd known they were going to Savannah to college together. He had not anticipated this. "No wonder his parents are here," he whispered as more cheering and clapping started. "And no wonder Montana looks like she's been crying for a few days."

"Does she?" Mister asked. "I hate that."

"They're so very young," Judge said, his voice trailing off as Ollie slid the diamond ring on Aurora's finger and cradled her face in his hands to kiss her. They certainly looked old then, and definitely old enough to get married and start a family.

Penny Walker got up and took the mic from Bishop, smiling fondly at her grandson and Aurora. "Gideon and I are so glad to be here with your family today," she said as the cheering quieted down. Judge didn't look at her or the newly engaged couple.

No, he searched the crowd for Etta, who wore a horrified look on her face. In truth, a lot of people looked like they'd been hit with a bolt of lightning. Tripp and Ivory Walker didn't, and neither did Bishop or Montana. So they'd known this was coming.

"I'm thrilled for Ollie and Rory, naturally. Gideon and I got married very young, so it can work out with a lot of dedication and hard work." She wore a stern look as she glanced at the two barely-adults again. "We all believe in you two."

Ollie stepped over and kissed his grandmother's cheek, but Penny didn't relinquish the mic to him. "I know it'll be a surprise to a lot of you," Penny said. "But Ollie and Rory are going to get married right here in this hall, in only thirty days from now."

Someone could've dropped a pin and everyone in the world could've heard it in the resulting silence.

"That's Christmas Eve," someone said, to which Penny nodded.

"That's right," she said. "Christmas Eve. Mark your calendars, because Ollie and Rory are moving to Savannah the day after Christmas, and they wanted to get this done as a way to start their new adventure together."

She gave the mic back to Bishop, who looked at it like it might turn into a snake. He looked out at everyone. "Duke is going to pray for us. Then we'll eat."

"Holy cow," Mister said as Duke got to his feet. "Holy *cow*, Judge."

"I know," Judge said, taking his first steps back into the hall. "Shush. Duke's praying."

He waited through the prayer, but a restless energy filled the whole barn. Once the last *amen* had been said, he looked at Mister still on the screen. "Do you want to stay on video? I'm going to go say congratulations."

"Yes," Mister said. "I'd like to as well."

"Okay," Judge said, trying very hard to live up to his name in that walk across part of the hall to Oliver and Aurora, who had already been mobbed by aunts and uncles. "Here goes nothing."

Chapter Thirty-Five

June pushed the creamed peas around on her plate, though they were one of her favorite foods. Everything since Sunday night had tasted so bland. She'd barely eaten anything, and she'd told herself it was because Adam didn't have anything in his house.

Then Cypress had come with her minivan and bags of snacks in the car, and still nothing tasted right. She'd been staying with her sister and her sister's family since Monday, and June was glad she could spend the holidays with her family.

She *was*.

The cloud of gloom that hung over her had everything to do with Judge Glover.

"Mom," Lucy Mae said, and June jerked her head up. "I told you she wasn't listening."

"I'm listening," June said, lifting a forkful of peas to her mouth.

"Really?" Lucy Mae folded her arms and leaned back. "Because I just said I was packing up everything I own and moving to one of the rings of Saturn, and you didn't even blink."

"She's right," Cypress said, and that annoyed June. Everything her sister had been doing and saying for the past few days had irritated her. June knew she wasn't really upset with her sister; she hated herself.

She hated the text she'd sent Judge on Sunday evening. She hated that he hadn't responded. He hadn't called. He hadn't argued. He'd just...disappeared. It wasn't like him at all.

"She said that, and you didn't even hear her."

"I'm just thinking about something," June said, swallowing the bland peas. She absolutely couldn't take another bite of those.

"Yeah, Judge Glover," Lucy Mae singsonged, a playful smile on her face.

June couldn't hold back the tide of tears, and a sob wrenched its way out of her throat. Lucy Mae's face changed in less than a second, and Cypress actually stood up and said, "Oh, my goodness. Is she choking?"

She was choking, but not on the dry turkey her brother-in-law had served her. She sucked at the air and couldn't find it.

"Momma," Lucy Mae said, putting her arm around June's shoulders. But she wasn't in the mood for comfort from her daughter. "What's going on?"

June shook her head and got to her feet. She couldn't breathe, and she couldn't think. She left her phone on the table and pointed to it. Then she ran out of the house and across the sunny patio in Cypress's back yard.

Instead of going straight back to the pool, June went left and ducked around the corner of the house. She pressed her back into the stucco and pulled in breath after breath. "How could he not have called?" she asked.

And more importantly, how could she even expect him to? She'd done something terrible to him. Absolutely terrible, and there was no way to undo it. How could she have done that to him? Had she really made such a terrible decision in that one awful moment?

For the first twenty-four hours, June had actually dared to hope Judge had gotten on a plane bound for California. She had no right to even think such a thing, and as she cried in the shade on the side of her sister's house, she knew she needed to set things right.

Maybe she could call him.

"He won't answer, will he?" she asked, tipping her head toward heaven. "Why have I done this? Why can't I figure out who I am?"

The clouds shifted above in the Santa Ana winds, and June watched the shapes in the sky and the shadows on the ground move. She wished she could drift just as easily as they did, find a new place to settle, and finally achieve the happiness she desired.

No, that wasn't what she wanted. She wanted to know how to be Juniper Nichols. That was all. Just Juniper Nichols.

Not Lucy Mae's mom. Not Judge Glover's girlfriend.

Not smart, savvy business owner. Not chocolate lover. Not genius with networks and LANs and servers.

Just Juniper Nichols.

And what would Juniper Nichols do in this situation?

The question entered her mind and burrowed in. When she'd been faced with a positive pregnancy test and no diamond ring on her finger, she'd gone straight to Adam to find out what they should do.

When Adam had walked out on her and Lucy Mae, she'd gone home to her parents to find out what she should do.

When she'd finished her program with cybersecurity and networking systems, she'd studied the market and found an underserved area in Texas. She'd packed up her daughter and moved a thousand miles to Three Rivers.

She'd rented a building and hired employees. She'd gotten a small business loan she'd since paid off.

She'd worked, and she'd worked hard.

"June?" Cypress called, and June pressed one hand over her mouth to silence her weeping. She didn't want to deal with her perfect older sister, with her humongous California home, her doting husband, and her two adorable children.

Cypress had always had everything together, while June's life had been unraveling one string at a time for years.

"Mom," Lucy Mae called. "I know you're out here, because you weren't wearing shoes!" She sounded angry, and June wondered what *she* could possibly have to be angry about. When June had tried to question her about the possible drug use and who these friends were that she'd been in a car with, Lucy Mae had shut her right down.

She was no Oliver Osburn with the *yes, ma'am, no, ma'am*, that was for sure. Lucy Mae had never held back when it came to June, and they'd yelled at each other several times as Lucy Mae grew into her own person.

Just another thing for June to feel guilty about. Yelling at her own daughter. Who did that, for crying out loud?

She'd put off Judge so many times. She'd asked Ida—a mom to twins with a husband who worked all the time—to take her two dogs so she could come here for the week.

"Mom!" Lucy Mae shouted. "You broke up with Judge for no reason! Why did you do that?" Her footsteps came closer, and June couldn't get away fast enough. She wasn't going to run again anyway.

She looked up at her daughter's angry face and wiped her tears away. Lucy Mae held up June's phone. "You broke up with him, which makes no sense. You're in love with him."

"So what if I am?" June snapped back. "I don't deserve a man like him anyway, and I don't know how to be with him when you need me."

"I don't need you."

"Yes, you do!" June yelled. "You were in a car with a driver who was high. High, Lucy Mae! You had to have known! Why would you put yourself in danger like that? That man died, Lucy Mae. He *died*. There's no redo from that. There's no restart. You can't go back in time and fix that."

Lucy Mae pressed her teeth together, her jaw bouncing hard with the pressure. "I didn't know."

June took a step closer to her daughter, so angry with her in that moment. "I'm not going to let us sweep things under the rug. Not us, Lucy Mae." She gestured wildly toward the house, though it wasn't the one where she'd grown up. "My parents did that my whole life. We *never* talked about anything important. Was it any wonder I ended up unmarried and pregnant at the age of eighteen? Even then, it was *hurry-up-and-get-married-so-the-neighbors-won't-know.*"

She drew in a shuddering breath. "Well, I don't care if the neighbors know. Maybe we can lean on them in hard times. They'll take Picasso and Remmy for us. They'll bring over food we don't have to make. We don't have to suffer behind closed doors."

"I didn't know," Lucy Mae said, the words a growl. "Because I'd been smoking that night too, Mom."

"I know that!" June said. "You think I don't know that? You were high too. It's the only way my extremely talented, smart, put-together daughter would get into a car with someone who had no business behind the wheel. Do you know that if he'd killed someone else, and he'd lived, he could've been charged with manslaughter? You go to prison for that, Lucy Mae. *Prison!*" She gestured wildly again.

Now that she'd shouted her feelings at her daughter, her chest began to expand properly again. "So yes, I broke up with Judge. I feel like everything is my fault. If I had been more available, you would've talked to me about pot, and I could've helped you understand the dangers of it. If I hadn't been so busy with my company and my boyfriend, I would've had the bandwidth to ask you who your friends were. Who you were hanging out with here in California. I would've had time to text Cypress to find out if you'd come here on the weekends. Something. Anything. I didn't do any of those things, because I'd rather spend time with my cowboy boyfriend and his amazing family."

Her chest heaved, and June couldn't help thinking she was simply digging a deeper hole for herself. Maybe she'd just bury herself down there and call it good. This was as good as she could do.

"Mom," Lucy Mae said. "You've dedicated your whole life to me. Don't think for a single second that I don't know how many times you've been asked out. I know, Mom. I haven't been a child for a long time."

June sighed and pushed her hand through her hair. She didn't care about that. She honestly didn't.

"Mom, you're different," Lucy Mae said. "Ever since you went out with Judge the first time, years ago. I could tell then how much you liked him, and he's literally been the most patient man on the planet."

"I can't," June said. "I feel too guilty."

"Stop it then," Lucy Mae said, handing her phone back to her.

"I feel guilty about you when I'm with him, and I feel guilty about him with everything else I do. He must be so angry."

"I'm sure he is," Lucy Mae said. "How are you going to fix it?"

"I can't fix it," June said.

"Call him."

June looked at her phone, a seedling of hope in her heart. She tapped and saw that she had called Judge fifteen minutes ago. She whipped her attention back to Lucy Mae. "You called him."

"I did." Lucy Mae reached up and wiped her eyes. "I can't stand watching you do this self-destruct thing you do with him. You've been so happy with him since you started dating him again, and I will literally never talk to you again if you don't fix things with him."

She turned and stalked away, leaving June to stare after her. "What did he say?" she called after Lucy Mae, but her daughter just went up the steps to the deck and then inside the house.

June took a deep breath and prayed Judge would hear his phone ringing. He was probably at the homestead or that beautiful barn where they held family parties for lunch.

Then she remembered that Texas sat two hours ahead of California, and lunch was probably over by now.

She tapped to call him, and the line rang once and picked up. Her heart shot to the back of her throat, and then plummeted to her feet when she got the chiming noises that indicated his number had been disconnected.

When the cool female voice confirmed it, June burst into tears again.

This time, she wasn't going to run away. This time, she marched back to the house and burst in through the sliding glass door. "His number is disconnected. I need help getting him back. Who has an idea?"

Lucy Mae looked up from her plate, a bright beam in her eye. "Momma, come sit down. Cypress was telling me something interesting."

June did, looking wildly from her mother to Cypress and then to Lucy Mae. "What?" she asked.

"Lucy Mae was telling me a little about Judge," Cypress said slowly, that voice grating against June's nerves. She swallowed her irritation and listened. She needed to get rid of some of her less desirable qualities if she wanted to be good enough for Judge Glover.

"And she says he's got a Christmas light show debuting online tomorrow night?"

June's pulse pivoted throughout her body. "Yes."

"And I don't know," Cypress said, pinching off a piece of her roll. "Someone I know is a literal genius with networks and servers. She can get inside anything and do all kinds of things most people don't understand."

"With only two clicks," Lucy Mae said.

June looked at her daughter again. "I can't mess up his show." That would only drive him further from her, not bring them closer together.

"No, of course not," Lucy Mae said.

"Don't you know how to send messages?" Cypress said. "Even to encrypted...lines?"

"I can usually get in through the backend server, yes," June said, waving her hand. "But that has nothing to do with the light show. That's the—" She froze, her brain finally catching up with her mouth. "That's the program Judge will see."

"There it is," Lucy Mae said. "See, mom? You don't

need the man's number. You can get into his server from any computer and send him a message."

June's stomach quivered. "What if he won't take me back?"

"He will," Lucy Mae said.

"How do you know?"

"Because he loves you," Lucy Mae and Cypress said together. Even her mother nodded, and she'd barely met Judge.

"If what Lucy Mae tells us is true," her mom said. "He'll take you back. You just have to be really, really apologetic and sincerely sorry."

"I am sincerely sorry," June said. She still wasn't quite sure who she was, but she knew she didn't need a label anymore. When June wanted to do something, she needed to dig in and figure out how to do it. Ask a lot of questions. Make mistakes, sure, but be brave enough to fix them.

Can I fix this? she prayed to know.

You're Juniper Nichols, she thought. *You can fix anything with a WiFi connection.* She drew a deep breath and hoped that Judge's heart was as wired in as his light show.

Chapter Thirty-Six

Judge clapped his hands on Ward's back as he hugged his cousin. "Thanks for coming, Ward."

"Of course," Ward said, embracing him back. "I wouldn't miss this for anything." He pulled away with a smile on his face. "Dot hasn't seen the show."

"Well, tell her it's the best you've ever seen." Judge chuckled, even though Ward had told him last week that this show was, indeed the best show he'd ever seen.

"I'm so excited," Dot bubbled as she approached. "I got the tables set up, Judge. Are we taking the treats out there?" She glanced at the trays of tasty snacks Judge had balanced on the porch railing.

"Are they cut?" Ward asked, reaching for the corner of a tray of Rice Krispy treats.

"Yes," Judge said. "And yes, Dot, we'll get them out there before the one with the hollow leg here eats them all."

"Hey, this is my first one," Ward said, and Judge simply cocked his eyebrows at him. "Fine," Ward amended. "The second."

"Third," Judge said. "I brought you one in the barn this morning."

"That was literally twelve hours ago," Ward said with a scoff. "That doesn't count." He picked up a stack of two trays and looked at his wife. "Do you need to get some insulin?"

"I already checked," Dot said, taking the two sheet pans of indoor s'mores Judge had made only a few minutes ago. They'd been such a big hit at Thanksgiving Day dinner, that several people had asked him if he'd have them at tonight's show.

He normally made Rice Krispy treats, because they only took three ingredients, and he could make huge batches of them in only a few minutes. With the enlarged family, Judge had made double the number of treats he normally did, and when he reached the clearing across the street from the Ranch House with a couple of trays of treats, he found the tables swamped with people already, many hands reaching for a square of cereal and marshmallow.

He slid his trays onto the table and backed up, enjoying the energy all these people brought to this curve of the ranch. He was used to the view of Three Rivers that sat right outside his front door, but some people didn't come over here all that often.

They took their treats and faced the town as the light in the sky continued to fade into darkness.

"This is so exciting," Sammy said as she stepped to his side. He reached for Russell, who grinned at Judge and said, "Ja, ja, ja."

"That's right," Judge said. "It's your favorite uncle, Uncle Judge." He met Sammy's eyes. "Thanks for coming. He can have a treat?"

"A little bit," Sammy said, smiling at her son. "He ate a lot for dinner, and he doesn't know when to stop. He'll eat until he pukes."

"Oh, I don't believe that," Judge said in a cutesy voice. "You don't do that, do you, bud?" Russell did, however, as Judge had witnessed it first-hand. He picked up a small square of the indoor s'mores and pinched off a square of cereal. Russell took it and put it in his mouth, his eyes getting bigger with all the sugar, chocolate, and cinnamon.

"Yeah, it's good, huh?" Judge laughed at the little boy. "Are you hoping for a girl this time?" he asked Sammy.

"Yes," she said without hesitation. "If I have another boy, I might burst into tears right there in the delivery room, and then that's it. Bear's not getting any more kids."

"What about the kids?" Bear asked, arriving on the scene. "Sorry I'm late, love. We got everyone out of that cabin and settled somewhere else."

"Are they coming here?" Judge asked, twisting to look past the Ranch House.

"Yep." Bear took his son from Judge. "Look at you, my sweet baby. Momma's got you all dressed up in your warm clothes."

"Dad, dad, dad," Russell babbled. He groaned and reached toward Judge, who handed him another single cereal square. He leaned back into his father and stuck the treat in his mouth.

"Of course," Bear said dryly. "This one only wants what makes his belly happy."

"I think it's his mouth," Judge said, giving Russell another bit of cereal.

"That's it, son," Bear said. "If I'm going to hold you tonight, you can't throw up on me." He turned away from Judge and headed for a seat, again warning his son not to throw up that night. Sammy patted Judge's arm and followed her husband. They took a couple of seats on the front row of chairs that Ward and Dot had helped Judge set up, right next to Preacher and Charlie, who held Stetson on her lap.

She held a book in front of him, but it had to be too dark for the child to see much. Judge turned and faced the house so he didn't have to look at the crowd. To his trained eye, he could see the outline of all the stars. He knew exactly which one would light up first, and he decided he better go check the speakers he'd put on the porch and corners of the house.

Normally, people would listen to the songs on the radio in their cars, tuned to a specific station. For the online distribution, Judge and June had figured out a way for people to turn their Internet to the right radio station, and all they had to do was download an extension.

It was an extra step Judge wasn't sure people would do —like driving up to Shiloh Ridge prevented him from getting the same number of views as others in the light show. But if they did, the music would come through their computer speakers just like it did in their cars.

Tonight, though, Judge needed the music to reach a hundred ears, and he went over to the speaker on the far corner of the house to check it. The blue light blazed on the back of it, and Judge could practically hear the crackling energy coming from it.

More voices reached his ears, and at least half a dozen people came from the back of the house and crossed toward the clearing. All the cowboys who worked the ranch and lived in their cabins had arrived.

For some reason, Judge's stomach swooped. He knew June wouldn't be coming. He was strong, but he wasn't made of iron, and he'd checked her Facebook page that morning. She'd posted a picture of herself, Lucy Mae, Cypress, and her mother, all of them grinning and wearing sunglasses. The caption had read, *Shopping in sunny CA the day after Thanksgiving.*

She'd looked so happy, and Judge wanted that for her, so he'd simply navigated away from her social media without doing anything.

Unless she'd gotten on a plane right after posting that, she wasn't in Texas tonight. He wondered if she'd try to watch the light show online. Even if she did, she wouldn't be able to see it, as Judge had decided he wasn't going to broadcast the show tonight.

Tonight was all about family. The residents of Three Rivers would get a push through the city email system tomorrow about the Christmas light displays, and Judge had decided to keep his name and location on the list.

He'd asked Steve Chelsea to list his as being online, and he'd done an interview with the director of the Christmas Festival a couple of days ago. He hoped he hadn't sounded like a fool, and he hoped everyone in Three Rivers would take less than eight minutes to tune into his show.

They didn't even have to waste any gas. Judge wondered how long it would be before everyone put their light shows online, and he hoped he hadn't caused any extra work for June.

He switched off the flashlight in his hand and headed back across the street. If the speakers didn't work, oh well. He wasn't going to obsess over this. He'd tested them before he'd gone to work on the ranch, and that was that.

He approached Ward in the second row, who'd saved him a seat. He sighed as he sat down, and Ward reached over and patted his leg. "It's going to be great."

"It's going to be whatever it will be," Judge said. "I don't think I'll do the show again after this year."

"No?" Ward tucked his hands into his jacket pockets. "Why not?"

"I'm tired," Judge said, and it summed up so much of his life. He was tired of the same day-to-day rigor of working the ranch. He was tired of thinking about June. He was tired of trying to riddle out where he'd gone wrong.

He was just tired.

An alarm on his phone went off, and Judge stood up. "All right," he called in a loud voice. He could be loud if he had to be; all the Glovers could be. "It's going to start in sixty seconds. It's on a timer. Thanks so much for coming tonight, and please, drink as much hot chocolate and eat as many treats as you want."

If they didn't, he'd be stuck with all of it in the Ranch House. He wasn't a diabetic, and he did love cereal, so he supposed that wouldn't be the worst thing ever.

He sat back down, and the buzz in the air increased with every second until the first note of the show. Then a swell of "ooh" went up into the air. Judge smiled and settled back into his seat.

He was really proud of this show, and he was going to enjoy it for the first time without taking a single note.

THE NEXT DAY, JUDGE TOOK HIS COFFEE INTO THE office to check on a few things before he went out onto the ranch. He was going to go into the family stables this morning, even if it made his heart boom in a strange way.

He just needed to check his email and see if the town had sent out the announcement that the light display shows were now up and running. They usually included the link to vote, and Judge wanted to check and see how many hits he'd gotten on the website to view his show.

It wouldn't be showing, of course, as the light shows didn't run until darkness fell. Judge had his timed to start at six o'clock and run until eleven, and he'd very clearly put that on the website where the show would be broadcast.

He clicked on the mouse and jiggled it to get the computer to wake. It did, but the program that Judge kept up and running for months out of the year—the software he used to program his show—was blank.

Nearly spilling his coffee as he tried to set it on the desk without looking, Judge sucked in a breath. He steadied his coffee and moved it far from the keyboard and other essential elements of the computer and gripped the mouse in earnest.

Something flashed on the screen, and Judge could only stare as words came up, seemingly being typed right in front of his face.

I knew I'd have to get up early to catch you, the words said. *I didn't see your show online last night.*

Judge wasn't sure what to do. He didn't know who was talking to him. The only thing he knew—he needed to get his show back online before he went to shovel out horse stalls.

"I didn't broadcast the show online last night," he said out loud as he typed. He did everything with only six fingers—his first two fingers and his thumb on both hands —and he wasn't nearly as fast as whoever had messaged him. "It was for family only."

I wish I could've been there. I put together a little show for you right now.

He leaned back in his chair as the words disappeared from the screen. A digital version of his show started on his screen, and he suddenly knew who could do this.

"June," he whispered. He'd seen his own show many times, but not this pixelated, computer-generated version of it, and he smiled at the perfect synchronization of the lights and the music. The show was over seven minutes long, and he wondered if he'd have to sit through the whole thing.

That question got answered quickly, as when the first song finished, the show deviated away from what he'd created.

The stars on the screen now lit up in the shape of words, spelling out the words, *I'm so sorry, Judge. I had a terrible moment on Sunday, where I thought I couldn't be with you and be Lucy Mae's mother. But I know I can be, if you'll just give me another chance.*

They flashed in red, then blue, then white, where they stayed while he read them again.

They faded, and the words *I love you. Please forgive me,* came up onto the screen.

Judge had never felt love and forgiveness as strongly as he had in that moment, and those emotions choked him in the back of his throat. He wanted to hear her voice, but he'd gotten rid of his other phone, something June obviously knew.

The most beautiful words in the world—*I love you*—disappeared, and June started typing again. *Your number is disconnected. If you give me your number, I'll call you. If you don't want to talk to me, well, that's it. You don't have to give me your number.*

Judge lunged forward to get his phone off the desk, as his number was new, and he wasn't sure he had it memorized. His fingers shook, and he cleared his throat, knowing he was going to have to talk to June in a matter of seconds.

He quickly typed out his new number and exploded to

his feet. He couldn't be sitting when June called. He wasn't even sure his voice was going to work. He paced away from the desk, only spinning back to it when his new phone rang.

He jogged over to the desk and picked it up. A number with a Texas area code sat there, and he swiped on the call. "June?"

"Judge," she said, her voice so wonderful and so clear over the line. She sniffled, and he wished she stood in front of him and he could kiss the tears from her eyelashes. "I'm sorry. I love you."

"I love you too," he blurted out, his heart beating so fast. "Where are you? Still in California?"

"Yes," she said, her voice so nasally. "I can't believe this. You're too good for me."

"Don't be ridiculous."

"You never responded to my text on Sunday."

"I sort of freaked out," Judge said, remembering how he'd chucked his phone and stormed out of the house.

"Do you think I've been leading you on?"

"No," he said softly, stepping over to the window. The stars looked so different in the sunshine. "I don't think you've been leading me on, June. I think you've been trying to figure out who you are without Lucy Mae."

"She's going to be the death of me," June whispered.

"I hope not before we get married," Judge said.

She said nothing, and Judge started to chuckle. "You do want to marry me, right June-Bug?"

"Yes," she said.

"And you want more kids, right?" He refrained from

saying they'd give her purpose for her life. She didn't need children to have purpose.

"Yes."

"I love you," he said. "Maybe I'll jump on a plane tonight."

"I just can't believe it," she said. "You're so forgiving."

"June," he said slowly, facing the house again. "I know who you are. I know what you've been struggling with since Lucy Mae graduated."

"So you've been expecting me to freak out in a bad moment."

Judge shook his head, hating that this conversation was happening long-distance. "No, I've not been waiting for you to have a bad moment, June. I understand why you did though. You were put in a very stressful situation, with a person who is the most important to you in the whole world. It just...threw you for a loop."

"Lucy Mae is not more important to me than you are."

"Oh, come on now, June-Bug. I thought we weren't going to say things we didn't mean."

Chapter Thirty-Seven

J une didn't hesitate for single moment before she said, "We did agree to that. I haven't said anything I don't mean."

Judge started to chuckle, and the next thing he said was as good as the words *I love you.*

"I wish you were here," he said.

Okay, *almost* as good.

She made another turn in the guest bedroom, the walls caging her about to be busted wide open, She couldn't wait to run down the hall to the kitchen and tell Cypress and Lucy Mae that she'd succeeded in getting Judge's new phone number.

Of course, they wouldn't be awake for another four hours, as it was just past four in the morning in California. She'd actually set an alarm for three a.m., and she'd drunk two cups of coffee while she waited for Judge to sit down in front of his computer.

"I wish I was there too," she said. "I'm so very sorry, John."

"Oh, don't start using my real name," he said in that Texas drawl that lit her up like nothing else. He really did possess the kindest heart and the most forgiving soul. He saw her in a way no one else did, and she hoped he always would.

"Would you...help me?" she asked. "Help me to be rational about things? I have to figure out how to...."

"Be yourself," Judge supplied. "June, that's all you need to be."

"I have figured out that much," she said. "What I haven't been able to figure out is who that is for each person in my life."

"How about you let me do that?" he asked. "At least for us."

June frowned, reached the window, and turned again. "What do you mean?"

"I mean, I have a perception of you, right? For example, you're the most beautiful woman in the world. You have a loving, kind heart. You know how to talk to teenagers, which I'm going to be honest, scare me to death. You know more about an Internet cable than anyone I know, and you make the very best lasagna on the planet."

June's heart warmed with each word that came out of his mouth. She smiled and shook her head. "That lasagna was frozen, out of a box."

"You're an excellent mother," he said as if she hadn't spoken at all. "A good friend. A kind boss. You make me feel like more of a man when I'm with you, and you have the kind of faith that can move mountains."

"That is not true," she whispered. "If I had faith, Judge, I wouldn't have freaked out on Sunday night."

"Tell me more about Sunday night," Judge said.

She didn't really want to, but she started with the words, "First off, dealing with Adam is very hard for me. So he stresses me out the moment I hear his voice." She sank onto the bed, which was actually too soft for her, and continued the story.

Several minutes later, she finished with, "And I was spinning. I couldn't stop thinking about how it could've been Lucy Mae who'd died in that car accident. I couldn't even remember the last thing I'd said to her, and I hated that I hadn't been talking to her every day. In my strange, malfunctioning mind, I seriously thought if I hadn't been dating you, I'd have been on the phone with her every night. I'd have heard all about these friends of hers, and I would've been able to prevent the car accident."

June sighed and hung her head. "It sounds so stupid when I say it out loud."

"I can help you," Judge said quietly. "And June-Bug, I'm so sorry about Lucy Mae. What's happening with that?"

"She's coming home with me tomorrow," June said. "I have to admit I'm not very happy about it. We got into an awful argument yesterday, and she told me she's been smoking pot here." Another sigh, but this time, June lifted her head. "She's going to finish the semester from Texas, and I guess we'll figure out what to do from there."

"You *will* figure it out," Judge said, and his confidence in her gave June a boost she needed.

"We land in Texas at one-thirty tomorrow," she said, plenty of hinting in her voice.

"I'll come pick you up."

"Would you?"

"I'd fly to you today if I could," he said quietly. "Of course I'm going to be there to pick you up tomorrow. I won't even have to miss church."

"You're too good for me," she said.

"Funny," he said. "I was thinking the same thing about you."

"DON'T FORGET YOUR BACKPACK," JUNE SAID, NODDING to the dark blue bag still in the overhead compartment. Lucy Mae didn't answer, and June wasn't surprised. She wasn't very excited to be back home instead of still living in California, but Lucy Mae needed a dose of reality.

She'd attended her friend's funeral on Saturday—a funeral for a man she'd known—and she'd been sobbing when she got back to Cypress's. She'd gone into her bedroom and laid in bed for the rest of the day. June had finally gone to check on her after a couple of hours, and they had experienced a tender moment, where Lucy Mae had admitted in a whisper that she needed help.

June knew that, and she knew exactly who to talk to in order to provide the help her daughter needed. Judge had told her surface details about his brother Cactus's struggles, and she knew Cactus saw a counselor. June would get the name and number of the therapist, and she'd find the perfect one for Lucy Mae.

She'd stick close to her daughter, hopefully without smothering her, and she'd show her what it meant to be a strong woman in today's world. She wouldn't fall apart over this. She'd get up and go to work every day. She'd make time for Judge. She'd be there for Lucy Mae.

This time, June didn't have to go running home to get help, and she didn't have to search for purpose in the arms of the wrong man.

She'd *chosen* Judge, and he'd chosen her.

Her heartbeat increased as they deplaned and made their way through the airport to the luggage carousels. Lucy Mae had packed everything she owned into a couple of new luggage pieces June had had to buy just to get everything home, and they waited in silence in the busyness around them.

Her bags finally came, and because June hadn't taken anything with her, they were able to manage them as they left the airport. As if God had timed everything down to the second, Judge pulled up to the curb as she emerged from the airport, and June's pulse went nuts at the sight of the big truck.

She dang near swooned at the sight of the sexy cowboy who came around the front of the vehicle. He wore a white shirt and tie, and June had never seen such a perfect sight. He beelined toward her, and she'd barely managed to release the handles on the luggage before he swept her into his arms. "I love you," he said, the words rushing out of him in a stream of air.

He pushed his hands through her hair and searched her face, as if trying to make sure she was okay. She smiled at him, and he lowered his head and kissed her. June heard Lucy Mae sigh in exasperation, but she didn't care.

She was kissing the cowboy she loved and wanted in her life.

Judge seemed to realize that they stood outside a public airport, and he pulled away. He sucked in a breath and turned toward Lucy Mae. He drew her into a tight embrace, which caused a surprised sound to come from her mouth.

"I'm so glad you're okay," he said. "I was so worried about you when I put your mother on that plane."

Lucy Mae wore nothing but shock in her eyes. "You...were?"

Judge pulled back and looked at her. "Yes, Lucy Mae. You mean so much to your mom, and your mom means so much to me. Of course I was worried about you."

And he thought he wasn't good with teenagers. Tears heated her eyes, but she kept them from spilling down her face.

"Come on," Judge said, reaching for the biggest bag. "We better get loaded up before the parking attendant gets mad at us for idling on the curb." Judge put all the bags in the back of the truck and then joined June and Lucy Mae in the cab.

"All right," he drawled. "Who's hungry? And follow-up question: Who here has not eaten at The Longhorn?"

"I could eat," Lucy Mae said, her voice thick. It took all of June's willpower not to turn around and see if her daughter was crying. Of course she was, and she should be. She'd caused a lot of problems in the past week because of her irresponsible and reckless behavior.

Even as June thought that, the hardness in her heart and mind melted away. She loved her daughter, and she only wanted the best for her. If that meant therapy and tough love, June was willing to do it. But it if meant kindness and a listening ear, June could do that too.

"Judge?" she asked, and Judge looked into the rearview mirror.

"Yeah?"

"You love my mom, right?"

"That's right." Judge glanced over to June and reached for her hand.

"So when you get married, will you...?" She trailed off, and June tensed, waiting for her to continue.

"Will I what?" he asked.

"Will you be my dad?" Lucy Mae asked. "I've never really had one, and I think you'd be pretty...cool to have as a dad."

June's tears returned, and this time she didn't hold them back. She let them flow down her face at the question, but especially at the answer Judge gave.

"Well, I'll try, sugar-bee," he said. "I've never been a dad, and I'm certainly not cool. Not only that, but you *do* have a dad already, and I know he loves you."

"How do you know?" she asked.

Judge looked in the rearview mirror again. "Who was

there on Sunday when you needed him? Who drove you to college? Who helped your mom calm down enough to let you do that summer engineering workshop?"

Lucy Mae sniffled, and June could hardly see anything through her tears. "I'd kind of like a full-time dad."

"I can try," Judge said again, and June realized that was all anyone was doing. Trying. She was trying. Lucy Mae was probably trying. Judge tried, each and every day.

She squeezed his hand, and said, "The light show looked like a million bucks online."

He perked up. "Yeah? You watched it last night?"

Chapter Thirty-Eight

✿❦✿

J udge laughed as he ran down the front steps of the Ranch House. Mister slid from his giant, black truck, a smile and a shiny pair of sunglasses on his face.

"Brother," Judge said, reaching him and drawing him into a hug. He didn't care that his emotions ran rampant from him. He didn't care if Mister saw them or felt them. His brother had been gone for over six months, and it would be good to have him home for the next week.

They clapped each other on the back, both of them laughing. "Come on," Judge said. "Sammy made sure there would be a hot meal for when you got here." He led the way into the house, calling to Bear and Sammy that Mister was here, as if they hadn't heard the growling grumble of his big engine.

"How was the drive?" Bear asked as he hugged Mister.

"It's not as long as you think," Mister said, moving to

embrace Sammy. "Somethin' smells way better than anything I've eaten in a while."

"It's your favorite," she said, clinging to him. "Bacon cheeseburgers and strawberry pie."

"Oh, Sammy, I wish you weren't already married to my brother." Mister laughed, and Judge marveled at all the changes in him. He had grown up while he'd been at Winterhaven. The anger that had followed him for so long was gone. Just...gone.

Judge couldn't detect a single ounce of darkness inside him, and that made his heart take flight too. He got down plates and busied himself in the kitchen to hide his emotions. June wasn't there yet, as he'd told her to come a half-hour after Mister's arrival.

The hamburgers hadn't gone on the grill yet, and they wouldn't eat until she arrived. Sammy had fried the bacon already, and that scent lingered in the air, prompting Judge's mouth to water. He set a roll of paper towels on the counter with the glistening strawberry pie and the sweet tea Bear had mixed up.

"All right," he said. "We don't have much time, and I'm going to need all the help I can get for this proposal."

Mister turned away from Sammy, now holding Smiles in his arms. The two of them grinned and gave Judge such joy. "What have you got?" Mister asked.

"I've got a ring," Judge said, opening the drawer that held all their odds and ends. He plucked the black velvet box from among a pair of nail clippers, a set of screwdrivers, and a measuring tape.

Mister's eyebrows went up. "That's it?"

"That's it." He looked at Bear and then Sammy, who both wore equally surprised expressions. "I told y'all I needed help with the proposal."

"I thought you meant, you know, help stalling her or something," Sammy said. "Like y'all stalled Dot out at the well for Ward."

"You have no plan?" Bear asked.

Mister reached for a piece of bacon and tore it in half. He gave part of it to Smiles, who grinned and ate it. He popped the other half into his mouth. "How about you get up on the roof behind that big star and shout down to her when she gets here?"

"Shut your mouth, Mister," Sammy said, stepping in front of him. "And stay away from that bacon." She glared at him and looked at Judge, her expression softening. "Judge, no woman wants to be 'shouted to' from a rooftop, even if it is a proposal."

"I could do something with the lights."

"It's the middle of the day," Bear said.

"It's kind of cloudy today," Judge said. "She'd be able to see them. I could put on her favorite song and program the stars to dance to the music. Then just sort of casually...ask her?"

"How long does it take you to program lights to a song?" Mister asked. "I remember you disappearing into that office for hours sometimes."

"Hours," Judge said miserably. He'd had June back in his life for almost a month since that terrible, no-good week without her. How could he not have planned something amazing for the proposal?

"It doesn't need to be long," Sammy said. "Go do a twenty second snippet. That shouldn't take hours."

Judge looked at the ring box and back to Sammy. "Will you stall her if she gets here before I'm done?"

"I'll do my best," Sammy said. "But you haven't given me a lot to work with. These two barely know how to have a normal conversation as it is."

Judge laughed as he jogged toward the office, mostly at Bear's growly protest that he couldn't have a conversation. His chair slid across the hard office floor as he sank into it at a run, and he pulled up June's favorite song.

He went to the most recognizable part—the chorus—and clipped the music so it was only twenty-four seconds long.

He loved the guitar and the upbeat sound of Randy Travis's *Forever and Ever Amen*. He could easily get the stars to beat along with the words and the rhythm, and his fingers flew as he wrote the program.

He added a loop to it, and he pressed start on it and jumped from his chair. "I got it," he yelled as he ran into the living room. "I just need to hook up the speakers." He dashed out the front door, his pulse nearly beating out of his body.

He plugged in the speakers and ran the wire to get the far ones on the corners of the house hooked up. With everything connected, Randy Travis's iconic voice filled the yard.

I've already forgotten every woman but you
Oh, darlin', I'm gonna love you forever
Forever and ever amen.

He ran down the sidewalk as the twenty-four-second clip continued to play, and he faced the house to check how everything went together. Sammy, Bear, and Mister joined him, and Bear sang along with the song in his rich tenor.

He started dancing with his wife, and Judge smiled at the pair of them. He wasn't sure he wanted to have as many kids as quickly as he could, the way Bear and Sammy were doing, but watching them, he could certainly see the love they had for one another.

They smiled and laughed together, and Bear said something as he twirled Sammy away from him that made her light up.

"This is great," Mister said, tapping his foot along to the beat as the loop started again. "It's perfect, Judge."

"Yeah?" He looked at Mister, still holding Smiles in his arms. "Can I just stand on the steps while she watches the show?"

"You can do whatever you want," Mister said. "You could've just shown her the ring and told her you love her. Asked. Done."

Judge's chest pinched. "Is this too much?" He'd never been all that worried about things before, but he wanted everything to be perfect for June.

Mister chuckled and shook his head. "Come on, Smiles. Let's go sneak more of that bacon and let Judge freak out on his own." He walked away, taking Bear and Sammy with him. They all returned to the house, and Judge followed them.

He grabbed the ring box from where he'd left it on the kitchen counter. "Okay, I'm going to go wait out front."

"That's a nice ring," Bear said.

"Mm." Judge leaned into the pillar at the top of the porch, wondering how time could move so slowly sometimes. Thankfully, he only had to wait about five minutes—which was a lot of the same Randy Travis song when the clip was only twenty-four seconds long—before June pulled up in her Nichols Networking van.

She smiled at him, checked something on the passenger seat, and started to get out.

Judge's pulse kicked heavy, booming beats through his chest, and he knew the moment June saw the flashing stars and heard the love song.

If you wonder how long I'll be faithful
Well, just listen to how this song ends
I'm gonna love you forever and ever
Forever and ever, amen.

The loop started again, but Judge went down the steps and slowly on down the sidewalk, his gaze stuck on June's.

"You rascal," she said above the music.

He held up the black, velvet box and grinned at her. He had to talk fairly loud to be heard over Randy Travis.

"I love you, Juniper Nichols. I want to be your husband, and I want you to be my wife." He popped open the box and got down on one knee. "Will you marry me?"

June started nodding even as tears wetted her cheeks. "Absolutely," she said.

With pure joy exploding through him, he got up and slipped the ring on her finger. He kissed her, his heart so full and expanding with every stroke of her mouth against his.

"I love you, Judge," she whispered, and he touched his lips to her neck.

"Forever and ever," he murmured.

"Amen," they said together.

Read on for a sneak peek at **THE WRANGLING OF THE WREATH**, which finally features Mister Glover and Libby Bellamore! Can they work out their differences and get on the same page?

Sneak Peek! The Wrangling of the Wreath Chapter One:

M ister Glover saw the outline of Three Rivers on the horizon, and something in his heart settled. Something he hadn't even realized had been kicking around inside his chest. He hadn't been terribly happy to leave Winterhaven, because he had friends there now. Brock put his dishes in the dishwasher every evening, and Josiah had given Mister some amazing advice about how to fall asleep faster.

He'd packed up and driven away, even when the boss wanted him to stay. Heck, he'd even been offered more money, and he'd have been paid the most out of anyone at Winterhaven had he accepted.

"I learned something, Dad," he whispered, the horizon blurring slightly in the heavy heat that had already arrived in the Texas Panhandle, though it wasn't even June yet. He'd learned that he could be a valuable resource—very valuable. He could put his head down and work without accolades. He could put up with a snoring roommate, and a messy cabin-mate, and a man who thought he was better than everyone else.

Not only could he put up with them, he could learn to love them for exactly who they were. In doing that, Mister felt like he'd learned to love himself better, flaws and all.

He smiled into the sunshine, and for the first time, a snippet in his letter from his deceased father made sense.

You'll need to go your own way, Mister. You've always done that, and it used to drive me and your mother insane. Then Grandmother would remind us of who you were, and we'd find a way to encourage you to seek and understand for yourself.

When he'd first read that paragraph, years ago, he hadn't known what his father meant. He'd never really thought he'd gone his own way. He'd had the opportunity to join the rodeo, because he was good with a rope and knew instinctively how to stay on a bull. So he'd joined.

He'd never really thought of it as "going his own way."

He'd returned to Shiloh Ridge, just like everyone else in his family. Cactus had gone to school for a long time, and he'd come back. Mister had too.

As his truck sped along the highway, Mister sure would like to ask Grandmother who she thought he was. How had she seen who he was when he was so young?

He wanted to honor his family name, do what was right, and be the type of person his grandmother had somehow seen, so long ago.

"I hope I'm at least better than I was," he murmured, though he already knew he was. He felt calmer inside, and while he had dreams and goals he wanted to accomplish, he didn't feel frantic to get them done.

He knew now that the joy came from the *doing*, not from the *finishing*.

His phone rang, saving himself from his inner thoughts, and he reached over to the infotainment screen and tapped to answer Preacher's call. "Tell me she's not having the baby," Mister said. Preacher and Charlie were due with their first child tomorrow, which was why Mister was moving back to Three Rivers and Shiloh Ridge Ranch today.

Despite the good life he enjoyed at Winterhaven with his cowboy friends and hard-working boss, Mister couldn't stand to be away from all the hustle and bustle on his family's ranch. He missed his brothers and sister and all of their spouses. He missed his cousins. He missed all the littles, and he'd missed eleven months of them growing up, changing, developing, and learning the wonders of mud, bugs, and baby calves.

In his opinion, cattle ranching—what they did at Shiloh Ridge—was better than dairy farming—what he'd done at Winterhaven. A quiet excitement brewed within him, and Mister couldn't wait to get back to the ranch and see all the changes. Bear had sent pictures of the house, but Mister knew from being gone this year that pictures and videos weren't anywhere near the same as seeing things in person.

A birthday party via video, where he could only see the chocolate cakes and the joy on his nephews' face? Or being there to taste, smell, hear, and bask in the familial spirit?

Yes, this year had been very difficult for Mister, and he thanked the Lord that he'd only felt it keenly in a few instances.

"She's not having the baby," Preacher said, chuckling. "Though she just glared at me *because* she's not having the baby."

"Oh, boy," Mister said, smiling. He pictured Charlie in the last selfie she'd sent him, and she had to be super uncomfortable. She'd told him to "hurry home" so he could "convince Preacher to let her start exercising or taking castor oil or something" to get the baby to come faster.

"We're just wondering where you are," Preacher said. "Charlie wants a few things from the grocery store, and I'm up to my eyeballs in the re-pasturization we're doing up here."

"Ward's got the whip cracking," Mister said, his grin only widening.

"That he does," Preacher said. "It's fine. It's good. But she can't drive to the store alone—"

"Yes, I can!" Charlie yelled, but Preacher just kept right on talking.

"—and I'm too busy to go. We thought you might be able to stop on your way through town."

"I can stop on my way through town," Mister echoed. "I can see it ahead of me. I'm maybe five miles out. Tell me what you need."

"Charlie will text you," Preacher said, and he sounded so happy too. So cheerful, and so...animated. For Preacher, that was saying something, as he preferred to live his life on the sidelines.

"Sounds good," Mister said. "I can't wait to see the new Kinder place too. It looks amazing in the pictures Bishop's been sending."

"It is pretty amazing what that man can do," Preacher said. "We're still a few months out from completion, but Montana told Char that they're actually *ahead* of schedule."

"They really are miracle workers," Mister said, his heart aching to see Bishop and Montana again. Their little boy Robbie had turned one over four months ago, and Mister had only been able to participate in watching the child blow out his single candle via video.

Judge, Preacher, and Ward had been the very best at keeping Mister involved in the family. He got to watch from afar all the birthday parties, the Sunday dinners, and the bridal shower for June, Judge's fiancée.

They'd set a date for August tenth to be married, and Mister knew that Judge had held off on setting a date until Mister had announced his plans to return to Texas. Guilt pulled through him, but Judge had told him August was the best time for June's family. It really had nothing to do with him.

"Okay, see you soon," Preacher said, and Mister let him end the call. A moment later the truck chirped a notification from the speakers, and a glance at the infotainment screen told him Charlie had texted.

"Read the text from Charlie," he said.

"Potato chips, the plain ones. Cool Ranch Doritos. Butter pecan ice cream. Thanks, Mister!"

Chips and ice cream. Mister grinned to himself, his need to get back to the ranch only doubling. He wouldn't have to dive right back into work, though summertime at Shiloh Ridge could make a man question his career choices. He'd take a few days to get moved home, go around and see everyone and everything that had changed, and then report to Ward and Preacher, the two foremen at the ranch, for work on Tuesday morning.

He continued his drive, pulling into Wilde & Organic only a few minutes later. The lot held plenty of cars for a Sunday afternoon, and Mister dang near fell over when he got out of the vehicle and had to breathe in the heat.

"My word," he said, gasping. "I'm going to die this summer." The weather hadn't really been better in Oklahoma, as it sat due east of Three Rivers, but he'd been driving in air-conditioned bliss for hours now.

He hurried inside the store and re-read Charlie's list. She only had a few things on it, and he quickly texted Judge to ask if he had anything he wanted. Mister wouldn't be moving back into the Ranch House, but he had planned for it to be his first stop.

Since Judge and June would be living there, and Bear and Sammy had moved into their new house a couple of months ago, there was room for Mister in the homestead. He'd be taking the suite Bear and Sammy had been living in, though Ranger had moved the ranch office and conference room across the landing to that area.

He'd needed the room for his own family, which had grown to four now. Bear and Sammy had four children and had needed a bigger place. Mister hadn't been able to come for the birth of their daughter, Heather, who they'd named after Sammy's sister. He couldn't wait to meet his niece, and he looked up from his phone, suddenly eager to get this shopping done.

Cactus had once told him that one of the best places to meet women was in the grocery store, but Mister had laughed him off. He wasn't looking to start dating anyway, and certainly not someone he met in the grocery store.

He hadn't met anyone in Oklahoma that had caught his eye, and Mister wondered if there would be anyone in Three Rivers that would. He'd grown up here and spent so many years of his life here. He felt like he knew so many people, though the town had grown a lot in the past several years.

An image of Liberty Bellamore filled his mind, and while Mister had thought she'd recede back to best friend status while he worked his days away at Winterhaven, he found that she hadn't.

He'd learned to control his frustration surrounding her, and he'd learned to enjoy their friendship again. He'd loved telling her about his life in Oklahoma, and he loved getting random pictures of the landscape around her. In fact, he smiled just thinking about her as he reached for a shopping cart.

"Welcome to Wilde and Organic," a woman said, handing him a quarter-sheet of paper. "We have half-pans of brownies on sale this afternoon."

"Sounds good," Mister said, taking the coupon. Charlie hadn't requested brownies, but Mister didn't know a Glover alive who would turn down a chocolatey treat.

He pushed a cart around, getting the things both Judge and Charlie wanted, then the brownies, and he finally just had the chips and Doritos left. He turned down the chip and snack aisle, the long row of bags of potato chips stretching in front of him.

"Plain," he muttered. Who liked plain potato chips?

"Mister?"

He turned toward the sound of the voice, already knowing who he'd find standing there. "Libby." She wore a pair of cutoff shorts with a red-and-blue-checkered tank top, with big work boots on her feet. Her hair wasn't braided or ponytailed, but fell around her face in beautiful brunette waves that made Mister's mouth turn dry.

She looked so much like the woman he'd known for decades. And yet...something about her was different too. Completely different, but he couldn't pinpoint what it was.

He also couldn't stop the smile as it bloomed on his face, and she dropped her basket with oranges and mint in it.

She laughed and grabbed onto him, pulling him into a wonderful hug that had him closing his eyes in bliss and inhaling the scent of her hair, her skin, her clothes. She'd definitely been working outside today, because she smelled like straw, sunshine, and sweat. It was the best scent in the whole world to Mister, and he wished he'd been out on the ranch with her today.

He sighed and said, "It's so good to see you." He started to laugh, and he lifted her right up off the ground and spun her around. Maybe Cactus had been onto something when he'd said Mister could meet someone special in the grocery store.

He set her down, and she backed up. She bent to get

her produce, and when her eyes met his again, a whole lightning storm started zapping in his chest.

"What are you doing here?" she asked, glancing at his shopping cart. "Are you back in Three Rivers for good?" The hope in her voice screamed in his ears, and Mister told himself it was because they were friends. Good friends.

Best friends.

She definitely fit in that box, but he could still feel her pushing and pulsing against the edges of it, wanting to become more. Maybe he just wanted her to be more, and that was him trying to break down the walls keeping her in the friendship position.

Not only that, he wasn't going to start anything with Libby he couldn't finish. Not again. He wasn't going to lose her again because of his childish behavior and stubbornness. He wasn't going to pressure her to go out with him. He wasn't going to ask her to set him up with anyone. He wasn't even going to make the first move.

He knew better now, so despite the thumping of his pulse and his own hope shooting toward the stars, he said, "Yeah, yep. Today's my first day back." He glanced at the chips in the rack beside him and grinned. "And wouldn't you know it? Everyone in my family is already putting me to work."

She chuckled and took in the groceries in his cart. "Getting brownies and ice cream is work? You've had it easy in Oklahoma, Mister."

He grinned at her, wondering if he'd heard something flirty in his name. He'd known her for so long, and he'd never heard anything off in her voice until Preacher had mentioned she'd asked about him.

He couldn't trust himself and his feelings right now, so he just said, "Nothing about being in Oklahoma was as easy as I've made it seem, Libs."

"No? What's been hard?"

Not seeing you in person, he thought, but he said, "Missing out on all the parties, the births, and the family stuff."

"You used to sometimes complain about the family stuff, and that was when it was a third of the size it is now."

Mister grinned at her, but he couldn't deny it. "I'm older now," he said simply. "I guess I didn't realize how wonderful it was to have so many people to enjoy life with." He wanted to ask her what she was doing later that weekend. Maybe they could go to lunch tomorrow. Lunch was an easy get-together, wasn't it?

You're not asking, he reminded himself, and besides, he couldn't commit to lunch—or any other date—because Libby had spoken true. His family was huge, and they'd all want to see him.

"Anyway," he said. "I just need to get these chips and get on up to the ranch. I'm not sure if you've ever been between a pregnant lady and her ice cream, but I know it's not a position I want to be in."

Sneak Peek! The Wrangling of the Wreath Chapter Two:

Liberty Bellamore could only stare at Mister Glover's mouth as he spoke. He'd grown in a full beard, just the kind Libby liked. He'd likely shave it before next Sunday, when she'd see him at church.

He was twice as handsome as she remembered, though he'd been sending her pictures as the beard had grown in. "I like the beard," she said, grinning at him. He'd grown one last year when he'd first left Three Rivers, but he'd shaved it after a while.

"Yeah?" He reached up and stroked his face, as if he didn't know he had hair there. "I'm thinking it's too hot for a beard."

"I'm sure you'll shave it soon enough," she teased. "You never did like that much facial hair."

"Yes, well, you dared me to see how long I could stand it this time. Goin' on five months now."

She giggled again and ducked her head, horrified at her

girlish, flirty behavior. Her mind screamed at her to *stop it!* and not only because she'd set very clear boundaries with Mister she wasn't going to cross again.

She cut off the sound and took a deep breath. Why had she come down this aisle? She was sure it wasn't because she'd seen this tall, dark, delectable cowboy studying the chips as if he couldn't read their English names.

"Are you going to make that tropical punch?" he asked, indicating her basket.

"Yes," she blurted out, seizing onto the topic. "I just... we're having a little picnic to celebrate Jack and Suzy's anniversary. I'm in charge of the punch, obviously." She lifted her basket, her face feeling so hot. Mister had to know more ingredients than oranges and mint were needed for the tropical punch he'd drunk many times.

"And chips," she finished lamely.

"Is your daddy makin' his famous spit-roasted pig?"

"Slaughtered it yesterday and everything." Libby smiled at Mister, enjoying this easy conversation. She needed it in her life. She craved it.

She also couldn't have it. Couldn't perpetuate it.

Get your chips and go, she commanded herself. *Quickly.*

She didn't think her family's news wouldn't reach Mister soon enough, but her legs literally shook at the idea of him finding out about Cory right here in the grocery store.

"Mildred's engaged," she said casually as she reached for the cheddar and sour cream chips she loved so much. She normally provided several different flavors of chips for her family to choose from, but she only carried a basket, and to get so many would require the cart Cory was filling with frozen lemonade, limeade, and orange juice.

"She is?" Mister asked, obviously surprised. "I thought you said she didn't like that guy that much."

"Oh, she's a big liar." Libby gave Mister a smile she hoped was friendly and not flirty and moved around his cart to get a bag of barbecue chips. "Once I figured that out, they were already talking about diamonds and dresses." She gave an exaggerated sigh. "They're getting married in November."

"Right during the Country Christmas?" Mister's shock only made Libby's pulse bounce erratically.

"Right before," she said. "So yes, I'm pretty mad at her."

"Wow," Mister said as she picked up another bag of chips, this time the Maui sweet onion flavor her brother Cord adored. Was three bags of chips enough? Had this conversation lasted long enough? Could she walk away now?

Her mind raced, and Libby had never been good under pressure. She didn't like confrontation, and she had no idea how she could possibly fill Mister in on everything that had happened in the past month or two.

Their texts had been friendly; the type of thing she'd send to an acquaintance, not a deep, personal friend. As he asked another question about Mildred with a pinch of hurt in his voice, Libby realized that he didn't view her as an acquaintance. He'd expected her to share her big family news with him, even though he'd been living in another state.

After all, that was what Libby and Mister had been doing for decades.

"She's getting married at the Old Apple Mill," Libby said, answering the question. "Our space at Golden Hour will already be set up for the Country Christmas." She glanced at him, not truly meeting his eyes. "So." She shrugged like that was no big deal, but Mister knew Libby would never get married anywhere but her family ranch.

She loved being a cowgirl, and she couldn't fathom a life without cattle, horses, and dogs in it.

"Where will she live?" Mister asked. "Are you going to lose that house you love?"

"No, Scott is a scientist at HealNow," Libby said, plucking a plain bag of chips from the shelf. "He has one of those nice, new homes on the north side of town. Kind of out by your sister-in-law's sister." She dared to look at him, and oh, how he made her heart pulse in her chest.

She stubbornly tamped against it, because she couldn't have feelings for this man anymore. It wasn't fair to him, and it wasn't fair to her.

And there's Cory, her mind shrieked.

"Bethany Rose and Doug Culver?" Libby said, providing the names for him. "There's a new subdivision out there. Scott lives out there, and since Mildred doesn't *really* work the ranch—not the way I do or Jack and Cord do—she's going to move in with him once they get married."

Mister edged closer to her, tugging on his cart from the front of it instead of using the handle. He hadn't picked up a single bag of chips yet, and Libby really wished he would.

He came far too close to her, which only made her skin prickle and ripple with want.

"I'm glad," he said, his voice throaty and deeper now. He seemed...older. More mature. Wiser. She realized he didn't give in to every thought in his head, as she watched his emotions blaze through his eyes but his mouth stay shut. Before he'd left for Winterhaven, whatever he'd been thinking would've just spilled from his mouth.

She also realized he hadn't told her a single thing about him. He'd been asking her questions about Mildred and her family and what she was doing at the grocery store. Before, everything was about Mister.

He'd conquered another bull. He'd won the National Championship. He'd gotten his shiny, bejeweled belt buckle in the mail and did she want to see it? He'd gotten an article accepted in a magazine.

Even when he'd first moved to Oklahoma, his texts had been about the farm, his roommates, and the work. Libby wasn't sure when they'd changed, but standing there in the snack aisle with him, she realized she hadn't heard about him or his life in quite some time now.

Months, probably.

"You love that house," he said. "Have you kept it red?"

"Yes," she managed to push out of her narrow throat. "I like the brick red."

"I know you do," he said. "You also like to switch things up sometimes." He grinned at her and his gaze softened. "It really is so good to see you. I've missed you more than I realized."

Before she could answer, a man called, "Libby."

She looked past Mister's shoulder, wanting to lunge at him and tell him not to look. But he was already turning in the direction of the voice too.

Another man strode toward them, pushing the cart filled with the other items she needed to make the tropical punch, as well as provide all the sides for the family picnic. Cory had met her parents before, but Libby had not introduced him to the whole family.

That was happening today. In mere hours.

"Did you get the chips, darlin'?" Cory drawled, barely glancing at Mister. Funny how Libby couldn't get herself to look away from him.

His face transformed instantly, and she caught a momentary bout of shock before he covered it smoothly away.

"Howdy." Cory went right past Mister to her. "Four bags, honey? I don't think that's enough. You said Cord will eat those onion ones by himself." He took the bag of chips from her hand and twisted to put it in the cart.

"Hello," Mister said diplomatically, and that single word thawed Libby.

She did lunge forward then, stepping partially in front of Cory. "Mister," she said, clearing her throat. "Cory." She looked at him. "Cory, this is Mister Glover. Remember I've talked about him?"

Cory finally looked at Mister, and his eyes lit up. "Yes, of course. The friend in Oklahoma." He reached out to shake Mister's hand.

His eyebrows had furrowed, but Libby plowed forward. "Mister, this is Cory Blanchard."

"You *haven't* talked about him," Mister said, taking Cory's hand and pumping it a couple of times before releasing it.

Cory chuckled, as if nothing was amiss in this snack aisle. Nothing to see here. Only Libby's utter humiliation and embarrassment that she had feelings for someone she had no right to feel anything for.

"That Libs," he said. "She likes to keep things a little secret." Cory put his arm around her waist, and Libby wanted the floor in Wilde & Organic to swallow her right down. "She thinks a forbidden relationship is more exciting."

"Forbidden relationship?" Mister's eyes bored into the top of Libby's head, because she couldn't raise it to face him head-on.

"He's my boyfriend," Libby muttered, the words nowhere near loud enough to reach Mister's ears.

"I'm the boyfriend," Cory repeated, much louder. So loud it made Libby cringe.

Mister took a step back, but she still didn't dare look at his face. "So nice to meet you," he said, his voice diplomatic and guarded. "I should get these things found and on my way. My sister-in-law is due with a baby tomorrow, and I don't know if you've ever made a pregnant woman wait for her potato chips, but it isn't pretty."

He chuckled in a way that sounded natural to a casual observer. But Libby wasn't a casual observer. She knew the force behind the laughter and how much it took for Mister to do it.

When she finally got the courage to look up, Mister

had retreated behind his cart and gripped the handle with both hands. "I just need to find the Cool Ranch Doritos...."

"Oh, they're down here farther," Cory said, so upbeat and so oblivious to Libby. He slid his hand away from her body and went down the aisle easily. He picked up the blue bag of chips and turned just as Mister started to go by her.

"Boyfriend?" he asked out of the corner of his mouth. "Seems like you've been holdin' out on me, my friend." He didn't slow down or stop as he walked by, and his words left a burning hole in her stomach.

She wasn't his friend, and he now knew it. Friends would've shared the news that they'd started seeing someone over two months ago. If they were friends, she wouldn't have blindsided him with a boyfriend in the grocery store.

Libby turned away from the two men exchanging chips and pleasantries. Her eyes filled with tears, and she loathed herself on a whole new level. *Why did he have to be here at the same time we were?* she thought.

Of all the times he could've stopped by to get chips for Charlie, why did You have to let it be now? Libby wouldn't get an answer from the Lord, she knew that. No matter how hard she tried to converse with Him or how many times she asked what she should do, she didn't get an answer.

This time would be no different.

"Let's see what we've got," Cory said. "You said at least eight bags, baby, and you have four."

She let him take her basket and move the chips into the cart. She let him pick out the rest of the chips while she studied cans of peanuts and cashews on the other side of the aisle. She couldn't let him see her crying, that was for certain.

Libby felt hollow inside, and she clutched her arms around herself, trying to keep all the pieces together. She'd lost her connection to God. She didn't feel worthy of His love anymore, and she didn't know what to do about it. She still went to church, but there was nothing there for her.

She was empty and floating through the wind, desperate for something or someone to hold onto, and no one came. Nothing appeared.

"Okay," Cory said, breaking into her thoughts. "Libby?" He put his hand on her hip, and she flinched away from him. "What's wrong? Are you okay?" He came around and stood beside her, facing her.

Looking up at him, she found concern and compassion in his dark brown eyes. He wore his hair a little too long, but she hadn't minded. He was a great kisser, and a lot of fun. He liked to go hiking and biking and while she wasn't terribly into outdoor sports, she did like being under the open sky and in the fresh air.

He wasn't a cowboy either, and Libby had thought she could make that concession, because he did possess good looks, and he worked hard, and he was kind to her. He cared about her.

She couldn't hide from him any longer. She couldn't hide from herself either. "I'm not feeling well," she said, her tears spilling over and tracking down her face. "I'm sorry, Cory."

"Hey, it's okay." He put his arms around her, and Libby let him.

"No," she said. "It's not okay."

"Why are you sorry?"

She drew in a deep breath and stepped out of his arms. It wasn't fair to take comfort from him. She needed to stand up and support herself. "That was Mister Glover, Cory."

He frowned as he peered at her. "Yeah, okay."

She shook her head, a fresh set of tears threatening to spill down her face. She pulled them back in and laced everything tight. She hated the crusty feeling of saltwater on her face, and she wiped it away. "He's my very best friend in the whole world. Or he was."

She knew she wasn't making sense. "I didn't tell him about us, because somewhere in the back of my mind, I was hoping that when he came back to town...."

Cory fell back a step, as if she'd pushed him. "You were hoping when he came back, the two of you would become an *us*."

Libby nodded. "Yes," she admitted. "I've liked him for a long time." She looked up into Cory's eyes, which weren't nearly as warm now. "It's just a silly crush. I'm sure it'll pass."

She'd been telling herself that for five years now.

Cory sighed and looked across the aisle. A mother and her two kids came toward them, and neither Libby nor Cory moved, though their cart sat on one side of the aisle and they stood on the other.

She obviously knew something was wrong here, and she met Libby's eyes with her wide ones. Libby shook her head slightly, and the mother herded her children through the narrow space to get to the goldfish down at the other end.

"Well," he finally said. "What do you want to do? Do you want to break-up with me?"

Libby had no idea what she wanted to do. She thought of Cory, and how charming he'd been. He'd swept her off her feet when she'd least expected it, and she did have fun with him.

But seeing Mister....

No one was Mister Glover, and she knew that deep down in her core.

"Let's just go to the picnic," she said.

"I don't want to go meet your whole family if this isn't going to work out between us," Cory said, moving over to the shopping cart. He looked at her, his unspoken words loud enough for her to hear.

You have to choose, Libby.

Now.

Help me, she prayed, and Libby closed her eyes and thought about what she wanted her future to look like. Her therapist had her do these types of visualization techniques, and she'd gotten very good at them.

She did see the brick red house in her future. The ranch she loved, with the job she loved, wrangling cattle and setting up for the Country Christmas.

And when she went home, it was to a tall, dark, handsome cowboy who'd known her for so long, he knew her better than she knew herself.

"I don't think you should come to the picnic," Libby whispered.

Cory blinked, obviously surprised, and then he scoffed. "Fine." With that, he left the cart full of groceries right there in the snack aisle and walked out.

Libby stood there frozen for another moment, then she went over to the cart and steadied herself against it. Her breath stuttered out of her lungs, and her next thought was that perhaps Mister hadn't left Wilde & Organic yet.

Perhaps she could find him and tell him what had just happened and invite him to the family picnic instead.

She looked toward the end of the aisle, and then she hurried away from the cart of groceries, her goal singular: *Find Mister. Find Mister right now.*

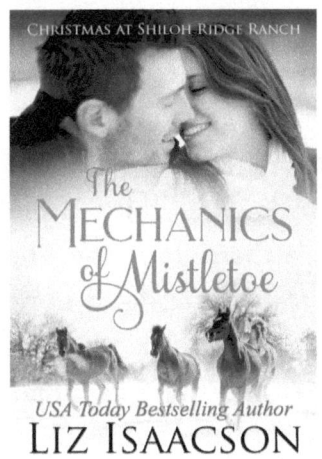

The Mechanics of Mistletoe (Book 1): Bear Glover can be a grizzly or a teddy, and he's always thought he'd be just fine working his generational family ranch and going back to the ancient homestead alone. But his crush on Samantha Benton won't go away. She's a genius with a wrench on Bear's tractors...and his heart. Can he tame his wild side and get the girl, or will he be left broken-hearted this Christmas season?

the HORSEPOWER of the Holiday

USA Today Bestselling Author
LIZ ISAACSON

The Horsepower of the Holiday (Book 2): Ranger Glover has worked at Shiloh Ridge Ranch his entire life. The cowboys do everything from horseback there, but when he goes to town to trade in some trucks, somehow Oakley Hatch persuades him to take some ATVs back to the ranch. (Bear is NOT happy.)

She's a former race car driver who's got Ranger all revved up... Can he remember who he is and get Oakley to slow down enough to fall in love, or will there simply be too much horsepower in the holiday this year for a real relationship?

The Construction of Cheer (Book 3): Bishop Glover is the youngest brother, and he usually keeps his head down and gets the job done. When Montana Martin shows up at Shiloh Ridge Ranch looking for work, he finds himself inventing construction projects that need doing just to keep her coming around. (Again, Bear is NOT happy.) She wants to build her own construction firm, but she ends up carving a place for herself inside Bishop's heart. Can he convince her *he's* all she needs this Christmas season, or will her cheer rest solely on the success of her business?

The Secret of Santa (Book 4): He's a fun-loving cowboy with a heart of gold. She's the woman who keeps putting him on hold. Can Ace and Holly Ann make a relationship work this Christmas?

The Harmony of Holly (Book 5): He's as prickly as his name, but the new woman in town has caught his eye. Can Cactus shelve his temper and shed his cowboy hermit skin fast enough to make a relationship with Willa work?

CHRISTMAS AT SHILOH RIDGE RANCH

The Chemistry of Christmas

USA Today Bestselling Author
LIZ ISAACSON

The Chemistry of Christmas (Book 6): He's the black sheep of the family, and she's a chemist who understands formulas, not emotions. Can Preacher and Charlie take their quirks and turn them into a strong relationship this Christmas?

The Delivery of Decor (Book 7): When he falls, he falls hard and deep. She literally drives away from every relationship she's ever had. Can Ward somehow get Dot to stay this Christmas?

CHRISTMAS AT SHILOH RIDGE RANCH

The BLESSING of Babies

USA Today Bestselling Author
LIZ ISAACSON

The Blessing of Babies (Book 8): Don't miss out on a single moment of the Glover family saga in this bridge story linking Ward and Judge's love stories!

The Glovers love God, country, dogs, horses, and family. Not necessarily in that order. ;)

Many of them are married now, with babies on the way, and there are lessons to be learned, forgiveness to be had and given, and new names coming to the family tree in southern Three Rivers!

The Networking of the Nativity (Book 9): He's had a crush on her for years. She doesn't want to date until her daughter is out of the house. Will June take a change on Judge when the success of his Christmas light display depends on her networking abilities?

The Wrangling of the Wreath (Book 10): He's been so busy trying to find Miss Right. She's been right in front of him the whole time. This Christmas, can Mister and Libby take their relationship out of the best friend zone?

The Hope of Her Heart (Book 11): She's the only Glover without a significant other. He's been searching for someone who can love him *and* his daughter. Can Etta and August make a meaningful connection this Christmas?

Rhett's Make-Believe Marriage (Book 1): She needs a husband to be credible as a matchmaker. He wants to help a neighbor. Will their fake marriage take them out of the friend zone?

USA Today Bestselling Author
LIZ ISAACSON

Tripp's Trivial Tie (Book 2): She needs a husband to keep her son. He's wanted to take their relationship to the next level, but she's always pushing him away. Will their trivial tie take them all the way to happily-ever-after?

USA Today Bestselling Author
LIZ ISAACSON

Liam's Invented I-Do (Book 3): She's desperate to save her ranch. He wants to help her any way he can. Will their invented I-Do open doors that have previously been closed and lead to a happily-ever-after for both of them?

Jeremiah's Bogus Bride (Book 4): He wants to prove to his brothers that he's not broken. She just wants him. Will a fake marriage heal him or push her further away?

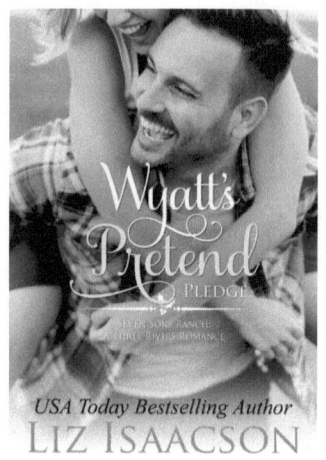

Wyatt's Pretend Pledge (Book 5): To get her inheritance, she needs a husband. He's wanted to fly with her for ages. Can their pretend pledge turn into something real?

Skyler's Wanna-Be Wife (Book 6): She needs a new last name to stay in school. He's willing to help a fellow student. Can this wanna-be wife show the playboy that some things should be taken seriously?

USA Today Bestselling Author
LIZ ISAACSON

Micah's Mock Matrimony (Book 7): They were just actors auditioning for a play. The marriage was just for the audition – until a clerical error results in a legal marriage. Can these two ex-lovers negotiate this new ground between them and achieve new roles in each other's lives?

Her Cowboy Billionaire Birthday Wish (Book 1): All the maid at Whiskey Mountain Lodge wants for her birthday is a handsome cowboy billionaire. And Colton can make that wish come true—if only he hadn't escaped to Coral Canyon after being left at the altar...

Her Cowboy Billionaire Butler (Book 2): She broke up with him to date another man...who broke her heart. He's a former CEO with nothing to do who can't get her out of his head. Can Wes and Bree find a way toward happily-ever-after at Whiskey Mountain Lodge?

Her Cowboy Billionaire Best Friend's Brother (Book 3): She's best friends with the single dad cowboy's brother and has watched two friends find love with the sexy new cowboys in town. When Gray Hammond comes to Whiskey Mountain Lodge with his son, will Elise finally get her own happily-ever-after with one of the Hammond brothers?

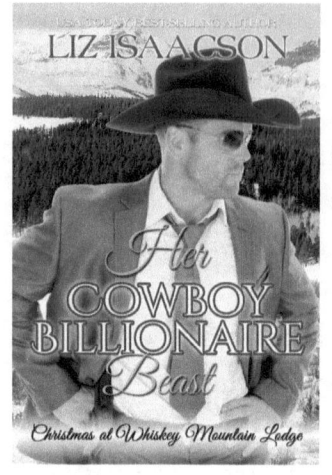

Her Cowboy Billionaire Beast (Book 4): A cowboy billionaire beast, his new manager, and the Christmas traditions that soften his heart and bring them together.

Her Cowboy Billionaire Bad Boy (Book 5): A cowboy billionaire cop who's a stickler for rules, the woman he pulls over when he's not even on duty, and the personal mandates he has to break to keep her in his life...

Books in the Christmas in Coral Canyon Romance series

Her Cowboy Billionaire Best Friend (Book 1): Graham Whittaker returns to Coral Canyon a few days after Christmas—after the death of his father. He takes over the energy company his dad built from the ground up and buys a high-end lodge to live in—only a mile from the home of his once-best friend, Laney McAllister. They were best friends once, but Laney's always entertained feelings for him, and spending so much time with him while they make Christmas memories puts her heart in danger of getting broken again...

Her Cowboy Billionaire Boss (Book 2): Since the death of his wife a few years ago, Eli Whittaker has been running from one job to another, unable to find somewhere for him and his son to settle. Meg Palmer is Stockton's nanny, and she comes with her boss, Eli, to the lodge, her longtime crush on the man no different in Wyoming than it was on the beach. When she confesses her feelings for him and gets nothing in return, she's crushed, embarrassed, and unsure if she can stay in Coral Canyon for Christmas. Then Eli starts to show some feelings for her too...

Her Cowboy Billionaire Boyfriend (Book 3): Andrew Whittaker is the public face for the Whittaker Brothers' family energy company, and with his older brother's robot about to be announced, he needs a press secretary to help him get everything ready and tour the state to make the announcements. When he's hit by a protest sign being carried by the company's biggest opponent, Rebecca Collings, he learns with a few clicks that she has the background they need. He offers her the job of press secretary when she thought she was going to be arrested, and not only because the spark between them in so hot Andrew can't see straight.

Can Becca and Andrew work together and keep their relationship a secret? Or will hearts break in this classic romance retelling reminiscent of *Two Weeks Notice*?

Her Cowboy Billionaire Bodyguard (Book 4): Beau Whittaker has watched his brothers find love one by one, but every attempt he's made has ended in disaster. Lily Everett has been in the spotlight since childhood and has half a dozen platinum records with her two sisters. She's taking a break from the brutal music industry and hiding out in Wyoming while her ex-husband continues to cause trouble for her. When she hears of Beau Whittaker and what he offers his clients, she wants to meet him. Beau is instantly attracted to Lily, but he tried a relationship with his last client that left a scar that still hasn't healed...

Can Lily use the spirit of Christmas to discover what matters most? Will Beau open his heart to the possibility of love with someone so different from him?

Her Cowboy Billionaire Bull Rider (Book 5): Todd Christopherson has just retired from the professional rodeo circuit and returned to his hometown of Coral Canyon. Problem is, he's got no family there anymore, no land, and no job. Not that he needs a job-- he's got plenty of money from his illustrious career riding bulls.

Then Todd gets thrown during a routine horseback ride up the canyon, and his only support as he recovers physically is the beautiful Violet Everett. She's no nurse, but she does the best she can for the handsome cowboy. **Will she lose her heart to the billionaire bull rider? Can Todd trust that God led him to Coral Canyon...and Vi?**

Her Cowboy Billionaire Bachelor (Book 6): Rose Everett isn't sure what to do with her life now that her country music career is on hold. After all, with both of her sisters in Coral Canyon, and one about to have a baby, they're not making albums anymore.

Liam Murphy has been working for Doctors Without Borders, but he's back in the US now, and looking to start a new clinic in Coral Canyon, where he spent his summers.

When Rose wins a date with Liam in a bachelor auction, their relationship blooms and grows quickly. **Can Liam and Rose find a solution to their problems that doesn't involve one of them leaving Coral Canyon with a broken heart?**

Her Cowboy Billionaire Blind Date (Book 7): Her sons want her to be happy, but she's too old to be set up on a blind date...isn't she?

Amanda Whittaker has been looking for a second chance at love since the death of her husband several years ago. Finley Barber is a cowboy in every sense of the word. Born and raised on a racehorse farm in Kentucky, he's since moved to Dog Valley and started his own breeding stable for champion horses. He hasn't dated in years, and everything about Amanda makes him nervous.

Will Amanda take the leap of faith required to be with Finn? Or will he become just another boyfriend who doesn't make the cut?

Her Cowboy Billionaire Best Man (Book 8): When Celia Abbott-Armstrong runs into a gorgeous cowboy at her best friend's wedding, she decides she's ready to start dating again.

But the cowboy is Zach Zuckerman, and the Zuckermans and Abbotts have been at war for generations.

Can Zach and Celia find a way to reconcile their family's differences so they can have a future together?

Second Chance Ranch: A Three Rivers Ranch Romance (Book 1): After his deployment, injured and discharged Major Squire Ackerman returns to Three Rivers Ranch, wanting to forgive Kelly for ignoring him a decade ago. He'd like to provide the stable life she needs, but with old wounds opening and a ranch on the brink of financial collapse, it will take patience and faith to make their second chance possible.

Third Time's the Charm: A Three Rivers Ranch Romance (Book 2): First Lieutenant Peter Marshall has a truckload of debt and no way to provide for a family, but Chelsea helps him see past all the obstacles, all the scars. With so many unknowns, can Pete and Chelsea develop the love, acceptance, and faith needed to find their happily ever after?

Fourth and Long: A Three Rivers Ranch Romance (Book 3): Commander Brett Murphy goes to Three Rivers Ranch to find some rest and relaxation with his Army buddies. Having his ex-wife show up with a seven-year-old she claims is his son is anything but the R&R he craves. Kate needs to make amends, and Brett needs to find forgiveness, but are they too late to find their happily ever after?

Fifth Generation Cowboy: A Three Rivers Ranch Romance (Book 4): Tom Lovell has watched his friends find their true happiness on Three Rivers Ranch, but everywhere he looks, he only sees friends. Rose Reyes has been bringing her daughter out to the ranch for equine therapy for months, but it doesn't seem to be working. Her challenges with Mari are just as frustrating as ever. Could Tom be exactly what Rose needs? Can he remove his friendship blinders and find love with someone who's been right in front of him all this time?

Sixth Street Love Affair: A Three Rivers Ranch Romance (Book 5): After losing his wife a few years back, Garth Ahlstrom thinks he's ready for a second chance at love. But Juliette Thompson has a secret that could destroy their budding relationship. Can they find the strength, patience, and faith to make things work?

LIZ ISAACSON

A THREE RIVERS RANCH ROMANCE

The Seventh Sergeant: A Three Rivers Ranch Romance (Book 6): Life has finally started to settle down for Sergeant Reese Sanders after his devastating injury overseas. Discharged from the Army and now with a good job at Courage Reins, he's finally found happiness—until a horrific fall puts him right back where he was years ago: Injured and depressed. Carly Watters, Reese's new veteran care coordinator, dislikes small towns almost as much as she loathes cowboys. But she finds herself faced with both when she gets assigned to Reese's case. Do they have the humility and faith to make their relationship more than professional?

Eight Second Ride: A Three Rivers Ranch Romance (Book 7): Ethan Greene loves his work at Three Rivers Ranch, but he can't seem to find the right woman to settle down with. When sassy yet vulnerable Brynn Bowman shows up at the ranch to recruit him back to the rodeo circuit, he takes a different approach with the barrel racing champion. His patience and newfound faith pay off when a friendship--and more--starts with Brynn. But she wants out of the rodeo circuit right when Ethan wants to rejoin. Can they find the path God wants them to take and still stay together?

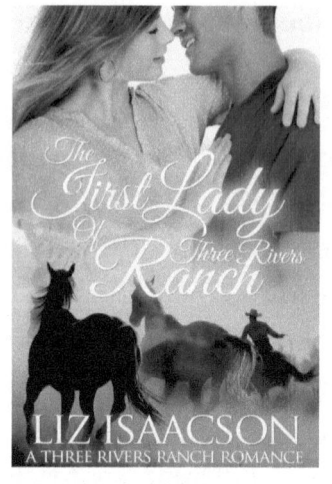

The First Lady of Three Rivers Ranch: A Three Rivers Ranch Romance (Book 8): Heidi Duffin has been dreaming about opening her own bakery since she was thirteen years old. She scrimped and saved for years to afford baking and pastry school in San Francisco. And now she only has one year left before she's a certified pastry chef. Frank Ackerman's father has recently retired, and he's taken over the largest cattle ranch in the Texas Panhandle. A horseman through and through, he's also nearing thirty-one and looking for someone to bring love and joy to a homestead that's been dominated by men for a decade. But when he convinces Heidi to come clean the cowboy cabins, she changes all that. But the siren's call of a bakery is still loud in Heidi's ears, even if she's also seeing a future with Frank. Can she rely on her faith in ways she's never had to before or will their relationship end when summer does?

Christmas in Three Rivers: A Three Rivers Ranch Romance (Book 9): Isn't Christmas the best time to fall in love? The cowboys of Three Rivers Ranch think so. Join four of them as they journey toward their path to happily ever after in four, all-new novellas in the Amazon #1 Bestselling Three Rivers Ranch Romance series.

THE NINTH INNING: The Christmas season has never felt like such a burden to boutique owner Andrea Larsen. But with Mama gone and the holidays upon her, Andy finds herself wishing she hadn't been so quick to judge her former boyfriend, cowboy Lawrence Collins. Well, Lawrence hasn't forgotten about Andy either, and he devises a plan to get her out to the ranch so they can reconnect. Do they have the faith and humility to patch things up and start a new relationship?

TEN DAYS IN TOWN: Sandy Keller is tired of the dating scene in Three Rivers. Though she owns the pancake house, she's looking for a fresh start, which means an escape from the town where she grew up. When her older brother's best friend, Tad Jorgensen, comes to town for the holidays, it is a balm to his weary soul. A helicopter tour guide who experienced a near-death experience, he's looking to start over too--but in Three Rivers. Can Sandy and Tad navigate their troubles to find the path God wants them to take--and discover true love--in only ten days?

ELEVEN YEAR REUNION: Pastry chef extraordinaire, Grace Lewis has moved to Three Rivers to help Heidi Ackerman open a bakery in Three Rivers. Grace relishes the idea of starting over in a town where no one knows about her failed cupcakery. She doesn't expect to run into her old high school boyfriend, Jonathan Carver. A carpenter working at Three Rivers Ranch, Jon's in town against his will. But with Grace now on the scene, Jon's thinking life in Three Rivers is suddenly looking up. But with her focus on baking and his disdain for small towns, can they make their eleven year reunion stick?

THE TWELFTH TOWN: Newscaster Taryn Tucker has had enough of life on-screen. She's bounced from town to town before arriving in Three Rivers, completely alone and completely anonymous--just the way she now likes it. She takes a job cleaning at Three Rivers Ranch, hoping for a chance to figure out who she is and where God wants her. When she meets happy-go-lucky cowhand Kenny Stockton, she doesn't expect sparks to fly. Kenny's always been "the best friend" for his female friends, but the pull between him and Taryn can't be denied. Will they have the courage and faith necessary to make their opposite worlds mesh?

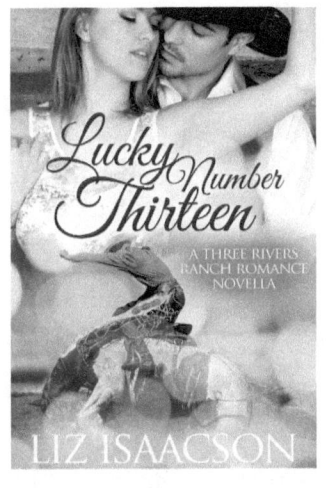

Lucky Number Thirteen: A Three Rivers Ranch Romance (Book 10): Tanner Wolf, a rodeo champion ten times over, is excited to be riding in Three Rivers for the first time since he left his philandering ways and found religion. Seeing his old friends Ethan and Brynn is therapuetic--until a terrible accident lands him in the hospital. With his rodeo career over, Tanner thinks maybe he'll stay in town--and it's not just because his nurse, Summer Hamblin, is the prettiest woman he's ever met. But Summer's the queen of first dates, and as she looks for a way to make a relationship with the transient rodeo star work Summer's not sure she has the fortitude to go on a second date. Can they find love among the tragedy?

The Curse of February Fourteenth: A Three Rivers Ranch Romance (Book 11): Cal Hodgkins, cowboy veterinarian at Bowman's Breeds, isn't planning to meet anyone at the masked dance in small-town Three Rivers. He just wants to get his bachelor friends off his back and sit on the sidelines to drink his punch. But when he sees a woman dressed in gorgeous butterfly wings and cowgirl boots with blue stitching, he's smitten. Too bad she runs away from the dance before he can get her name, leaving only her boot behind...

Fifteen Minutes of Fame: A Three Rivers Ranch Romance (Book 12): Navy Richards is thirty-five years of tired—tired of dating the same men, working a demanding job, and getting her heart broken over and over again. Her aunt has always spoken highly of the matchmaker in Three Rivers, Texas, so she takes a six-month sabbatical from her high-stress job as a pediatric nurse, hops on a bus, and meets with the matchmaker. Then she meets Gavin Redd. He's handsome, he's hardworking, and he's a cowboy. But is he an Aquarius too? Navy's not making a move until she knows for sure...

Sixteen Steps to Fall in Love: A Three Rivers Ranch Romance (Book 13): A chance encounter at a dog park sheds new light on the tall, talented Boone that Nicole can't ignore. As they get to know each other better and start to dig into each other's past, Nicole is the one who wants to run. This time from her growing admiration and attachment to Boone. From her aging parents. From herself.

But Boone feels the attraction between them too, and he decides he's tired of running and ready to make Three Rivers his permanent home. **Can Boone and Nicole use their faith to overcome their differences and find a happily-ever-after together?**

The Sleigh on Seventeenth Street: A Three Rivers Ranch Romance (Book 14): A cowboy with skills as an electrician tries a relationship with a down-on-her luck plumber. Can Dylan and Camila make water and electricity play nicely together this Christmas season? Or will they get shocked as they try to make their relationship work?

Books in the Last Chance Ranch Romance
series

Last Chance Ranch (Book 1): A cowgirl down on her luck hires a man who's good with horses and under the hood of a car. Can Hudson fine tune Scarlett's heart as they work together? Or will things backfire and make everything worse at Last Chance Ranch?

Last Chance Cowboy (Book 2): A billionaire cowboy without a home meets a woman who secretly makes food videos to pay her debts...Can Carson and Adele do more than fight in the kitchens at Last Chance Ranch?

Last Chance Wedding (Book 3): A female carpenter needs a husband just for a few days... Can Jeri and Sawyer navigate the minefield of a pretend marriage before their feelings become real?

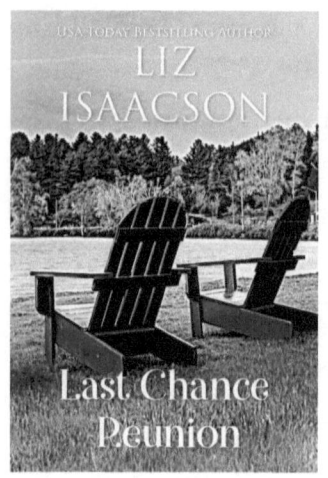

Last Chance Reunion (Book 4): An Army cowboy, the woman he dated years ago, and their last chance at Last Chance Ranch... Can Dave and Sissy put aside hurt feelings and make their second chance romance work?

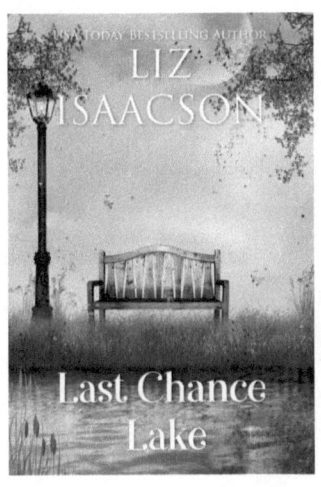

Last Chance Lake (Book 5):
A former dairy farmer and the marketing director on the ranch have to work together to make the cow cuddling program a success. But can Karla let Cache into her life? Or will she keep all her secrets from him - and keep *him* a secret too?

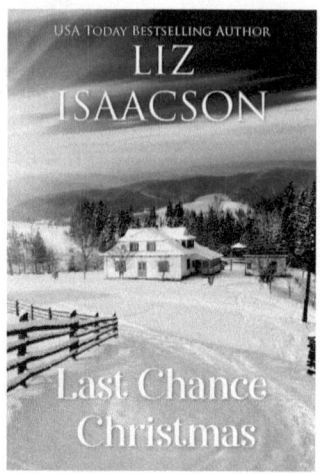

Last Chance Christmas (Book 6): She's tired of having her heart broken by cowboys. He waited too long to ask her out. Can Lance fix things quickly, or will Amber leave Last Chance Ranch before he can tell her how he feels?

Books in the Steeple Ridge Romance Series:

Her Billionaire Cowboy (Book 1): Tucker Jenkins has had enough of tall buildings, traffic, and has traded in his technology firm in New York City for Steeple Ridge Horse Farm in rural Vermont. Missy Marino has worked at the farm since she was a teen, and she's always dreamed of owning it. But her ex-husband left her with a truckload of debt, making her fantasies of owning the farm unfulfilled. Tucker didn't come to the country to find a new wife, but he supposes a woman could help him start over in Steeple Ridge. Will Tucker and Missy be able to navigate the shaky ground between them to find a new beginning?

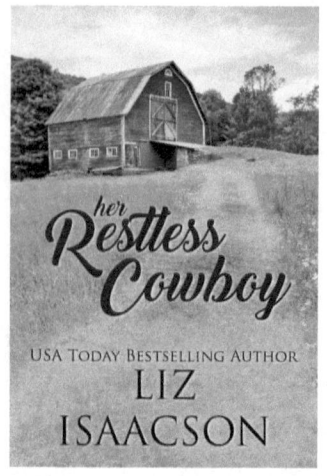

USA TODAY BESTSELLING AUTHOR
LIZ ISAACSON

Her Restless Cowboy: A Butters Brothers Novel, Steeple Ridge Romance (Book 2): Ben Buttars is the youngest of the four Buttars brothers who come to Steeple Ridge Farm, and he finally feels like he's landed somewhere he can make a life for himself. Reagan Cantwell is a decade older than Ben and the recreational direction for the town of Island Park. Though Ben is young, he knows what he wants—and that's Rae. Can she figure out how to put what matters most in her life—family and faith—above her job before she loses Ben?

Her Faithful Cowboy: A Butters Brothers Novel, Steeple Ridge Romance (Book 3): Sam Buttars has spent the last decade making sure he and his brothers stay together. They've been at Steeple Ridge for a while now, but with the youngest married and happy, the siren's call to return to his parents' farm in Wyoming is loud in Sam's ears. He'd just go if it weren't for beautiful Bonnie Sherman, who roped his heart the first time he saw her. Do Sam and Bonnie have the faith to find comfort in each other instead of in the people who've already passed?

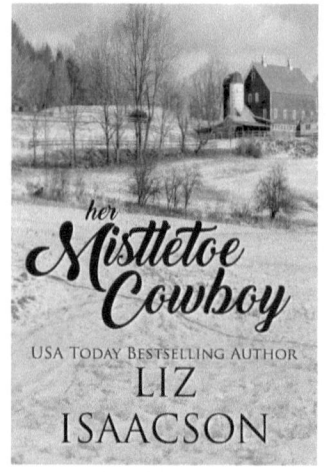

Her Mistletoe Cowboy: A Butters Brothers Novel, Steeple Ridge Romance (Book 4): Logan Buttars has always been good-natured and happy-go-lucky. After watching two of his brothers settle down, he recognizes a void in his life he didn't know about. Veterinarian Layla Guyman has appreciated Logan's friendship and easy way with animals when he comes into the clinic to get the service dogs. But with his future at Steeple Ridge in the balance, she's not sure a relationship with him is worth the risk. Can she rely on her faith and employ patience to tame Logan's wild heart?

Her Patient Cowboy: A Butters Brothers Novel, Steeple Ridge Romance (Book 5): Darren Buttars is cool, collected, and quiet—and utterly devastated when his girlfriend of nine months, Farrah Irvine, breaks up with him because he wanted her to ride her horse in a parade. But Farrah doesn't ride anymore, a fact she made very clear to Darren. She returned to her childhood home with so much baggage, she doesn't know where to start with the unpacking. Darren's the only Buttars brother who isn't married, and he wants to make Island Park his permanent home—with Farrah. Can they find their way through the heartache to achieve a happily-ever-after together?

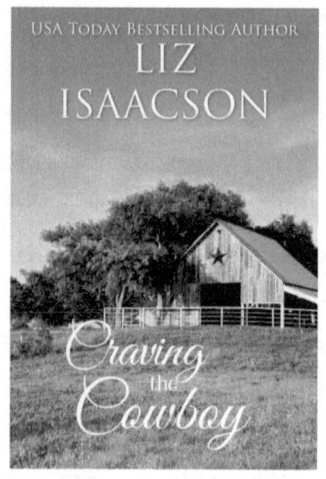

Craving the Cowboy (Book 1): Dwayne Carver is set to inherit his family's ranch in the heart of Texas Hill Country, and in order to keep up with his ranch duties and fulfill his dreams of owning a horse farm, he hires top trainer Felicity Lightburne. They get along great, and she can envision herself on this new farm—at least until her mother falls ill and she has to return to help her. Can Dwayne and Felicity work through their differences to find their happily-ever-after?

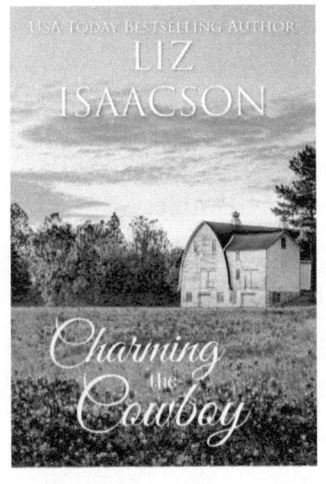

Charming the Cowboy (Book 2): Third grade teacher Heather Carver has had her eye on Levi Rhodes for a couple of years now, but he seems to be blind to her attempts to charm him. When she breaks her arm while on his horse ranch, Heather infiltrates Levi's life in ways he's never thought of, and his strict anti-female stance slips. Will Heather heal his emotional scars and he care for her physical ones so they can have a real relationship?

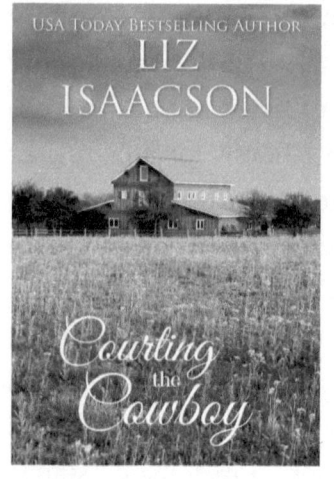

Courting the Cowboy (Book 3): Frustrated with the cowboy-only dating scene in Grape Seed Falls, May Sotheby joins TexasFaithful.com, hoping to find her soul mate without having to relocate--or deal with cowboy hats and boots. She has no idea that Kurt Pemberton, foreman at Grape Seed Ranch, is the man she starts communicating with... Will May be able to follow her heart and get Kurt to forgive her so they can be together?

Claiming the Cowboy, Royal Brothers Book 1 (Grape Seed Falls Romance Book 4): Unwilling to be tied down, farrier Robin Cook has managed to pack her entire life into a two-hundred-and-eighty square-foot house, and that includes her Yorkie. Cowboy and co-foreman, Shane Royal has had his heart set on Robin for three years, even though she flat-out turned him down the last time he asked her to dinner. But she's back at Grape Seed Ranch for five weeks as she works her horse-shoeing magic, and he's still interested, despite a bitter life lesson that left a bad taste for marriage in his mouth.

Robin's interested in him too. But can she find room for Shane in her tiny house--and can he take a chance on her with his tired heart?

Catching the Cowboy, Royal Brothers Book 2 (Grape Seed Falls Romance Book 5): Dylan Royal is good at two things: whistling and caring for cattle. When his cows are being attacked by an unknown wild animal, he calls Texas Parks & Wildlife for help. He wasn't expecting a beautiful mammologist to show up, all flirty and fun and everything Dylan didn't know he wanted in his life.

Hazel Brewster has gone on more first dates than anyone in Grape Seed Falls, and she thinks maybe Dylan deserves a second... Can they find their way through wild animals, huge life changes, and their emotional pasts to find their forever future?

Cheering the Cowboy, Royal Brothers Book 3 (Grape Seed Falls Romance Book 6): Austin Royal loves his life on his new ranch with his brothers. But he doesn't love that Shayleigh Hatch came with the property, nor that he has to take the blame for the fact that he now owns her childhood ranch. They rarely have a conversation that doesn't leave him furious and frustrated--and yet he's still attracted to Shay in a strange, new way.

Shay inexplicably likes him too, which utterly confuses and angers her. As they work to make this Christmas the best the Triple Towers Ranch has ever seen, can they also navigate through their rocky relationship to smoother waters?

Praise for Liz Isaacson

Choosing the Cowboy (Book 7): With financial trouble and personal issues around every corner, can Maggie Duffin and Chase Carver rely on their faith to find their happily-ever-after?

A spinoff from the #1 bestselling Three Rivers Ranch Romance novels, also by USA Today bestselling author Liz Isaacson.

Books in the Horseshoe Home Ranch Romance Series:

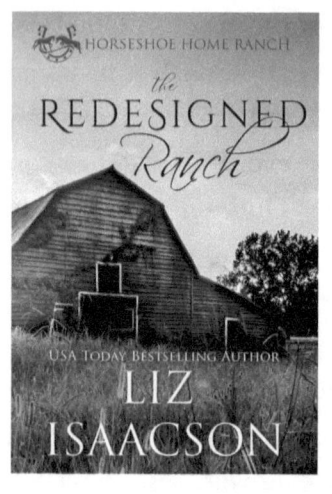

The Redesigned Ranch (Book 1): Jace Lovell only has one thing left after his fiancé abandons him at the altar: his job at Horseshoe Home Ranch. Belle Edmunds is back in Gold Valley and she's desperate to build a portfolio that she can use to start her own firm in Montana. Jace isn't anywhere near forgiving his fiancé, and he's not sure he's ready for a new relationship with someone as fiery and beautiful as Belle. Can she employ her patience while he figures out how to forgive so they can find their own brand of happily-ever-after?

The Snowstorm in Gold Valley (Book 2): Professional snowboarder Sterling Maughan has sequestered himself in his family's cabin in the exclusive mountain community above Gold Valley, Montana after a devastating fall that ended his career. Norah Watson cleans Sterling's cabin and the more time they spend together, the more Sterling is interested in all things Norah. As his body heals, so does his faith. Will Norah be able to trust Sterling so they can have a chance at true love?

The Cabin on Bear Mountain (Book 3): Landon Edmunds has been a cowboy his whole life. An accident five years ago ended his successful rodeo career, and now he's looking to start a horse ranch-- and he's looking outside of Montana. Which would be great if God hadn't brought Megan Palmer back to Gold Valley right when Landon is looking to leave. Megan and Landon work together well, and as sparks fly, she's sure God brought her back to Gold Valley so she could find her happily ever after. Through serious discussion and prayer, can Landon and Megan find their future together?

Be sure to check out the spinoff series, the Brush Creek Brides romances after you read FALLING FOR HIS BEST FRIEND. Start with A WEDDING FOR THE WIDOWER.

The Cowboy at the Creek (Book 4): Twelve years ago, Owen Carr left Gold Valley—and his long-time girlfriend—in favor of a country music career in Nashville. Married and divorced, Natalie teaches ballet at the dance studio in Gold Valley, but she never auditioned for the professional company the way she dreamed of doing. With Owen back, she realizes all the opportunities she missed out on when he left all those years ago—including a future with him. Can they mend broken bridges in order to have a second chance at love?

The Wedding in the Winter (Book 5): Caleb Chamberlain has spent the last five years recovering from a horrible breakup, his alcoholism that stemmed from it, and the car accident that left him hospitalized. He's finally on the right track in his life—until Holly Gray, his twin brother's ex-fiance mistakes him for Nathan.

Holly's back in Gold Valley to get the required veterinarian hours to apply for her graduate program. When the herd at Horseshoe Home comes down with pneumonia, Caleb and Holly are forced to work together in close quarters. Holly's over Nathan, but she hasn't forgiven him—or the woman she believes broke up their relationship. Can Caleb and Holly navigate such a rough past to find their happily-ever-after?

The Long Way Home (Book 6): Ty Barker has been dancing through the last thirty years of his life--and he's suddenly realized he's alone. River Lee Whitely is back in Gold Valley with her two little girls after a divorce that's left deep scars. She has a job at Silver Creek that requires her to be able to ride a horse, and she nearly tramples Ty at her first lesson. That's just fine by him, because River Lee is the girl Ty has never gotten over. Ty realizes River Lee needs time to settle into her new job, her new home, her new life as a single parent, but going slow has never been his style. But for River Lee, can Ty take the necessary steps to keep her in his life?

Christmas at the Ranch (Book 7): Archer Bailey has already lost one job to Emersyn Enders, so he deliberately doesn't tell her about the cowhand job up at Horseshoe Home Ranch. Emery's temporary job is ending, but her obligations to her physically disabled sister aren't. As Archer and Emery work together, its clear that the sparks flying between them aren't all from their friendly competition over a job. Will Emery and Archer be able to navigate the ranch, their close quarters, and their individual circumstances to find love this holiday season?

The Love of a Cowboy (Book 8): Cowboy Elliott Hawthorne has just lost his best friend and cabin mate to the worst thing imaginable— marriage. When his brother calls about an accident with their father, Elliott rushes down to Gold Valley from the ranch only to be met with the most beautiful woman he's ever seen. His father's new physical therapist, London Marsh, likes the handsome face and gentle spirit she sees in Elliott too. Can Elliott and London navigate difficult family situations to find a happily-ever-after?

Books in the Brush Creek Brides Romance
Series:

Brush Creek Cowboy: Brush Creek Cowboys Romance (Book 1): Former rodeo champion and cowboy Walker Thompson trains horses at Brush Creek Horse Ranch, where he lives a simple life in his cabin with his ten-year-old son. A widower of six years, he's worked with Tess Wagner, a widow who came to Brush Creek to escape the turmoil of her life to give her seven-year-old son a slower pace of life. But Tess's breast cancer is back...

Walker will have to decide if he'd rather spend even a short time with Tess than not have her in his life at all. Tess wants to feel God's love and power, but can she discover and accept God's will in order to find her happy ending?

The Cowboy's Challenge: Brush Creek Brides Romance (Book 2): Cowboy and professional roper Justin Jackman has found solitude at Brush Creek Horse Ranch, preferring his time with the animals he trains over dating. With two failed engagements in his past, he's not really interested in getting his heart stomped on again. But when  flirty and fun Renee Martin picks him up at a church ice cream bar--on a bet, no less--he finds himself more than just a little interested. His Gen-X attitudes are attractive to her; her Millennial behaviors drive him nuts. Can Justin look past their differences and take a chance on another engagement?

A Cowboy Proposal: Brush Creek Brides Romance (Book 3): Ted Caldwell has been a retired bronc rider for years, and he thought he was perfectly happy training horses to buck at Brush Creek Ranch. He was wrong. When he meets April Nox, who comes to the ranch to hide her pregnancy from all her friends back in Jackson Hole, Ted realizes he has a huge family-shaped hole in his life. April is embarrassed, heartbroken, and trying to find her extinguished faith. She's never ridden a horse and wants nothing to do with a cowboy ever again. Can Ted and April create a family of happiness and love from a tragedy?

A New Family for the Cowboy: Brush Creek Brides Romance (Book 4): Blake Gibbons oversees all the agriculture at Brush Creek Horse Ranch, sometimes moonlighting as a general contractor. When he meets Erin Shields, new in town, at her aunt's bakery, he's instantly smitten. Erin moved to Brush Creek after a divorce that left

her penniless, homeless, and a single mother of three children under age eight. She's nowhere near ready to start dating again, but the longer Blake hangs around the bakery, the more she starts to like him. Can Blake and Erin find a way to blend their lifestyles and become a family?

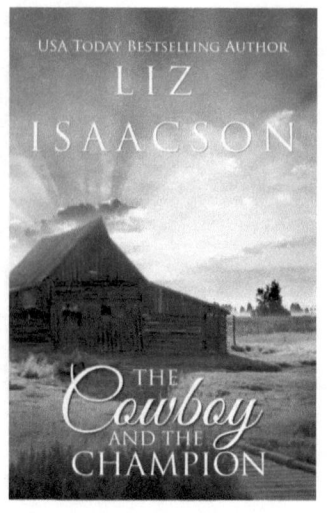

The Cowboy and the Champion: Brush Creek Brides Romance (Book 5): Emmett Graves has always had a positive outlook on life. He adores training horses to become barrel racing champions during the day and cuddling with his cat at night. Fresh off her professional rodeo retirement, Molly Brady comes to Brush Creek Horse Ranch as Emmett's protege. He's not thrilled, and she's allergic to cats. Oh, and she'd like to stay cowboy-free, thank you very much. But Emmett's about as cowboy as they come.... Can Emmett and Molly work together without falling in love?

Schooled by the Cowboy: Brush Creek Brides Romance (Book 6): Grant Ford spends his days training cattle—when he's not camped out at the elementary school hoping to catch a glimpse of his ex-girlfriend. When principal Shannon Sharpe confronts him and asks him to stay away from the school, the spark between them is instant and hot. Shan-

non's expecting a transfer very soon, but she also needs a summer outdoor coordinator—and Grant fits the bill. Just because he's handsome and everything Shannon's ever wanted in a cowboy husband means nothing. Will Grant and Shannon be able to survive the summer or will the Utah heat be too much for them to handle?

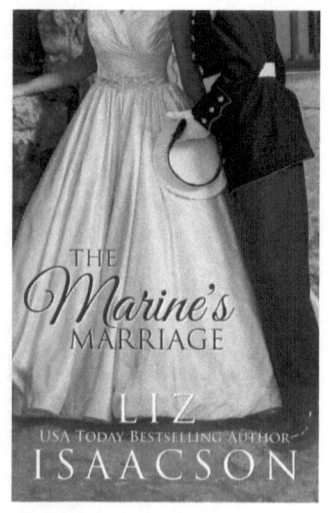

The Marine's Marriage: A Fuller Family Novel - Brush Creek Brides Romance (Book 1): Tate Benson can't believe he's come to Nowhere, Utah, to fix up a house that hasn't been inhabited in years. But he has. Because he's retired from the Marines and looking to start a life as a police officer in small-town Brush Creek. Wren Fuller has her hands full most days running her family's company. When Tate calls and demands a maid for that morning, she decides to have the calls forwarded to her cell and go help him out. She didn't know he was moving in next door, and she's completely unprepared for his handsomeness, his kind heart, and his wounded soul.Can Tate and Wren weather a relationship when they're also next-door neighbors?

The Firefighter's Fiancé: A Fuller Family Novel - Brush Creek Brides Romance (Book 2): Cora Wesley comes to Brush Creek, hoping to get some in-the-wild firefighting training as she prepares to put in her application to be a hotshot. When she meets Brennan Fuller, the spark between them is hot and instant. As they get to know  each other, her deadline is constantly looming over them, and Brennan starts to wonder if he can break ranks in the family business. He's okay mowing lawns and hanging out with his brothers, but he dreams of being able to go to college and become a landscape architect, but he's just not sure it can be done. Will Cora and Brennan be able to endure their trials to find true love?

The Trooper's Treasure: A Fuller Family Novel - Brush Creek Brides Romance (Book 3): Dawn Fuller has made some mistakes in her life, and she's not proud of the way McDermott Boyd found her off the road one day last year. She's spent a hard year wrestling with her choices and trying to fix them, glad for McDermott's acceptance and friendship. He lost his wife years ago, done his best with his daughter, and now he's ready to move on. Can McDermott help Dawn find a way past her former mistakes and down a path that leads to love, family, and happiness?

The Detective's Date: A Fuller Family Novel - Brush Creek Brides Romance (Book 4): Dahlia Reid is one of the best detectives Brush Creek and the surrounding towns has ever had. She's given up on the idea of marriage—and pleasing her mother—and has dedicated herself fully to her job. Which is great, since one of the most perplexing

cases of her career has come to town. Kyler Fuller thinks he's finally ready to move past the woman who ghosted him years ago. He's cut his hair, and he's ready to start dating. Too bad every woman he's been out with is about as interesting as a lamppost—until Dahlia. He finds her beautiful, her quick wit a breath of fresh air, and her intelligence sexy. Can Kyler and Dahlia use their faith to find a way through the obstacles threatening to keep them apart?

The Paramedic's Partner: A Fuller Family Novel - Brush Creek Brides Romance (Book 5): Jazzy Fuller has always been overshadowed by her prettier, more popular twin, Fabiana. Fabi meets paramedic Max Robinson at the park and sets a date with him only to come down with the flu. So she convinces Jazzy to cut her hair and take her place on the date. And the spark between Jazzy and Max is hot and instant...if only he knew she wasn't her sister, Fabi.

Max drives the ambulance for the town of Brush Creek with is partner Ed Moon, and neither of them have been all that lucky in love. Until Max suggests to who he thinks is Fabi that they should double with Ed and Jazzy. They do, and Fabi is smitten with the steady, strong Ed Moon. As each twin falls further and further in love with their respective paramedic, it becomes obvious they'll need to come clean about the switcheroo sooner rather than later...or risk losing their hearts.

The Chief's Catch: A Fuller Family Novel - Brush Creek Brides Romance (Book 6): Berlin Fuller has struck out with the dating scene in Brush Creek more times than she cares to admit. When she makes a deal with her friends that they can choose the next man she goes out with, she didn't dream they'd pick surly Cole Fairbanks, the new Chief of Police.

His friends call him the Beast and challenge him to complete ten dates that summer or give up his bonus check. When Berlin approaches him, stuttering about the deal with her friends and claiming they don't actually have to go out, he's intrigued. As the summer passes, Cole finds himself burning both ends of the candle to keep up with his job and his new relationship. When he unleashes the Beast one time too many, Berlin will have to decide if she can tame him or if she should walk away.

About Liz

Liz Isaacson writes inspirational romance, usually set in Texas, or Montana, or anywhere else horses and cowboys exist. She lives in Utah, where she writes full-time, walks her two dogs daily, and eats a lot of peanut butter M&Ms while writing. Find her on her website at lizisaacson.com.